SPINDLE

THE TWO MONARCHIES SEQUENCE, BOOK ONE

W.R. GINGELL

IN THE TWO MONARCHIES SEQUENCE

#1: Spindle
#2: Blackfoot
#3: Staff and Crown
#4: Clockwork Magician
#5: Masque
#6: Castle and Key

With humble thanks to Diana Wynne Jones, whom I greatly wish I could have met.
We writers learn via osmosis, and I would have liked to bask in that sunshine a little longer.

1

Polyhymnia knew perfectly well that she was dreaming. Her hair was in pigtails and she was wearing a smock, suggesting a dream age of perhaps twelve or thirteen. The dream itself was a distant memory of a history lesson with Lady Cimone, her teacher. She had been amused for a brief moment to find herself daydreaming during the lesson—dreaming, as it were, within a dream, while Lady Cimone pointed out the various flaws in Civet's latest sally against Parras.

Oh, I remember this, thought Poly suddenly. *Parras tossed over one of our outposts, and we walked right into an ambush trying to retaliate.*

Pain, in her left ear. Poly clutched the injured member in surprise. "Ow!" She hadn't remembered *that*.

"Perhaps you could pay attention to your lesson, now that you're awake?" suggested Lady Cimone. She always did prefer boxing ears to using a cane. Maybe it was her idea of the personal touch. "This is important, Poly."

Poly let her younger dream-self murmur the appropriate response, her attention snatched away, because a gold-edged rift was beginning to form in the blue wall behind Lady Cimone.

The lady caught the direction of her gaze and gave a sharp

glance behind her. "Bother!" she said. She seemed annoyed rather than taken aback.

Before long the perpendicular rift was tall enough to admit a human, and Poly wasn't quite surprised when a young man did step through. He was wearing a long, mud-splattered black coat that looked as though it had seen one too many days travelling, and he had an inquiring, dishevelled look. His forehead was wide and square, with dark hair springing upwards and sideways from it, and his mouth was both determined and wistful, though the triangular set of his chin spoke more to determination than wistfulness. Poly shut her mouth, which had dropped open, and took an involuntary step backwards as the man edged carefully into the room. He was glowing with residual magic, sparking a plethora of alarm bells in Poly's head.

He stepped purposefully toward Poly and said, "Shoo," at Lady Cimone.

The Lady smiled a little grimly and said, "I am no more a dream than you are, young man. Kindly be polite."

Poly became her normal, older self in confusion, and the dream-memory of the younger her melted away, leaving Lady Cimone and the young man behind in the resulting void. The young man seemed almost as bemused as Poly felt, but Lady Cimone was looking, as usual, serene and omniscient.

"I tried my best, but I'm afraid he got you," she said to Poly. "You'll have to go with the wizard for now. Your parents said they'd try to find you somewhere along the way, but things might be a little more difficult than they expected. Try not to forget everything the minute you wake up, child."

"But—" Poly began, but Lady Cimone was already gone. Poly put her hands on her hips and surveyed the young wizard, who was still standing where he was, disturbingly real for a dream figure.

"Huh," he said. "Didn't expect that. Come here, princess."

Poly could have said, 'I'm not the princess', but it didn't seem worth arguing with a dream. Instead, she said, "I don't think so," and slipped up and out of the dream.

It should have woken her. For a moment, she thought it had. She was standing in her own small, rounded chamber, stranded aimlessly between her bookcases. Through her window-slit the outside world looked sunny and normal. Then she saw the translucent something coating her hands from fingers to elbow, and belatedly felt the odd, sideways pull that had brought her here.

"Bother," she said aloud. The translucent something wasn't quite magic, but it seemed to be the dream equivalent. In real life, Poly had no magic. It was the one consistent way to tell dream from reality when her dreams became too realistic.

Poly wriggled her fingers and the translucency shivered coolly across them with a sense of familiarity. When had she started dreaming about magic so often? In fact, when had she started dreaming for so long at a time? She felt as though she'd been dreaming for years.

Time to wake up, Poly decided. She let herself slip upwards and awake, and again found herself sliding sideways to the pull of something strong and unfamiliar.

Someone said, "No you don't, darling. Back to sleep with you."

Poly gave a little gasp of indignation and fought against the pull. It was ridiculous to allow her dreams to be hijacked by an unpleasant dream entity of her own creation. Where was it coming from?

She dragged herself around, seeking the owner of the voice, and felt the reality of her dream-chamber wobble around her. A nasty quiver of surprise shook her at the sight of the hooded, murky figure that was cobwebbed in the doorway, more shadow than substance.

To give herself time to become brave, Poly asked aloud, "Now, what are you? I know I didn't dream you up."

"You must have," said the hooded figure, its voice soft and amused. "Here I am."

Too smooth for words, Poly thought, sharp with fear. There was a prickle at her back that made her think the wizard from the previous level was making his way through to her again. A panicked, nightmare quality had settled over the dream like a wet blanket, weighing her down, and for a brief moment Poly found herself unable to think.

The same soft voice said, "Darling, you're being difficult. There's no need for things to become uncivilized. Be a good girl and go back to sleep."

"I don't like you," Poly said experimentally.

"That's hurtful, darling," said the voice reproachfully. "As it happens, I'm really quite fond of you. However, needs must, and you really must *go to sleep*."

The reasonable tone to the shadow's voice was hard to resist. Her bed was somehow in the middle of the tower room where it didn't belong, and Poly felt herself take one step toward it.

The sheets should have been cool and smooth when she slid between them. Instead, they were fuzzy and warm, and Poly felt her eyes gum together in a last warning of approaching slumber, the prickle at her back fading in the warmth.

"Huh," said a second voice. "This is all very interesting. Who are you? No. Not who. What?"

"Undefined element," said the hooded shadow thoughtfully. Poly could vaguely see it through her gummy eyes, outlined in the brilliant gold of the wizard's magic. "You are not valid here. Retreat or assimilate."

"Tosh," said the wizard mildly. "You're what? A remnant? Go away."

"No, I don't think so," said the shadow.

It seemed to Poly, mired in sleep, that an impossibly strong magic was stirring in the room—no, in the very air—around her. It was bright, fiery, and entirely translucent. The wizard said, "Yow!" and did something golden and magical with more haste than precision. Poly stirred, fighting against sleep, and saw his face briefly appear above her. He said, "Well, better get on with it, then."

Poly tried to say, 'Get on with what?' but found that she couldn't move her lips. It took her a shocked moment to realise that she couldn't move her lips because she was being kissed. It took another to realise that she was waking up—*really* waking up. Gold magic fizzed from her lips to her toes, and everything familiar…disappeared.

A DREAM RETREATED, scurrying away with important thoughts that wouldn't stay to be remembered. Stale, stuffy air tickled Poly's nose. Something inflexible held her head in place, cupping it through the strands of her hair, and something warm and equally inflexible pressed against her lips. In between waking and sleeping, Poly came to the startling conclusion that she was being kissed. It was not a gentle kiss or a lover's kiss; it was a quick, hard, punctilious sort of kiss that suggested the kisser had better things to do and would like to get on with it, please.

She made herself lie still, heart pounding, until the pressure lessened. Then she vigorously jabbed her knee up into the kisser's stomach. There was a pained huff of air in her face and the intruder curled defensively, groaning. Poly whipped herself away, ripping through bedclothes that tore like rotten wool as she half-fell, half-scrambled to the floor.

Her glasses weren't on her nose where they ought to have been, leaving the world a confusing blur of grey and gold without sense or structure. Poly stumbled through the blur with her arms outstretched, feeling a whispy tickle of cobwebs—or was that hair?—across her fingers, and thought that the flagstones beneath her feet sank slightly.

There was a shuffling behind her, then someone's arms grabbed for her waist. Poly stomped frantically in the general direction of her assailant's feet and felt the heel of her shoe crush her assailant's toes. He shouted in agony, and Poly tore herself away, stumbling towards a bulky blur that seemed to be the bed. Her skirts were confusingly voluminous and fine, catching at her ankles, and a silky curtain of what Poly was almost certain was hair swirled around her as she ran behind the bed. From the safety of the bed, she squinted hopelessly at the fuzzy outline of the intruder. He seemed to be clutching his foot.

"Who are you?" she demanded, skirts bunched in both hands and ready to run again if he moved.

"She told you not to forget," he said bitterly. By the movement of his foot, he was cautiously trying to ascertain if she had broken his toes.

Poly felt an entirely vicious satisfaction. "What are you doing in my bedroom?"

"I came to rescue you," he said, gingerly setting the injured foot down. "And I didn't expect to be lamed, either. I thought princesses were meant to be charming."

"I don't need rescuing from bed, thank you very much," Poly said, her voice very slightly wobbling. It was discomposing to find that she had gone to bed fully dressed. It wasn't even her dress, she thought briefly, finding that her fingers were nervously clutching fine, cool satin.

Then it occurred to her that the wizard thought she was the princess. She stiffly released the fabric, her stomach twisting, and grasped at the bedhead instead. It was soft beneath her clutching fingers, and when she staggered forward a little at the unexpectedness of it, it collapsed into soggy dust, bereaving her at once of both support and cover.

"Now you've done it," said the fuzzy figure disagreeably. "The whole place'll start, now. I wish you'd stop darting about: I'm not going to chase you over and under the furniture. Don't you want your glasses?"

Poly did, badly. Standing in a pile of disintegrated bed with something hairlike whispering terrifyingly around her, she wanted them so earnestly that she was somehow not surprised to find them in her hand. And yet, disintegration and hairlike tickle blurrily threatening seemed better than the idea of seeing the threat in all its detailed danger, and Poly hesitated. It was only when she saw the intruder straighten and step toward her that she made herself shove her glasses back onto her nose, smudges and all.

The world sprang into sharp focus, making it desperately hard to ignore the long black tendrils that danced and swayed in her peripheral. Poly focused her gaze somewhat tremulously on the wizard, her shoulders stiff with fear, and saw that he was looking distinctly offended.

"How did you do that?" he demanded.

A long black strand curled around Poly's wrist softly, and she swallowed. In a little above a whisper, she asked, "Do what?"

"Don't do that, either," he said, but Poly, who had already taken one step backwards, then another, found herself backing into a small mahogany table.

No: *through* it. The table collapsed softly in half and crumbled to dust, coating the hem of her satin dress. Poly, stumbling backwards with her arms desperately outstretched for balance, stepped on something that jerked her head painfully backwards, and tumbled into the dusty mess.

There was hair everywhere. She was sitting in it, surrounded by it, her palms resting against it when she pushed herself up from the flagstones. Poly whimpered—a necessary weakness to prevent the greater one of screaming—and raised shaking hands to comb through what should have been chin length hair.

It was no longer chin length. Her fingers, patting downwards from the pate of her head, met with hair strands to her shoulders, then her ribs, then her waist, until she lost the flow of it in the swirls of hair she was sitting on.

She'd trodden on her own hair.

"My—hair—"

"Yes, yes, princess, very impressive, but we need to go now."

"I'm not going anywhere with you," said Poly, her eyes wide. Her hair was moving in gentle little undulations that stirred the dust and caught in the sharp edges of the flagstones. She looked down at her fingers, hoping to see translucent magic dripping from them, but they were frighteningly normal.

"Real, then," she said. "Why is my hair moving?"

"Huh," he said. "Interesting. What have you done to it?"

"What have *I* done to it? Nothing! *Why is it moving?*"

"You can't sit there and play with your hair. The castle is falling down."

"It's double-blocked and reinforced with multiple layers of magic," said Poly, breathing too fast. "It can't be falling down."

She knew the castle couldn't be falling down. It was ridiculous to consider the thought. But the air was thrumming oddly—had been doing so for some time, she thought—and when Poly looked around, gathering her wits, she saw that the room was disintegrating. Wall hangings were dropping softly to the flagstones in soft, woolly pieces, dressers were making wood scented piles of dust around the room, and great, sandy waterfalls tumbled from the top of each wall as the stones crumbled. Even the flagstones beneath her feet felt fragile. With the corrosion came a sense of strong, ancient magic, and Poly knew with certainty that she was no longer in the time she had been in yesterday. Years—no, *centuries* must have passed to make the castle collapse like this. She knew that everyone she had ever known was dead and gone, and that, strangely, the wizard had been telling the truth. He *had* come to rescue her.

There was a prickling across her skull. Poly saw her hair rise and unfurl in her peripheral, threading through the stale, humming air, but her eyes were heavy and it was difficult to feel as frightened as she should have felt.

"The castle is falling apart," she said quietly.

"Told you so," said the wizard. The words didn't quite seem to match the shapes his lips were making, and she wondered if she was in shock. "Magic was the only thing holding it up; now that the spell's broken, the stored time will crush it to powder. We need to leave."

Poly saw the golden pulse of magic that meant he was about to Shift them both from the castle and resisted instinctively. There was a bright point in the room that was pulling at her. The room itself, unfamiliar and familiar all at once, prodded at her consciousness, forcing her to think.

Poly felt the wizard's magic tug at her again, and resisted still. The wizard had called her princess, and she was certainly in the princess' room. The satin ensemble: that was the princess', too. But that bright spot—three rectangular aberrations in the dust of an old bookshelf—ah, that was *hers*.

Poly dug the rectangles out of the dust and found herself looking down at three books. Her books, to be precise. The princess had taken these three some time ago when Poly had been so foolish as to admit they had once belonged to her enchantress mother. Persephone had always been resentful when someone proved more interesting than herself, and when it was discovered that Poly hadn't inherited the enchantress trait, she had doubled her attentions. Persephone's jealousy, not to mention a nasty way with magic, had made Poly's life a short, interesting, and bitter one as the princess' lady-in-waiting.

She was still gazing at her books when the wizard's voice said in her ear, "What did you do to my spell?"

Poly hunched her shoulders against the tickle of his breath on her ear. "I didn't do anything to it."

When she turned around the wizard was looking at her with glassy, distant eyes. "Yes, you did. You're a very bothersome young woman."

Poly would have liked to tell him that if his spells didn't work it was his own fault, but she had learned from bitter experience that it was unwise for a person without magical abilities to antagonise those who *did*. The princess had made the lives of her ladies-in-waiting unpleasant enough, but that two of those ladies-in-waiting also had magic while Poly didn't, had made her the odd man out. She had learned very quickly that there are a hundred ways in which someone with magic can make someone without very uncomfortable.

Poly yawned and swayed slightly. The thrumming had become a steady hum in her head, lulling her to sleep even as she delved through her memories. An insistent prodding in one shoulder woke her slightly—the wizard was poking her experimentally with his forefinger.

"Oh, you are awake," he said, tilting his head back to gaze at her as though he were inspecting an insect.

Poly blinked sleepily and frowned, her hair rising and curling in the air. She distantly felt the wizard slide between tendrils of her hair to curl one arm around her waist, then there was a swift, disorienting Shift, and they were outside the castle. Poly, jolted forcibly back into the present by the sudden change, watched in shaken silence as the castle collapsed in a mushrooming cloud of dust and rubble. Her hair blew up and away in a rush of dusty air that made her sneeze, then gradually wafted back around her. She thought it was still moving slightly even when the breeze petered out.

The wizard had moved on to pick about in the rubble when it came to Poly's attention that something sharply uncomfortable was digging into her ribs. She shook herself, eyes heavy, and blinked down at the three books that were clasped in her arms. They were the same size and neatly stacked, corners safely pointing outwards, but as she pulled them away from herself, something rolled woodenly across the cover boards. Poly caught it before it fell into the rubble and found herself holding a small wooden spindle. It had delicate curls carved into the whorl and a design of leaves etched along the barrel: it was a spindle for decoration, not real use.

The wizard looked up from his rubble-trawling. "What's that?"

"Nothing," Poly said automatically, curling her fingers back around the spindle.

He shrugged and turned his back, gazing away from the

castle. Poly looked up, conscious of a feeling of stifling closeness, and discovered that an impossibly tall, thorny hedge had grown up where the moat used to be. So tall and curving was it that it blocked both light and sight of the first two suns in the triad. The weakest, third sun was still in sight, but its light was more drear than bright.

Poly clutched her books closer in cold disbelief, following the line of the hedge until she could see that it stretched around the entire castle, pile of rubble that the castle now was. The stillness in the air suggested that the foliage was miles thick.

Poly swallowed, her throat dry. What in the world had happened to the castle, and why did it feel like it was her fault?

"How did you get through that?" she asked the wizard, finding a more comfortable question to ask.

"The incantation they used had a mistake in it," the wizard murmured, looking at her with unfocused eyes and then away again without recognition. "Be quiet. I need to find it again."

Poly frowned, pushing up her glasses. If there had been a mistake in the incantation, it had righted itself.

"Wizard." His eyes were still unfocused, and Poly could see his magic pushing at the thorn hedge. A little louder, she repeated, "Wizard?"

"Luck."

"Pardon?"

"Luck," he repeated, pushing her aside to prowl further along the hedge. "It's my name. Use it. I'm not a wizard."

"Luck, then," persisted Poly. She'd put a lot of effort into being invisible at the castle, but it was quite another thing to be ignored on sight and without effort. "There isn't a gap in the hedge magic anymore."

That made his eyes focus sharply on her, and she saw with some interest that they were deep green instead of gold as she had first thought. He asked, "Can you see the hedge magic?"

"Of course!" Poly said, surprised. She had thought that

everyone could see and touch magic as easily as they saw and touched water.

"Interesting!" he said, and promptly turned his back on the hedge to gaze rather disconcertingly at her. Poly found that she preferred being looked at as though she wasn't there. The way Luck was looking at her made her think of the way Wizard Timokin used to look at his dissection specimens: interesting, but just a specimen after all.

Luck's magic grew immensely, surrounding her, and Poly felt her hair rising and spreading out tendrils to meet it. Gold threads mixed with the silky black threads of her hair, joyfully twining together with a buzz that startled her, and Luck gave a short, sudden yelp.

"What did you do?"

"N-nothing," Poly stammered.

"Yes, you did," contradicted Luck, frowning. "What have you done to my magic? It's gone all peculiar."

The force of his magic became narrower, more subtle; probing at her memories, her thoughts. Then it was sliding, cold and precise, into her consciousness.

Poly gasped and slapped at the magic.

Luck yelped again, this time in pain, and snatched the tendrils back into himself. "Stop that!"

His magic, which was swirling angrily about his person, now bore a slightly brownish tint.

"You've no business poking at my mind," Poly said fiercely. She knew that she had hit back harder than the offence warranted.

"Why is it that every time I touch you, you slap me?" wondered Luck.

"I didn't slap you," Poly protested, flushing. The way he managed to construe everything as her fault was off-putting. "I kicked you, and it was because you kissed me. I don't go around just kicking people, you know."

"It wouldn't surprise me," Luck remarked. "Nothing about you would surprise me. You're a horribly violent princess."

Poly, gasping at the unfairness of it, took far too long to think of a reply.

At last, she said sourly, "My name is Polyhymnia. You might as well call me Poly if we're being so informal."

She didn't want to secede the title of Princess until she knew why Luck was addressing her by it, but it was jarring to hear the title every other time he spoke to her.

Luck blinked. "Huh. Alright," he said, and added, "Stay still, I want to try something."

He did something tricky with his gold magic and Poly found herself imprisoned in a closed spell circle.

"Let me go at once!" she demanded, hot and cold by turns with anger and fear. It wasn't the first time she had been captured in a spell circle: the Princess had been fond of using them to carry out punishments. Living with the princess had taught her very quickly that rugs on the floor were best travelled around rather than over, and that one's bed should always be thoroughly inspected unless one actually *liked* being strangled by one's bedclothes, or snuggled in the clammy embrace of a faintly smirking selkie who was just as surprised to find himself in bed with a human girl but by no means as unwilling.

Therefore, it was with something approaching terror that Poly saw a golden tide flood Luck's eyes. His magic gathered strength with truly horrifying speed, and a great, pulsing mass of power hurtled toward her. Poly shrieked and instinctively, ridiculously, threw up her hands to catch it. She found herself with a glowing gold mass cupped between her hands, her heart pounding madly in her ears. Her hair roiled around her in a state of excitement, a span longer than it had been when she woke.

Luck laughed gleefully, to her indignation. "Wonderful! This is supposed to be impossible. Dear Polyprincess. No, stop wriggling, I haven't finished yet."

Poly was about to tell him furiously that he had *better* be finished, when another surge of magic hurtled toward her. There was no catching it or stopping it—it was a solid wall of magic, just waiting to break. Her hair unfurled to meet it and the two met with a shock Poly felt to her bones.

Her breath caught in the back of her throat, but this time it was with a sigh of contentment, not fear. This wave was gone just as suddenly as the first, and Poly's hair was once again heavy with magic, streaks of silky gold among the dusky strands.

Luck gazed at her, an odd look in his eyes. "Magic likes you. *My* magic likes you. Huh."

Poly ran a lock of hair through her fingers, feeling the silkiness of the magic. It refused the call of her fingers and sank deeper into the strands. She could feel a powerful, painless pulling at her hair and knew that it was Luck trying to call his magic back to him. It resisted his call as well, hair and magic thread merging indistinguishably with each other.

A few moments later her hair was the same slate black it had always been, and Luck was standing by the thorn hedge, watching her with narrow eyes.

"I'll want that bit of magic back later," he said.

"It wouldn't let go," Poly said, but she wasn't sorry. "I did try."

Luck flickered and was suddenly, invasively closer, a coil of her hair curled around his fingers.

"It's growing," he said, in interest. "It was shorter in the castle, and shorter again when we were in your dream. I think some of the sleep spell is still holding on."

Poly had a nightmarish vision of herself sleeping again, perhaps for hundreds of years, and the slight fuzziness in her head cleared long enough for it to occur to her that she didn't know how long she had been asleep. In the moment of clarity, it seemed to her that there was something else she should be remembering: something important, something too dangerous to be left unremembered.

Poly tried to force the memory but the fuzziness in her head was too thick. She sighed, and asked Luck the one question she could remember.

"How long have I been asleep? I only meant to have a little rest because of the Midsummer Night Festival."

Luck slid her a narrow-eyed look. "My time scales are relative, but even I don't call three hundred years a little rest."

Poly sat down numbly on a block of marble. She had felt that the castle was chilled with age and decay, but her mind had refused to believe that she could have been asleep for quite so long.

"What about the people? Lady Cimone, Melisande and Giselle?"

Luck, frowning at the hedge, asked, "Who are Melisande and Giselle?"

"The—my ladies-in-waiting."

"Oh. They're dead," said Luck. "There was a massive battle after you went under the enchantment: no one knows what happened, but the battlefield went up in enchanted amber. It's still frozen today; someone knew their stuff. The country's run by a parliament now—I suppose they thought we were less likely to embalm several thousand people if there was enough red tape to keep us tied by the heels. The Old Parrasians and Royalists cause a few annoyances, but the red tape keeps them in line as well."

Strangely enough, the idea that Civet was no longer a monarchy evoked only a feeling of slightly vindictive pleasure in Poly. The princess would have been appalled.

She said, "Good. It was about time."

Luck's green eyes flicked to her and away again. "Maybe. Every four years there's an election to decide which party will represent the country, but since both parties have a complete council of wizards, the balance of power hasn't really changed."

"At least you can vote them out," Poly said. The thing with royal families and magic bloodlines was that once one king or queen was dead, you could be sure that there would be another, just as powerful, in his or her place.

"Yes, but they're all the same," said Luck. The way his lips moved out of synchronisation with his words was beginning to give Poly a headache. "Confound the hedge, where's this glitch!"

"I told you," Poly said, inured to repeating herself. No one at the castle had listened to her either. "There isn't one anymore. It used to be *there*, but I think it was only one way."

"Huh. They did a different casting for the inside. Now what?"

"Can't you just Shift us out like you did in the castle?"

"No. Shifting through magic this thick is impossible. I'll do a Journey spell once we get away from the hedge." He eyed the hedge thoughtfully. "It should have disintegrated when the castle did. It's got something to do with you, Poly; you make magic behave oddly."

"I don't do it on purpose," sighed Poly, wondering what else she was destined to take the blame for. She was sure that she had never been able to influence magic before she was bespelled: it would have made life a lot easier if she *had* been able to do so. "Anyway—" she added, but Luck was no longer listening.

He was surrounded by a swirling and thoughtful mass of golden magic, his eyes tinted slightly with the same gold.

Moments later he startled Poly by giving a joyful yell. "I've got it! Come along, Poly."

Poly found herself swept off her feet, quite literally.

"Put me down!" she demanded. Her hair seemed to have other ideas, however: it curled around Luck's shoulders, cocooning them together in a blanket of hair and magic.

"Very nice," said Luck approvingly, oblivious to her blush. "No, leave my legs free, Poly; I need to walk."

"Tell my hair!" Poly snapped, her cheeks uncomfortably hot. She thought she could still feel the pressure of Luck's lips on her own, and she didn't like being cocooned to him. "I'm not doing anything!"

"Legs," Luck said, peering down at the hair lashing his legs together. Much to Poly's relief, the tendrils loosened reluctantly. "Huh. Very unusual. Off we go."

Poly gave a suppressed squeak as Luck dashed at the hedge, clutching his coat lapels. Then they were ploughing through huge, thorned branches and green-black foliage. She could feel the magic of the hedge prodding at her magicked hair, sensing the Poly-ness to it, and it struck her that the hedge had been tuned to her particularly, and no one else. As she realized that, she began to feel the hedge probing deeper, sensing the difference that was Luck. As if in response, her hair tightened.

"Luck—"

"I know. Put your arms around my neck."

Poly muttered, but did as she was told, wriggling her arms to twine through hair and around his neck. As she did so, Luck caught a breath to match his breathing with hers, and Poly felt the scrutiny of the hedge lessen slightly.

At first, she thought they had managed to confuse it, but then she saw it experimentally reaching for Luck's uncovered legs and gasped, "Run!"

"Too late," said Luck's voice matter-of-factly in her ear, and Poly braced herself for the onslaught of magic.

But Luck was still striding forward, exuding surges of magic that were more powerful than anything she had ever seen. A light-headed feeling of relief made Poly's head spin: Luck meant it was too late for the hedge.

The next minute they were breaking out into the full light of the triad. Luck put Poly down some distance away from the hedge, breathing easily despite the huge waves of magic that were still rolling off him. Her hair didn't take kindly to the idea of separation, curling tendrils around his neck just as he freed one wrist and sliding insidiously around his waist just as he managed to free his neck.

"Poly," he said at last, plaintively.

"I'm *trying*," said Poly, harassed and pink faced, and trying not to notice Luck's other arm around her waist. In desperation, she gave her hair the same sort of mental slap she had given Luck's magic when it became nosy, and it released him with sulky slowness.

Poly sat down wearily, feeling as though she couldn't keep her eyes open another second, and said, "*That* was *harrowing*."

Luck looked stung and slightly hurt, but Poly was too tired to feel herself able to frame a sensible explanation and she didn't know why he should take it so personally, after all. So she simply curled up in a cocoon of hair, her books tucked in close to her chest, and fell asleep.

2

When Poly woke up the next morning, it was because of a pain in her nose and the fact that she didn't seem to be able to breath. Gasping, she opened her eyes to find Luck crouched beside her, pinching her nose and frowning.

"Ow! Luck, *ow!*"

"You like your sleep, don't you?" he remarked, sitting back on his heels.

Poly's voice was small and pained. "You pinched my nose!"

"You wouldn't wake up. Huh. It must be a side effect of the enchantment."

Poly gazed at him balefully. That was no reason for suffocating her in her sleep. There were *spells* for waking people up.

"No, don't glare at me," Luck said. "I'm only trying to help."

"My nose will fall off."

"Rubbish," said Luck briskly, seizing her chin. "No, don't wriggle, Poly. I want to look at that curse."

Poly, finding her personal space thus encroached upon, ventured a dismayed, "But—"

Luck twitched her chin slightly to the side, fingers sharp and unheeding. "Huh. There's something very unusual here." His face lunged closer, invasive and accusatory. "What are you holding, Poly?"

"What? Nothing."

"Yes, that's what you said yesterday; but it's not true."

Poly looked askance at him, and he looked back, unperturbed. But there was something in her hand, come to think of it. She uncurled the hand with a frown, fingers stiffly reluctant, and they both gazed down at a small wooden spindle.

"Huh. That's a bit of a disappointment," said Luck. "Not a lick of magic in it."

Poly wondered, "Where did that come from? It looks familiar."

"It should," said Luck, losing interest in the spindle and reacquainting himself with her face. "You've been carrying it around since yesterday. Stop blinking, Poly."

"I can't have been carrying it around since yesterday," objected Poly, trying desperately not to blink. The attempt proved counterproductive, and she tried not to blush under a particularly glazed look from Luck. "I'd remember."

"You didn't remember me from the dream."

"What dream?"

"Yes," said Luck. "Well, it's no good trying to poke around from the outside. I'll have to keep an eye on it as we walk."

"Walk? You said you could do a Journey spell once we were out of the hedge."

Luck gave her a blank look that suggested she was babbling. "You must have misunderstood. Anyway, I can't."

"Why not?" she demanded, determined at least to get an answer out of him.

"Journey spells make me ill," Luck said, with dignity. "It's time for breakfast. Eat your eggs before they go cold."

And there *were* eggs. They were sitting lopsidedly on a sloped boulder nearby, dribbling golden yolk down a flimsy plate and surrounded by a decent amount of bacon and two slices of toast. Poly was too hungry to be surprised. She was even too hungry to ask where Luck had produced the eggs from, or why she hadn't seen the change in his magic. She had a small, terrified feeling that it was such a small effort for him that it hadn't even registered.

Poly, who had a basic knowledge of the theory of producing somethings out of nothing—not to mention *cooked* somethings—began to feel that she might have been safer with the princess than she was with this wizard.

She wasn't even sure he was a wizard, if it came to that. His magic was just a little bit too golden and strong and abundant to make him a mere wizard. Poly thought she might be glad of the princess' mantle if it came to travelling with an enchanter, since a princess must command respect, after all.

She was still hoping rather doubtfully that this would be the case when she finished scraping the last golden drops of egg from her plate with a strip of buttered toast.

Luck said, "You eat more than a Capital foot soldier," and it came to her attention that he was watching her in fascination.

"I haven't eaten in three hundred years," said Poly, trying for dignity despite the flush of heat that had crawled into her cheeks. "I was hungry."

"Yes, you have," Luck said. "The enchantment had a sustenance clause built into it. I don't suppose you know exactly what sort of enchantment it was that they laid on you, by the bye?"

"I thought *you* knew," Poly said, in a rather accusatory tone. He was the wizard, after all. Or enchanter, if one subscribed to the view that the worst possible outcome was the one most likely to occur.

"I don't know everything," said Luck, levelling a vaguer-than-usual gaze at her. "Your enchantment is three hundred years old. It's based on an ancient sort of ritual that dates back even further, and it's all convoluted with a curse as well. There are only a few scraps of information on it apart from the spellpaper that bound the enchantment in place. I searched the whole Capital Library looking for clues."

Certain that she was about to be told again that it was her fault, Poly asked hastily, "Where did you get the spellpaper?"

"The Head of the Wizard Council gave it to me," Luck said, removing the golden gaze, much to her relief. She wondered if he'd been trying another sneaky spell on her, and thought that yes, he probably had. "The elections are only half a year away and everyone's digging for filthy rumours and backstory about the opposing party. Then you turned up like a gritty little pearl just waiting to throw everyone out of balance, and suddenly the Council's housecleaning doesn't seem quite so perfect."

I'm housekeeping, Poly thought, her eyes narrow and somehow hot. *Well!*

"Why did he give it to you? Why not just find me himself?"

Luck shrugged. "Probably didn't want to be assassinated. Or kicked, if it comes to that."

"Very well, then," Poly said briskly, still annoyed and ridiculously hurt. "Thank you for rescuing me, and I'll be quite all right by myself now. You can go on without me."

"No, I can't. I have to bring you back to the Capital with me. It's in my contract."

"C-contract? Oh!"

That was even worse. As if it wasn't enough that someone had decided to use her as a common-or-garden ingredient in an enchantment, now she was being bartered and arranged for as if she were simply a commodity.

"Don't be silly, Poly," said Luck. "If I don't take you back with me, Mordion won't give me the books."

A shock of cold surprise fizzed through Poly from her head to her toes, freezing out the anger. "*Who* is giving you books?"

"Mordion. You don't know him."

There was an unpleasant feeling in her stomach. Poly said, "Do you know, I think I might."

"Rubbish. You can't."

Poly bit down on a sharp retort since Luck was quite right: it was very unlikely that the Mordion she had known could still be alive after three hundred years.

However, the memory of what that Mordion had been capable of inspired in her a fear powerful enough to say, "I'm not going anywhere with you."

Luck blinked at her as if he were seeing her for the first time, and said with interest, "Huh. We'll see."

There was a momentary build-up of ridiculously powerful magic that Poly's hair extended, quivering, to meet. Displaced air huffed coolly in her face, and then everything...stopped.

"Right," said Luck, and Poly, whose only sense had been one of stillness and relief that nothing seemed to have happened, found to her stupefaction that she could no longer move.

"Let me go!"

"No," Luck said, busily drawing loose threads of magic back into himself. "For one thing, you're too dangerous: also, you'd probably kick me. Here we go—"

This time the Shift was nothing like instantaneous. Every moment was marked and precise, drawing out in the suddenly thick air until Poly was convinced that she was not breathing the air so much as drinking it. Her spindle dropped from her fingers with a preciseness that felt almost deliberate, and in the same moment one of the books she had rescued fell into her open palm, binding down. The pages flicked through the thick air until at last they rested on an ink illustration. It swam in Poly's gaze, black and definite against the vellum, but her dazed eyes didn't have time to register which picture it was, because at that exact moment there was a sharp snap and a tug.

Poly tumbled into grass, free and breathless, and found with some relief that the air had regained its customary consistency.

Luck's voice, somewhere above her head, said, "Huh. That was interesting."

Her head was resting on something soft. Poly allowed herself to enjoy the comfort until it occurred to her that her headrest was rising and falling in a rhythmic manner that suggested...breathing.

Oh. Poly sat up hastily. It was Luck's stomach that her head had been cushioned on.

"A lesson in history, princess," said Luck, without seeming to notice either that she'd been reclining on him, or that she'd moved. He was dreamily watching the clouds, and Poly thought that she could have continued using his stomach as a cushion without him noticing. "Roughly three hundred years ago—"

Poly sighed. "I was alive then. I *know*—"

"You'd just gone to sleep. Don't interrupt. Roughly three hundred years ago, just after you'd gone to sleep, someone cast a huge enchantment with sharp edges and a wobbly middle that should have stopped it from working altogether."

Silence fell briefly, and when Poly looked down at Luck, he'd gone back to gazing at the clouds. Just as she thought he'd forgotten her, he said, "If the magic they used hadn't been so powerful, the enchantment would have collapsed. As it was, it ran away with Civet, and before Parras knew what was happening there was a feral army marching for the border and killing everything it came into contact with."

"You said there was an enchanted battlefield—"

"Two days," said Luck, as if she hadn't spoken. "That's how long it took Parras to capitulate and accept terms. There were still enough Civetan knights who hadn't gone rabid to make sure the terms were kept up, but when they went to stop the army, they couldn't. Idiots. I could have told them that."

Poly felt sick. "We invaded Parras?"

"Fortunately for the rest of Parras, something or someone finally interfered with the enchantment and the whole battlefield went up in enchanted amber. The Parrasians who weren't dead were safe, but the enchanted Civetans were all trapped."

"So when you talk about Civet and our capital city—"

"New Civet and the Capital," nodded Luck. He sat up, grass clinging to his hair. "They moved it further into what was Parras and had a Council run the country instead of royals. As far as we knew all the royals were dead, anyway. The enchanted battlefield stayed where it was. Officially, it's a civic reminder, but I think they just couldn't clean it up."

Poly nodded numbly, meeting Luck's eyes briefly and finding only vague disinterest there.

"Impressive work," he said. Poly thought she must have imagined the swift green glance that momentarily pierced his blank disinterest. "The kind of thing that makes you think there were a couple of enchanters mixed up in it all."

Poly said, "Oh," rather listlessly. She wished Luck would get to the point.

"I mention it," continued Luck dreamily, "So that next time you throw off one of my small Shifters, you know which direction to go."

"Throw off—I didn't throw off your Shift spell!"

"The Capital is in Old Parras, for your information. Also, they don't like people Shifting in and out because it makes security difficult, so there are magical filters that tend to shred people who try to get in. I don't particularly like the idea of being shredded."

Poly reached unconsciously for her books and found them all stacked neatly together. She must have imagined that stretched out period of time before the Shifter brought them here. "I didn't—"

"Next time," added Luck, seizing her chin between two fingers, "try to get us closer to the Capital, not further away. And I want to know how you pushed my Shifter off course—there's nothing of it in your eyes."

Poly pushed her glasses up on her nose, using the movement to jerk her chin away from his fingers. Unfortunately, scowling at Luck didn't remind him about the small issue of personal space—he merely shuffled invasively closer again to peer into her eyes.

"I didn't do anything to your spell," she said, edging back. "Whatever went wrong, it's your own fault. I wasn't even *moving*."

"Funny, that. Can't find any traces of it on you."

"I told you," said Poly. "I didn't do anything."

Luck gazed at her with his head tilted back. "I know you did it, I just can't see how."

Oh, bother you then, Poly thought. She waited until Luck sat back on the grassy hill again before she asked, "Where are we?"

"*I* don't know," said Luck annoyingly. "*I* didn't do it."

"I didn't either," muttered Poly, because Luck had stopped listening. He was flicking at a butterflower with one pensive finger, eyes vague and just a little bit golden.

"Interesting," he said.

Poly asked, "What's interesting?" without much hope of Luck answering.

He seemed to have forgotten about her again, and was engaged in ruthlessly pulling up handful after handful of green, sweet smelling grass. It was only after he thoughtfully began putting grass blades in his mouth that Poly realised the grass wasn't in fact sweet smelling. It didn't smell like anything, if it came to that. She blinked and took a closer look at the clumps of grass that Luck had uprooted. They were so bright and vibrant that they *must* smell sweet and grassy. Had the grass tricked her into thinking it had a smell, or had her own mind been playing tricks on her?

She asked Luck, who didn't seem to hear and only replied, "Yes, but I want to know *why*."

"Let me know when you find out," she said, a little sourly, and left him to his grass tasting.

She wended her way from the ridge she and Luck had arrived on, to the very top of the hill, intent on reaching its summery apex. The triad was almost offensively cheerful here, caressing the bonny faces of the butterflowers as she passed them and glancing vibrantly off every grass stalk. The breeze was delightfully pleasant, and Poly wondered if her mind had created these impressions, too. She thought they became a little less strong as she wondered about them.

From the top of the hill Poly saw nearly a dozen hilltops

decked in summery green, each more sunny and cheerful than the last.

"Oh, really!" she said to the general splendour. "Don't you think you're trying just a bit too hard?"

Some of the distant hilltops were wooded and tree lined, others bare and grassy, but all alike had a splendour of obnoxiously healthy countryside that Poly found a little smug. She narrowed her eyes at them, fancying that the surrounding hills were just a little...unreal, perhaps?

"I wonder," she said aloud. And then, "*Oh!* It's not that they don't smell. It's *why* don't they smell!"

Poly looked at the hilltops surrounding her with narrowed eyes. There was some sort of insect buzzing away in the distance, surprising her with the knowledge that it was the first she had seen since she and Luck arrived at this place. Adding to the air of unreality was the fact that the bare, grassy mounds furthest away were a little fuzzy. Were they quite real? She wasn't sure anymore.

Busy with her thoughts, it was a few minutes before Poly realised that the distant insect buzzing from one hilltop to the other, was in fact a person. The figure was travelling in short bursts of blue-green magic, disappearing on one hilltop and appearing on the next almost instantaneously. Moreover, it seemed to be quickly coming closer, as if intent on discovering what kind of insect *she* was.

As it came sporadically closer Poly was able to discern the bright starbursts that exploded in its magic: whoever it was, he or she was quite mad.

Soon she could see that the thing was a man, dressed in a hermit's cassock that was ragged and indecently short of his knobbly knees. A wild bush of a beard stuck out of his thin face, threaded with flowers here and there. He was chasing a brilliantly blue butterfly, making little darting snatches at it and cackling gleefully when he missed, Shifting when he had to.

Poly was watching him with a mixture of bemusement and suppressed laughter, wondering if she ought to call Luck, when with frightening suddenness, the hermit was *there*, his face so close that his resounding "Hah!" fogged Poly's glasses.

To her mortification, Poly shrieked and leapt backwards, her hair expanding like a cloud in immediate response to the threat. Then Luck was somehow in front of her, his strong, bright magic pulsing around him.

"Bravo!" yelled the hermit.

Poly bit back a giggle despite the hammering of her heart. The hermit was projecting droplets of spit freely—and, by the look on Luck's face, quite forcefully.

The hermit didn't seem to realise, or perhaps he didn't care. He continued to gurgle and clap his hands in glee, yelling, "Bravo! Bravo! No, Eureka! Hah! Eureka!"

Luck pointedly wiped his face with a conjured handkerchief, but the hermit paid no attention to the fact. Poly, taking courage from the fact that he seemed to be rather more mad than dangerous, was able to quiet her hair, and at last stepped out from behind Luck.

At the sight of her the man giggled again and said: "I knew I was right. I *told* you I was right. Every three years it snows, and then it happens!"

Luck, looking put upon, said in a long-suffering voice, "Poly, I don't suppose that one of those books you picked up in the castle was called *Angwynelle*, by any chance?"

"It snows!" burbled the hermit, oblivious to the cloudless blue sky and the full radiating heat of the suns. "Every three years, and then you know what happens. The snowflakes come!"

Remembering that it *had* been *Angwynelle* that had fallen open in her hand, and that the hermit was disturbingly familiar, Poly said guiltily, "Yes, but it can't be *that*—"

"Well it is," Luck said, wiping another wet speck from his nose. "I told you that you'd ruined my shift spell."

He seemed mildly pleased by the fact.

"But the hermit is a character in a book, not a real person!"

protested Poly. She had read *Angwynelle* enough times to recognise a character as memorable as the hermit.

"You don't think *he's* real, do you?" asked Luck. "He's a figment."

But the hermit's bony fingers, which were tugging at Poly's hair and rapping her smartly on the skull, *felt* real. He looked up at her with bright, wild eyes, and said, "I'm just as real as you are, my darling snowflakes. Or just as unreal. In point of fact, I'm even more real than you are."

"You're just a character in a book," Poly told him, a little rudely. She had already felt the oddness to the place, the way things seemed to be just a little too beautiful and faded around the edges. It occurred to her rather horribly that if she and Luck travelled as far as they could possibly travel, they would find nothing but empty green hills until they finally came upon the hermit again.

The hermit gurgled, unoffended. "Bravo, little snowflake! Encore! But I'm still more real than you are, you know. You're not even as real as a snowflake."

"Yes, I am," argued Poly. The hermit's way of speaking made her head spin.

"Wrong!" shouted the hermit, showering Poly with a fine mist of moisture. "Wrong and false! Ipso facto and tripe! I'm *far* more real than you are. You're here in my little patch of words, and I'm all that exists here, so *you* don't exist. I might not exist in your world, but you're in mine now. Hah! A snowflake is a snowflake whether it's made of ice or letters, so a snowflake is more real than you are, too. So there."

"He makes a disturbing amount of sense," said Luck, eyeing the hermit in some fascination. He asked, "Is there a way out?"

"Yes, my snowflakes," burbled the man, shivering out of existence and appearing again beside what appeared to be a rather shakily fenced goat corral. "Come along, come along, come along! You mustn't melt, you know; I would never get the water out of my nice new carpet."

He had fizzed in and out of existence several more times before they caught up with him, and then skipped from one foot to the other in impatience when they stopped. "Hurry up, snowflakes! Through the gate before you melt!"

"That's a goat pen," said Poly.

"Hah!" said the hermit. "That's all *you* know! It's not a pen. Pen! Hahahaha! Not even a quill. Not it, oh no! It's a door."

"He's right, you know," Luck said, green eyes beginning to tinge slightly gold. "It's an opening between two paragraphs, and it's outward bound."

The hermit clapped his hands, producing a blackbird feather with a flourish of starburst magic. He carefully tucked it behind one of Poly's ears as if it were a jewelled earring and said, "This is yours, little snowflake. Such a long time to wait, wasn't it? But now everything will come about again, so long as you're right, right, right!"

"I suppose so," said Poly, dubiously touching the feather.

The hermit, suddenly anxious, said, "Said too much, didn't I? I wasn't supposed to, was I? Right, right, right, that's all I was supposed to say. You have to go now. Off, off, off! Off you go!"

"The book first, I think," said Luck, holding out his hand for it and ignoring the harried shooing motions that the hermit was making.

"It's mine!" Poly objected, annoyed to find that he expected her to give her book up at his mere request.

Luck shot her a golden look, and then the book was in his outstretched hand without more than a whisper of magic.

"I'll want it back later," she said, but Luck had already lost interest in her. He was watching the hermit's increasingly erratic antics.

"What's wrong with him?"

"Does it matter?" asked Poly, and encountered a reproachful look from the hermit. "I mean—well, you're a character. You're written that way. It doesn't have to matter *why*."

"I'm written very specifically," said the hermit proudly. "Clever little snowflake, aren't you? Go away."

Since he emphasized the command by shoving Poly into the outbound passage, Poly was left with very little to say to this. Scenery blurred, and Luck must have grabbed her in passing, because when they tumbled back into the real world his arms were rucked uncomfortably under her arms and she had formed a closer acquaintance with his mud-stained coat.

Poly was obliged to dissuade her hair from clasping Luck to her side before he could disentangle his arms, by which time she was feeling hot and bothered and misused.

"Don't look at me like that," said Luck, his eyes very green. "I don't particularly like being conjoined to you, either."

Poly, who hadn't thought she was *looking* in any specific way, blushed.

Taking unfair advantage of her confusion, he added, "I thought princesses were meant to take lessons in charm and deportment."

It was rather a shock to be reminded that she was meant to be the princess. Poly had to close her mouth, which had automatically opened to correct Luck, before she said something unconsidered. She wanted badly to know why she had been used in an enchantment, and what exactly that enchantment was. Answers would undoubtedly be more forthcoming for a princess than a lady-in-waiting.

"I thought that wizards were meant to be versed in international diplomacy," she pointed out instead, feeling that it was time she put her foot down if she meant to be the princess. "You laid hands on a royal personage—"

"I didn't; I kissed you," interposed Luck, curling a portion of Poly's hair around one finger and closely observing it.

"That's what I said."

Luck disengaged his left wrist from the last of her hair and let go of the lock he held. "Then I seem to have been laying my lips on you, not my hands. Come along, Poly, and stop arguing. We have a long way to walk."

Out of the unreal ambience of the hermit's chapter the triad was glowing warm and welcoming, creating its usual three-pronged shadows. The plains spread out before them, the grass flowing in great, slow waves as the gentle wind swept close to the ground, warm and scented. There were wildflowers among the grass plumes: butterflowers, pettypips, occasional patches of lavender, and even a few flowers Poly didn't recognise. She amused herself as they walked by naming as many of them as she could remember. Gwyn the gardener had taught her their names long ago, when he found infant Poly in his garden, happily engaged in eating his prized roses. Poly had spent almost as much time with Gwyn as she had with her parents in those young years.

Poly smiled, remembering his leathered old face, and with faint surprise discovered that tears were gliding down her cheeks in gentle sorrow at this memory.

In an effort to stop them, she curled her arms more tightly around her remaining books and asked Luck, "When will we cross the border?"

She seemed to remember that the border was where the southern plains met the northern forests. Much of the tension between Civet and her neighbouring country of Parras had been over claims that the already land rich Civet was poaching forest land along the border by felling trees. Poly remembered Lady Cimone's curled lip at the rumours and realised with surprise and sudden understanding that the Lady had known all along what her country was capable of. It was unsettling, because one always felt that one's country was on the side of right and justice.

"You're not paying attention, Poly. There isn't a border anymore. *Why are you sleeping?*"

Luck's last words were sharp and laced with a cutting edge of his gold magic, and Poly, who had indeed been falling quietly asleep as she walked, mis-stepped in the shock between waking and sleeping, and tumbled over a small bump in the ground.

Luck hauled her up by one arm, and said, "Poly, you're deliberately making a nuisance of yourself."

"But I'm not!" Poly protested, stumbling blindly without her glasses. A moment later they were thrust onto her nose, and Luck's annoyed face swam into sight. "I was just walking, and you were talking, and then I was asleep."

The annoyance in Luck's face faded, to be replaced with a thoughtful look.

"We were talking about Civet," he said. "But what were you thinking?"

"The same, I suppose."

"No, you weren't. You're always thinking something different from what you're saying. Why were you crying?"

Poly, who had thought Luck hadn't noticed her tears at all, decided that his vague look wasn't entirely to be trusted.

"I was just remembering."

"Remembering what?"

"Castle things," Poly said, purposely vague. Gwyn, like Lady Cimone, was something she preferred not to discuss with anyone, particularly Luck.

Luck gave her one of his long, green, thoughtful looks, but when he spoke it was to change the subject entirely.

"Do you have that spindle about you?"

Poly gazed at him in mild puzzlement. "What spindle?"

"Yes, exactly," said Luck. "You're determined to sleep, and a wizard could find that offensive."

Poly opened her mouth, closed it again, and at last said plaintively, "But you said you weren't a wizard!"

"I'm not," said Luck, unexpectedly lunging at the skirts of her gown. His hand found the single, tiny slit of a pocket and tugged something out of it. "And I find it offensive that you keep falling asleep."

Poly, looking in confusion at a familiarly carved spindle that she hadn't remembered just moments ago, protested, "I can't *help* it! Luck, how did that get in my pocket? Did you put it there? I'm sure I've—"

"—seen it before. Yes, you have. Poly, you're incorrigible. You should be waking up, not falling asleep again."

"Maybe you didn't wake me up properly."

"Of course I woke you up properly!" Luck said, pinioning her with a hard look. "My kisses are notoriously effective."

"Oh, is that what they are? Do you wake up a lot of cursed girls, then?"

"Spindle."

"What?"

"Spindle."

"What spi—ow! Let me go! What is that? Where did it come from?"

"Well, this is just ridiculous," said Luck.

His fingers were wrapped tightly around her hand, and somehow there was a spindle pinched uncomfortably between her fingers and Luck's. More uncomfortable still was Luck's fascinated gaze: a gaze that was entirely too close and interested and golden.

He said, "You're such a delightful little puzzle, Poly! We have experiments to do when we stop for the night. And I have to kiss you again."

"No we don't, and no *you* don't," said Poly positively.

"Also, we'll need scones."

"How are scones relevant?"

Luck gave her a blank look. "Scones are always relevant."

Poly was relieved when he stepped back and released her, though she wasn't quite sure if the preoccupied air he sank into was comforting or worrying. At any rate, that blank look from Luck was the last sign he gave Poly that he remembered her existence for quite some time.

She didn't mind; it gave her time to try and remember exactly what had happened the day she went to sleep. The last thing Poly remembered was laying down on her neatly made bed to rest briefly before the rigors of the Midsummer Night's Festival. She had been wearing her own grey cotton, she was certain—a waiting-lady's dress with too many petticoats and too much whalebone, but certainly her own dress. How had she ended up in the princess' dress, not to mention the princess' bed?

It wasn't that the dress wasn't pretty. It was embroidered satin, light and cool, with huge, fluffy petticoats to add to the airy, summer feel of the gown, and a creamy ruff that sat softly against her neck. Although it was now very much the worse for wear, it had once been one of the princess' favourite party ensembles. It wasn't at all suitable for striding through the countryside, however, and Poly, constantly curling a section of the skirt around her wrist to keep it out of the way, knew she would never have dared to wear the thing. She could only imagine what Persephone would have done to her if she'd been caught wearing it.

No, Poly had gone to sleep wearing her own grey striped cotton dress, one hand lying on the taut bodice of whalebone and piping, the other tucked behind her more austere ruff. She remembered gazing up at the ceiling with the thought of caramel corn puffs threading through her mind. So when had her dress been switched? Poly thought she had woken up again, but had she? Was that just one more dream in her three-hundred-year night?

3

It was noon by the time a blot sprang up on the horizon ahead of them, the triad sitting above it like three red-gold juggling balls.

Poly gazed at it in blank surprise. "Oh. What's that?"

"A dirty little town," said Luck, rousing from his own preoccupation. "I want to visit it."

"Why?"

"You can't wear that," he added, his eyes travelling over the overblown green gown. "You'll have to change."

"Into what? I haven't got another dress."

"Transform it," said Luck, giving her a vague, puzzled look.

"I haven't got magic," Poly told him, sighing. He ought to know that.

"Yes, you do."

"I've never had magic. Believe me, I would know."

"Rubbish. You must have." Luck's eyes were very green and narrow, but much to Poly's dismay, curls of gold were beginning to lick at his pupils. "Poly—No, Poly, don't run away."

"Don't you touch me!"

"I'm not going to touch you, I just want to—"

"No!"

"Poly—"

"*No!* I've had quite enough of magic, thank you very much."

Luck gazed at her thoughtfully for a moment, then asked with interest, "How are you going to stop me?"

Poly sat down, a miserable pouf of green satin and white petticoats, and regarded him balefully. "I can't," she said, in a gruff voice.

"You're angry again." Luck's voice sounded surprised.

Poly threw him an incredulous look and folded her arms. Luck tilted his head back to look at her, his eyes almost completely golden and unfocused, and she felt the whisper of his magic slithering around the outskirts of her mind, too close for comfort. Apparently, Luck's disregard for personal space extended to his magical as well as his physical aspect. She caught a whisp of the golden magic between her fingers, felt it slip over her fingertips like silk, then pinched and tore it away from herself.

Luck gasped, then groaned through his teeth. "*Don't* do that!"

"Don't slither around me like that!"

There was a brief silence while they both glared at each other. Then Luck hazarded, "Do you like the dress?"

Poly had the feeling that he was still trying to discover why she was angry, and in spite of herself she was amused. "No," she said. "It's huge and useless and annoying."

"Oh. Well, what do you usually wear?"

"Something sensible. Small ruff. Grey pinstripes, no ruffles. Big pockets."

"Grey? Why do you want to wear grey?"

"I don't know, it sort of fades into the background," suggested Poly, remembering too late that the princess would scarcely have liked to fade into *any* background, and that she was meant to be the princess. Soft colours had helped her to survive in the castle.

He gave her a dubious look. "All right. Picture it in your mind."

Poly did so, remembering the no nonsense quality of dress

with its big pockets, stiff whale-boned bodice and quiet, narrow sleeves. A pleasant little shiver shook her as a cool tingle of magic trickled down her back, and when she opened her eyes again, the grey pinstripe was falling in neat folds around her on the grass.

After that, it was delightfully easy to slide her remaining two books each into a pocket. Poly huffed a little sigh of relief to find her arms free again.

"Blue would have been better," said Luck. He was surveying her with a frown, but when her eyes met his, his head snapped around. "Well, come on, then."

It was late afternoon when they entered the town. It had proved to be further away than it looked, to Poly's dismay. Her legs were shaking with weariness by then, but she didn't seem to be actually sleepy, and Poly came to the conclusion that she was merely out of condition. Luck didn't have any such difficulties and continued to stride ahead of her until it was evident to Poly that he'd forgotten about her again. His head swung from side to side, his eyes wide and vague, and with his dishevelled hair and mud-spattered coat buttoned crookedly, he looked just a little mad. As they walked further into the town, Poly found herself thinking that it was just as well: there was a suggestion of menace to the dirty streets that she didn't care for, and so long as Luck looked wilder and more dangerous than anything they were likely to meet, she was inclined to think that they would be safe.

She hurried along behind and collided painfully with him when he stopped suddenly outside a tea shop, her glasses jerking off the end of her nose.

Luck snatched at her glasses as they tumbled and passed them back to her. "Oh, there you are, Poly. I wondered where you'd got to."

"What are you looking for?" Poly panted.

"Tea!" said Luck.

He ducked into the shop and Poly dashed after him willy-nilly, shoving her glasses back on. She found herself pushed down into a seat at a tiny corner table that surprised her by being spotlessly clean.

"Tea for two," Luck told the little boy that came to wait on them. "And scones. Lots of scones."

"What are you looking for?" Poly repeated, when the little boy had gone. It hadn't escaped her notice that Luck had dodged her questions at least twice today.

Luck looked at her with bright eyes and said, "Magic. A great big snarl of it. It wasn't here when I passed through before."

"What is it?"

"Don't know."

"*Where* is it?"

He shrugged and ran a careless hand through his already untidy hair, forming new spikes. "Don't know that either. It's snagged on every thread of magic through the town and pulled them off centre. I thought you could see magic? Why can't you see it?"

Poly blinked and pulled back defensively from Luck's intent gaze, thankful when the boy returned with a plate piled high with scones to provide a distraction.

"More scones!" said Luck firmly, and the little boy scuttled away again. Luck buttered four scones, coating them with raspberry jam and thick cream, his eyes still on Poly. "Well?"

Poly jumped. "Well, what?"

"Have a scone," said Luck, shoving one into her hand. "They're good. Why can't you see the tangle?"

"Um," said Poly, trying to pull her thoughts together. Luck's golden gaze was distinctly off-putting. She pushed away the discomfort, as well as the thought that Luck was taking advantage of her distraction to eat all the scones, and concentrated.

The little boy returned once but Poly didn't take any notice of him. Luck's huge golden glow of magic was *there*, and *there* was the warm blue-and-brown swirl of someone (the baker, probably) just through the kitchen doors beside them. Something had caught in the blue-and-brown, snagging a very tiny thread with it, and as Poly gazed at it, it occurred to her that many other threads were caught up in it as well. It was a huge, tangled mess of magic with a pulsing ball of something at its centre.

"You do see it," remarked Luck. "Huh. Interesting."

Her concentration broken, Poly yawned and focused sleepily on him again. Things were beginning to take on a muffled consistency, but she noticed that all the scones were gone and glared at Luck, who gave her a wide, glassy look back.

"Don't fall asleep, Poly," he said, starting to his feet and for the door. "It's time to go."

Poly darted after him, hastily eating the scone in her hand as she hurried to keep up. No doubt she was fortunate Luck hadn't eaten that, too.

She didn't have either the time or effort for disgruntlement after that. Luck fairly dashed down the streets, one dizzying turn after another, and Poly had to put all her effort into keeping up with him. It was far from dignified, and more than one pedestrian turned and gazed after them in astonishment as they thundered past. Once, they startled a horse into trying to bolt, and the strident abuse of its rider followed them for several streets.

Luck's legs were longer than hers, and Poly had just despaired of catching up when she collided with him again at a street corner. Luck gasped a little on impact but caught her glasses again and straightened Poly with one distracted arm. His head was swivelling between two different streets, his eyes wild and fascinated. Poly only had time to shove her glasses back on before he grabbed her hand with a gleeful laugh and dragged her after him.

"This way!"

They ploughed through a group of silent, watchful men some way down a darkened back street, but Luck didn't notice, intent on his prize. Despite the lingering gaze of those men, Poly couldn't help grinning as she was dragged mercilessly in Luck's wake: she wondered exactly how much Luck could miss when he was concentrating on something else.

She thought she had almost worked out their course by the time they stopped briefly at a dubious old wood and metal staircase. It ran up the outside of a building, barely held against the rotting woodwork by a few rusted brackets and shaking in the light breeze. For an unsettled moment Poly thought Luck would drag her up that as well, and while they dithered, a small cannonball shot out of the shadows and artfully careened into Luck.

Poly saw the dirty little hand that slipped into Luck's waistcoat pocket and opened her mouth in warning, but it wasn't needed. The thief, attempting to pull out his hand again, had quickly discovered that he couldn't. A look of horror spread over his pinched little face, and he tried again to free his hand, this time with more desperation and less stealth.

Poly saw the glimmer of gold thread and gave a sudden, delighted chuckle. There was magic lining the pocket: Luck had thief-proofed it.

The urchin looked up at her desperately, his eyes pleading, but Luck darted off again obliviously, dragging both Poly and the urchin behind him. Poly gave herself up to the irresistible pull, giggling madly, and the urchin stumbled along with her, his eyes wide with panic and by no means sharing her enjoyment of the situation.

At last, they tumbled into a blind alley where Luck skidded to a stop, spinning in a tight circle that towed Poly and the urchin helplessly behind him.

He looked distinctly offended, as if the walls had moved to spite him, and said, "No, this can't be right."

Poly threw an amused look around, taking in the few doors of disreputable appearance and the one small, likewise disreputable puppy that was tied by a piece of thin rope to a dirty drainpipe. She disengaged her hand from Luck's while he was distractedly turning in another circle, and wandered a little further, charmed by the puppy. It was a caramel-coloured mongrel with a cheerful, wiry little beard of fur on its tiny chin, and it stood on its hind legs for her. Poly crouched beside it, offering a friendly hand, and heard the sounds of a scuffle from Luck's end of the alley. She looked up, discovering to her delight that Luck had finally noticed the pickpocket, and was chasing him in a tight circle as the boy scampered close to Luck's coat in a vain attempt to evade capture. It was rather like watching a dog chase its own tail.

"Poly! Poly, what is this?"

Luck seized the child by the scruff of the neck at last, and tugged his hand free from the waistcoat pocket.

"It's a little boy," Poly told him. "A pickpocket. You picked him up several streets back."

"Did I?" Luck gazed down at the child in bemusement. "I thought my coat felt a bit heavier. Well, I suppose you won't do that again in a hurry, will you?"

The pickpocket shook his head soundlessly, desperately. Luck dropped his hand and made a vague shooing motion.

"Off you go, then," he said mildly. The pickpocket took to his heels without waiting to be told a second time and Luck turned his attention to the walled alley. "It's gone. Poly, can you see anything?"

Poly tore her gaze away from the wriggling bundle of muddy fur that was attempting, with great determination, to lick her face, and threw a cursory look around. "No. It's all gone. Even the threads are gone."

"Huh. That's what I thought. What is *that*?"

"It's a puppy. I think it likes me."

"It looks like a dirty mop head," opined Luck, eyeing it with disfavour. His horrified gaze fell on a lock of Poly's hair that the puppy was gleefully chewing on, and to Poly's great amusement, looked as if he were about to be sick. "Make it stop!"

Poly gave the puppy's lean little stomach a brisk rub, ignoring Luck. She was surprised that the puppy was still attached to its lead; this little scrap of doghood was still coming into its first, sharp teeth. By this stage it should have been chewing everything around it to ribbons, including the thin black rope that tethered it to the drainpipe.

"One of the doors has something on it," she told Luck, to distract him from his fascinated horror.

He blinked. "Hmm? Oh, that's just a sigil. It means the owner sells spells."

"Journey spells and such?"

"Yes," said Luck. "Convenient, isn't it?"

He had begun to look thoughtful, which worried Poly slightly.

The puppy, annoyed by her preoccupation, uttered a shrill little bark and leapt up to lick her face, trailing its string lead over her arm. Poly felt the pull of savage cold where it touched her, and gasped in pain, tumbling the puppy from her lap. It barked at her again, the cock of its ears offended, and Luck's eyes flicked to them both for a vague moment before he raised his hand to knock on the marked door.

There were a few minutes of silent waiting, while Poly tentatively reached out to the puppy again and Luck traced the sigil on the door thoughtfully. Then a shuffling and clanking of locks announced the arrival of the proprietor, who cracked the door open just enough to display a scowl.

"Wot?"

"Spells," said Luck, just as much to the point. "I want one. A long-distance Journey spell with the capacity for two. And your dog. I want to buy it."

Poly looked suspiciously at Luck, but not so suspiciously as the proprietor. "Wot d'you want the mongrel for?"

"My wife likes it," said Luck, unblinking. "It's her birthday."

The proprietor sent a doubtful look in Poly's direction, and she gave him a wide, sunny smile in return. She didn't know what Luck was up to, but if it meant that she would have the puppy it was worth going along with. She cuddled it closer, aware of the man's eyes on her, and the puppy took this opportunity to lick her face thoroughly.

"Why should I sell you my dog?"

"Because I'll give you a gold covey for it," said Luck reasonably. "And another for the Journey spell, *if* it's a good one."

The proprietor glared at them both suspiciously for another long moment, but at last grudgingly nodded, as if he were doing them a great favour. Poly had to bite the inside of her cheek to check the laugh that wanted to come out. She didn't know what a covey was, but if it was gold, it was worth far more than a draggled little puppy, no matter how wildly prices had inflated in three hundred years.

The proprietor of this particular establishment must have been more than passingly familiar with the principle that what sounded too good to be true probably *was*, because he kept one, suspicious eye on Luck as he ushered him into the dingy hall. Poly smiled blandly and stayed where she was; the man, with a last dubious glance at her, followed Luck.

It was peaceful, if somewhat dirty, in the alley. Poly, who wasn't really used to grimy little alleys, looked around with some interest, absentmindedly patting the puppy. There were odd little scuffling noises from the other side of one wall, but since it seemed likely that this was a perfectly normal occurrence for disreputable back alleys, Poly didn't allow herself to be frightened.

When she turned her attention back to her new puppy, Poly found that it was thoughtfully chewing on the stiff front point of her bodice. She sighed and gently disengaged its mouth, careful to avoid catching the tiny white teeth in a stray thread, and found that it had chewed a small hole right through the bodice.

"What a nasty little piece of mischief you are," she told it.

She found that she was rubbing the arm that had come into contact with the puppy's lead and stopped herself with a frown. The skin of her arm was unblemished, and it was only when she wasn't thinking about it particularly that she seemed to feel the burning cold arc across her skin again. She had been around enough magic to know that the residual burn wasn't necessarily a pertinent development; she thought, however, with a sour smile, that it might be just as well to get Luck to untie the puppy when it came right down to it. Let him have a taste of his own medicine.

Poly was still meditating on that particular idea with no small amount of satisfaction when Luck returned and surprised her at it. She scrambled to her feet, hastily arranging her expression into something less obviously bloodthirsty, but Luck gave her a clear, green look anyway.

He wiggled a rolled scroll at her and said, "Come along, Poly. Untie the dog: his owner will change his mind in a minute."

Poly opened her mouth to protest, but Luck was already halfway back down the alley. She sighed to herself. Of *course* Luck would get out of it. She set her teeth and yanked at the slipknot, flinching away when the thin rope slithered to the cobbles—a normal, harmless piece of string. Poly gazed at her unhurt fingers for a moment and then picked up the end of the string again, feeling silly. The puppy, pulled up mid-frolic, yapped shrilly and raced in a bumbling circle.

Poly giggled, but said: "Save your energy. You'll need it."

Luck had already disappeared, which meant more running. Poly huffed out a breath and tugged the puppy into an unenthusiastic trot, hoping that Luck would be in sight when she reached the next intersection. Colliding with a warm body just around the corner, she thought for a relieved second that Luck had made another of his sudden, inexplicable stops.

Unfortunately, the face that was looking down at her was dashingly bearded and completely unfamiliar.

"Hello darling," said the stranger. Poly recognised the tone in one cold blink, and the level calculation of the devastating smile in another. There were a hundred courtiers just like him on any given day at the castle, surrounding Persephone with their practised smiles and carefully concealed motives. This was one of the carefully dashing ones that liked to steal kisses in the stairwells, and his hands were already on her shoulders.

Poly kicked him in the shins and wrenched her shoulders away, ready to run when she could. The puppy was growling—a low, guttural sound that didn't match its diminutive size—but heroically refrained from either tangling her ankles in its lead or snapping ridiculously at the stranger's heels.

The smile hadn't gone from the stranger's face, which worried Poly slightly. What worried her more, however, was that he had moved to block her way, and that five other men had unaccountably segued from the brickwork around them. Last time something like this happened, she had only escaped because Gwyn had found her, and because everyone knew that you didn't gainsay Gwyn and his very large, very sharp hoe. Where was Luck?

The stranger sauntered toward her again, still with the faint smile on his face, and Poly found that she had been backed neatly against an unyielding brick wall. When had that happened? She had a moment's sick recollection of the impact, and the stranger swinging her by the forearms, ostensibly to lessen the force. It was more likely that he'd done it to propel her into the street behind him, where he would more easily be able to box her in. That meant he'd been waiting for her—or perhaps for Luck.

"That wasn't very nice, darling," said the stranger. He stood too close, amused at her stiff discomfort, and cupped one cheek in his palm, caressing it with his thumb. "You're a mite stiff and old fashioned, but that's a fine gown. I'm sure you've got some pretty flim-flams tucked away in those big pockets of yours. Out with 'em."

The puppy, Poly was absolutely determined not to part with. On the other hand, she was just as little inclined to be robbed of her mother's books. She tugged on the puppy's string unobtrusively, trying to hide it in her skirts, but it had stopped growling and was frantically whining instead, pulling with such force on the lead that it had almost freed itself from the collar.

"And the dog," said the stranger softly, his smile warm while his eyes were cold.

Ah. It wasn't about her after all. Whatever Luck had recognised in this little puppy, someone else had also recognised. An unfamiliar hum seemed to buzz through her head at the realisation, and Poly found that her hair had begun a slow, whispering movement around her shoulders.

"You'd better let me go now," she told the man, pleased to find her voice clear and steady. Strands of her hair were already snaking up and over her shoulder, and as she watched a few tendrils coiled around his wrist.

The stranger saw it too, with a curious, half-cocked smile, and said over his shoulder: "I think she likes me, boys."

It was because of this remark that Poly didn't feel sorry for him when he began to scream. She thought, distantly, that her hair must be tightening around his wrist quite nastily. She had a feeling that it was also doing something else—that she was *making* it do something else—that wasn't quite nice.

"Make it stop!" he gasped. "Lady, mercy!"

Poly hesitated, and in her hesitation was lost. She saw the dirty gleam of light on a blade just as the man slashed desperately at the coil of hair around his wrist. A shaft of agony and loss pierced her chest, tearing a scream from her: a short, staccato sound that didn't have time to echo against the surrounding buildings before there was a warm, golden presence between herself and the stranger.

Luck's voice said, in sharp, icy fragments, "Did you *cut. Her. Hair?*"

Poly, choking on fiercely suppressed sobs, clutched at his arm and sent the stranger a murderous glare.

He wasn't looking at her. His eyes, very wide and wary, were fixed on Luck. Poly couldn't see Luck's eyes, but she knew that by now they would be eddying molten gold if the searing heat of magic at present emanating from him was anything to judge by.

"Your pardon," said the stranger, and he said the words carefully, dropping them delicately into the air like an artist tinting paint with small, perfect drops of colour. The other men had already melted away into the back streets. "I mistook the lady for someone else."

"Give her the hair," said Luck, still very softly.

The stranger did so, and Poly saw on his wrist deep, bleeding punctures that certainly hadn't been there before. Had she done that?

She took the limp hank of hair with cold fingers and tucked it away in her pocket, where it curled around something confusingly wooden and curved. Poly uncomprehendingly felt the outline of it with her fingers and found that it was a spindle. She released it, and a whisper of thought slipped away.

Distantly she heard Luck say, "You can go now," and saw the stranger slip away, his desire for haste fighting against his habitual swagger to produce an uneven quickstep.

Someone said, "Poly."

Poly looked at Luck blankly, static buzzing in her ears. She could feel the shorn lock of hair in a thin strand of pure ice from the hair tip to her toes, and gradually became aware that the tingle of warmth in her hand was because Luck was holding it.

She blinked, and Luck said, "Oh, you *are* in there. Hold the dog, Poly. Things are going to get blurry."

4

Luck led Poly by the hand through a vague oil painting of scenery that seemed to smear the lines of the town's dingy grey with the fresh green of grass and the vague outline of a mountain.

She only remembered four steps, but when Luck dropped her hand and said, "I think that's about it for me," the town was nowhere in sight, and a mountain had sprung up behind them. Poly, still trancelike, wondered if it was possible that she had walked through walls and perhaps a mountain as well. She was dimly aware that the thought wasn't carrying the weight it should carry, but the aching loss of that single hank of hair was still dragging at her mind with leaden fingers.

Someone dug through her pocket as she murmured a protest, then there were fingers in her hair and Luck's face swam into view again. He plaited the cut piece of hair back into the rest, strands of gold glowing momentarily and then fading to black as the hair re-joined.

Poly closed her eyes, feeling the comfortable warmth seep into her numb limbs, and when she opened them the world was in focus once again.

"You disappeared," said Luck. "Don't do it again. People notice and try to take advantage."

"I didn't disappear," Poly told him wearily. She was beginning to *feel* as though she'd walked through a mountain. "You ran too fast, and those men were *waiting* for us."

"Huh," said Luck, cocking his head. "Were they, though?"

His eyes lost focus, and Poly, wanting to catch him while she still could, asked, "Did we walk through a mountain?"

"You need to take better care of your hair," advised Luck, his gaze narrowed for a brief moment. "Binding your magic into it was reasonably clever, but it has its drawbacks."

"Luck." Poly waited until he was looking at her before she said, very clearly: "I do *not* have magic. Any magic in my hair is from you."

Luck observed her in unblinking silence, said, "Huh," again, and promptly lost interest in her. Poly thought, wearily, that he still didn't believe her.

She found that she was still clutching the puppy to her chest and put it down gently on the grass. Luck was lost in his own thoughts—and, for a wonder, standing still—so Poly had time to observe her surroundings a little more precisely. Her observation brought her to the conclusion that Luck was planning on stopping for the day. Hard by the mountain, set against a rocky outcrop, was a wooden three-sided arbour with a roof that was old but serviceable, and a crude, well used stone fireplace.

Rest for the weary traveller, or a trap? wondered the sceptical side of Poly's mind, but she wandered toward the shelter anyway. Behind it, and very far in the distance, was a mountain range, scraggled and uneven against horizon—the one they had walked through, if Poly's memory served her correctly.

From the frame of the shelter, she could see a wide, gently sloping plain that gradually curved up to the base of another range; this one much closer and higher. Above it, Poly fancied that she saw a reddish haze.

Luck's voice said, too close to her ear, "What are you looking at?"

Poly twitched herself away in annoyance, rubbing her ear. "The horizon is orange."

"Sunset. You can untie the dog now, Poly."

"It can't be sunset: I can still see both the lower suns."

Luck looked vaguely puzzled. "Can you? Huh. It seems later than that." It struck Poly that he was slightly unsteady on his feet, and she would have felt sorry for him if he hadn't added: "Unleash the dog, Poly."

"I don't want to," she said bluntly, remembering the cold burn of the thin rope when she first touched it.

A thoughtful, gold edged gaze was levelled at her. "Poly, you're being difficult again."

"No, I'm not. If you want the dog unleashed, do it yourself."

"I see that diplomatic processes have broken down again. Poly, that lead is a very powerful antimagic spell."

"Antimagic magic doesn't make sense," said Poly, trying to be exasperated with him. Luck had begun to sway on his feet, a fixed look on his face, and she didn't particularly want to feel sorry for him. "It'd eat itself."

Luck blinked rapidly. "That's a good point. Why doesn't it eat itself? Magic…antimagic…there must be a buffer. Poly, unleash the dog."

Luck was right, Poly thought crossly. Diplomatic processes *had* broken down. In fact, if they broke down any further, Luck was going to find himself with a black eye.

"Why don't you do it?" she demanded.

"I told you. Antimagic magic that doesn't eat itself. It's set to attack the person who uncollars the dog."

"And you don't want to be attacked," nodded Poly.

"No."

"Luck, I don't want to be attacked either."

"It only eats magic," said Luck, with a very clear, green look. "You should be fine, shouldn't you?"

Oh, very clever, thought Poly bitterly. *Hoist with my own petard.* Aloud, she said: "*Fine.*"

The puppy was busily chasing its tail in a corner of the shelter, but when she emitted a short, sharp whistle, it cocked its ears and galloped joyfully toward her, trailing its lead. There was nowhere to sit except in the dirt, so Poly pushed aside the thought that this was her only clean dress (in fact, her only dress of *any* kind) and sat down cross-legged to receive the puppy's eager attentions. Luck was watching closely, she was sure, despite the fact that he seemed to be teasing out stray threads of magic from his cuff while swaying slightly on the balls of his feet. She had to resist the urge to hunch her shoulders against his attention.

The collar was laughably easy to unhook, but the puppy sat very still for the operation anyway, gazing up at her with strangely anxious eyes as she released it. The collar promptly slithered from the puppy's neck to the ground, slipping free of the metal clasp on the lead. The lead itself hung innocently from her fingers.

Luck said, "Huh. That was underwhelming. You can let it go now, Poly."

"No, I can't," said Poly quietly. The lead stuck to her hand in a nasty, icy way that suggested frostbite, and the iron clasp at the end of it had begun to sway gently although her hand was still.

"Of course you can."

And with such a compelling voice, his eyes swimming with gold, Luck should have been irresistible. But his magic swirled around him in the wrong colour, and Poly wondered what had gone wrong instead of doing as she was told without thinking about it.

Luck said, more persuasively, "Let it go, Poly. You don't have any magic; you told me so."

The hint of suggestion mingled with the fact that Poly *knew* she hadn't any magic probably would have worked if the clasp hadn't chosen that moment to rise, snakelike, and begin a slow, achingly cold spiral around her wrist. After that it was hard to be convinced of anything but pain and cold.

Poly heard her own breath, ragged and too fast in an attempt not to cry, and thought despairingly, *It should eat itself. Why doesn't it eat itself?*

Then the pain faded, leaving a curl of iron etched on her skin fully to the elbow, and Poly was able to catch her breath, confused and relieved all at once. She climbed to her feet mechanically, still clutching the puppy.

"What do you know, it *did* eat itself," said Luck, his voice agreeably surprised.

Poly inspected the silvery spiral on her arm, reminding herself to *breathe*, and above all, not to hit Luck. "What happened to my arm?"

"I think it might have gotten cross-threaded."

Luck seized her arm, jerking her unexpectedly closer, and followed the curling trail of iron with one finger, his head cocked.

"Why did it stop?" Poly asked uneasily. She had a horrible feeling that if it started again, it wouldn't stop.

Luck gave a sudden, gleeful chuckle. "I don't know. Oh, I like this!"

"Will it start again?"

"No. I told you, it's cross-threaded."

"I don't know what that means!"

"Don't be cross, Poly, it makes you scowl."

Poly took a brief moment to count to ten. Then, very politely, she asked, "Will the mark go away?"

"There *must* still be some curse left," said Luck, his eyes very bright. "Huh. I was right. That's very, very sneaky."

"What's sneaky?"

"Dog!" said Luck suddenly. "Where is it?"

Poly considered refusing to tell him until he answered at least one of her questions satisfactorily, but she had the idea that Luck would simply refuse to understand her. She silently hefted the hand that held the puppy up to Luck's notice, then sat down wearily to observe events.

That did attract Luck's attention. "Don't sit down, Poly," he said. "We've got work to do."

"If it can't be done sitting down, it can wait," she told him grimly. Taking advantage of the change in its position, the puppy launched itself gleefully at her face, its tail madly wagging. "Hallo, darling," she said, acknowledging the small whines of joy with a light tousling of its floppy ears.

-hallo, hallo, hallo!-

Poly froze for a bare second, and her fingers were seized in needle-sharp milk teeth.

-haha! mine! hahaha!-

"Stop it wriggling," complained Luck, watching the dog with disfavour.

Poly looked up at him a little blindly, surprised that he hadn't heard.

-don't want him to hear- said the muddy little voice. *-you smell pretty-*

-Oh. Thank you?- Poly thought, and found that she was fighting back giggles. *-I'm Poly. What's your name?-*

-polly. polleeee-

-Yes- Poly said patiently, as the diminutive tail whipped furiously back and forth. *-Poly. That's me. But who are you?-*

-onepiece. have food?- It sounded hopeful, and the oscillation of its tail, if possible, only increased.

"He wants something to eat," she told Luck.

He directed an accusing look at Onepiece, then turned it on Poly. "Don't get attached to it."

"Why not?"

"It's not a dog, you know."

"It *looks* like a dog," Poly pointed out. Onepiece—if that really was his name—didn't even faintly smack of magic. She told Luck so, by way of a clincher, and he clicked his tongue thoughtfully.

"Huh. It doesn't, does it?" Luck blinked twice, rapidly, and then Poly saw his eyes begin to sparkle, which worried her. "Do you want to know why not?"

Poly, resigned to finding out why whether or not she really wanted to be told, asked, "Why not?"

"I think it's because you're touching it," said Luck, his eyes deep green with interest and a fascinated curl to his lips. "I'm glad I met you, Poly: you're far more interesting than I thought you would be."

Poly said ironically, "Thank you *so* much", but Luck wasn't listening anymore.

Muttering to himself, he ran an absent hand through his dishevelled hair, and though his magic was still brownish and his eyes tired, he seemed to vibrate with furious energy.

"Antimagic magic that eats itself, and a tangle of magic that disappears in half a heartbeat," he said, bright eyed. "It's all connected and probably a trap, but now we have an antimagic arm that shouldn't be a problem. Is it the dog or the spell?"

There was a tentative presence in Poly's mind once again. -*who talking to?*-

-*Himself, I think*- said Poly, with more amusement than ire. Even if Luck *had* been talking to her, she wouldn't have been much the wiser.

-*oh*- The puppy seemed to gaze critically at Luck, and then offered, -*swollen brain?*-

-*Most likely*- Poly said dryly. She briefly listened to Luck argue with himself, then asked Onepiece: -*What are you?*-

-*dog!*- said the tiny animal, fiercely. -*dog!*-

Well, that answered *that* question, thought Poly, intrigued to find that Luck was correct. Onepiece, whatever he was, was certainly not a real dog. -*What happened to you, darling?*-

Poly was startled to realise that she could hear a small sniffle in her mind through Onepiece's audible whine.

-*found me and chained me with burning cold. then forgot until I saw you. sparklyPoly and I remembered*-

-*What did you remember?*-

He buried his nose in his paws. -*me. remembered me*-

Poly, chilled and sick, cuddled him fiercely, eliciting a childish giggle in her mind and a profusion of face-licking. -*Poor darling*- she said. -*How old are you?*-

Onepiece shook his ears and gave the equivalent of a mental shrug. -*light comes and goes. is big cold*- Poly heard faint, laborious counting -*four times. snow on snout four times*-

-And how long have you had a snout?- Poly asked.

-*always*- said Onepiece, but she heard the uncertainty in his voice. -*snout and fur is* warm-

Poly sighed and patted him gently on the head. Luck looked as though he had finished the conversation with himself some minutes ago and was now gazing enquiringly in her direction.

She said hastily, "Oh, are you talking to me?"

"Pay attention, Poly," said Luck reproachfully.

Poly raised her brows but politely refrained from pointing out the glaringly obvious hypocrisy of the command because Luck was looking vaguely injured. "What?"

"Give me the animal."

"Why?" asked Poly, deeply suspicious. She had the feeling that Luck was about to begin experimenting with magic again, and although she was glad that the magic wasn't directed at her, she didn't particularly like the thought of it being directed at Onepiece, either.

"Because I told you to," said Luck, in a mildly puzzled tone of voice.

Poly gazed at him thoughtfully for a long moment. Luck, his face decidedly pale, paid no attention, and at last she observed, "People always do what you tell them to, don't they?"

He didn't seem to notice *that* question either. He really was very good at avoiding questions. If he didn't change the subject, he ignored them completely.

By way of trying a new tack, she said, "Your magic's gone all funny."

That earned her a baffled look. Luck said, "Poly, you're being deliberately difficult again."

She sighed, giving in to the inevitable, and proffered the silently protesting Onepiece, who insisted in her head that he didn't want to, didn't want to, didn't *want* to!

"It's alright, darling, he won't hurt you," she said soothingly, and at Luck's startled look, added, "I was talking to Onepiece. You're not going to hurt him, are you?"

-heard that!-

"Probably not," said Luck agreeably.

-poly! poly, help!-

-Shush, now- she admonished Onepiece.

He ceased his mental cries of distress but commenced a long, miserable whine in place of it as Luck seized him cavalierly by the scruff, lifting him out of Poly's hands.

She said, "*Ooof!* That's strong!"

"Huh. Gratifying," remarked Luck, dangling the miserable Onepiece before his eyes.

It was hard to see the puppy in the haze of magic that surrounded him, glittering and bright. Luck's magic was golden and warm, but Onepiece's was clear, colourless, and utterly impossible to look at for more than a few seconds.

"Moderate your intake, Poly," said Luck, busily drawing tiny glowing sigils in the air. He swayed on his feet as he scrawled but didn't seem to notice.

"Oh," Poly said breathlessly, her hair wafting forward. Onepiece wriggled in Luck's grasp, snapping playfully at the strands, and Poly heard his giggle again. "How?"

"Relax. Stop staring."

Poly blinked rapidly and found that Luck was right. Ever since the dirty town where she had had to search for the snarl of magic that was Onepiece, Poly had been concentrating too hard. She took off her glasses to turn the world into a blur and slowly let go of the tension, relaxing something beyond her eyes until the sparkle of Onepiece's magic was a pretty glitter instead of an aching blaze.

When she put on her glasses once more, Onepiece was floating aloft in a ring of sigils, looking startled but not displeased. Poly felt rather than heard the constant stream of wonder and fascination running through his mind, and thought sourly that it was all right for Onepiece—he *had* magic. He had a good chance of avoiding anything Luck could throw at him.

She was still darkly considering the unfairness of life when there was a silent kind of *pop!* inside the sigil circle, and Onepiece was no longer a puppy. Instead, a thin child of about five years old hung helplessly in the air, huge brown eyes gazing around him in horror and shock.

He threw back his head and howled, pedalling clumsily with limbs that were unfamiliar and useless, and Poly reached for him without thinking, her antimagic hand snatching away the floating sigils and catching the dirty child before he could fall to the ground.

Luck watched her with a detached kind of interest and said, "Huh. I didn't expect that."

"Change him back," said Poly quietly.

Onepiece's hands tried and failed to cling to her, the fingers weak from disuse and lack of practise, and she cuddled him closer, one arm supporting the scrawny backside and the other around a back that showed far too many ribs. His howl didn't cease, but softened into a constant, keening whine that was further smothered in her neck, where Onepiece had buried his head.

"He's not a dog, Poly."

"I don't care," she said, in a voice like flint. Heat built from her shoulder to her fingertips, and Poly found herself flexing the fingers of her antimagic arm. The spiral blazed around her arm, a white-hot heat that somehow managed not to burn her, and she said to Luck again, "Change. Him. *Back*."

Luck took one step backwards, for once very much awake, his

eyes watchful and green. There wasn't a hint of magic to him, and Poly thought with a fizz of surprise that she had really startled him. The fizz caused the antimagic spiral to lose something of its heat, but she wasn't sorry to see it go. She curled the arm back around Onepiece.

Luck relaxed slightly, exuding magic cautiously, and Onepiece quivered in Poly's arms, bare skin rippling into fur. When the change had finished, her armful was considerably lighter and Onepiece's nose significantly wetter where it pressed against her neck.

She said to Luck, "I need an apron. One big front pocket, please."

And when it was done, and Onepiece was sniffling quietly in the pocket, because Luck was still silent and now quite pale, she said, "Sorry."

5

The next morning Poly woke heavily, slowly, and unconvincingly. She yawned, fighting off the cobwebs of a dream that had seemed menacing at the time but became more ridiculous the further awake she grew.

As she stirred, Onepiece poked his nose out of the pocket he'd been sleeping in to snuff the morning air and impart the pleasing intelligence that he wanted to pee on a tree.

Poly lifted him out of her pocket and sat up, passing a weary hand over her face. Luck already sat at the other end of the shelter, his legs stretched out in front of him and his magic still tangled in skeins of brown and gold, but although he was pale he also seemed quite cheerful.

His eyes met hers, as if he'd been watching and waiting for her to wake up, and when she sat up, he immediately said, "I need to look at that curse of yours again."

Poly resisted the urge to ask why, since she was certain he wouldn't tell her anyway, and decided not to give Luck the chance to find her 'difficult' today. Accordingly, she heroically held her tongue on the subject of her growling stomach and didn't make a fuss when Luck's scrutiny of the curse consisted in cupping her face with his hands and peering intently into her eyes as he had done before.

She did sigh faintly, but Luck didn't seem to hear and after a while Poly got the impression that he was no longer quite there behind his eyes. It didn't seem to be a very important point until it occurred to her to wonder: if Luck wasn't *there,* where was he?

-trying to get in- sent Onepiece helpfully, crouching nearby in order, if the furious scratching was any indicator, to share his fleas with her.

Gloomily unsurprised, Poly reached out the part of herself that had found Onepiece effortlessly, and discovered a second presence hovering nearby, humming furiously with power.

-Onepiece says you want to get in- she thought at it, and the buzzing presence sharpened on her with an almost battering interest.

-Oh, there you are- it said, and swooped right on past her into a warm, cosy nook that Poly recognised, in some surprise, to be her mind.

The presence that was Luck solidified into Luck's person, and Poly did the same hastily, forming metaphysical limbs just in time to drag him away from an interesting little corner that was stacked high with thin folders in shiny poison-red.

-You have a lot of bad memories- observed Luck, leaving the red folders in favour of a bright four-tiered mobile of planets that spun lazily despite the fact that there was no breeze, metaphysical or otherwise.

Poly eyed the red folders dubiously. *-Those are bad memories?-*

-Yes-

-Can I get rid of them?- Poly flipped through the top few, and a flurry of thoughts and impressions flowed through her fingertips unpleasantly.

-No. I've tried that-

-Is this what my mind looks like?-

-Not really- said Luck, cautiously poking at the mobile to

throw the planets out of alignment. The planets seemed to think about this for a moment, then gently but firmly wafted back into their correct positions. *-It's an abstract form to help enchanters store and find things more easily-*

-Oh- said Poly blankly. *-Then **you** made it look like this?-*

-Of course not. You did. Poly, why did you have short-sword instruction with one of the tower guards?-

Poly looked around in dismay to find that he was sorting through the top drawer of a desk that had been set into a bookshelf. She darted across the room and slapped the drawer shut, nearly catching Luck's fingers as she did so.

-You said you wanted to look at the curse- she reminded him.

-Oh yes- said Luck. *-It's over there-*

When Poly looked *over there*, it was with the disagreeable feeling that she'd been uneasily ignoring that side of the room from the first moment she entered her mind. Now she knew why: an entire wall was thick with opaque nothingness, shifting and forming almost-shapes. It pulsed, and Poly had the horrible idea that it was actually growing—as if to take over her mind in a slow, inching crawl.

-What's it doing?-

-It's growing- said Luck, confirming her suspicions. He didn't sound very much surprised.

*-Should it **be** growing?-*

-Of course not. It shouldn't even be there. It should have dissipated when I kissed you-

-If it's still there, why did I wake up?- Poly demanded. Even when Luck answered questions he somehow *didn't*.

-Because I kissed you. Be quiet, Poly; I need to concentrate-

She sat back in silence, dissatisfied and worried, to watch Luck at work, even if there wasn't much to watch. He merely sat cross legged in front of the pulsing mass of curse and stared at it.

Business as usual, then, thought Poly sourly.

His magic was still wrong and confused, so when she became tired of looking at the bruised strands, she sighed and began to straighten it out, combing the strands between her fingers as though they were hair. Luck gave her one, swift look that startled her, but since he went back to ignoring her almost immediately, Poly kept straightening and soothing until the strands glowed and became gold again.

When she at last looked up from her work, Onepiece had arrived and Luck had more or less gone again. The less was the fact that his meta-body was still present; the more was that his meta-eyes had gone as blank and empty as his real eyes.

-*Where's he gone this time?*- she asked Onepiece uneasily. She didn't particularly like the idea of Luck roaming about in her mind where she couldn't keep an eye on him.

-*sleep*- said the puppy, hiding behind her skirts again.

Poly thought that this had more to do with the nastily swirling curse than it did with Luck, and it occurred to her with a sick, sinking feeling, that the curse was closer to Luck than it had previously been.

-*What do you mean, sleep?*-

-*went too far in*- said Onepiece, shrugging. He didn't sound particularly sorry, which distantly amused Poly. -*sneaky curse. maybe should kiss him?*-

-*I don't think so*- Poly said decidedly.

She made her way to Luck's side with one wary eye on the gently rolling curse, and knelt beside him, sparring for time by laying him on his back.

First, she tried gently patting his cheeks. It was such a natural reaction, and Luck's cheeks felt so normal and entirely *real* that it took Poly another few moments to realise that it was utterly useless. Neither her hands nor Luck's cheeks were actually *real* in here.

-*Oh, this is ridiculous!*- she said in exasperation. -*Onepiece, what can I do?* **Except**- she added sternly, catching the mulish glint in Onepiece's brown eyes, -**Except** *kissing him*-

-*magic*- said Onepiece happily, after a momentary pause.

Poly sighed. -*I don't have any magic*-

-not yours. his-

-But—oh! Oh, I see! Onepiece, you're a clever boy!-

Onepiece wagged his tail furiously and pranced a few steps forward on his hind legs. -clever boy, oh yes! clever, clever Onepiece!-

Poly spared him a brief pat on the head, her lips curving in spite of herself. She turned her attention back to Luck just in time to see a thread of magic trail by, unravelling at a languid pace from the bulk of his magic. Luck wasn't asleep, then. He was lost somewhere in the curse, and he was using his own magic as a line to try and find his way back.

She gently touched the thread and pinched, bringing the unravelling to a slow and gentle stop. Then she tugged twice, sharply, on it. There was a moment of taut uncertainty before the thread pulled at her fingers once, twice. Poly swiftly wound it in, and a moment later Luck blinked heavily, his eyes too green and his cheeks too white.

He stared at the manifestation of a ceiling broodingly for some time before he said: -I seem to have misjudged the sneakiness of your curse- He sent a narrowed green glance in Poly's direction and added, eyes narrowing still further, -Or there's something you're not telling me, Poly-

-There's a lot I don't tell you- said Poly frankly. -But nothing pertinent-

-Well, **something's** making the curse hold on when it should die away- Luck said. -My casting was flawless. Besides, you woke up! Why did you do that?-

Poly found herself somewhat maliciously repeating what he'd said earlier, -I suppose because you kissed me-

-Yes, and that was flawless, too- added Luck. -Poly, there's something very odd about you-

-**Must** we sit here and discuss it in my mind?-

-Yes. I can't get back out just yet.-

-Oh. Why?-

-Why is the dog here? It keeps panting and drooling-

-Dogs do that- Poly told him reasonably. She snapped her

fingers at Onepiece as if he really was just a dog and he bounded happily into her lap, unresentful.

-Well, make it stop. It puts me off-

-*Him*- corrected Poly, more from habit than actual conviction that the reminder would do any good.

She briefly checked Luck's faint halo of magic for any traces of brown, but it was pale gold all the way through. In that case, it was mostly likely exhaustion that was keeping him here. Poly remembered Persephone's pallor after the princess produced her first item-based spell and thought ruefully that if Luck was anything like as exhausted, she was likely to have company for a while longer. At least an exhausted Luck was less likely to pry into things that wouldn't bear scrutiny.

Poly found herself stiff and sore by the time Luck was rested enough to pull himself back to his own body. She had been right: an exhausted Luck was much easier to deal with than a well-rested one. Most of his activity consisted in gazing thoughtfully at the ceiling manifestation and blinking occasionally, while Poly crossed her ankles and amused Onepiece with her fingers.

That pastime eventually produced a few tiny drops of blood that the puppy contritely licked away, and when Luck vanished without warning Poly blinked herself back outside too, stretching cautiously. She wriggled fingers that were entirely unscathed and was slightly abashed to find herself surprised.

"Right!" said Luck, startling Onepiece into a brief growl. "Journey spell."

He strode out of the shelter while Poly was still trying to gather her legs together in a semblance of order sufficient to stand, and she was relieved to find that while she'd been stretching, he had been fetching breakfast. There was a fresh supply of bacon and eggs for her, piled even higher than yesterday's ration, and for Onepiece there was a papery bowl of stew that tottered drunkenly on shaky paper supports.

When breakfast was satisfyingly gone, Poly set her plate down, and it disappeared before her fingers quite left the edge of

the porcelain, making Onepiece first jump and then gulp faster with an anxious look at his own bowl.

From outside the shelter, Poly heard Luck say, "Huh. Poly? Poly, come here."

She found him some distance from the shelter, squinting up at the mountains where a clear line of sight ran through the ranges. It converged on a peak in the far distance which, to Poly's straining eyes, seemed to be haloed by a slight tinge of orange. The Journey spell pointed straight at it, for which Poly was grateful: she had a brief, unpleasant memory from yesterday of walking through another mountain. She would be glad not to do that again.

Luck, pinching the end of the Journey spell closest to him, looked faintly startled. "I need a hand," he said. "Specifically, the antimagic one. Reach in the other end, will you?"

"What am I looking for?" asked Poly, obligingly reaching her spiral-bound hand into the scroll. It passed through effortlessly until she was up to the elbow in scroll.

"Small glass vial. It'll have a lead stopper in the top and a lead seal on the side. Pull it out."

Poly did so, rummaging around the smooth sides of the scroll, and wasn't surprised to find it bigger on the inside than it was on the outside. By the time she felt the vial under her fingertips she was on tiptoes and straining with her arm shoulder deep in the scroll.

"Got it. But it's tight."

"Rip it out," said Luck carelessly, and Poly looked at him sharply because his magic was anything *but* careless just then.

Oh well, she thought, and tore the vial from its socket. Nothing happened, so she pulled her arm out all the way, sinking back onto her heels, and observed the tiny glass bottle. Top heavy with lead, it swirled with a vaguely yellow gaseous substance.

Unimpressed, Poly asked, "What now?"

"Put it in my pocket," said Luck. "No, not that one: the big breast one in my overcoat."

Poly dropped the vial into his front pocket and saw what looked like a wince pass fleetingly over Luck's face, prompting her to ask, "Luck, why am I doing this?"

Luck gave her a blank look. "This time you need to feel around for a scrap of paper: it should be wrapped around a wick."

"Yes, but *why*?"

"Because I need that piece of paper," said Luck.

"Yes, but why didn't you get it out yourself?"

"Didn't know it was there, then. Paper, Poly."

She sighed and twitched the tiny scrap away from a smooth wick, withdrawing her arm and displaying it to Luck.

"Good. Now tear it up."

She did so with raised brows and scattered the pieces with a flick of her fingers. It occurred to her that Luck waited until she finished before he released the scroll.

"Was it another antimagic spell?" she asked, watching Luck carefully. From the corner of her eye, she saw the scroll unfurl, spit a few useless drops of magic, and fizzle out.

Luck, watching the scroll with unfocused eyes, didn't seem to notice her gaze. "No. It was a bomb."

Poly took a moment to count to ten, afraid that she would do something unbecoming in a princess if she didn't. Then, she asked, very carefully, "What was it I pulled out of the scroll?"

"The trigger and the accelerant."

"I see. I suppose it didn't occur to you to tell me I was putting my hand into a bomb?"

"I didn't want you to worry. Come along, Poly, it's time to leave."

It's going to take more than ten, thought Poly a little wildly, as Luck strode away.

-*are staying?*- asked Onepiece, his voice hopeful.

"No," said Poly. "We're going with him, even if it's only to hit him."

. . .

The passage through the mountains wasn't as straightforward as it had looked from the shelter. When closer, the gentle, meandering incline that Poly had seen turned out to be rather steeper than expected. And despite the fact that the path looked quite clear and straight through the mountains on either side, the reality consisted of zigzags to avoid the narrow, ankle-breaking gullies and steep banks that sprang out of nowhere.

Onepiece enjoyed himself immensely, leaping from tuft to tuft with his tongue lolling out, but Poly found it a struggle in her skirts and whaleboned bodice, and even Luck slowed down a little. Long before the shelter below was out of sight, Poly's underarms were chafed from the carefully set sleeves of her grey gown and sweat had soaked through the back of it.

Her shoes, which were meant for courtyards and not mountain climbing, soon pinched painfully at every step. Poly abandoned them after a few unpleasant hours, refusing to believe that even a princess would be expected to put up with the agony simply for appearances sake, but endured the dress for some time longer in the hope that she could induce Luck to change it into something more comfortable when they stopped to rest.

However, as the morning wore into afternoon it became increasingly obvious that Luck had forgotten about lunch, rest, and possibly even his travelling companions as well. He was still striding effortlessly ahead when Onepiece became too tired to trot any further and wheedled his way into Poly's apron pocket, and Poly, making a determined effort to catch up, came to the conclusion that Luck was using a Keep Away spell. He always stayed just that little bit ahead no matter how hard she tried to match his pace.

When it became evident that no rest break was forthcoming, much less something to eat, Poly stopped by a large sun warmed rock and hefted her tired body up on it to rest anyway. She was curious to see how long it would take Luck to notice she was no longer following—if he ever *did* notice.

-*are there?*- asked Onepiece, poking his nose out and yawning.

Poly thought enviously that it looked like he'd just woken up. "Just a rest stop," she told him, absentmindedly patting his head. "You can go back to sleep."

He sniffed the air curiously but evidently decided to believe her, because he tucked his nose back into the pocket, and after a few moments of furious scrabbling to get comfortable, seemed to fall asleep again. Meanwhile, Poly studied her grass-stained toes and wished she didn't feel quite so hungry.

It was only a few minutes later when Luck wandered into sight again. He sat down next to Poly without having to jump himself up and didn't complain about having to return for her, which Poly thought was tantamount to an apology, coming from Luck.

They sat in silence until Luck said, "You haven't got shoes."

"They hurt. They're on a rock back there somewhere."

"Oh." Luck grew silent again, and Poly had an idea that he was trying to hazard her out. "I could have got you more."

"I couldn't catch up," she reminded him, without rancour.

"Huh. I'll have to turn that off: I forgot that you don't twitter at me. I expected a princess to twitter more."

"No, we only twitter at lapdogs and suitors," said Poly, successfully repressing a small, pointed grin at Persephone's expense.

"Oh," said Luck. "I'll remember that. Do you want shoes?"

"Not until we reach civilisation," Poly replied carelessly, resolving to enjoy the freedom of bare toes for just a little longer. "But I need a different frock."

Luck looked blank but was obliging. "All right. What do you want?"

"Something light and loose," said Poly. "Whatever girls are wearing now. I don't mind, just so long as I can *breathe* again."

When the cool touch of magic had come and gone, Poly found herself in a loose-fitting smock with short, full sleeves and a hemline somewhat higher than she'd expected. Mad from a bright, butterflower yellow, it had even bigger pockets than her old grey gown. When she checked, she found that both Onepiece and her books were already in them, Onepiece muttering at the change in his sleep.

Her pantaloons, somewhat sad and dusty and decidedly lacking in ankle-ruff, were noticeable by a good two inches. Poly supposed that girls now were wearing their pantaloons daringly below the knee and considering it somewhat less daring than it had seemed three hundred years ago.

She retied the laces of her pantaloons at the knee, exposing a rather white expanse of slender leg, and observed the lower half of her shins below the yellow cotton. She thought she might easily be able to get used to this style of dress.

As they climbed higher Poly began to notice sheep on the slopes around them. At first it was one or two, then little clusters of five and six, and before long every expanse of green around them was dotted with a multitude of fat white sheep.

The lambing must have gone well, thought Poly, eyeing the flocks with a professional eye, because there were a great many of them. They were old enough to walk properly while still young enough to be adorable, and Poly found the corners of her mouth lifting slightly at the familiarity of the sight. Civet had run its economy solely on the wool trade, leaving such high-profit animals as skerries and gnau to Parras for the less costly and more sure return of wool. Gnau leather was highly sought after and certain to turn a truly startling profit if only one could stop the creatures dropping dead from fright every time a crow cawed overhead as it flew past, and while skerry fleece was even more popular than gnau leather, the animals were tiny, and required delicate shearing to salvage as much of the fleece as possible. Wool was not exactly exotic or even very comfortable, but everyone used it, and the benefits of mass production had easily allowed Civet to keep financially equivalent to the more luxury-based economy of Parras.

Of course, thought Poly, wrinkling her brow, that was before three hundred years of sleep, and expansion, and *New Civet*.

Mind you, the sheep-scattered mountains certainly seemed to suggest that New Civet had followed Civet's rather than Parras' example. She wondered if they would come across any skerry when they climbed higher into what had once been Parras.

Unfortunately, all they came across as they climbed higher was rain. It was late spring, Poly guessed, judging from the bright green of new foliage and the gusts of wind that came with the rain, so the rain wasn't bitterly cold. It did make her hair feel twice as heavy, however, and she began to fear for the remaining books she had carefully concealed in her pockets. They were old and delicate, and certainly not to be bandied about in inclement weather.

Poly patted her pockets absently, finding the bright yellow material already soaked with moisture, and sucked in a shallow breath of regret. No doubt they were already ruined. She tried not to mind too much, but a small sniff escaped her anyway. Onepiece, once again trotting under his own power, kept up a constant stream of complaint in the back of her mind.

Poly had been rather blindly wiping the rain from her glasses for some time when Luck stopped abruptly. This time she stopped herself from tumbling into him with a quick half step to the side and reflected crossly that things would be much easier if Luck were to call marching orders. Or if he would walk by her side like any normal male instead of striding on ahead.

"It's raining," he said. Poly thought he sounded surprised.

"It's been raining for the past half hour," she told him, amused in spite of herself.

"I don't like being rained on."

"Oh. Well, there's not much you can do about it, you know."

Luck tilted his head back to observe her, a puzzled line between his brows. "Of course there is," he said.

He sketched a tiny figure in the palm of his hand, then blew out his cheeks and huffed it toward a convenient rock ledge that was currently running along the path beside them.

As Poly watched in astonishment, a white, tentlike structure bloomed, just a little taller than Luck and twice as long as it was high. She reached out a hand to touch the insubstantial stuff, expecting to feel her fingers pass through something like mist, only to discover that the pearly whiteness was in fact cold and springy.

"What is it?" she asked Luck, but he had already stepped through a thin gap in the stuff.

A puff of warm, displaced air succeeded him, inducing Poly to follow after him without wondering further about anything but warm—and above all, *dry*—shelter. She found her clothes dry and soft immediately upon stepping inside, which pleased her greatly, even if Onepiece, following close behind and about to vigorously shake himself, looked affronted and decidedly less pleased about the business. He trotted after her as she walked curiously around the shelter, her fingers lightly touching its taut surface, and was interested enough to try burrowing at the white sheen that stretched below them and indented with each footstep before springing back.

Luck, sealing the parting with two pinched fingers, shot the dog a green-eyed look. "Don't do that."

Onepiece gave a small, growling bark but did as he was told, and sulkily climbed into Poly's lap when she sat down. His flowing train of thought-speech said: -*poor Onepiece, poor puppy. white is tight and warm but it's sneezy*-

Poly amused him with her fingers for some minutes, twinkling them past his nose and tapping his paws while he watched in fascination and tried to capture them between his tiny teeth, before she said casually, "You have them too, darling."

Onepiece looked suspicious. -*have fingers, yes. clumsy and heavy*-

"Well, they needn't be clumsy," Poly said reasonably. "Your legs must have been heavy and clumsy once. How is it you can walk and jump now?"

-*lots of walking*- said Onepiece shortly, and she had a brief inrush of hazy memories that spoke of aching bones and aching cold.

"It's just the same with fingers," she told him. "You must use them, or they'll stay clumsy."

-*dog is warm*- Onepiece said sulkily.

"It's warm in here."

There was a barely audible huff from the puppy. -*huh. fingers. no use*-

"Rubbish," said Luck, making them both jump.

He sat down next to Poly, stretching out his long legs comfortably in front of him, and roughed Onepiece's ears. Onepiece gave a sigh of pleasure and flopped forward on Poly's knees.

"Can't do that with paws," pointed out Luck, giving the puppy one last scratch. He seized Poly's hand and threaded his fingers through hers, displaying their linked hands to Onepiece. "Can't do this with paws, either."

Onepiece's stream of consciousness slowed, stopped, and threw out one hiccough of an idea. -*mum?*-

Poly thought she caught the sense of a very tiny, human Onepiece holding the much larger hand of someone else, and was taken aback at the wave of longing that swept over the puppy.

"Perhaps," she said. "But you'll have to be human again."

There was a moment of utter silence from the puppy, while Poly became aware that Luck not only still held her hand, but was now tracing the spiral of antimagic with one finger, a frown on his face. Then an overwhelming surge of clear magic shook the shelter, and the tiny, naked boy that was Onepiece was back again, huddled in her lap. His eyes were at first wild and frightened, but when Poly wrapped her arms around him, disengaging her fingers from Luck's, he gazed up at her in perfect contentment.

"Clothes, I think," she said to Luck.

. . .

That night, Poly had nightmares again. They woke her up, gasping, with the image of hundreds of frozen faces caught in amber coloured magic seared through her mind, and for a confused moment she couldn't tell where she was. There was green, and misty white, then there was warm orange interposed over both, and Poly came to the slow, heavy realisation that she was clutching a spindle in her antimagic hand, wooden spike digging bluntly into the silver curlicues and the pattern of the spindle embossed on her palm. She decided that it was too much trouble to wonder why she was holding a spindle, and automatically pushed it into one pocket to look at later.

While the world decided whether it was going to be green or orange, Poly pushed herself up blearily, carefully avoiding Onepiece, who had curled up under her arm in his dog form. She spared a brief thought to wonder where the little trousers Luck had magicked for him were, and if they would appear again the next time Onepiece turned human. Then the world outside the shelter made one last massive effort and decided to be orange, and Luck groaned.

Poly sat up properly, crossing her legs and pawing at her eyes, and pushed her glasses on in order to look at him. His magic had gone wrong again, but this time it was blackened instead of brownish, as if whole strands of it had gone badly over-ripe.

Luck sat up with a paper white face and fixed heavy, reproachful eyes on her. "Poly, you'll be the death of me."

Poly drew in a small, exasperated breath. "I didn't do anything. You've got *Angwynelle*."

"It wasn't the book," said Luck, climbing slowly to his feet.

He walked unsteadily past Poly and shouldered his way through the slit in the white membrane, letting a flash of orange briefly into the tent. She heard him, a moment later, being very sick.

When Luck came back, he seemed less pale, but his magic was still as black as ever. He looked even more rumpled than usual this morning, and Poly wasn't sure which she wanted to straighten more: his magic or his hair.

Luck swiftly put any such charitable ideas out of her mind by narrowing his eyes at her saying accusingly, "You hijacked my spell. Why are you always hijacking my spells?"

"What happened?" she asked, resigned to the fact that he wouldn't believe she'd had nothing to do with his spell, hijacked or otherwise.

"We're at the Frozen Battlefield," he said.

6

The unwelcome recollection of thousands of frozen, orange-glazed faces sprang immediately to Poly's mind.

Shaken, she said, "You said something about a frozen battlefield back at the castle. Was that the glow I saw on the horizon yesterday?"

"You've been putting my spells off for days," said Luck darkly, his shoulders hunched. "You kick me and threaten me and —whoops—!"

Poly watched him bolt for the slit again with the horrible feeling that this time at least, she just might be responsible. Her dream was simply too coincidental for the two occurrences not to be linked, whether or not it seemed possible.

She sighed, following Luck outside, and began to straighten the worst of the blackened threads of his magic. Luck merely groaned at her and threw up again.

When he had finished, he wiped his mouth and said with great precision, "You are a plague, madam."

He slumped against the tent, eyeing her owlishly, and if Poly didn't know that he was entirely sober, she could have been persuaded that he was drunk.

Spindle

He pulled at the tent uselessly in an attempt to rise, and said at last, "Help me up, Poly."

She thought about putting her nose in the air with a remark about plagues but thought better of it. Instead, Poly helped him up and propped him against the dubious support of the tent.

When she tried to back away, Luck said, "No, Poly, don't go."

His blackened magic fizzed around him with sparks of gold and tar, and Poly felt a slight tug, nearly light enough to resist. Nearly, but not quite. She took one step back toward him.

"We have experiments to conduct," he added.

This intelligence gave Poly enough of a snap to break free. "No more experiments!" she told him firmly. "Especially not when your magic is doing *that*."

Luck muttered darkly at the failure of his spell. Then he reached out physically and tugged her forward by the ears, pulling her closer as much through the agency of surprise as superior force.

"Ow! Stop it!" Poly demanded, outraged.

Luck, without letting go of her ears, simply said, "No," and enforced one last step toward him that brought her far too close to be able to box his ears. Poly couldn't decide if that were a good thing or not. He said, "Tilt your head up, Poly: I can't see."

Poly, very frostily, said, "See what?"

"The curse. It sits in the corners of your eyes and laughs at me."

"Ow! Luck, what are you doing? Let go!"

"I'm kissing you again," said Luck, reasonably. "I told you—"

"No!" snapped Poly, snatching his hands away.

She gave him a short, effective shove in the chest that had him far too busy trying to stand to follow her, and stomped away before she did something hazardous to her health, like punch Luck in the nose. Then she stomped right back, drew a circle in the moist dirt, and stood inside it.

"Pay attention," she told Luck grimly. "Pretend this is a magic circle."

"All right," said Luck obligingly. He was still swaying on his feet, but his colour had improved.

"Magic circles have an equidistant circumference, don't they?"

Luck regarded her with gold flecked eyes and nodded.

"All right. This represents my personal space. You," she added, fixing him with a repressive glare that didn't seem to repress him very much, "Are to stay outside it at all times."

"Huh," said Luck. He appeared to think about it for a few minutes, then offered, "You need a glove."

"A—*pardon?*"

"Glove, glove. Women wear 'em to parties."

Poly sat down in the dirt, bewildered, and began to straighten Luck's magic again, as much in the conviction that Luck wasn't going to make sense until his magic was right again as the desire to be doing *something* with her hands other than hurt Luck. "Why do I need gloves?"

Luck, who seemed to be going back to sleep, opened his eyes a gold edged slit, and said, "You'll only need one. It'll make a statement."

Poly managed, "Yes, but—" before the glove materialized and fell into her lap with a whisper of sound.

She should have asked again, but the single glove was a beautiful thing made out of light, clingy material that laced up from the wrist to just beyond her elbow, and Poly decided after a moment's appreciative observation that she didn't much care why she was wearing it.

Between the fingers of her other hand and her teeth, she managed to get the article laced and tied over her antimagic arm. It covered the spiral of antimagic completely, but left her unblemished fingers free—which, Poly realised belatedly, must have been the purpose of it.

She went back to unravelling Luck's tangled magic, admiring her new accoutrement as her fingers flew. Luck didn't object, or even move; the bruising to his magic was worse than it had been after the Shift spell that took them straight through the mountain. Poly wondered, as she combed her fingers gently through the insubstantial threads, just exactly how far they had travelled this time. She could see the glow of orange in the corners of her eyes, and found herself thankful that she hadn't had the leisure yet to look around, since she was sneakingly sure that she wouldn't like what she saw when she did so.

There was a stir in the already magic fraught air, suggesting that Onepiece had woken, and a moment later, Poly heard his sleepy voice in her head. *-poly. there's orange deadthings-*

"It's all right, darling; they can't hurt you," Poly said soothingly, hoping that she was right.

"They've been stuck for nearly three hundred years," observed Luck, adding his mite to the conversation, much to her surprise. "They won't come out just to watch you eat breakfast."

-breakfast?- the puppy's ears perked up hopefully. *-breakfast where? chops'n'sausages?-*

Luck looked slightly ill again, and Poly said hastily, "You can have breakfast when Luck feels well enough to get it."

*-yes, but **hungry**-* said Onepiece sadly, climbing into her lap.

He sniffed cautiously at her gloved hand and muttered his disapproval, but Poly ignored him. Luck's magic was very nearly tidy again. It only needed—*snap!*

That, thought Poly in satisfaction, shaking the whole out as if it were a freshly laundered pillowcase to be folded. Luck's eyes widened, and he looked more awake and aware than she had ever seen him before.

"Better?" she asked, but she already knew the answer, so it didn't matter when Luck said, "Go look at the frozen people, Poly," and dashed back into the tent.

Onepiece followed him, presumably in pursuit of breakfast, and Poly was left to pick herself up, wondering if Luck ever said thank you. She thought not.

When she could no longer avoid doing so, Poly turned her eyes on her surroundings. The tent was now freestanding instead of leaning into the shadow of an escarpment—behind it a vast expanse of green hills. Poly came to the conclusion that they were now well atop the mountain she had sighted through the ranges yesterday. It was bigger than she'd expected, and significantly hillier. When she turned stiffly, reluctantly following her orange peripheral sight, the first impression she had was one of unexpected stillness and warmth.

There must have been thousands of people suspended in the orange glow before her: each one still and lifeless, not moving by so much as a single hair. The amber stuff itself stretched further than she could see, both to the right and to the left. Even the sky had taken on an orange tint above it.

Poly stared, appalled, at bodies of men and women alike, frozen in lifeless youth. None of them were kitted out as soldiers. It occurred to her that the Frozen Battlefield was singularly misnamed: it was neither cold, nor peopled by soldiers. She looked carefully at the faces within sight, searching for any trace of horror or surprise, but the only emotion she could pick out with any clarity on each of the faces was a fierce kind of radiance that was as alien as it was frightening. Poly began to have second thoughts about her assumption that this was no battlefield.

She wandered further along the edge of the orange substance, wondering what the amberness would be like to touch but unwilling to find out for certain. It *looked* gelatinous, but that could just be the impression created by the smooth-edged surface. These people had certainly not suffocated. They looked like they had been enveloped and extinguished all in a moment, caught unawares in their terrifying rapture.

It must be magic. Only, thought Poly with her brows drawn together, it didn't *feel* like magic. Her eyes, running over face after face, snagged on three grouped together, and she was conscious of a mind-numbing shock. It was Persephone. Persephone as beautiful as she had ever looked, and twice as alive in the triumphant brilliance that mirrored every other face around her. Beside and a little behind her were the king and queen, their faces likewise aglow; but Poly spared them only a glance, because there beside the princess, between Persephone and her mother, was a space. It leapt out at her, a vaguely man shaped disturbance in the gelatinous amber, and her eyes followed the logical path the escapee must have taken.

There! There was a disturbance in the surface of the amber, a slight dip running from the ground to somewhere roughly a foot above Poly's head: the kind of indent that might have happened if someone had stepped out of a jellylike substance just before it was quite set. The thought should have brought with it some relief, but Poly thought of one of those fiercely happy people roaming at large in New Civet, and shuddered.

She hurried back to the safety of Luck and the white tent and found herself in time for breakfast. For once, the thought of eating didn't appeal to Poly, and at last, chasing blueberries around a bowl with a broad silver spoon, she said to Luck, "One of them got out."

He opened his mouth, and Poly could see his lips beginning to form the word 'rubbish'. Then he seemed to think better of it. "Where?"

"A hundred yards or so eastward. There's a man-sized hollow space and a ripple in the surface."

Luck thoughtfully rubbed his head, forming wild spikes. He didn't speak immediately, and when Poly passed him her unfinished bowl of breakfast berries he ate them automatically, drumming the spoon against the side of the bowl in a manner as aimless as it was annoying.

Then he said, "No one's ever noticed one of them missing before. Huh."

He said it more in interest than in disbelief, and Poly, letting him mull it over, went on to her next point of unease. "What's *wrong* with them? They're all—"

"Disgustingly happy," nodded Luck. "I'm sure I've told you about this before."

"No, you said that Civet took to the battlefield and that something went wrong. You said no one knew what happened."

"Someone does. There are little clues all through the Capital Library."

"What sort of clues?" asked Poly curiously, allowing the conversation to be waylaid briefly. "And why?"

"Notes in margins, redacted Governmental Spellpapers that get *un*-redacted if you know how. Passages in ancient books. Some of the notes and passages are older than the original spellpaper attached to your curse."

"*Older*? How?"

There was a very wide-awake glitter in Luck's green eyes. "Some of 'em are older than you, too, Poly."

"How can some of the clues be older than me if it all happened after I went to sleep?"

"Well, that's the question, isn't it? Mordion handed me a nice little piece of the puzzle when he gave me your Spellpaper."

Poly stared at him. "What has it got to do with me? I wasn't even there!"

"Exactly!" said Luck, as if it made perfect sense. "You weren't there. That's what made it all clear."

"Made *what* clear?" demanded Poly, bewildered; but Luck was already tossing the breakfast bowls into non-existence as he stood.

"I want to see the man-shaped hole. Come along, Poly."

Poly did so, sighing, with Onepiece trotting at her heels, and pointed out the area to Luck. "There. Between those two."

"Huh," said Luck. "There *is* a hole. Crafty."

He ran a finger over the indent, startling Poly because she hadn't expected him to touch the stuff. Then he *licked* the amber.

Poly dropped her head into one hand, pinching the bridge of her nose. "Luck—"

"Oh," said Luck. "Ah. That tastes familiar. Give me your hand, Poly."

He grabbed her hand without waiting for her to comply, and slapped it onto the surface of the amber, palm open.

She let out another sigh, this one exasperated. "Luck, what did I *just say* about personal space?"

Luck returned one of his best glassy looks just as Poly, her fingers pressed firmly against the amber by his, felt a tremor go through the stuff.

"What—"

The tremble became a roar, buzzing through Poly's fingers all the way to her teeth, and when she tried to pull her hand away, Luck let her. The roar didn't stop, to her dismay: if anything, it doubled. She clutched her one stinging hand in the other and watched, frozen, while the hundreds of suspended Civetans shivered as one and then disintegrated into fine amber dust.

There was a sudden emptiness. Poly, her eyes as wide and glassy as Luck's, saw the particles snatched away on a light breeze. The grass where the amber had been was shrivelled and black, and that blackness went on as far as she could see.

"I told you it tasted familiar," said Luck. He sounded pleased with himself.

Poly looked at him sickly. "Did I kill them all?"

"What? No, of course not. They've been dead for hundreds of years. They only looked alive because of the amber."

"Oh," said Poly, and found that she was whispering. She added vaguely, "My hand is cold."

"That's because the non-magic catalyst had magic locked inside it," Luck told her, gazing at the black expanse in front of them with distant eyes. "It was tuned to you. As a matter of fact, I expected it to—oh, there it is."

It? thought Poly with a sinking heart. She followed Luck's eyes and saw a haze sweeping across the new barrenness, a long, gentle wave of what could have been blackened stubble, following the swells in the ground as it rode the breeze. It was only when it rose, wavelike, that Poly realized it wasn't riding the breeze: it was carried along of its own volition, gathering from the most distant edges of the Frozen Battlefield to approach them.

Poly shook out her antimagic arm, willing it into warm, reassuring life, and had a moment of nasty surprise when it didn't respond.

"Won't work," said Luck, his eyes still on the gathering blackness.

A stab of anger pierced through the fear in Poly. "What did you do?"

"I made an anti-antimagic glove." Luck sounded pleased with himself. "Now you can't accidentally kill any of my spells, and no one can tell you've got it."

Poly fumbled with the strings of the glove, horribly aware that she wouldn't be able to get it off in time, and asked in calm desperation, "How do we stop *that*, then?"

"Stop it?" Luck looked surprised. "We don't want to stop it. Anyway, I'm not sure it's all exactly *magic*, as such."

It was too late now, anyway, thought Poly. The wave of blackness had reached them. It rose to surround them, high and black and shifting...and stopped.

"Oh, I like this!" said Luck, prodding at the stuff with his magic.

Poly wanted to hit him.

The dark, shifting pieces of stubble began to take on the same amber glow that the Frozen Battlefield had had before they dismantled it, and she wondered briefly if it had let go of the others in order to trap herself and Luck. Then everything flickered once, twice (was that Luck or the stubble? Poly wondered dazedly) and they were suddenly surrounded by forest.

"Huh," said Luck. "Interesting. I'm sure this is impossible."

"Did we shift again?" asked Poly, looking around with wide eyes. The ground beneath them was still blackened battlefield in a small circle extending outward from their feet until it became, without warning, mossy forest floor. It gave Poly the impression that they were surrounded by a cylindrical window.

To her left were two teens, a boy and a girl, both perhaps just a few years younger than herself. The boy was dark haired and bespectacled, fiddling with a ticking black box, and as she watched, he slapped at the hand of the red-haired girl, who was enthusiastically trying to turn a knob on the box. She scowled at him darkly, reminding Poly vaguely of someone she knew, then caught sight of Poly and Luck.

She squealed, the scowl vanishing as swiftly as it had come. "It worked! Peter, it worked!"

"I told you it would," said Peter, with a slight air of superiority. He looked up, his grey gaze meeting hers, and Poly felt a shock that sang right to her toes.

The first coherent thought that sprang to her mind was, *Ma was right. He* ***was*** *cocksure when he was a boy!* The second was to wonder what exactly her parents were doing here, mingled with the question of why they were so *young*. The overarching thought, however, was that *this* was why Dad had made sure that she could pick him and Ma out of an imprint no matter what year the imprint was from.

"Do you know who we are?" asked Peter cautiously.

Poly nodded, short and sharp, with the idea that if she were careful enough, Luck might never need know they were her parents.

Peter nodded back, squeezing the red-headed girl's hand to keep her quiet, and it occurred to Poly that he was being as careful as she was. "The tickerbox will shift us on again in a bit, but Glenna was certain that we could meet up before it did."

Glenna, her eyes roaming up and down Poly, looked fiercely pleased. "I would have been nicer to you if I'd known," she said.

Poly's gaze shifted enquiringly to Peter, who looked annoyed with himself. "Sorry, we keep forgetting what part of your time line we've met with. Are you two already—I mean, is he your husband?"

"Good grief, no!" said Poly, horrified. "He's a wizard who um, rescued me."

Peter grinned. "Hallo, Luck. You look even less civilized than usual."

Luck, whose eyes had narrowed, grinned back, startling Poly. "Past or future?"

"Um." Peter thought about it, polishing his glasses, and said at last, "Well, both, I think: we haven't gone far enough to tell, yet. You should see us again soon actually, only we'll probably be younger by then. We'll need somewhere to stay for a while, and we probably won't know who you are."

Luck's eyes went golden again, and something shifted in the forest, sending ripples over the amber window.

Peter said apologetically, "It won't work, you know. The tickerbox isn't magic, it's clockwork."

"You've made a hole in time," observed Luck, looking sharply from Peter to Glenna. "Who are you?"

Poly shot her youthful father a warning look, but he was already shrugging. "That's not allowed. Actually, it's a big kind of Not Allowed. Poly, we've only got a few more minutes before we shift again, and I don't know when we'll end up. Once the window dissipates, all the magic trapped inside is going to hit you: I'm afraid there's rather a lot. I had to push a big bunch of it into the tickerbox to solidify the resin in time, and it seems to have leaked through. It might be a bit strong."

Poly's eyes snapped to his face. "*You* put those people in amber?"

"*We* did," said Glenna, in a gruff little voice. "They would have killed everyone. Or enslaved them. It was all very nasty and we don't want to talk about it."

A flicker disrupted their faces briefly, and Poly felt the tug of dismay at her heart. "What happened to you both?" she asked hastily, before they could disappear.

"Peter pushed too much magic into the tickerbox trying to time-travel us," Glenna said matter-of-factly. "He does that a lot, as a matter of fact. It burned out one of the baby engines that was regulating—"

"It's a *secondary* engine!" interrupted Peter, looking annoyed. "And it happened to be the one that was controlling time and interval, so we've been ducking in and around all over the place. Mostly we've been going backwards but I'm pretty sure we'll come forward again before too many years. Either that or I've managed to fix it by the time we're older. Anyway, we'll be seeing you."

There was a surge through the surface of the window, and Poly's parents became harder to see.

"No, no, don't go yet," said Luck, very awake and excited. "There were notes, clues, little bits and pieces in books and such: old ones."

Peter, pushing up his glasses in sudden interest, moved closer and must have made some reply to Luck, but Poly found herself being addressed by her mother, who said quietly, "I'm sorry we leave—left, that is—you there. I think anything that wasn't originally tuned to the tickerbox gets left behind. We haven't been able to carry anything with us out of the different times yet. Peter says he'll figure it out, but I suppose we won't, if we left you behind."

"Lady Cimone looked after me," said Poly, smiling through the pain in her heart.

The window twisted and rippled more furiously than before, distorting Glenna's tight-clasped hands and suspiciously wet eyes. Luck and Peter murmured back and forth rapidly, then Peter stepped back and grabbed Glenna's hand.

"See you soon," he said to Poly, and grinned. "Or later. I've lost track."

The inrush of eager magic following the disintegration of Peter's time spell left Poly shaken and distinctly euphoric. Into the silence Onepiece wailed—terrified, confused and alone. He threw himself at her, and it was only when he had been attended to with all the proper cuddles and reassurances that Poly heard the irregular *taptaptap* of something nestled in her hair. Startled, her hand flew to her hair, and felt something round and hard and cool threaded onto a lock of her hair. She twitched it into sight and frowned down at the five or six amber beads that had somehow joined the blackbird feather a little below her right ear.

"Now where did *you* come from?" she muttered to herself.

She didn't really need the sudden, interested, and entirely too close inspection that Luck gave the beads to be certain that they were a small reminder of the amber magic she'd received from her father, however. She sent Luck a narrowed look that was meant to remind him about poking his nose where it wasn't wanted, but Luck only stared back at her with liquid gold eyes that failed to comprehend anything but the magical puzzle she had presented him with.

"They tuned it to you," he said, eyeing the beads with fascination. "Nothing has changed that amber slab for three hundred years, and you disintegrated it with a touch! They tuned it with magic and something else. Something crafty. Poly! Who were they?"

"Peter said I'm not allowed to tell you," Poly reminded him, scruffing Onepiece's ears with affectionate fingers. She was disinclined to disobey her father: she still relished the relative safety of being known as the princess.

Luck's eyes narrowed. "Do you always do what Peter tells you to do?"

Poly bit back an unwise laugh and said, "Well, yes, actually."

"Huh." Luck sounded disgruntled. "You don't do anything *I* tell you to do."

"Perhaps you should *ask* me instead of *telling* me," suggested Poly sweetly.

Luck gave her another of those clear green looks that meant he'd heard but refused to acknowledge as much, and said, "You can't be the princess when we get to the village."

Poly, caught between two disparate ideas, said dazedly, "Can't be the—*what* village? What do you mean, I can't be the princess?"

"My village. I'm sure I told you about it." He ignored her

mutter that No, he *hadn't*, and added, "They won't know what to do with a princess. Also, someone is trying to kill you."

A small, drawn-out growl from Onepiece surprised them both. *-no one is **allowed** to hurt poly. i will bite and bite and **bite**-*

Poly pulled gently on the puppy's ears to quiet the growl, remembering the Journey spell that had been a bomb, and found her voice to say, "Perhaps they're trying to kill you."

She could fully sympathise with the urge to kill Luck.

"They've had years to kill me off if they wanted to," said Luck. "It only started after I kissed you."

"I suppose that makes it my fault," said Poly, with a faint smile. "All right. Who am I supposed to be?"

"You can be one of my housekeeper's nieces," said Luck carelessly. "She's got a gaggle of them that live in the Capital and send her dozens of letters every week. If people think you come from the Capital it'll explain why you talk so oddly."

Startled, Poly asked, "But won't she mind?" and added belatedly, "I do not talk oddly!"

"Knowing Josie, she's probably already prepared a room for you," Luck said. "She's the most frighteningly prescient woman it's ever been my misfortune to meet. I think she scries the coalscuttle."

Poly, torn between a desire to know if it really was possible to scry with a coalscuttle and another to know what Luck meant when he said she spoke oddly, found herself left behind once again while Luck strode across the blackened expanse of newly liberated field. Onepiece scrabbled to be let down and hared after him, short legs pumping enthusiastically, and when Poly hastened after them both it was agreeably easy to catch up with Luck, suggesting that he had turned off his Keep Away spell.

While Luck strode along without talking, a vague crease between his brows, Poly asked Onepiece, *-Do I speak oddly?-*

Onepiece gave the mental equivalent of a shrug, his thoughts cartwheeling gleefully after a lone butterfly, the first to brave the blackened ground in search of flowers.

"You flatten your vowels," said Luck, surprising Poly by attending. "You sound like you just stepped out of Ye Olde Civet."

"I did just step out of Ye Olde Civet," Poly told him.

"Well, you need to sound like you just stepped out of Mrs. Terry's Finishing School for Elegant Young Ladies. Or better still, Trenthams." Luck pursed his lips and added unexpectedly, *"Rounded tones, young gels! Rounded tones!"*

Poly stifled a giggle not entirely successfully and protested, "That's just silly! I'd sound like a courtier putting on airs!"

"That's another thing," nodded Luck. He sounded like he was warming to his subject. "Finished ladies are meant to sound flowery. You're all blunt edges and vinegar."

"Then I'll have to be an *un*finished young lady," said Poly, refusing to be ashamed. "Onepiece, do *not* eat that!"

Onepiece froze, a piece of matted and unidentifiable miscellany between his canines. *-poly want some?-*

"No, Poly does *not* want some!" she said tartly. "Put it down, darling: you can have something nice later when we stop for the night. Look at it, it's got amber all over it."

Onepiece dithered for a moment before reluctantly dropping the clod of matted amber. As it blended into the blackened grass Poly heard him sigh mentally, but he trotted back to them cheerily enough, and she knew he was thinking about his promised treat.

"And keep the glove on," said Luck, prompting Poly to realise that she'd been unconsciously tugging at the crossed laces of the glove, which had become uncomfortably tight. "People aren't supposed to be able to absorb antimagic. I'd rather not have a little bird mentioning around the Capital that the foreign princess can absorb antimagic."

"I've never heard of antimagic before," Poly said, in accusatory tones.

Luck, unoffended, said, "They called it static magic, or something. It was new in your time, anyway: well, newly discovered."

Poly frowned, her fingers unconsciously fiddling with something smooth and wooden in her pocket, and thought that static magic sounded vaguely familiar. "I want to know why it curled around my arm," she said broodingly.

"I want to know what you're fiddling with," said Luck, with one of his sharper, leaner looks.

He grabbed her gloved wrist, half tugging it from her pocket, and Poly applied the heel of her foot to his toes with some energy. It didn't have as much effect barefoot, but Luck still yelled and let go—more, Poly thought, after a startled moment, because Onepiece had attached himself to Luck's heel with his tiny needled teeth than because of her attack.

"Yow! Ouch!" said Luck, attempting to fend off Onepiece with the foot that Poly had battered. "Get off, you miscreant mongrel! Poly! Yow. I forgot you have a habit of attacking me."

Poly made a bubble with her outstretched arms. "Personal space! Do you assault every woman you meet?"

"No, just you," said Luck agreeably, at last detaching Onepiece from his boot.

Poly could hear a surprisingly proficient stream of invective aimed at Luck from the puppy's usually sunny mind, and gave him a mental shake.

-*Language, Onepiece!*-

"You were fiddling with that spindle again, weren't you?"

Poly sighed. Everything with Luck seemed to be a riddle. She ignored this one, and instead inquired, "When will we arrive?"

Luck blinked. "Arrive?"

"You said we were going to your village."

"Oh. Did I? I suppose we must be, then. It's on the edge of the forest, so don't go wandering off."

-*like forest*- said Onepiece's voice.

Luck eyed the puppy with disfavour. "You can wander off if you want, but I'd rather not have to rescue Poly from a wyvern or a gaggle of mandrake. Not to mention another bout of enchanted sleep."

Poly considered mentioning that mandrake didn't come in

gaggles and weren't likely to attack even if they *did*, but she had an idea that Luck's village was likely to be less normal than most if only because he lived there.

Instead, she repeated, "When will we get there?"

"About sunset. If it hasn't moved again."

Oh, for pity's sake! thought Poly crossly. Who ever heard of a town that moved itself about?

Onepiece must have caught the emotion if not the sense of her thoughts, because he pranced up to her feet with the irreverent thought: -*wizards. all squirly brain. no sense*-

"I'm not a wizard," said Luck, shooting them both one of his sharper green looks.

Onepiece yipped and danced sideways toward Poly, who brazened out the look by demanding, "Why don't you want people to know about the antimagic part of my arm?"

"There are three types of magic," said Luck. Poly thought he was doing his usual sidestep until he added, "One is common: two are rare. Antimagic is one of the rare ones."

"I thought antimagic was—" Poly floundered and finished lamely, "I don't know, sort of *not* magic. My arm *breaks* spells, doesn't it?"

"Well, it is," reiterated Luck unhelpfully. "And then there's unmagic, which is just as tricky and even more powerful."

Poly said gloomily, "I think you're making it up. Unmagic! How ridiculous!"

Luck gave her a glassy look that made her flush and said, "Maybe they'll ask you next time they name a variation. Magic is common enough, but antimagic and unmagic are rare. Antimagic affects magic, and unmagic affects them both; and when you've got all three together something, somewhere goes boom. Certain people in the Capital like things that go boom: that's why I don't want it to get about that I'm strolling through the village with someone capable of altering antimagic."

"Oh." Poly pondered the idea meditatively and was faintly surprised to find that she agreed with Luck. She pulled the laces of her glove a little tighter. "What type of magic do enchanters have?"

"Normal magic. We have more than wizards, but it's the same thing. I'm stuffed with it," he added off-handedly. "Enchantresses are different: they tend to have antimagic rather than magic. Not you, though."

"That's because I'm not an enchantress," Poly said. She was getting rather tired of correcting Luck. "What sort of people have unmagic?"

"No one *has* unmagic," said Luck. "It just sort of floats about trying to cause trouble. But I'm beginning to rethink that, too."

"Oh," said Poly again, trying to look as if she understood.

Luck's explanations had a tendency to leave her more in the dark than she had been previously. She had her doubts as to whether Luck's elucidation upon the distinctions between different types of magic was entirely accurate, but she didn't know how to say so without offending him. With any luck the Capital would have a comprehensive library that could be placed at the disposal of a recently rescued princess, and Poly could make the study herself. She would have asked Luck to clarify what exactly he meant by 'floating around causing trouble', but his eyes had glazed and he was turning his head from side to side as if to pick out a landmark in the blackened expanse of battlefield.

Poly looked more closely, ignoring the flare of sudden bright magic from Luck, and thought that perhaps he *was*. There was a distinct lack of magic in the old battlefield, but if she looked very hard, Poly could see myriad fragments of magic that looked like the loose ends of a weaving at the far edges of the burnt grass. She remembered vaguely from early lessons with Lady Cimone that the land was undergirded with magic. Whatever her parents had done, they had done thoroughly: they'd cut a section of the mountain away from its very foundations.

"Will it join back again?" she asked Luck, watching the trailing threads of magic as they reached out wistfully.

Luck blinked at her and said, "It *has* moved. It was through and over two weeks ago, and now it's under and side-slipped."

"What a pity," said Poly, matter-of-factly, for once able to follow Luck's twisted trail of thought to the conclusion that the village wasn't where he expected it to be. Apparently even Luck's village found him irritating enough to hide from him. "Will the edges join again?"

"What edges?" Luck said, tilting his head back. "The village doesn't have edges. It's sort of spiral."

"Not the village," Poly said patiently. "The battlefield."

Luck tucked his chin back in and walked on, this time angling them sharply to the left. "Don't know. Can't stop now, Poly, it's still moving. No time to fiddle with magic."

Poly's lips twitched in appreciative amusement, but she forbore to point out that she was not the culprit when it came to fiddling with magic. Instead, she gave her immediate attention to following Luck's increasingly erratic lead.

Once they reached the edge of the battlefield and plunged into deep, sweet-smelling grass it became more erratic still as Luck followed cunning little scarves of the underlying land magic that dipped and danced and threaded between each other bewilderingly. Poly was careful to follow him closely, finding Onepiece's sharp, startled warning of -*oopsiedaisy! country's gone squirly*- unnecessary, since she had already discovered for herself that the land was twitching beneath them. She picked up the puppy, unwilling to run the risk of losing him in one of the more unexpected twitches, and touched some of the brilliant scarves of land magic as they passed them. A few were loose and came away in her fingers, more substantial than she expected, and Poly studied them curiously, wondering exactly where Luck had led her. They didn't seem to be exactly walking through the hills as they had been, nor did it feel as though Luck had started a travel spell.

-*It feels like we've gone* **deeper**- she said to Onepiece, curling the loose, fluttering pieces of magic around her fingers, where they coiled silkily and seemed to cling to her skin.

-*forest magic*- said Onepiece in suspicious tones, sniffing loudly at air that was somehow richer than it had been. -*all forest underneath. sneaky sneaky forest pretending to be hills*-

-Oh- Poly looked around dubiously and almost lost sight of a faintly hazy Luck, which was worrisome enough to prompt her to cling to his coat pocket. There was no reason for him to be disappearing in clear country without a tree in sight.

Luck reached back and grabbed her hand without taking his eyes off the seething countryside, leaving Poly rather relieved. At least this time he didn't seem to find it necessary to haul her along at breakneck speed.

The countryside was still curling at the corners of her eyes by the time the last sun disappeared over the horizon. Poly let Onepiece out of her pocket to pee behind a clump of wildflowers, but she wasn't comfortable until he was back in sight. And when Luck went to sleep for the night, close enough that Poly's hair tried to curl around him too, Poly didn't quibble about the matter of Personal Space. For once, Luck's obnoxious proximity was comforting.

7

As late morning merged into afternoon the next day, Luck's village sprang out of the grasslands, complete with a darkening of trees behind it. It came upon them suddenly enough to startle Poly, who couldn't rid herself of the idea that it had been waiting, crouched out of sight on purpose to make her jump. The *squirly*ness that Onepiece had complained of was all but gone and the countryside now seemed less rarefied and dangerously magical. Poly still sensed a lingering oddity at the corners of her eyes, but Luck seemed more relaxed and even Onepiece poked his nose out of her pocket to gaze around in obvious approval.

Luck beat a summons on the gate that boomed around them with such unabashed clarity that it must have been amplified by magical means, but the sound had scarcely faded when he forced the gates open himself, with a massive crack of gold-lightening magic that split the enchantments in two. Through the open gates, Poly saw the gatekeeper approaching on the run. He looked more resigned than afraid, prompting her to think that this was an impatience that Luck had been guilty of on more than one occasion. When he saw them he stopped running altogether.

"They'll have heard it," he said to Luck, when he came within earshot, jerking his thumb toward the centre of the village.

It sounded, thought Poly, like a warning.

"Can't be helped," said Luck, ignoring the fact that it could have been helped with just a moment's patience.

Poly, struggling to keep up, noticed that he had lengthened his stride and found herself impressed: whoever *they* were, *they* had Luck on the run.

She wasn't long left in suspense: even as the gatekeeper ushered them along the main street, curtains began to flutter; and before long the streets flooded with excited villagers, who, for reasons best known to themselves, seemed actually *glad* to see Luck. There was such a babble of voices that Poly couldn't make out any individual remarks addressed to Luck, but from the sheer amount of bowing and eyelash batting that seemed to be going on, she concluded that most of the addresses could be shuffled under either of the twin headings: "Oh, Powerful and Lofty Enchanter, how good to see you again," and "Oh, Intriguing and Handsome Enchanter, how good to see you again."

She was vastly amused to be the subject of more than one venomous look, since Luck had forgotten to let go of her hand and couldn't be brought to realise as much no matter how she tugged—and more than slightly discomforted to find that she herself was attracting not a few admiring looks from the young male populace. Poly wasn't used to being looked at admiringly: she was used to padding silently at the edges of society and avoiding any kind of looks, admiring or otherwise. Fortunately for the quiet blush she could feel making its way into her cheeks, a determined dash on Luck's part drove them through the crowd and into a house without any more ado.

Poly, bewildered in the sudden silence, said, "Good grief, they act as though you're one of the Immortals! Anyone would think you'd been patriarch for hundreds of years!"

"Well," said Luck apologetically, "That's probably because I *am*."

More unbalanced still, Poly found that now she was the one clutching Luck's hand, and hurriedly let go. "Immortal or a patriarch?"

"Not exactly immortal," Luck admitted. "I'll die. Eventually. Maybe. I've been the village enchanter for about a hundred and twenty years or so."

Poly gazed at him for a long moment, but all she could find to say was, "You're still only half as old as me, then."

Someone stifled a giggle, but Luck said approvingly, "Yes. I knew you'd understand!"

"Well, I don't," Poly said positively, and this time someone definitely laughed.

"Luck, let the poor girl sit down!" said a comfortably fat voice.

To Poly's relief, the voice was neither adoring nor awed. She turned her head and found that besides the gatekeeper, who had managed to slip in with them, the room contained another two people. One was a young, scowling girl with chestnut hair. The other was the owner of the fat voice: plump, but not as plump as her voice had led Poly to believe. Her brown hair, which was confined in an entirely sensible bun, was touched with a shade of red. She pulled a chair forward for Poly in a self-possessed way that made Poly think that this house belonged to her, but Luck was throwing his travel-stained overcoat carelessly over a pile of what appeared to be assorted rubbish, and Poly couldn't picture this neat, bustling woman allowing that kind of mess in her own household. No, it was more likely that this was Luck's housekeeper.

"I'm Josie," said the woman, confirming the guess. "Norris, my husband: he keeps the gate. And Margaret, our girl. You must be my newest niece."

Poly smiled mechanically at Margaret, who stared back in unsmiling challenge—good grief, not another of Luck's bevy!— and with more warmth at Norris, who had a slow, curling smile that wrinkled the corners of his eyes.

"I don't mean to pry," said Josie, with sharp black eyes that suggested that she *did* mean to, and would enjoy doing so, "But should I be welcoming the son of my niece, or a young nephew? The neighbours will ask."

"I told you she was fiendishly knowing," observed Luck dispassionately, appearing for a moment through a doorway before disappearing again.

The sharp look was friendly enough, and Poly had no qualms about drawing Onepiece out of her apron pocket. She was rather surprised that Josie had noticed the puppy.

-food?- said Onepiece hopefully, prompting another sharp look from Josie.

"A nephew, I think," Poly said, silently promising: *-Food later-* to Onepiece. "Will it matter—"

"No," said Josie. "We've more than a few *talented* children in the village, pet. It comes with being so close to the forest, of course."

"Of course," echoed Poly, wondering what exactly the forest had to do with the matter.

Still, if Onepiece's predilection for trotting about in the guise of a small puppy could pass without comment, it would be a very good thing. Poly had been surprised to find within herself the deep, furious determination that Onepiece would be a little boy again, little by excruciating little. If Luck could be persuaded to stay still for just a few days, she was certain that the village was the very place to do it.

Someone asked in a flat voice, "Where's she going to sleep?"

Poly's eyes involuntarily went to Margaret, who had spoken and was now watching her with mingled dislike and suspicion.

"There's no room in my bed," the girl added, tilting her chin just slightly when Josie's thoughtful gaze turned on her.

"She can sleep in mine," said Luck, breezing back into the conversation carelessly. There was a moment's startled silence when all eyes turned on him in various astonishment and horror, before he added, "It's still here somewhere: that tricky wire thing with a mattress."

"The one you use when you're up all hours working on a spell," nodded Josie. She wasn't quite twinkling, but when her eyes met Poly's over Margaret's head, there was a brief second of shared, amused frustration. Josie, it would seem, had been putting up with Luck for quite some time. "You can set it up in Margaret's room," she added, in a brisk tone that permitted no argument from either Poly or Margaret. Poly wouldn't have argued in any case, but Margaret, she was sure, would have if she *could* have. "Norris, you'd best be off to the gatehouse again."

Norris did as he was told, too, but with a quiet amusement in his deep grey eyes that suggested he did so entirely under his own volition. Perhaps he did: Poly had an idea that despite appearances, he was no more under the thumb than Luck was.

Before he left, he tugged a tangle of tubing and wire from one of Luck's piles of rubbish with casual force and propped it against the same pile with a wink in Poly's direction. She smiled back gladly at him, feeling less overwhelmed, and picked it up before Josie had to tell Margaret to do so. The girl would have done it, but she would have hated Poly just that much more.

Poly sighed, remembering just the same look in Persephone's eyes.

-*bite?*- suggested Onepiece. His tiny hackles had gone up and she could feel his stomach vibrating with a silent growl. -*sharp-shiny eyes. puckleberry mouth. not nice to poly-*

-*Be nice*- Poly told him, but she felt comforted. She followed Margaret down a pokey hall that made her feel giddy and Onepiece sneeze, and firmly shouldered open the door that the other girl would have carelessly let swing shut in her face.

The room was white and cheerful—and, for the most part, tidy. Poly wondered if Margaret was naturally tidy or if Josie made inspections, and in the middle of wondering came to the sudden, startling conclusion that they were no longer in Luck's house.

There were two circumstances that led to this conclusion. The first, that the view from the window was now distinctly the gatehouse, was immediately noticeable. Poly, remembering the stride of Luck's long legs, knew that they had left the gatehouse behind very quickly once the village had been breached. The second and more disturbing sign that all was not quite correct, was that the doorway, once shouldered through and closed, lay flush with the wall and showed no signs of any actual opening. When Poly examined it more closely, she saw that the doorway had been drawn—and not particularly well drawn—on the wallpaper with a stick of charcoal. Even the round knob was a swirl of hastily scribbled black charcoal.

When Poly had finished studying it she found Margaret smirking at her. She felt a flicker of amusement: Margaret evidently thought she had scored a point.

She reached curiously for the drawn-in doorknob, feeling it somehow round and solid in her hand just as Margaret said, "It's only one way. Luck doesn't like people wandering—Oh! You can't —How did you do that?"

Her voice was angry, and Poly, who had automatically turned the doorknob that she found in her hand, gazed ruefully at the open door. Well, *that* had done a mischief.

"Magic likes me," she said.

"Magic doesn't *like* people," returned Margaret, her eyes hard and angry.

Poly silently closed the door again and began to puzzle out the wire bed in one corner of the room, while Margaret fidgeted in the silence.

Finally, the girl asked abruptly, "How did you meet Luck, anyway?"

The tone of her voice seemed to suggest that it had been an engineered meeting.

Poly dismissed her first, wildly incendiary instinct to tell Margaret that she and Luck had first met when he kissed her awake, and said merely, "Oh, it's a long story. Luck was passing by when I happened to need some help, that's all. He's taking me to the Capital."

"What about the dog?"

"He's not really a dog," Poly said, scruffing Onepiece's ears.

"I know that. Why is he travelling with *you*?"

Poly blinked, startled. "I don't quite know. Luck bought him at a dirty little town and I somehow adopted him."

"Luck does that," said Margaret, shrugging. "Buys things that interest him and then throws them away when he's solved them or gets bored with them."

"I suppose it's a good thing Luck gave Onepiece to me, then," remarked Poly, amused both by Margaret's proprietary knowledge and the toss of the head that accompanied it.

Between Luck, Onepiece, and now Margaret, she was beginning to feel as though she was running a nursery.

She felt a tinge of unease from Onepiece's pocket and heard the thread of a thought from him that asked a garbled question. -*No, darling*- she said, in as firm of a voice as she could project. -*I promise I won't get bored with you. And I would never give you away like a parcel of goods: who would protect me then?*-

There was an immediate buoyancy from the puppy, who demanded to be let down so that he could thoroughly sniff out the room—in order, thought Poly with a small, half frowning smile, to assure himself that no dangers attended her.

"You can change back into a boy after dinner," she told him, this time aloud, and Onepiece paused mid-sniff, considering the idea. Poly added enticingly, "Then you can check the windows as well, and maybe try to walk a few steps."

Onepiece huffed a breath through his nose and said: -*dinner? yesyesyes*-

Poly didn't see Luck again until dinner time. Margaret stuck to her like a furry-bean to skerry fleece, less for the love of her company than, Poly suspected, the determination to prevent Poly wandering back within reach of Luck. She was cheerfully untroubled by this state of affairs, quite ready to enjoy a holiday from Luck's startling and quite often dangerous company, and ruthlessly used Margaret as her guide to wander up and down the village. Luck had described it as 'sort of spiral', but Poly came to the conclusion that Luck had either not wandered the boundaries of the village in quite some time, or that his long years of service had addled his brains. The village seemed to resemble nothing so much as a crooked dogleg. From what Poly could see in the distance, the impressive wall bounding the front of the village extended only partway around it. The rest seemed to be bordered merely by forest, prompting her to wonder exactly what use a wall and gate were if they didn't surround a village entirely.

When she mentioned as much to Margaret, the girl looked at her in as much surprise as disdain.

"Well, there's the forest," she said.

The village itself was almost overwhelming. There was magic *everywhere*, doing everything imaginable, and almost every resident she saw possessed at least rudimentary magic of his or her own. The constant flicker of magic was there at the corners of her eyes no matter which way she turned, and Poly wasn't sure if it was the surfeit of magic that made it all seem a little skewed, or if magic was just a little different here in Luck's village. The constant pressure of magic tired her quickly, but Onepiece was delighted to explore each new sight and smell, and he pranced ahead of the girls, uttering his short, gruff little bark whenever something moved more quickly than he expected.

And Margaret, after all, wasn't a bad guide. Despite her evident lack of sense when it came to Luck, she wasn't actually *stupid*, and Poly even found herself smiling involuntarily at some of Margaret's more acerbic comments on her unfortunate neighbours. She wondered if the girl knew how much alike she and her mother were.

By the time they arrived back at Luck's house, she and Margaret, if not exactly fast friends, were beginning to tolerate one another. This happy state of affairs was considerably helped by the fact that Luck, who managed to be waist deep in a cupboard that was only inches deep on the outside, didn't seem to notice Poly's arrival any more than Margaret's.

In fact, it was only after Margaret had gone unwillingly to prepare dinner that Luck became aware of Poly's existence. She had perched herself tiredly on what seemed to be a rounded metal bulwark in one corner of the room, amused to watch Luck's peregrinations to and fro as he pieced together a complicated and sprawling spell, but after turning in a confused circle three times in a row, eyes glazed, he caught sight of her.

At once his eyes sharpened. "Poly! Where did you go? Why weren't you here? The balance has been off all afternoon!"

"I've been exploring," Poly told him, unwilling to bestir herself to ask what balance he was talking about. "Margaret was showing me the village."

"Well, she shouldn't have been," said Luck, irritably. "I *needed* you."

Poly wondered if she should feel flattered and decided against it. Most likely Luck wanted her to do something unpleasant. "If it's another bomb, I don't want anything to do with it," she said, yawning.

She crossed her legs and arranged the brilliant yellow material of her skirt over her shins and bare feet. She'd forgotten to ask Luck to magic her another pair of shoes before they got to the village, and she had been uneasily aware of more than one pair of eyes watching her bare ankles as she and Margaret walked.

Luck gazed at her with untroubled green eyes. "Why would it be a bomb?"

Poly, feeling an absurd urge to laugh, decided that she was far too tired, and said, "Oh, I don't know. The magic here is very strange and I think I want to go to bed."

Luck's face was suddenly decidedly closer, causing Poly to jerk back against the wall to avoid him. She opened her mouth to protest and found that she was yawning again instead.

"Huh," said Luck, leaking golden magic. He sounded smug, and, Poly thought, slightly pleased. "Your balance is off, too. The curse is being sneaky again."

"Personal space, Luck," Poly said wearily, fighting back

another yawn in order to add, "What do you mean about the curse?"

-threads are coming loose- said Onepiece, trotting into the room from the direction of the kitchen. He brought with him the mouth-watering scent of baked potatoes and melting cheese.

"Fine print," said Luck, at the same time. "Governmental spellpapers are tricky, too. To wake you up I had to smudge things a bit with some of the sub-clauses in the spellpaper, and the curse has been thinking about things all the while, trying to find out how I tricked it."

Poly found that she understood and was pleased with herself. "And now it has?"

"I need the spellpaper, but it's hiding from me," complained Luck. He ran his fingers vigorously through his hair, sending dust and cobwebs dancing in the late rays of sunshine that lit the room. "It was in my library when I left, and now it's moved. One of the gremlins must have got it."

Poly put her chin in her palm and observed Luck with sleepy interest. "Do the gremlins often move things?"

"Sometimes. Sometimes they just eat them. Or poop on them. Wake up, Poly; it's rude to fall asleep when I'm talking to you."

-and there's dinner- said Onepiece anxiously, turning small circles below her as if getting up the nerve to attempt the high scramble onto the metal bulwark.

Poly reached down and lifted him into her lap. "It's all right, darling; I'm only a little sleepy. Luck will fix it. Is dinner ready?"

"We're too busy for dinner," said Luck, ignoring Onepiece's prompt and enthusiastic affirmative. "The dog can eat if it wants to eat."

"*I* want to eat," protested Poly, awake enough to feel indignant at Luck's use of the plural.

"Rubbish. There's too much to do and you've been gone all day. Hold out your hand, Poly."

Poly instinctively drew back, curling the fingers of both hands into her palms. "Why?"

"I want to try something," said Luck.

Poly thought, in sleepy fatalism, *He always sounds so* reasonable. *Then you're up to your elbows in a bomb, or walking through a mountain.*

"You're fading, Poly!" Luck's voice was sharp, but distant, and when Poly tried to focus on his face, it blurred. "If you don't wake up, I'll have to kiss you again, and you won't like that."

There was a far-off whine, then a tiny, forceful personality battered at the cobwebs of sleep that were winding, thick and fast, around Poly's mind. She tried to reach out to it, vaguely aware that it needed reassuring, but couldn't form her thoughts enough to break through. Poly had a moment—or perhaps it was a day or maybe even a week—to feel fuzzily panicked, before a sharp pain in one finger shocked her back into herself.

Luck's magic swarmed around her, huge and golden and *everywhere*, and a frightened little voice babbled, -*sorrysorrysorry! pollee! pollee?*- but all Poly could see was the bead of blood as it slipped silkily down her finger and dropped, dropped, dropped...

Poly fell. It was like falling in a dream, except that instead of waking up, she hit reality.

Or in this case, she thought, looking around swiftly and more than slightly shaken: the past. She was in her bedroom, her hands automatically straightening her grey, everyday ensemble, and if the messy locks of her shorn hair were any indicator, she had been lying on her bed and napping until recently.

Poly felt a cold chill of intuition. It was the Midsummer Night's Eve Festival tonight: it must be, because her younger body was not *very* much younger, and her hair had been slashed off the morning before the festival. Moreover, this particular grey dress had been new for the occasion. But Poly didn't remember waking up until Luck kissed her.

This, then, was a memory that had been buried away very, very carefully. The question was, had it been buried by the curse as a kind of magical side effect, or on purpose by the person who had cursed her?

Poly didn't waste time trying to find her way back to Luck and Onepiece because she could feel Luck's magic somewhere in the back of her mind, warm and reassuring. Even further back was the idea that this was *important*.

Poly was faintly aware of her younger mind gently ticking over, thoughts flitting past as her fingers ran perfunctorily through her hair. Curious, she let herself sink into her younger mind, and heard her thoughts say, *Haircut, then strawberries, then the Carvery.*

The haircut was understandable, Poly thought, remembering ruefully the appalling mess that Persephone had made of her hair. And Persephone rang for strawberries at the same time every day—which strawberries were crushed and applied to her face in preparation for whatever evening entertainment she chose to attend.

But why the Carvery? wondered Poly, listening intently to the memory-thoughts as they flowed past.

*...a birthday present I like...*said Poly's thoughts, accompanied by a flourish of pictures.

Poly grinned a small, meta-grin at the back of her own mind as her past self bore her along inexorably, passing down old corridors that were now lost to her. She'd been getting herself a birthday present. Images flitted past until her younger mind settled on one: a small wooden spindle that had carved curlicues and a lovely curve to it. Now that was interesting. Why a spindle?

The outdoor corridors were busier than usual. Brightly dressed pages from various houses dodged through the strolling courtiers and around stone colonnades, shouting shrilly at each other over the hubbub of talk. The scent of roses wafted on the warm air, achingly familiar, and Poly felt her younger self smile at the scene as she swept quietly along the outskirts, her grey gown sweeping grey shadows to make her comfortably invisible.

he pages dashed past her as if she weren't there, and Poly, skirting the courtiers with even less trouble, remembered with a faint feeling of surprise that no one ever *did* see her. She had become so used to Luck's invasive notice that the quiet safety of invisibility had all the quality of an old, favourite cloak stuffed to the back of the closet: still useful once in a while, but no longer worn every day.

Poly found herself enjoying the sensation, and it was something of a shock when she realized that someone *had* seen her. She noticed the fact before her younger self did, with a slight sick tug where her stomach would have been if she were corporeal.

Mordion, dressed all in silky dark blue, lounged with pantherlike grace against one of the colonnades, and if she was not mistaken, he had been watching her for quite some time. Beautiful and deadly, he had had a reputation for breaking hearts that made him even more attractive to most of the women in court.

Immediate experience clashed with fractured memory, and with a cold chill, Poly remembered a sliver of the day. In a few seconds, Mordion would uncoil himself from the colonnade, attracting her notice, and stroll across the crowded walkway, parting the courtiers without effort.

He did so, and Poly's memory merged with the scene, her head jerking back slightly as younger Poly realized his intent to cross her path. Poly noted approvingly the small, swift sidestep that her body gave in an attempt to forestall the meeting, and even more approvingly the scowl she felt forming on her face.

Brief fragments of memory flashed past her mind as younger Poly remembered indications of Mordion's interest over the last few weeks. The Shearing Day feast, where he had sat opposite her and gazed at her beneath his lashes, carefully dropping his eyes *just* after she caught him at it. The Princess' walking picnic, where Mordion walked ostensibly with Persephone, conversing suavely, but still managed to help Poly over every bit of stony ground that she came even conceivably close to, murmuring charmingly in her ear at the same time.

But why me? said younger Poly's thoughts. Poly watched the flow of her own thoughts intently as they rippled around one stubborn idea that stood, rocklike, at the centre of her mind: the idea that Mordion had a habit of flirting with women who, in some way or other, benefited him.

There was Lady Angela, whose father was a very rich and influential backer of promising young mages attempting the treacherous climb to glory in the Mage's Council. He was noted for his highly select dinner parties, at which you could always be certain of finding the most prominent members of the council—and, occasionally, the king and queen. That was ten years ago from this time, and Mordion had been merely a new interest in the court: beautiful, certainly, but neither very rich or terribly powerful. Poly recalled Lady Cimone saying rather dryly that Lady Angela had opened a very useful door for him, and now she understood why.

After Lady Angela, Mordion had briefly squired the Massey sisters to a succession of Harvest festivities, raising eyebrows by flirting outrageously with both girls. Gossip began to circulate that there would be a marriage between him and the elder girl, Helen. Poly, who was at the age of eleven entering her second year of service as lady-in-waiting to the youthful princess, and already a silent watcher, distrusted gossip. She was almost certain that Mordion was more interested in the younger, less beautiful, Mary.

There was nothing concrete to suggest that he distinguished Mary particularly, nor was there evidence that he had taken advantage of either of the sisters in any way. There wasn't really even anything to prove that he had squired them for any other reason than idle amusement, but Poly, sneaking out to watch the Harvest Night dancing from a tree that overlooked the courtyard in one quiet, shadowy corner, found herself overlooking more than just the dancing.

At first, she was quite alone, content to pick tangberries and turn her fingers orange with the juice while she watched gauze and muslin flutter on the courtyard below. Then, so suddenly that Poly dropped one of her tangberries, a gentleman in blue masterfully swept his partner into the shadows of the tree. They were already talking when they stopped, and Poly heard the voice of Mary Massey say, "It's not the same at all! I would like it back, thank you very much."

"Darling, you wanted it gone," murmured Mordion. He sounded very reasonable, and Poly wondered if Mary wanted to hit him for it as badly as she did. "You begged me until I agreed."

Mary Massey, quiet and proud, said, "I know, but now I would like it back. I don't think I quite understood what it meant."

Mordion's bowed head spoke regret. "I'm afraid it's too late: it's gone."

"Gone?" Poly thought Mary sounded empty, her voice dead and cold. "I see. I think I would like to be alone now."

Mordion was either kind enough or clever enough to take the dismissal with one of his more breathtaking smiles and a lingering kiss that Mary allowed with a lack of embarrassment that suggested it wasn't the first kiss she and Mordion had stolen in the shadows. The kiss tilted Mordion's head at just the right angle; his eyes met Poly's over Mary's shoulder. He winked at her, but Poly gazed back at him with cold dislike until one of Mordion's eyebrows winged up. He chuckled.

"Goodnight, darling," he said, and Poly wasn't sure if he was talking to Mary or herself.

Mary, without looking up, bid him a good night in return, and sat quietly on the lowest branch of Poly's tangberry tree. Poly was watching Mordion melt back into the party when she realised that Mary had begun to cry in a silent, calm sort of a way with her head leaning into the tree trunk and the tears running down her cheeks.

A month later Mordion had enrolled in the Royal Players and was tearing across the stage in the company of the wildest young actors the castle had ever seen; daring enough to be popular but somehow never there when anything definitely disgraceful occurred. His clever use of magic began to be remarked upon.

Poly, watching his steady rather than meteoric rise in polite circles, never forgot to be wary of him. The thought remained in her mind now: Mordion had a habit of associating with people who, in some way or another, benefitted him. Now Mordion was chief Mage of the Mage's Council, and he was showing an interest in her.

Why me? said younger Poly's thoughts, while older Poly, sorting through the memories as they flashed past, echoed the question.

Poly didn't offer Mordion her hand, but somehow he managed to kiss it anyway. He did the kissing with great skill, holding her eyes as he did so in a smouldering sort of way, the older Poly thought grimly, that was meant to make her heart flutter. She was pleased to note that her heart did no such thing.

Younger Poly stared him down, nostrils flaring; daring him, if the militant thoughts were anything to judge by, to just *try* and wink at her.

One of Mordion's brows went flying up, and his blue eyes narrowed with amusement.

By way of retaliation, he said, "Charming! I really must compliment your coiffure!"

"I'm starting a fashion," Poly heard her voice say dryly. "What do you want, Mordion?"

"Your company, amongst other things," said Mordion easily, tucking her hand into his arm.

Poly took it away again and slipped her hands into her pockets. "I'm busy."

"How fortunate that I'm not!" he remarked affably, with a glinting smile. "I'm free to attend the most beautiful lady in court about her business."

Poly saw the flash of her younger self's thoughts suggesting the remark that in *that* case, he should go and find the most beautiful lady in court and leave her in peace, but a sideways glance at Mordion stopped the remark on young Poly's tongue.

Mordion, a predatory smile lingering on his lips, said, "Very sensible of you, darling. Although, I admit that I would have liked the opportunity to describe your attractions to you one by one."

Poly began to feel very afraid. Her younger self had not blushed—which pleased her, since it meant that she hadn't fallen prey to Mordion's skilled assault in spite of herself—but Mordion was showing no signs of being rebuffed despite her marked rudeness. It took her a little while to realise that she was feeling so frightened because younger Poly was frightened as well.

A flash of memory showed Poly the man-shaped void in the amber, and she seemed to hear Luck's voice saying again that *Mordion* had promised him books to rescue her.

He *did it,* thought Poly, lightheaded with shock. It was ridiculously clear: she should have known it the moment Luck mentioned Mordion's name. The surprise made a buzzing in her ears that separated her from her younger self, and Poly tried to cling to the memory, but it was too late.

She floated up, up, up, leaving her past self to the mercies of Mordion.

8

Poly woke with a gasp and a shiver, feeling as though she'd been doused with cold water. She was lying on the dusty floorboards, and Onepiece was howling. One of her amber beads, she noticed mechanically, had come free and was caught between floorboards, cracked and a little blackened. It was empty of magic.

Poly's gaze travelled away from it and focused on her finger through dusty glasses, aware that it was throbbing uncomfortably. It took her a moment to focus on a smeared patch of scarlet on the tip of it.

"It was the dog that bit you," said Luck. "I didn't have anything to do with it."

Poly automatically reached for Onepiece, sitting up dizzily to gather him into her lap, and said, "It's alright, darling. I'm back."

-poly poly *POLY!-* wept the puppy, burrowing into the crook of her arm.

"You would have kicked me for that," Luck remarked gloomily. "The dog bites you, and you cuddle it."

Poly gave a sudden chuckle. "I'm glad you didn't bite me," she said. "Onepiece, you were very helpful. Thank you."

"Targeted sensory programming," said Luck. He hauled her up by one arm, more enthusiastically than gently, his eyes bright.

Onepiece chose that moment to turn human, and Poly was left to juggle his half-human, half-canine body with one arm while Luck propelled her forcefully at one of the plastered walls in the room.

"Yow!" said Poly, as plaster loomed and then vanished. "Luck—!"

"The wall is slightly out of synch with our timeline," Luck explained, without stopping.

There was a kind of grating gurgle from Onepiece, and Poly realised in some surprise that he was laughing. *-sneezy-* said his thoughts.

"Use your outside voice," Poly told him automatically, gazing around at the room she had been propelled into.

It was a library, messy and disorganized, with haphazard piles of books stacked crazily against every wall but the one they had entered by. That wall was almost translucently see-through and gave a brick-and-plaster patterned view of the other room.

Onepiece said, "*Zee!*" forcefully in his deep little voice, clicking his teeth, and looked pleased with himself.

Poly said, "Clever boy!" and found herself being vigorously licked. She couldn't help the involuntary grimace or the quick shoulder swipe she gave to dry her cheek, and Onepiece muttered aloud incoherently for a moment before she heard his voice in her head.

-kisses- he said reproachfully.

"That's a puppy kiss. Little boys kiss like this: *mwah!*"

Onepiece gave the throaty chuckle that passed for his giggle, shoulders hunching automatically as his eyes crinkled.

"*Mwah!*" he said, planting a sloppy kiss on her cheek in return. "*Mwah! Mwah!*"

Poly successfully resisted the urge to wipe off her cheek this time but swung him by the wrists to avoid another assault. He hung from her hands happily, gazing about the library with his mouth gaping and padding lightly at the floorboards with his bare feet. At least this time the trousers and shirt that Luck had originally magicked for him had appeared along with his human body. There would be time to work on the shoes later.

Poly hefted Onepiece until his feet were over hers and walked him around the room while he rattled his chuckle to the surrounding books and wobbled unsteadily on weak legs. They passed Luck as he was crouched by one of the book piles, and Onepiece, with gleeful abandon, tossed a *mwah!* in his direction.

Luck recoiled, his face surprised and offended in equal proportions, and Poly giggled helplessly.

"Why's it doing that?" he demanded. "Poly, you're encouraging the dog to mock me."

"Puh!" said Onepiece, taking a false step and dragging Poly one unsteady step sideways.

"He was blowing you a kiss," Poly said breathlessly, recovering her balance with difficulty. "I was showing him how to kiss."

"Puh!"

"Yes, darling, very clever."

"Well, tell it not to," Luck told her, eyeing Onepiece warily. "If it wants to learn how to kiss, we can give it a demonstration when we're not busy."

"He knows how to puppy kiss," explained Poly, gently swinging Onepiece's feet back onto her own. "I was showing him how to kiss like a little boy."

"Hm," said Luck. "Maybe not, then. Poly, stop playing with the dog: the gremlins have moved the books I want. I need you to find them."

"*Eee!*" insisted Onepiece. "Puh. *Eee.*"

"Lee, darling," said Poly. "Put your tongue behind your teeth. Po-*lee*. Luck, why am I finding the books that *you* lost?"

"Puh. *Lee!*"

"I didn't lose them," Luck said irritably, dashing one hand through his hair. "I *told* you: the gremlins moved them. Maybe they ate them. Poly, I *need* my books. There were passages in them about Targeted Sensory Programming and Sensory Recall that I need to have another look at. You've done something very beautiful, and I don't know how you've done it. Ah. That's what I was going to ask you: where did you go?"

"Back," Poly said. "The morning before I was cursed, actually. It was a memory, but I didn't remember it until now."

"Huh," said Luck, tilting his head back to gaze at her. His hand dropped from the bookshelf, and he took a narrow-eyed step forward. "Interesting."

Poly was ready to back away, but fortunately this time Luck was content to poke experimentally at the amber beads in her hair with one finger. In fact, the most offensive thing he did was to tug sharply at the hank of hair that was threaded through the amber, and then stare at her punctured finger. Once he said, "Blood," in a disapproving tone of voice; then he said, "Huh," and let her go again.

"*Puh*-lee," muttered Onepiece, smacking his lips and giggling gutturally at the sound. "Puhpuhpuh. Pollee. Yuck."

Luck shot the puppy a narrow golden look and said, "I don't think your magic is trying to break the curse."

"The magic I don't have?" asked Poly sweetly, twitching the lock of hair away from Luck's fingers.

"Yes, that magic," said Luck, sublimely inattentive. "I think it's trying to get *you* to break the curse. You've hidden memories and programmed yourself to remember them by visual or sensory stimulus using whatever magic you have to hand. I can't tell what you've linked it to, though. That's the tricky bit. You made us skip to the Frozen Battlefield overnight and pushed my Shifter wrong to make us visit the hermit. I think you programmed yourself to get us to certain places."

"I didn't program anything," Poly told him mildly. "I don't have magic, Luck."

"You've got memories you can't remember," Luck said. "You wouldn't know."

Poly opened her mouth and closed it again. At length, she

said, "Well, yes. But why would I try to get us to the Frozen Battlefield? How was that supposed to help break the curse? And how on earth could the hermit help?"

Luck was silent for so long that she knew he couldn't think of a reason.

At last, he said, "I need my books, Poly. One's called *Self-Programming: Establishing Markers*, and the other is a little red book with a flowery title like *Psychoanalogy and Neuro-Linguistic* something or other. And look for that spellpaper."

Poly considered asking whether either of the ridiculously complicated titles involved magic of any kind but reflected that Luck would most likely be throwing magic at her whether or not she found the books, and that it was undoubtedly easier to find them than to have Luck complaining every few minutes that the gremlins had eaten them.

Poly found a big book with brightly coloured pictures and set Onepiece down in a corner with it, ignoring Luck's glare. The puppy accepted it shakily and pawed at it with his fingers, but watched her owlishly as she searched the shelves, mumbling under his breath. When she next looked over, he was fully immersed in the pictures, and she was able to turn her attention to the task of finding Luck's missing books. Since she didn't place any faith in the existence of Luck's 'gremlins', it seemed sensible to start in one corner of the room and search the piles of books from top to bottom.

Halfway through the third pile of books Poly began to be aware that there was a faint halo to them, and a cautious rather than thorough examination leading her to believe that there was another, slightly odd layer to the books, she sat back with a sigh, and asked in resignation, "Luck, are there two layers of books?"

Luck, leaning into the wall with one shoulder, absorbed in a tiny blue book and swatting absently at specks of dust that drifted frequently by his nose, said an absent, "Hm?"

Poly assumed, more for the sake of giving him the benefit of the doubt than because she really believed it, that he had been looking for the books also, and had been distracted by an old favourite.

"The books. Are there two layers?"

"Two layers. Out of synch," he murmured.

"Well, it's *untidy*," Poly said. She unlaced the glove from her antimagic hand and tugged it away briskly, tucking it into her apron pocket. No doubt it would be covered in Onepiece's camel-brown hairs before long; her apron was already littered with them. The silver spiral around her arm glittered and sparked with silver all the way to the centre of her palm, free and eager to be used, and Poly reached through the halo, through the gap in synchronicity, and grasped something that wriggled. The books pulsed, wavered, and doubled in amount, tumbling in a cascade to the dusty floorboards.

Onepiece gave his rough chuckle and made an explosive sound with his lips, flinging his thin hands into the air. The action overbalanced him and sent him sliding into a pile of books, much to his amused surprise, and Poly had to stop herself from involuntarily stepping over to pick him up. It was useless expecting him to learn to be a boy again if she was constantly holding him up.

He made an inarticulate noise, then a raspberry as he tried to blow away the dust that clung to his face, and said silently to her, *-shelves all tucked up. daft wizard. empty dusty-*

Poly opened her sight a little wider, gazing at the walls until she could see what the puppy meant. The faint shadow of what could have been three or four bookcases was etched into the ivory render of the walls—vague scrolling that *could* have been swirls of render, but wasn't quite.

"Clever boy!" she told Onepiece approvingly, and the puppy grinned a wide, slack grin at her.

She ran the palm of her antimagic hand over the rendered wall, and the rough, sandpapery feel of render gradually gave way to the smoothness of painted wood. *There!* There was one of the shelves, solid and firm beneath her fingers. Poly gave a tiny chuckle of satisfaction and curled her fingers around the shelf, tugging briskly.

The bookcase moved, groaning and unwilling, and segued from the wall into solid self-existence, scrolled and white-painted with a top shelf that was just out of Poly's reach. She heard Luck muttering crossly about walls that wouldn't stay still, but since his only other reaction to the disturbance was to wriggle his shoulders against a tottering tower of books that had nudged subtly into him, she merely pulled out the other three bookcases one by one, ruthlessly tumbling books out of the way.

"Yik!" said a shrill voice as the last bookcase ground out of the wall.

Something soft and small pelted into Poly's hair, and she looked up to see myriad tiny, sharp teeth grimacing at her out of a dirty ivory face. The creature was only five inches tall and naked. It was vaguely humanoid but sexless, with a bush of what might have been hair but was more likely to be dust bunnies glued haphazardly to its head. It had a second woodchip grasped in its tiny paw, and the vaguely threatening chittering it made with its toothy mouth seemed to suggest that it was on the point of hurling that at her, too.

Poly narrowed her eyes at it, and slowly raised her index finger. "*No*," she said sternly. "No throwing."

The creature gibbered, dancing on its flat, toeless feet, and made small, darting motions at her forefinger. It looked very much as though it were trying to nerve itself up to throw the woodchip.

"No," Poly said again, more slowly.

"Yikyikyik!"

"Bookshelf is for books," Poly said calmly, looking into the jewel green orbs that stared at her beadily. "Not for Yiketty yiks."

"Yiketty yik," it said sadly, dropping the woodchip.

Poly wasn't sure if it was conceding defeat, or making a bid for sympathy.

Following her instinct that anyone in Luck's house was bound to be undernourished, she suggested, "Food?"

"*Yik!*"

"All right," conceded Poly. Onepiece said *-food!-* distantly in her head, and she saw a scrabble of book cover and pages as he shrank back to his puppy form. "Wait here."

-me too, me too! haha, food!-

Onepiece followed her through the vague wall manifestation and then danced ahead into the kitchen, precipitating a small shriek and hasty footsteps.

Margaret appeared in the doorway, brandishing a kitchen knife, and said, trying to be cross, "The next time he scrabbles around my feet like that, he'll be chopped up and put in the pot with the rest of the meat!"

-chopchop!- said Onepiece gleefully, still dancing around her feet. *-inna pot!-*

"Exactly! Poly, can you tell Luck that dinner will be ready in a quarter hour?"

"I can *try*," Poly said doubtfully. "I don't know that he'll listen, though: he's reading a little blue book and all I can get from him are two-word answers and a grunt every now and then."

"He's in the library? Well, that's the last we'll see of him today," Margaret said pessimistically. "Are you having your dinner there?"

Poly made a rueful grimace. "Probably. Luck's lost two books he wants me to find, and the library is a mess. I'll probably have to clean it before I can find anything."

"Rather you than me!" said Margaret with an unsympathetic laugh. "What did you come out for? Does Luck need something?"

"Do you have anything in the kitchen that a—" Poly paused, sighed, and gave in to the inevitable, "—that a gremlin would find tasty?"

"Pulled out the bookshelves, did you? Well, that'll cause a bit of a mess around the house. Give 'em cheese; they like that. You won't get any peace until you put the bookcases back into the walls, though; they live in them, you see."

"Well, they'll have to live somewhere else," said Poly, with a determination she didn't quite feel.

She accepted the lump of cheese that Margaret gave her, ignoring the knowing smile and shrug that went along with it, and returned to the library.

When she got back, she was greeted by a row of silent, beady eyes that watched her intently from the top three shelves of the fourth bookcase. The original gremlin had been joined by roughly twenty more of the creatures, and they sat with their bare bottoms on the painted wood, dangling their flat feet into the dusty air.

"Yik," said the first gremlin, precipitating a chorus of *yikyikyik!*s that threatened to pierce Poly's eardrums.

She held up her index finger again sternly and, much to her satisfaction, an awed silence fell as twenty-odd gremlins stared at her finger as if bewitched.

"Huh," said Luck, flicking over a page. "They don't do that for me."

His voice was absorbed and uninterested, but it produced a violent response from the gremlins, who chittered and shrieked at him until Luck looked up from his book with a decided snap of gold to his eyes. This quietened all but the boldest of them, and even they berated at a mutter instead of a shriek.

Poly, deciding that this was possibly the best behaviour she could expect of them, hastily broke the cheese into smaller portions and gave it out with congratulatory murmurs. The first gremlin to receive his cheese clasped it beatifically in webbed, fingerless hands and crooned, "Ah she!"

"Shee!" crooned the others, bobbing their heads.

It was a relief to think that they knew more words than the continual *yikyik*, but Poly found their wide, adoring gaze slightly nerve wracking, and said, touching a hand to the middle of her chest, "Poly. Not she. Poly."

The mutter of 'Poly' was passed between the gremlins with much tooth snapping satisfaction until one of them held up his lump of cheese with a victorious cry of, "Polyolyoly! Ollyollyolly!"

The others took up the cry, brandishing their choooo, and charged back into the walls, shrieking and *yik*-ing. Poly was left feeling rather uncertain, but since she saw neither a trace of webbed hand nor dust-bunny hair despite all her knocking and tidying and dusting, she let herself assume, a little uneasily, that she had pleased them.

-*inna walls*- said Onepiece in her head, sniffing cautiously at the render of the walls. -*all yikyik and cheese and She Poly*-

"Oh dear," Poly said, with a tingle of foreboding. "I hope I haven't sent them on a rampage."

-*yes, but not in bookcase anymore*- pointed out Onepiece prosaically.

Later, Poly retired to the kitchen to fetch dinner, and grinned to find that she had caught Margaret with her head out the kitchen window, berating a would-be caller in a loud whisper.

"But Meg, you promised!" protested the lad.

He was a boy with big round glasses and a natural expression of hopefulness that was at present somewhat strained, and Poly thought he looked rather nice.

Margaret tossed her head at him and said, "Yes, but Luck's home, Puss: you'll have to go with someone else. Oh, Poly, there you are. I've put it all on a tray for you."

Poly said thank you cheerfully and nodded at the boy in a friendly way that made him blush darkly, much to her amusement. She wandered back to the library with leisurely slowness, wondering how many boys Margaret was dangling on a string while she tried to attract Luck's notice. The thought was a rather stringent one, and she wondered for a moment if she was jealous of Margaret—because unless she counted Mordion, Poly hadn't even had *one* boy to dangle on a string.

But then, thought Poly hopefully, *I never wanted one. Not a courtier, anyway.*

The thought cheered her up. It would have been a rather dismal thing to find herself jealous of a petty sort of girl like Margaret.

Well, she thought fairmindedly, *Not petty. Just proprietary.* Besides, Luck didn't seem to notice her any more than he noticed the other village girls, unless Poly construed his not running away from Margaret as notice. In which case, Margaret was to be pitied rather than envied.

She picked her way through stacks of books, placing Luck's dinner beside him on the floorboards, and received a sweet, absent smile from Luck that meant he hadn't really noticed her. If *that* was what Margaret had to contend with, Poly did pity her.

Poly went back to her own piles of books, nibbling at her cheesy potatoes whenever the hunger pangs struck her, and before long found that her dinner had turned leathery with cold. She eyed her plate ruefully, comparing it with Luck's, which was still full and now congealed in solidified fat, and realised that Onepiece had gone to sleep curled up in his corner. Mentally apostrophizing herself for a thoughtlessness as bad as Luck's, she picked him up and bore him off to bed, forestalling his sleepy mutters with a gentle caress of his ears.

It was cold and dark outside the library, surprising Poly with the lateness of the hour, and when she tiptoed into Margaret's room the girl was already in bed and heavily enough asleep not to wake at the opening of the bedroom door. Poly deposited Onepiece on the bed, covering him with the sheets just in case he turned human in his sleep, and stretched limbs that had, she now realised, become stiff and sore. How long had she and Luck been immured in the library? She'd lost track of the time, sorting madly to make order from chaos, and somehow it hadn't seemed important to keep track of the rapidly advancing hour. Perhaps— heaven forbid!—Luck's absentmindedness was catching.

Poly grimaced at her smudged reflection in Margaret's bureau mirror and decided that it was necessary to escape the dusty air of the house. She'd taken many moonlit walks back at the castle, letting the silence and coolness of the night slide over her refreshingly. It had helped to wash away Persephone's petty snipes and the continual, battering assault of tiny, unkind magics from Melisande and Giselle. Here in Luck's village, she was less likely to be remarked upon if she slipped out, and Poly was quite certain that Luck wouldn't notice her absence.

Poly made her way quietly back through Luck's living room and out the front door. She was uncertain of what lay beyond Margaret's real bedroom door and was unwilling to risk bumbling around someone else's home late at night. It didn't occur to her until she shut the front door that Luck might have some kind of magic lock on it, but when her convulsive grab at the doorknob turned it easily, she was able to huff out a breath of relief and feel thankful that at least Luck had thought to include her in the house spells, even if he couldn't remember to make sure that she had dinner.

It was pleasantly cold outside, but the touch of a cool breeze on her unfamiliarly bare arms reminded Poly fleetingly that the butterflower yellow dress Luck had made her was the only one she presently owned, and that her complete lack of both coin and apparel would have to be brought up with Luck tomorrow. But in the meantime, the moonlit village was quietly welcome, and Poly strolled through the tightly knit houses until she found herself at the outskirts of the village. The houses here were bigger, single level dwellings that spread sideways in contrast to the neat, two-level condominiums at the centre of the village. Behind them the forest stretched out, silent and massive.

Poly wandered closer to the shadowed trees, but when her hair uncoiled itself from the plait she'd confined it in and reached out waveringly to the forest she backed away rather quickly. There had been quite enough magic for one day.

To her surprise, this time she didn't encounter the village wall as she walked. The village had seemed somehow smaller yesterday too, and Poly, wondering just what Luck had meant when he described the village as spiral, made an addendum to the list of things she needed to mention to him tomorrow. She had a shrewd idea that Luck worked on a different set of vocabulary to the rest of the world.

There were even *fields* in the village, for heaven's sake! Margaret had only shown the portion of the village that she considered pertinent—which tended to be shops and the houses of her cronies—and it was rather a surprise to find herself following deep ruts in the grass that served for tracks between the crops.

They were smallish fields, perhaps only a quarter mile square each, but they were full and whispering in the moonlight, just like fields should be. Poly amused herself by trying sleepily to guess what was in each field, but with indifferent success: after the familiarity of paddock after paddock of sheep, one green, rustling crop looked much like another. Besides, the villagers seemed to have a ridiculously eclectic mix of crops, some of which, Poly thought doubtfully, she was *almost* sure were not in season.

A closer look at the fields showed a webbing of unfamiliar magic surrounding the crops that intrigued her enough to bring a halt to her stroll while she tried to puzzle out the thread of one of the closer spells.

One of the threads was Luck's, Poly was certain. She stretched out a finger to trace the single thread, and it gave a little beneath the pressure, taut but elastic. The other strands were myriad and completely unfamiliar, and they all had that slight skew to them that she'd noticed before. Despite Poly's best efforts, she couldn't tell what the spell was for.

She was still gazing at the webbing and yawning behind her hand when it occurred to her that she was very nearly asleep where she crouched. The thought spurred her to rise rather hastily and turn homeward with a quicker step than before, an unwelcome vision of herself laying asleep and forgotten between rows of corn (or was it cotton?) slowly creeping into her mind.

Poly hurried back through the rustling green stalks, mentally scolding herself for the stupidity of taking to the open air at night when she was plagued by a sleep curse. She wasn't the only one taking the air, however; as she hurried homeward, Poly saw a broad-shouldered shadow struggling through the only empty, unploughed field in sight. The thread of stray, wrong magic that had drawn Poly's attention to that fact was quivering with barely suppressed hunger.

Poly shivered and disintegrated it with her antimagic hand as she passed. Poacher or mischief maker aside, she didn't care for the type of magic that had made the nasty little trap. She heard running footsteps and saw a shadow vault over the fence, and walked a little faster with the uneasy suspicion that she might have freed a poacher from the rightful grasp of his victim.

The way back home seemed twice as fast as the way there, and Poly, who thought she'd managed to become thoroughly lost, was grateful to find herself trailing up the main road to Luck's cottage in very short order. Luck was outside waiting for her, which explained the quicker journey back: he gave her a quick, critical look over and nodded decisively as if he were satisfied.

Poly was too sleepy to really care what it was he was satisfied about, and when he opened the door for her in a rare moment of thoughtfulness, she merely murmured goodnight and took herself off to bed.

THE ACRID BURN of smelling salts woke Poly to a world that was far too warm. She sneezed three times, constricting a thin, bony little body that protested its displeasure in semi-articulated grunts, and battled her way out of tangled bedsheets, almost falling out of the regrettably narrow bed.

"You're lively this morning," remarked Luck.

He was looking bright and cheerful, thought Poly sourly, and his hair was standing up almost straight. She had an idea that he hadn't been to bed at all.

"I'm in my *chemise*!" said Margaret's voice indignantly.

She looked as though she wasn't sure whether to be pleased or offended to find Luck in her bedroom. Luck gave her one of his wide, glassy looks until she scowled and dragged the sheets up to her chin, then turned back to Poly.

"Wake up, Poly. I need you."

Poly put up one hand to rub her sleepy eyes and was bewildered to find that she had just knocked off her glasses.

"I put them on you," Luck said unnecessarily, pushing them back on her nose with surprising proficiency. He looked pleased with himself. "Wake up, Poly. There's something sideways around the village and we haven't finished in the library."

"Luck, I'm not dressed! No, let me go: I won't be pulled around the house in my chemise!"

"I don't care what you wear," argued Luck, still tugging. "I just want my books."

"Well, I want breakfast. And so does Onepiece."

"Yus," said Onepiece explosively, clinging to Poly's chemise in a way that threatened to become embarrassing. "Fist!"

"Yes, darling; you'll get breakfast," soothed Poly, disengaging Onepiece's grubby little fingers and twitching her own fingers out of Luck's hand. "No, out! *Out*, Luck! I will come to the library when I'm dressed."

Luck protested, but she pushed him firmly out the door and shut it just as firmly behind him. When she turned around, Margaret was watching her, open mouthed.

Grey eyes met blue: Margaret's mouth shut with a snap, and she said in the friendliest tones Poly had yet heard from her, "We need to get you some new clothes, Poly: you can't keep wearing that yellow thing every day. Luck has an account at every store in the village, so we might as well go shopping this afternoon." She met Poly's surprised thanks with a shrug and a humorous, "Oh well, if people think we're related you can't go around dressed like that. It looks like Luck chose it."

"He did," admitted Poly, feeling oddly protective of the yellow frock. "I think it's pretty."

Margaret eyed the dress appraisingly as Poly pulled it over her chemise. "Well, it's certainly *bright*. Here, these slippers should fit; you can't go about barefoot. Should I ask about the glove?"

"Probably not," Poly said ruefully, gazing down at the lacy article.

"All right, we'll get dresses that match it. What about the hair?"

"What about it?"

"Well, it's *moving*. Is it a spell?"

The thought of her unnervingly active hair as an aid to beauty struck Poly as exquisitely humorous. "A hundred strokes a night and Gaipur Lotion, you mean? No, Luck threw some magic at me and it stuck."

"His magic did all that?"

"Not all of it," Poly said reluctantly. She crouched beside the bed to neaten Onepiece's choppy brown hair and hefted him to his feet, ignoring his internal burbling with an iron will. She thought he was a little stronger today and wondered if it was just her imagination: certainly he was still as unbalanced as ever. "It was, well, *different* when I woke up. Onepiece, if you want to speak, speak aloud."

Onepiece made a rude noise at her and said *'mwah'* sweetly to Margaret, who looked startled and giggled. "Oh, isn't he the sweetest thing? Does he do that at Luck?"

Poly grinned. "Just last night. I don't think I've ever seen Luck so startled."

"I'll just *bet*," said Margaret wistfully. "What I wouldn't give to have seen it! You'd better let me braid that, Poly: we're all Talented, but self-governing hair is out of the way even here."

Poly, who had been distractedly trying to finger comb her hair and keep Onepiece from falling over at the same time, accepted the offer thankfully, hauling Onepiece along with her by his shirt collar. When she sat down the boy seized her knees, fingers thin and sharp, and tried cheerfully to not fall over.

"There's a Happening tomorrow," Margaret said offhandedly, catching an escaped whisp of hair that had been tickling Poly's ear. Fortunately, Poly's hair seemed to be ambivalent toward Margaret's particular magic, which sped up the braiding process considerably. "If we can find you something ready-made, you should come with me. Luck'll be having callers until at least midday, and besides, everybody wants to meet you."

"Oh! A Happening," said Poly, all at sea with the implied capital letter.

Margaret gave a sniff of laughter. "I keep forgetting how quaint and old fashioned you are, Poly: you sound just like one of the old table tabbies. A Happening is just dinner and maybe a dance. You don't even need a really plummy dress, so long as it's smart."

If she took 'plummy' to mean fine, Poly thought she could just about understand that. Language hadn't changed so very much in the last three hundred years, but travelling with someone as succinct as Luck had made her forget the small matter of colloquialisms.

"Won't the hostess mind?" she asked Margaret, a little at random.

The thought that language hadn't changed much was sticking in her mind, because language *did* change over three hundred years. No one who had studied the Elder Books at the castle's library could think otherwise; those ancient tomes, heavy with years and almost entirely incomprehensible with outdated spelling and extinct words, were a written testament to the changeability of language.

Margaret tied a ribbon into Poly's braid end, letting it drop with a heavy thump, and said, "The Prime Lady, you mean? No, as far as they're concerned, a bucket's as good as a drop. You're done," she added unnecessarily, since Poly continued to sit, lost in her musings.

Poly blinked a little and murmured thanks. Fortunately,

Margaret didn't seem to expect to be repaid in kind, and she was able to make her way back to the library shortly thereafter.

By the time Poly and Margaret set out on their shopping expedition there was a line of people sprawling from the front door all the way out the garden gate. Margaret, who had come to fetch Poly from the library, caught sight of them through the front window and hastily bundled Poly out by the kitchen door. "This way, Poly! If they can't raise Luck, they'll fetch whoever they can."

"What do they want?" asked Poly, peering over the hedge only to be tugged away by the other girl.

"Charms. Spells. Some of them need magic mended or the forest pushed back. Luck's contract says that they can call from first bell to midday to be seen to, but sometimes Luck forgets about them all morning and then keeps going until last bell."

Poly was about to remark that anyone who wanted the forest pushed back should perhaps hire a woodcutter instead of Luck when she remembered the quiet intent of the forest, and the way her hair had reached out to it. Perhaps the forest, like the village, was a little more than it seemed.

"Is that what he does when he's home?" she asked instead, obeying Margaret's insistent hand-wavings to scurry along half bent behind the shelter of the hedge.

"No, mostly he tries to get out of it when he's home," Margaret said carelessly.

They rounded the street corner and she straightened, briskly tugging the wrinkles out of her bodice and setting her hat at a more flirtatious angle. Poly, following suit, regretted having no hat: back at the castle hats had not been worn, and she thought they were a delightful nonsense. Some of the older court ladies had worn turbans, but the girls had worn their hair long and uncapped, threaded with flowers or jewels—or, if the lady was an enchantress, sparkling spells.

Poly smoothed her hair instead, uneasily noticing that a

whole fat skein had already escaped from the braid, and followed in the wake of Margaret's bobbing straw hat, feeling oddly bereft without Onepiece's constant nattering in her mind.

"Are you sure your mother doesn't mind watching Onepiece?" she asked anxiously.

It was perhaps the fourth time she had asked, and although she didn't see Margaret roll her eyes Poly could hear the laugh in her voice as Margaret said, "Trust me, Mum is having the time of her life. She adores having a little person to cook for and clean and bully. No, not that one, Poly: Mistress Holly specializes in frumpy old tabby clientele. *We* want Hobsons."

Poly followed her dutifully, though she hadn't seen anything wrong with Mistress Holly's quiet, long-sleeved displays. She found herself, after the confusing silver tinkle of a bell somewhere above her head, enveloped in a close, bright world of fabric and dress dummies. Something sharp pierced her foot through the borrowed shoes, and Poly curled her toes, instinctively looking down to find the source of the pain. A bright, steely gleam proclaimed the presence of a pin, which she picked up and passed to the effervescent lady who bustled over to them at the sound of the bell.

"Thank you, dear!" said that lady warmly, attaching the pin to her collar, where it nestled among several others. "Mika always misses one or two."

She gestured behind her as she spoke, and it took Poly a few, blinking moments to recognize that the tiny, furry bundle of clothes nestled among the draping fabric, was, in fact, a monkey. It was picking at the carpet with the same studious intensity that it would have searched for fleas, and as Poly watched, it drew a wickedly sharp pin from the carpet, and leapt, chattering, to its owner's shoulder.

The lady patted it absently on the head, provoking the monkey to display its teeth as it secured the pin in her collar with the others, and said, "You must be Poly, dear: Mrs Hobson, very much at your service. Josie mentioned that you might find your way here today. Blue and green, I think. Bespoke or ready-made?"

"Two ready-made and two bespoke," said Margaret, forestalling Poly. "Luck's account."

Poly felt her lips quirk ruefully at the corners and reflected once again that Margaret and Josie really were very much alike. She allowed herself to be bustled up onto a step stool and hoped fervently that dressmaking had become more expedited with the passing of three hundred years, not to mention the loss of whalebone and stuffing as regular accoutrements to a frock. Judging from the flush of pleasure mantling Mrs Hobson's cheeks and the dreamy look of an artist in her usually sharp black eyes, however, Poly rather thought not.

Poly was pinned into a dress of moss green velvet with silver trim at the cuffs, her feet encased in the softest of new slippers, when the door swung open madly, violently ringing the bell, and a young man strode into the room.

"Good heavens! A maiden!" One bright blue eye laughed at Poly from between the fingers that the young man put over his face. "Madam, I protest I wasn't looking!"

Poly met the dazzlingly blue gaze and felt a pleasant shock that made her say more prosaically than usual, "Well, there's not really much to see."

"I beg to differ," he said, with a frankly admiring gaze.

Poly hoped rather desperately that her cheeks weren't as hot as they felt, and was grateful when Margaret said, "Oh, don't tease her, Michael. She's not village: she won't understand you."

Wondering if she should feel insulted, Poly said calmly, "I won't take offence, I promise, even if I'm *not village*."

Margaret grinned at her, informing Poly that she had reacted appropriately. "Don't you think it's a little dark?" she asked, nodding at the green velvet.

Poly's fingers curled into the velvet protectively. She *liked* darker colours. The frock was pretty and quiet at the same time, and the silver trim added a touch of distinction to the greenness that was pleasing.

"It's warm," she said instead. "And it will wear well."

"What tosh!" said Margaret indignantly. "That's no reason to buy a gown!"

"It sets off your eyes," said Michael, leaning casually into the window and giving Poly an unabashed lookover. "Grey eyes, slate black hair, and moss green velvet—" he kissed his hand with a flourish. "And *what* hair! What have you got in there? Spells?"

"Little bits and pieces of magic," said Poly. She self-consciously touched a hand to her hair and dropped it in annoyance when she realised what she was doing. "Mostly from Luck but some of it came from my—from a boy we met, and I found some floating outside the village."

Michael cocked his head. "Free magic, eh? What—"

"Oh, Michael, what do you want? We're *busy*."

"Well, if you don't want your invitations, I suppose I'll leave you to your shopping," said Michael, without moving. "I have patterns to cut, too, you know."

He winked at Poly, who much to her own mortification found herself blushing again, and turned to greet Margaret's sharp eyed interest with wide, innocent eyes.

"What invitations?" Margaret demanded, abandoning Poly's prospective wardrobe for more important considerations. "Who is having a party, and why do you know about it before me?"

"Sheer charm of manner and the small fact that me Ma happens to be the one giving the party. Two weeks from now, last bell. Are you coming?"

"*If* I have nothing better to do," Margaret told him loftily, her tone belying the anticipation in her eyes.

"I was asking *Poly*," said Michael provocatively. "I don't much mind whether or not you come, Miss Margaret; only me Ma told me to ask."

"Fibber," said Margaret, but without heat. "If I didn't talk with you no one would. You need me there."

He shrugged and tilted his head enquiringly at Poly, who said, "I'd love to come. Will your mother mind if I bring along one very small boy?"

"Mind? She'll love it. She's always complaining about how big and ugly I've gotten. She'll cuddle and cook and bring out ancient sweeties. You won't be able to get away."

"Onepiece will love it," said Poly, laughing.

"In the interests of making sure that Onepiece isn't the only one in the village enjoying himself," began Michael, a gleam in his blue eyes that brought out a responsive twinkle in Poly's, "may I inveigle the promise of a dance from you tomorrow? Just a small one, and I promise it won't be painful."

Poly opened her mouth to agree gladly, a warm little burr of contentment in her throat, when it occurred to her in a dashing moment that she didn't know any of the current dances.

Quiet in her disappointment, she shrugged and said, "I don't know the right dances. Sorry."

"Oh, I make up my own anyway," said Michael easily. He gave her a small, curving, devastating smile and added, "And now that you've promised me a dance there's no getting out of it. Goodbye, Poly; goodbye, Miss Meg. Buy the dress!"

"That boy!" said Margaret when he had gone. Despite the stringency of her tone, she was smiling. "Don't listen to his nonsense, Poly; he's a flirt and a constant bother."

"So I gathered," murmured Poly, trying not to think about laughing blue eyes and a curving, mischievous smile. Her mouth twisted wryly as she said, more for her own benefit than Margaret's, "I hope I know better than to be won over by a charming smile and a few compliments."

But she bought the dress.

9

"What is last bell?"

Luck's dishevelled head appeared from behind an untidy pile of books. "Poly! You look different. What did you do? No, never mind—where were you yesterday afternoon? The—"

"I know, I know," sighed Poly, resigned to the inevitable. "The balance was out all day. What is last bell?"

"No—well, yes, actually; but that's not what—I was imprisoned all afternoon, Poly. In my own house. The hordes just kept coming and coming. And there's still something sideways in the village! People are beginning to complain. Where were you?"

"Shopping with Margaret," said Poly, automatically straightening two books that had fallen down on one of her carefully ordered shelves. There hadn't been sight or sound from the gremlins since she left the cheese out for them yesterday, and she had slept well—and better yet, woken without Luck's help. It was looking like a beautiful day. "Apparently my taste is outmoded and my clothing outdated. Have those people been lining up since dawn?"

"Probably," said Luck, with a slightly wild look. "The line

doubles in size every time I look out the window. Last bell? Last bell is the ceasefire order."

"Last bell is the end of the work day," Poly mused aloud, making a mental note. That reminded her of another lingering question, and she asked curiously, "Luck, how is it that we could understand each other when we met? Language doesn't work like that; things must have changed while I was asleep."

"Oh, that. I put a spell on you."

Poly blinked rapidly, then said with deceptive calmness: "You put a *spell* on me?"

"It was that or learning to speak Ye Olde Civet again. They stopped speaking that way a few years after I was born, you know. It was easier to put a spell on you."

Poly briefly remembered Luck's lips moving just out of synch with his words on the day she met him, and a small part of her was obliquely satisfied at a solved puzzle.

A larger part, rising in indignation, caused her to say, "You're running a spell on me and you didn't even *ask*?"

Luck stopped looking hunted for long enough to say, "No, it stopped working a few days back when your brain caught up with the dialect. All I had to do was start it; when you stole some of my magic you took over the spell yourself."

Poly wavered between pointing out firmly that Luck had *thrown* magic at her, and that she had not in fact stolen it, and reiterating just once more that as she didn't possess magic it was impossible for her to have kept up a spell, outside magic or no.

Instead, she said, "You've no right to run spells on me, Luck! My personal space extends to not putting spells on me."

"Huh," said Luck. "You should have said. Poly, what are you— no, this is my sanctuary! A few more minutes and they might think that I've already gone out. Poly!"

But Poly, with reprisals in mind, had already passed through the library wall. The line of villagers was stretching out of sight through the window when she peeked out, and when she opened the door an older woman with a worried face gazed up at her in dawning relief.

"Luck can see you now," she told the woman.

A barely audible sigh slipped through the woman's lips. "Pebbles and primroses, I thought I wouldn't get in before last bell! You're Josie's niece, aren't you? Hmm," she added, without giving Poly a chance to reply, "You don't much favour her."

Poly met the shrewd blue gaze and came to two conclusions. "You're Michael's Ma," she said slowly, ushering the woman into the house. "No, I'm not Josie's niece. You knew that already."

"I might have guessed," she said, smiling infectiously. "But then, I've known Josie for some time. Come to tea with me one afternoon, dear: you can tell me who you really are. Just between you, me, and the bees. I suppose my lump of a son didn't mention me by name—no? You can call me Annie."

Poly shook the hand that was offered and called out somewhat unnecessarily to Luck, "Your first visitor is here, Luck!"

"I'm not at home," said Luck's voice sulkily, but he came out of the library anyway.

One of his grubby, once white cuffs was torn, and there was blood on his wrist from what Poly strongly suspected was a gremlin bite.

"Luck, what did you do to the gremlins? I just got them settled!"

"They mounted a pincer movement from the ancient history corner and stole my pocket watch," said Luck irritably. "I'm *wounded*, Poly. Possibly infected."

"Show me," Poly ordered, and took a leaf out of Luck's book by seizing his wrist without waiting for permission.

"It's too late, I'm probably already dying," Luck said. "Have I met you? What do you need? I don't do love spells."

Correctly assuming that these questions were for Annie's benefit, Poly ignored them and tilted Luck's wrist to the light. He said an absentminded *ouch* but didn't otherwise acknowledge the inspection.

"We've met," said Annie. "I wouldn't bother you, wizard, but it *is* getting quite urgent."

Poly, discovering with some surprise that Luck was right, and the bite really *was* infected, heard the note of deference in Annie's voice and owned herself even more surprised. She touched the slightly bleeding bite carefully, exciting the tiny specks of magic that were ferociously attacking the surrounding skin, and lent one ear to the conversation.

"You're the one with the jinxed field," Luck was saying. "Slightly sideways strawberries or something like that. Standard for something that close to the Forest."

To Poly, carefully drawing out shards of burrowing magic, it sounded as if he had said it with a capital. Not forest, but The Forest.

"The Forest isn't the problem," said Annie. "It's the jinx itself; it's gone sideways."

Luck's green eyes glazed a little, warning the initiated that he had begun to grow bored with the subject. "It's a jinx; it's meant to go sideways. There's a standard clause in the bill of sale allowing for a variance of eight degrees within the first ten years of sale."

"It's a family plot, and the variance in the last year alone is fifteen degrees," Annie said rapidly. Perhaps she wasn't as uninitiated as Poly had assumed. "Premium planting for the strawberries began early this month, but Michael hasn't been able to so much as turn the soil without the risk of turning himself inside out, or the field tricking him into thinking that he's a strawberry and ought to plant himself."

"Huh," said Luck. "Clever. When did you last have an incident?"

"Night before last," said Annie, stirring in Poly the memory of a captured intruder she had freed from a malicious bit of magic. "He got away, but it was a close thing."

Poly looked up rather guiltily. "That might have been my fault. Is your field the only one that's unploughed?"

"For the last fortnight," Annie nodded, her eyes narrowed. "Fault, child? What fault?"

"I was out for a walk and saw someone caught in a piece of nasty magic, so I disintegrated it. I didn't really think until it was too late that it could have been a thief."

Annie laughed out loud, a warm gurgle. "Thief, my eye! That was Michael! He was trying to fertilise and turn the sod, but after a few square feet the jinx had him fast and wouldn't let him out. He says that a beautiful shadowy damsel with the oddest magic he's ever seen passed by and released him with a wave of her hand."

Poly was surprised into a chuckle. That sounded just like the blue-eyed boy she had met yesterday.

Annie's eyes twinkled at her in amused comprehension as she added, "Of course, I asked him how he knew she was beautiful if she was shadowy, and he said it was too great of an adventure for her *not* to have been beautiful. We've been at a loss to know whom to thank."

"Poly," said Luck sharply, "Have you been taking off your glove in public? What did I tell you about that?"

"Absolutely nothing," Poly told him. "And it wasn't in public, it was in the fields after midnight."

"Rubbish. I must have. Anyway, you're not to do it; I don't care how many boys you're trying to save."

Poly counted carefully to ten in her head before she picked up Luck's wrist again. "We were talking about Annie's jinx, Luck. Hold still please."

"Oh," said Luck vaguely. He was gazing down with blank eyes, whether at her or his wrist, Poly wasn't certain. "All right. I'll have a look at it. Goodbye."

"I'm obliged," said Annie, with a respectful nod that came just short of being a curtsey.

Her eyes, bright and inquisitive, dwelt on them both for a while longer until she caught Poly's eye, whereupon she mimed drinking tea in what seemed to be a silent encouragement not to forget their engagement for afternoon tea. Poly gave her a warm smile in return, as much for her own sake as for the chance of meeting Michael again, and tugged the last gnawing thread of magic from Luck's wrist as Annie closed the front door behind her.

"Well, you've done it now," said Luck gloomily, passing his other hand over the bite. When his fingers fell away the bite was an old scar, fading quickly. "Now they'll all know I'm here. Batten the hatches, Poly; you're going to be my assistant."

By the end of the day Poly almost regretted the loss of temper that caused her to call Annie in. Visitors had flowed in and out of the parlour like a stream, never ending and inquisitive, and Luck had kept her busy fetching this and that. The visits were made even more nerve wracking by the fact that a good many of them seemed to be young men who had come upon the flimsiest of pretexts, and who were more pleased to be talking to Poly than Luck. Two of them were bold enough to strike up a proper conversation with her, but the rest of them were content to gaze bashfully at her and blush every time she accidently caught their eyes.

Later in the afternoon Onepiece staggered into the room, gleefully supporting himself on the walls and leaving grubby handprints on the plaster. As much as Luck expected *this* fetched and *that* pinched did Onepiece expect congratulations and encouragement and kisses; between the two of them Poly found herself very nearly exhausted by the end of the day.

It was only when Margaret, dressed in deep blue muslin that admirably complimented her chestnut style of prettiness, bounced into the room and enquired wasn't Poly ready *yet?* that Poly remembered the reason for that little curl of excitement in her stomach that refused to be quite banished.

"Oh, good, you're here," said Luck, oblivious to dress and conversation alike. "Hold this."

Since *this* was a greasy carriage wheel, Margaret's look of horror and subsequent relief at the tolling of Last Bell were entirely understandable.

Poly, amusedly aware that Luck hadn't, or wouldn't hear the bell, said calmly, "Last bell, Luck."

"Can't be. It's only lunch time."

"I'm going to a party at—"

"Mistress Pritchard's."

"—at Mistress Pritchard's. If you want me, that's where I'll be."

"But I want you now!" Luck objected. "Margaret, too: it's a three-person job."

The unfortunate owner of the spelled wheel, aware that he was encroaching upon forbidden time and possibly eager to be at the party himself, said hastily, "I'll call for it tomorrow," and made good his escape.

"Yes, but it's last bell, and Margaret is in her party frock," said Poly patiently. "Even the nice man who owns the spell has gone."

Luck looked around blankly and said, "Huh. Where did he go?"

"Home, most likely."

"Bell," added Onepiece crossly, earning a warm smile from Poly.

"That's right, darling. If Josie says you've been good, you may come to the party."

"Good!" Onepiece said forcefully. "*Ver'* good!"

"Rubbish," said Luck. "I heard the screams from the library."

-angryhungry gremlins. looking for Poly-

Poly glanced guiltily toward the library. "Oh dear! I forgot to feed them this morning. The poor things!"

"Ah. That must be why one of them took a bite out of my arm, then."

"Perhaps," said Poly, refusing to feel guilty for that as well. More than likely, Luck had antagonised them. "I'll be back later tonight, Luck."

"Tomorrow, belike," interposed Margaret humorously.

Luck frowned and said, "In that case, I'll go with you."

He refused to be persuaded that Poly had no intention of staying out so late, becoming increasingly mulish when Margaret pointed out that if she danced with even *half* the boys who would be present tonight, Poly couldn't hope to be home before midnight, and in the end it was easier just to let him accompany them than it was to try and change his mind.

When Poly, exasperated, headed for the kitchen to appropriate fresh supplies of cheese for the gremlins, Luck tugged his cuffs, creating a snap of magic that turned his bloodied and battered clothes into something just as old but less shabby.

That made Poly more exasperated than before. She wasn't entirely sure why the idea of Luck's vague green eyes watching her dance with Michael made her uncomfortable, but it did. And since she fully intended to dance with Michael the most pleasing option had seemed to be Luck staying at home.

Yet here he was when she came back into the room, setting a threadbare and entirely ridiculous object over his spiked hair (Margaret called it a *top hat,* whatever that was) and smiling dreamily at her.

Margaret, watching him in awe, protested weakly, "But you never come to night-time happenings!"

"Rubbish. Of course I do. Come along, Margaret; come along, Poly. Dog, heel."

"Mistress Pritchard is the *best* Prime Lady," confided Margaret, as they were ushered by a grinning youth through an avenue of scented blue flowers and into a glittering backyard. "Her son is the best magicker of fairy lights, and her daughter makes the most divine lemon tarts you ever tasted. *She* does absolutely nothing, of course, just sits there and smiles plumply at everyone; but the food is always better and so are the dances."

Luck didn't volunteer any information, but since he disappeared in the direction of the decorated supper table very soon afterward, Poly was left to the reflection that the food must be very good indeed. That, or Luck had noticed the bevy of pretty young girls who had brightened considerably at his appearance and were now making a spectacle of themselves, much to the amusement of their elders.

Onepiece said, "Sparkle," in an unconvinced tone, as though unsure whether he should be approving or not, but when Poly helped him stagger over to the supper table, he chuckled long and gleefully.

"Sticky!" he explained, attempting to fit more lemon tart into his mouth than it would conveniently hold and inevitably finishing with the better part of the lemon butter smeared over his face.

"So I see," said Poly with a rueful smile.

She looked around briefly, telling herself that she was observing the revels and *not* looking for a certain pair of blue eyes, and was too late to catch Onepiece before he fell against her stickily in a valiant attempt to seize the centrepiece of separate, wobbling jellies.

"A woman after my own tastes!" said a laughing voice in her ear, and Michael was unaccountably there beside her, heaving Onepiece to his feet with a supreme lack of concern for the liberal amount of lemon tart that transferred in the process. "I would plunge headfirst into the dairy delight of Miss Pritchard's flummery if possible, but I see you've sensibly been content to absorb her lemon tart via osmosis instead."

Poly laughed and thanked him, reaching automatically for Onepiece, but Michael levered him onto one hip and pulled her into a three-fold embrace instead, spinning them all into the dance.

He said, "Oh, we'd better dance now that we're all sticky. We're clearly meant to be together. Besides, if I don't dance with you, Miss Margaret will make me dance with her."

Since Margaret whirled past them in the dance at that

moment with a laughing, audacious wink, Poly took leave to doubt this, and said as much.

"Well, I had to say *something* to salve my wounded pride," he said, and added easily, "How do you think I get any of the ladies to dance with me, if not out of pity?"

"Tosh," said Onepiece, his gruff little voice displeased.

Poly wondered where he had picked up such a word. This time she felt the last remnants of the language spell whisper the meaning of it in the back of her mind, and found that she agreed.

"I believe you could dance with any of the girls here tonight," she told him frankly. She hadn't missed the lingering, envious glances of the other girls—and if several of the young men seemed to be watching *her*, many more girls were watching Michael.

"Oh well, one has to be modest, after all," said Michael, grinning. "Me ma says you're coming to tea. When?"

"I'm not exactly sure," confessed Poly, allowing Michael to swing her in a close, fast arc that was thrilling more because she was afraid of losing her footing than because it pulled her closer to Michael. It was a pleasant surprise to find that the *derringer* was still performed (even if it was done so as an old curiosity), but the way Michael danced it was quite different to what she was used to. Poly found it difficult to speak and mind her step at the same time. "She didn't tell me what day would be convenient."

Michael gave her a sparkling smile. "Every day is convenient when it comes to you."

"Every day is convenient when you're not the one baking the scones," Poly told him dryly, and was pleased to surprise a laugh out of him.

"I yield me, lady! Half-week, then: me Ma does all her baking in the morning, so you're sure to be fed, at least."

Poly nodded, her eyes sparkling, and curtsied to mark the end of the *derringer*. Unfortunately, it didn't occur to her in time that her court curtsey might no longer be in vogue, and she was mortified to find that while she was making the low, graceful salute, the other girls had merely bobbed and ducked their heads.

Michael's lips curled in a sparkling smile again, whether in interest or amusement, Poly wasn't sure. She was relieved when Margaret, who had finished the dance quite close to them, said, "Ooh, pretty! I didn't know anyone knew how to do those nowadays."

"Well, Miss Margaret," said Michael, distracted long enough for Poly to rise and recover Onepiece, "I suppose I'd better dance with you now. Can't have you going partnerless, can we?"

"Speak for yourself!" said Margaret, with a toss of her head, but she accepted the hand he held out with a saucy smile.

Poly left the green with the smiling thought that they were really very much alike. They laughed and sparkled their way through the dance with a hundred carefully haughty nose tilts from Margaret and as many challenging chin tilts from Michael.

Poly watched them from a secluded bench beneath a weeping willow because it was easier to watch them than to observe the throng as she would usually have done; there were far too many eyes on her for it to be a pleasant exercise. Onepiece, who was beginning to gain a rather remarkable control of his features, and who had learned from who-knows-where the art of sticking out his tongue, made creatively rude faces at the starers as he stood on the bench beside her. Poly muffled her laughter and tugged at his shirt until he plopped down in her lap.

"Pah," he said. "Bosky rude."

"Yes, but it's not polite to notice," said Poly. She was very familiar with the politics that made up the basis of a civil cosmos. "They'll stop staring when they know us better."

Onepiece said "Pah!" again, making her think that he'd possibly spent too much time with Luck, and added internally: - *not staring because of **that**. staring because-*

"Because?" prompted Poly.

Onepiece seemed to be struggling with an idea too complex for his young mind. He blew out his cheeks and bounced impatiently on her lap as his lips pursed and re-pursed with the wrong words.

-*easier as dog*- he complained. -*that one wants to dance with you. that one wants to kiss you*-

"Good grief!" said Poly faintly, ignoring the '*mwah*' with which Onepiece saw fit to embellish his remark. "How ridiculous! Who told you such a thing?"

-*not told*- said Onepiece, performing a creditable shrug. -*heard. too loud front thoughts*-

Poly said, "Good grief!" again, unintentionally encountering the eyes of both indicated men as she flitted a nervous look over the company. The first, a youngish man with a mop of curly red hair, blushed and dropped his eyes, but the other one—the one Onepiece insisted wanted to kiss her—a little older, with pleasant lines beside his eyes, held her gaze and smiled. She looked away, but not quickly enough: he had already started through the dancers toward her and Onepiece.

"Pah!"

"Be polite," admonished Poly.

She was feeling more than a little unsettled but couldn't convince herself that the feeling was an unpleasant one. The faster beat of her heart wasn't mere diffidence: it was oddly thrilling to discover that she was considered attractive by not one man, but two.

Onepiece must have heard the 'front thoughts', because he looked as though he wanted say 'pah' again. He caught her eyes as his lips opened, and sensibly refrained.

Instead, he wriggled violently, muttering, "Food. Yum," until Poly allowed him to slide from her lap and totter away to the supper table.

By the beaming looks of indulgence he was receiving from the elderly ladies there, it seemed apparent that he would be well looked after, so Poly turned her attention to the bolder of her two admirers, who had reached bowing distance and was doing just that.

This time, she was careful to give just a friendly nod instead of her full curtsey, hoping fervently that he wouldn't ask her to dance. After that one, half familiar *derringer* the music had become faster and wilder, and she wasn't sure she could have kept up with the tempo even if she *did* know the dances.

But he said, "Dance with me?" anyway, and at Poly's regretful admission that she was unacquainted with the dance, assured her with the same words Michael had used, "I make up the steps anyway."

Since she couldn't imagine that everyone made up their own dance steps to the popular jigs of the day, Poly hazarded a guess that it was a general phrase of reassurance, and somewhat doubtfully assented.

Much to Poly's surprise, her partner *did* traverse the dance to his own steps. Certainly no other couple (with the possible exception of Michael and Margaret) was doing anything so free and complicated.

He said, "I'm Colin," and led her easily through an opening sequence of steps that she followed almost instinctively by the casual direction of his capable hands.

Push and pull were easy to recognise and follow, Poly decided: a simple matter of tension that made obvious the direction in which she was expected to move. Having Colin's arm around her waist was less simple, since it was as much a matter of confusion at his proximity as it was difficulty in following the gentler pressure exerted.

"Poly," she said distractedly as they narrowly avoided colliding with another couple. "Sorry!"

"Never apologise," he said, smiling infectiously down at her and using her own hands to direct a series of shimmying movements that Poly would never have guessed herself capable of if left to her own talents. Her astonishment seemed to amuse him: his smile widened, softening in the crease around his eyes, and he added with a deprecating half shrug, "It's always the gentleman's fault. If the gentleman can't lead, his lady can't follow."

"Perhaps someone should mention that to Luck," remarked Poly. "I don't think he knows."

One of his eyebrows rose just a fraction. "You're on good terms with the wizard."

"I wouldn't say *good*, exactly," Poly said, rather resenting the eyebrow.

"First name basis," explained Colin, his thin lips quirking at the resentment. "We all call him the wizard."

"Oh. He's not, you know."

He nodded. "We know what he is. We call him wizard to help us forget that he could kill any of us with a twitch of his finger, and that he'll probably outlive our grandchildren's grandchildren."

"Oh," said Poly again. "It's bad for him. He forgets that people are people."

"Well, I don't suppose we really are, to him," Colin said, shrugging elegantly in time with the tempo. "He's different."

"No wonder he's so spoilt," she said severely. "He thinks he's the most important person in the three monarchies—"

"Three monarchies?"

"Two monarchies," Poly corrected herself. "And all the cries of *hail wizard* don't help."

"You must be the first woman in the village to say so," Colin said, looking at her curiously. "Will you take him in hand, Miss Poly? Cure him of his wayward habits?"

"Good grief, no!" said Poly hastily. "I'm only just beginning to understand the importance of time, and I'd hate to waste it on a lost cause."

This time he looked amused. "Then I can only hope that you don't find the rest of the village a similar waste of time, since I would regret not having your better acquaintance."

"Oh no, I'm finding it very instructive," Poly assured him, responding to the smile. "Margaret has been particularly helpful."

"And I've been charming and amusing," pursued Colin. "We're in a fair way to being redeemed."

She laughed, but said, "Luck's not so bad, I suppose; it's just that he's hard to live with in close quarters."

"Perhaps, but he has other qualities that make up for it."

"Yes," agreed Poly, but dubiously.

That made Colin smile again, and he was still smiling when he straightened from the salute bow at the close of the dance.

Much to her own surprise, Poly found that she didn't sit out more than two dances. Her partners were more often tongue-tied than not, but it didn't stop them from trying their luck, and Poly found the chance to sit down a real luxury.

Her last dance of the night was with Michael, who gave her a flamboyant bow to finish, and inquired, "Are you gaming tonight?"

"I *beg* your pardon?" She forgot to curtsey in her shock, gazing wide eyed at Michael with hazy memories of the dissolute gaming parties at the castle. They were possibly the only pleasure that the princess had been absolutely denied by her fond parents.

"There are only three sets of four dances and then the games," he said, watching her quizzically.

"Oh yes, the games," Poly said faintly, aware that her years had betrayed her again but unsure of anything except that cards and scantily dressed women were apparently *not* a part of the gaming to which Michael was alluding. "What sort of games are they?"

Michael's eyes glittered with excitement. "With Josie here it'll be something in the Forest. Scavengers, most likely."

There was that implied capital again, thought Poly. A gently undulating coil of hair slipped from her braid and tickled her ear in a bid for freedom, and she hastily tucked it behind her ear before Michael could notice it. "Why the forest?"

"Well, it's highly charged, dangerous, and has the added advantage of privacy," he said, teasing her with his eyes.

"Oh," said Poly, blinking. "You mean—"

"The games are too fast and competitive to allow much, but the younger ones sneak a kiss or two whenever they know Josie isn't watching."

"Just the younger ones?" asked Poly thoughtlessly, then blushed as his blue eyes laughed down at her.

"We can't let the younger ones have all the fun, now can we, Miss Poly!"

Much to her relief, he offered her his arm and turned his attention toward the supper table, where Onepiece was half hidden behind a tiny mountain of food. Poly bit her lips in amusement and saw Michael grin.

"Will you play?" he asked her, when her blush had had a chance to subside. Poly was grateful for that.

"I haven't really played that sort of game before."

"Just remember, then, that as in dancing, the games mainly depend on which partner you have."

Poly surprised herself by laughing. "You mean yourself!"

"Not to put too fine a point on it—yes. Come along, Miss Poly; you, me, and Onepiece will carry off the games in victory!"

Josie looked pleased to see her join the games and explained the rules in a stentorian voice, ostensibly for the benefit of everyone, but Poly felt the kindness toward herself. As far as she could tell, this particular game was something of a scavenger hunt, with an added element of piracy—namely, that any group could rob another of their carefully won prizes if they could do so by the use of trickery or first level magic. First level magic, Poly discovered, included small trickery, basic illusions, and any spells not directly affecting the other person.

There would be, added Josie with a gimlet eye on several young men in turn, No Question Of Violence. There was a suggestion of booing at the reminder, but most of the youthful participants replied with a rippling tide of mirth that ran through the crowd as it dispersed into the forest.

Fortunately, Michael was very familiar with the game, and a quick glance at the scavenger list didn't dismay him as it did Poly.

Onepiece didn't care either way, Poly thought in fond amusement: he snatched at nightflutters and glowbugs as they walked, disregarding frequent tumbles, and was as happy to be walking as searching.

As the little group wended their way toward the forest, they passed close by what Michael, earlier, had irreverently called the Ancienteers' Table. Unsurprisingly, Luck was there, deep in conversation with Norris, the both of them surrounded by a clear wall of odd magic that had figures sprawled across its length and breadth. Occasionally, one of them would sweep away a figure or a group of figures, replacing them with quick, decisive strokes of the finger.

"Norris is the only one Luck can have a decent game with," Michael told her in a low voice as they passed, and Poly, gazing a little closer, realised that Michael was right: it *was* a game.

"They're splicing spells," he added, catching her look of comprehension.

He kept his voice soft, and it occurred to Poly that he didn't particularly want to catch Luck's attention. Agreeing on general principle and wondering how many people were actually *afraid* of Luck as much as in awe of him, Poly turned a deaf ear to what she was fairly certain was Luck calling her name, and allowed herself to be swept away into the forest.

The forest was dark and cool and frightening. Poly felt a moment of perfect stillness after they entered the canopy of trees, then her hair slipped sinuously from its braided bonds. Onepiece crowed with gleeful laughter, catching at the wafting locks with both sticky hands as they grew rapidly, and Michael said softly, "Magical."

Poly would have agreed, feeling somehow more awake yet more perilously sleepy than she had since Luck woke her, but he wasn't looking at the forest.

Into the stillness and wafting of hair, she said, "I didn't expect this."

"You're cursed."

"Yes. A little bit."

"It's not broken yet."

"No."

"Your hair is growing," he added, gingerly touching a strand that came within his reach.

"Yes. Sorry about that."

Michael shook his head as if clearing it of the gently pervading mist that trailed the forest floor. "No. No, it's beautiful. I think it might be attracting the Forest's attention, though."

Poly shivered slightly, feeling the same aged depthlessness she had felt once in the castle before it collapsed into rubble. "Is that bad?"

"Well," said Michael, sounding as if he were holding his breath, "I suppose it depends on how the Forest is feeling."

"Capital letters again," said Poly, surprising a low chuckle from him.

"I suppose so. No, it doesn't have feelings exactly; sometimes things happen to people who wander in the Forest alone, though. Is it safe for you to go on?"

"I don't know," said Poly helplessly. "Luck's trying to break the curse completely, but so far we haven't had much success."

"How exciting! Have you tried starving it of magic? Can I try?"

The novelty of being *asked* before having an experiment performed on her made Poly smile as much as did Michael's eagerness. "What about the list?"

"Oh well, we should give the others a fighting chance, after all! Miss Margaret cries so easily!"

Poly gave an involuntary giggle. "So I noticed! All right then. Go ahead."

It looked like he was pulling on a thread, with two long, tapered fingers pinched and drawing away from her steadily, and at first Poly felt brighter and more awake than ever.

Onepiece grimaced encouragingly at her from the grassy knoll he'd found to sit on and said, "Wakey-wakey."

She felt so much better, in fact, that when the shaft of deadly fatigue pierced her heart, deadening her limbs, Poly slid bonelessly to the sweet-scented grass without time to feel more than cold surprise. For a moment there was silence, then a riot began over her head: howling, a quick, urgent voice, and a burst of potent magic that would have taken her breath away if she had had the energy to be impressed by it. Michael's face swam hazily above her, and Poly thought she felt his fingers touch her face lightly, then there was another snap of magic, distinctly Luck-tinted, and Michael's face disappeared.

This worried Poly distantly, and she tried to reach one sluggish hand out to him, but someone pushed the hand down impatiently.

"...and when I don't try something, it's because it won't work," said a voice of such coolness that Poly had difficulty in recognising it as Luck's.

She had the hazy impression that he was angry, which made her suddenly very much more concerned about Michael. A sharp, unpleasant smell assaulted her nose, sparking her mind and body into life, and Poly jerked her head away, suddenly wide awake.

"Michael? Are you all right?"

"He's fine," said Luck irritably, recapping the smelling salts. "I *called* you. Why didn't you listen?"

Poly blinked. "Oh, you *are* there. I thought I was dreaming. It's all right, Michael, you can let Onepiece go now."

Onepiece, struggling furiously, was lowered gently to the grass, and made a joyous leap for Poly's lap. Under stress he had reverted to his most familiar form, and she submitted ruefully to having her face licked before kissing the top of his head.

"I'm all right, darling," she told him soothingly.

Michael, looking distinctly ashamed, said, "I'm sorry, Poly. I thought I had it."

"It almost worked," she said, with a half shrug. "It's all right."

"No, it's not," Luck said. "I had the curse lulled and peaceful, and now you've started it thinking again. I *told* you not to go into the forest."

"Yes, you did," agreed Poly, able for once to acquiesce to one of his sweeping statements.

"Well, don't do it again. The balance is tricky enough without you wandering into random pockets of magic. If you tip it any further, I'll have to kiss you again."

"I won't," said Poly fervently, trying vainly to rise. Her hair was ridiculously long, and it had piled beneath her when she fell, making it a painful and difficult matter to sit up.

Michael's eyes narrowed in amusement as he helped her climb to her feet. "Wait, did he just threaten you with a kiss?"

"Yes," sighed Poly, gathering handfuls of grass strewn hair to avoid stepping on it. "It's a long story."

"Poly, you're not listening to me," complained Luck. "And *you*. Next time, mind your own business. Only an idiot would try to starve a curse inside the most powerful magical focus in the two monarchies."

Poly, gasping with indignation as much for her own sake as for Michael's, said heatedly, "He was only trying to help! And it almost worked!"

"Rubbish; it played along until it had what it wanted. Now I suppose you want me to take you home."

Poly eyed him frostily, but Michael said, as though he hadn't noticed the rudeness, "I'll walk you home, Miss Poly."

She was about to categorically deny any desire to return home at all, when Luck grabbed her hand with an exasperated noise and did something tricky with the forest around them. Poly, stupefied, found herself back in the library.

She said furiously, "How could you be so rude!"

"Books, Poly!" said Luck, throwing books willy-nilly over his shoulder from one of the bookcases she had tidied just before they left.

"Not those ones! There's one on the desk and another on the footstep. Luck, did you leave Onepiece behind?"

"This isn't the right one," Luck said, tossing the book that she'd left on the footstep. "The dog gets in the way; it's better off with your sweetheart. Yes, this one is right."

Declining to comment on the appellation of 'sweetheart', Poly insisted again, "How could you be so rude to Michael?"

Luck absently threw his top hat toward the desk, missed, and abandoned it heedlessly to the dust. "Who? Oh, the idiot. He shouldn't stick his nose into my business."

"It isn't your business, it's mine," argued Poly, snatching up the top hat with more than necessary violence and resisting the urge to hurl it at him.

A pearly gleam in the depths of the top hat caught her eye, and she was engaged in carefully tugging out its source from the inner band when a knock at the front door faintly penetrated the library. Poly extracted what turned out to be a spellpaper—no doubt the one Luck had been looking for; her own curse—and tucked it into her pocket as she rather thankfully went to answer the door.

When she opened it, she was greeted by Michael's mischievous face.

"Lost something?" he inquired.

Onepiece, looking sulky, was tucked under one of his arms.

Poly tried to apologise, but Michael became so ridiculous that she soon found herself laughing instead. Onepiece was handed over only on a promise to dance with Michael at the next happening, and Poly was able to go to bed with the pleasant feeling that not quite all was wrong with the world.

10

Poly woke the next morning to uncomfortable heat and a distinct feeling of claustrophobia. To add to her discomfort there was a tiny, sharp elbow digging into her ear, which suggested that Onepiece had turned boy some time after he curled up on her pillow but hadn't moved from the pillow. One of his legs dangled over the side of the bed, but the other had managed to work its way under the covers. The rest of him was wrapped snugly in what seemed to be...*hair*.

"Good grief!" groaned Poly, giving up the attempt to lift her head from the pillow after one painful effort.

"Oh, you are awake," said Luck, making her squeak in surprise. He was stretched out at the foot of her bed with an open book in one hand, his boots only *just* off the quilted blanket—and that, thought Poly crossly, must be why she couldn't move her legs. "I wouldn't try that again if I were you: it's lashed underneath the boards."

"Yes, I thought it might be. What do I do?"

"Lie very still, I suppose. Poly, the curse is being sneaky again, but I think you might have been sneakier."

Onepiece stirred and murmured, "Tosh," but that was more likely to be because it was his favourite word than because he'd understood Luck. Poly was left wondering if she agreed with the sentiment.

"I knew there was something niggling away in the back of my mind," continued Luck, disregarding Onepiece's sleepy mutterings. "Your hair is too helpful: it's keeping the curse at bay by growing. Even if you'd pumped all your magic into it, it shouldn't be that clever."

"How does growing keep the curse at bay?" asked Poly.

She'd given up trying to explain yet *again* to Luck that she didn't have magic, *hadn't* had magic, *wouldn't ever* have magic. His reiteration was insidious enough that Poly thought she might just come to believe him, in the end.

"It's using up all the power the curse is putting out: that's why you woke up by yourself this morning. Every time the curse pumps out more power, your hair starts to grow."

"My hair is feeding on the curse?"

"No. Well, yes, sort of. Don't go wandering off today, Poly; I need to check a few things."

Poly looked at him warily, feeling distinctly less safe now that she was lashed in place. "You mean you want to run more experiments on me. Well, you can't: I'm going to tea with Annie."

"Who's Annie?"

"Michael's Ma."

"Oh. No."

"What do you mean, no?"

"There's no time for tea, we have more important things to do."

"I didn't mean right now," said Poly, unable to repress the twinkle in her eye. "Darling, must you stick your elbow into my ear?"

There was a muttering from Onepiece, then the pressure was removed from her left ear and a warm little arm curled around her neck in what closely resembled a choke hold.

Poly, beginning to feel more than a little claustrophobic, said plaintively, "Luck, you're sitting on my legs."

"The dog's sitting on your neck," he objected.

"Yes, but he's not as heavy as you are. Luck, can't you do something about all this hair?"

Luck glanced up from his book again. "What? I suppose so."

Poly bit back the remark that if he *could*, why had he been sitting on her legs for the past quarter hour, and said as patiently as she knew how, "Then will you do so, please?"

Much to her relief, he said, "I suppose so," again, amiably enough, and slid off the bed. "The dog will have to move."

"*Sleepy*," said Onepiece firmly, clinging tighter to Poly's neck; then, surprisedly, "Hair!"

His mouth made puffing noises at the strands that were spread across his face, and two little arms windmilled, making knots in Poly's hair.

Poly heroically bore the tugging, though she opened her mouth once to warn Onepiece that he was about to fall off the bed, but gathered from the startled 'Whoops!' and a thump that her warning had been too late.

There was silence for a brief moment while Poly tried unsuccessfully to disentangle her arms from the piles of hair, expecting to hear a sniffle or a whine break the silence. Then there was a grating rattle that informed her Onepiece was laughing, and Luck said, "Stop wriggling, Poly; the dog's fine. It's found the gremlins."

Poly, left staring at the ceiling without the luxury of being able to turn her head more than minimally to the left or the right, was obliged to accept this remark in good faith, though the muted chuckles and a few, throaty '*yik yiks*' from Onepiece as he scrabbled beneath the bed seemed to bear it out. She hoped the gremlins didn't have anything that was catching.

Before long, Poly's unrelieved view of the ceiling was broken by the close-up view of Luck's shabby waistcoat and untied cravat as he bent over her. He had changed back into his clothes of the previous day. Unfortunately, it seemed that he hadn't taken the time to have them washed. She tried not to notice the jam stain on his waistcoat, and that his cuffs were still torn from his encounter with the gremlins, but when a more malodourous stain of possibly chemical origins passed by her nose just a little too close for comfort, Poly asked, "Doesn't Josie wash your clothes?"

"Yes, she does, blast her," said Luck's voice, somewhere above her head.

There was a slight tug at the crown of her head, and Poly felt a sudden lightness. It wasn't enough to allow her to move her head, but it did take the pressure off slightly. Below the bed, Onepiece sneezed, and a chorus of strongly disapproving little voices said, "*Yiketty yuk!*"

Luck added, in the voice of injury, "Every time I get a set of clothes properly worn in and comfortable she waylays me and makes me give them up. Interfering woman."

"How awful for you."

"Don't be facetious, Poly; it doesn't suit you."

There was another tug, and a corresponding lightness somewhere in the vicinity of her left ear. Poly tried craning her neck to see what Luck was doing, and the spotty waistcoat disappeared, to be replaced by Luck's face, eyes narrow and golden.

"Don't wriggle, Poly. I don't want to accidentally take off your ear."

"My *ear*? What are you doing?"

"Barham recommends separation and immediate cauterization," said Luck, displaying an impressively long tear in the waistcoat beneath his arm as he levered Poly's shoulder to turn her on her side.

"Cauterization of *what*?" demanded Poly, alarmed at the mention of searing immediately after the subject of her ears had been brought up.

"It's the balance that's the important thing: all of this is excess, so it doesn't matter if it comes off, but the original ratio of magic to hair has to remain the same. Balance, Poly."

As if I'm his apprentice, thought Poly, resisting the urge to roll her eyes. "Luck, what are you cauterizing? Are you burning my hair?"

"What? Of course not. That would be counterproductive."

Poly said, "Ow!" to a pinch at the nape of her neck and found herself tumbling irresistibly onto her face in a coil of soft hair.

"Huh," said Luck, hauling her back. "That was easier than I thought it would be. You weren't particularly fond of your hair, were you? Only it's a bit short now."

"Not particularly," said Poly, wondering if Luck's haircut would prove to be any neater than Persephone's had been.

She gave a slight, cautious shake of her head, and heavy strands fell away in sleek coils, leaving her feeling rather light-headed and weightless. When she ran her fingers crisply through it, her hair was sitting reasonably neatly just below her ears and had curled under slightly to tickle them.

"Oh!" she said in surprise. "That turned out better than I expected. Why didn't it hurt this time?"

"Because I'm not an idiot," said Luck, busily gathering up hair.

As fast as he gathered it, more was disappearing over the other side of the bed, and Poly thought that it was still as lively as ever until she saw the tiny, pale fingers and glittering eyes that peeped between the strands. The gremlin saw her: one slender finger was briefly placed over a toothy smile, and a crafty look was directed toward Luck. Poly looked away hastily, trying not to smile.

Luck added, "Anyway, I told you: it's the balance."

"Yes, you said that," agreed Poly, disentangling herself from heavy loops of hair. "I still don't know what you mean."

Luck shot her an irritable look. "That's because you don't pay attention when I'm trying to teach you things."

"What a whopper!" said Margaret, yawning. She was watching them both with interest, and Poly wondered when she'd woken up. "As Michael says: Pot. Kettle. Black. Why are you in my bedroom again, Luck? And is that *hair*?"

"A *lot* of hair," agreed Poly, surreptitiously sweeping more strands of the stuff to the floor for the gremlins.

Goodness knew what they wanted with it: perhaps they had nests in the walls that needed lining. She curled a few of the hairs around her fingers, expecting to feel the same silky life her hair had always had, but they were brittle and dead. She dropped them with a fastidious grimace, and then felt almost mechanically for the amber beads and the hermit's feather that now always swung below her right ear.

"Still there," said Luck, watching her with distant eyes. "They've shrunk, though."

"Your hair is still growing," Margaret said helpfully. She had evidently decided that Luck in the bedroom was going to be a regular occurrence and was brushing out her own hair without embarrassment in nothing but her chemise. "Will it keep doing that?"

"Probably," said Luck, just as Poly said hastily, "No!"

But grow it did, and by the time Poly was dressed, her hair was once more halfway down her back, shifting and whispering in the quietness of the hall to Onepiece's great delight. He trotted after her more steadily than usual with a hank of it curled in one long, skinny hand, and though the growth slowed down after that, her hair remained more lively than usual, and she didn't attempt to plait it.

A quick glance through the window on her way to the kitchen showed fewer supplicants today, for which Poly was thankful. There was no sign of Josie in the kitchen, but there was a pot of porridge sitting on a potholder and laced with a Keep Warm spell. Poly sat Onepiece at the table and turned to fetch the bowls and spoons, her stomach growling. By the time she turned back around, Onepiece was using his fingers to stealthily scoop porridge into his mouth with great dispatch, one eye on her and another on the gremlin that was crawling out of his pocket and making for the pot at top speed.

He gave a wordless howl when she took the pot away and

cleaned his hands, but when she gave him his own bowl and a spoon, he used them with enough proficiency to make her think that he'd merely been too hungry to wait for her. If Poly wasn't mistaken, he was also dexterous enough to feed the gremlin from his spoon once or twice when he thought she wasn't looking.

Luck wandered into the kitchen while they were still eating, his eyes distant and slightly gold. Between sitting on her bed earlier that morning and the present, he had changed his shirt for a slightly less shabby one, though his trousers were as dusty as ever; and his advent into the kitchen seemed to be for no other purpose than to vaguely watch Poly and Onepiece eat. Onepiece made a rude noise at him that sent splotches of porridge pattering onto Luck's hitherto clean tabletop and prompted a brief, narrower look from Luck, but Poly smiled at him and asked more in resignation than eagerness whether they would be travelling on again this week.

Luck gave her the long, sideways look that always made her feel like he was thinking something very different to what he was speaking, and asked surprisingly, "Don't you like it here?"

Poly was slightly ashamed to find that her first thought was of blue-eyed Michael. "Of course I do! But I thought you had to take me to the Capital to get your books."

"Well. Yes."

"Then—"

"Well, I can't pass you off to the Council with a curse dangling from you," Luck said irritably. "They don't like messy ends there. Not unless they're the ones making them."

"Oh. What will they do with me?"

"Huh," said Luck, his face suddenly blank. "I didn't think of that. They'll probably try to win your endorsement, just to get the Royalists off their backs."

The idea of anyone campaigning to put another Persephone on the throne struck Poly as dryly humorous.

"Of course, the Old Parrasians will probably try to assassinate you," added Luck, with what Poly found to be a distinct lack of concern. "Heaven knows what Black Velvet will do, but it'll be something subtle and annoying."

"But I don't want the throne!"

Luck shrugged. "Try and make *them* believe that. The Old Parrasians are a rabid bunch of warmongers and the Council's full of only slightly less rabid fungus-feeders. And that's reckoning without the Royalists."

"It sounds just like home," sighed Poly, feeling as though she had gone from the kiln to the furnace. She looked askance at Luck and asked, "How did you get mixed up in all this? And who are all these people?"

"I'm not mixed up in anything; I just want my books."

"I suppose that explains the bomb, then."

"What? Huh. Maybe we should let someone try to kill you again."

"No!" interrupted Onepiece, scowling inexpertly but ferociously at Luck. "No killing Poly!"

"It's all right, darling: no one is trying to kill me. Luck, how would that help?"

"Well, we'd be waiting for them this time. We might learn something useful."

"Or I might be dead," suggested Poly, giving Onepiece a hard look until he ceased to wobble his spoon threatening at Luck and began eating his porridge again.

"Rubbish," said Luck. "I wouldn't let them kill you."

"That makes me feel much better," Poly assured him.

"Not kill Poly!" Onepiece muttered into his porridge, sulkily this time. "I will *bite.*"

"I'm capable of looking after Poly without your help, dog," said Luck. "How many people are outside, Poly?"

"A few. Not as many as yesterday."

"Huh. Good. Poly, where's your spindle?" Poly blinked, confused, and Luck's head tilted consideringly. "You've forgotten it again, haven't you?"

"No, of course not!" Poly said sharply, feeling fed up. There was a faint fuzziness at the back of her mind that worried her. Why did Luck always speak in riddles? And why was he asking about a spindle?

"Where is it, then?"

"It's—it's—"

"Never mind," said Luck, lunging at her with surprising speed. "I know where it is."

He pulled a spindle out of her pocket and brandished it at her.

Poly, belatedly, said, "Stop that!"

She had, in fact, forgotten all about the spindle—couldn't remember putting such a thing in her pocket. However, that was no excuse for Luck to turn out her pockets.

"I thought so. Hold out your hand, Poly."

"Why?" Poly asked, suspiciously, curling the fingers of both hands.

"You can leave your glove on; I don't want the antimagic one."

"Luck—"

"Hand, Poly. Hand. Oh, never mind."

Poly found herself with one hand in Luck's, the spindle curled between her fingers and palm. "Let me go!"

"Sit still, Poly; I'm working on something."

Poly drew in a deep breath, counted to ten very carefully in her head, and relaxed both her hand and the warm glow of antimagic that had begun to fizz in her left arm.

This prompted Luck to look at her with faint surprise and something else that made Poly protest defensively, "Well, you would have done it anyway, so why should I waste time struggling?"

Luck's eyes went glassy and just a little bit gold. "Concentrate, Poly. When was the last time you thought about the castle?"

"The castle?" repeated Poly in surprise. Out of all the things she had come to expect from Luck's experiments, a conversation reminiscing on castle life was not one. Truth to tell, it had been some days since she'd thought of anyone from the castle, besides fleeting thoughts of Mordion or Persephone. It had faded into the colourless backdrop of her old life, thrust out by the invasive and unignorable presence that was Luck; and in a quieter manner by the dog-boy who was at present looking at her with oddly anxious eyes. "A few days, I suppose."

"Don't need castle," muttered Onepiece, *sotto voce*. "Have dog and wizard now."

"Huh," said Luck, his eyes glassier and more golden than ever. "Tell me about the king and queen."

Poly opened her mouth to reply, remembered that as far as Luck knew, the king and queen were her parents, and shut it again. At length she ventured, "As a ruling couple or as parents?"

"Ah, I forgot: that won't help. Tell me about the people instead."

"Well, there was Lady Cimone."

"Strapping, stern, matronly woman? We met. Very capable woman, that."

"Yes," said Poly, sighing faintly. Lady Cimone was one of the few things Poly *did* miss about castle life. "She knew ancient Glausian, Parrasian, and three dialects of Lacunan."

"Waste of time," said Luck. "There are spells for that."

"Yes, but learning them makes you *think*," said Poly—or at least, she thought she said it. Life had become somehow soft around the edges and a little bit confusing.

It took her some time to realise that she'd fallen asleep, and by then, someone was already shaking her shoulder.

"Lady? Lady, are you well?"

"Yes, just sleepy," yawned Poly.

She rubbed at her eyes, aware that she didn't recognise the voice but unable to see who it was. It was a nice voice, all velvet and deep and perhaps dangerous, and she wasn't really surprised when she opened her eyes to find a face just as beautiful and perhaps dangerous bent over her in concern.

"Crooked wizard!" said Onepiece's voice from the general vicinity of her lap. Poly looked down, her hand unconsciously reaching to pat him briefly on the head, and found that Onepiece had wound himself, mosslike, around her torso, and was sitting in her lap. "Tricksy tricks and leaves!" he continued, indignantly.

The dark-eyed face that had been bent over her smiled in amusement. "Has Luck been up to his tricks again?"

"I must be a less pleasant companion than I thought," murmured Poly, too interested in the fact that this person had called Luck by his name instead of the honorific 'wizard' to be more than wearily annoyed that Luck had been experimenting on her again.

She wondered briefly if Luck had put a sleep spell on her himself, or if castle memories had triggered the curse again, and lent only a perfunctory ear to the stranger's politely charming reply that she *couldn't* be.

"You don't know Luck very well, do you?" she remarked, still somewhat sleepily.

Certainly the curse had been triggered again: that must have been what Luck was testing for. So Mordion had been clever enough to make sure that every time she remembered something from the castle, it would trigger the curse again. Evidently, thought Poly bitterly, it hadn't been enough to curse her. Mordion had planned and replanned for every possible event, including her awakening.

The stranger laughed. "You mean he doesn't find *anyone* congenial company."

"That's right," Poly agreed. Her mind was slowly but surely waking up, and it now seemed odd to find a stranger leaning over her in Luck's kitchen. "Are you looking for Luck? He's receiving, but I think he's in the library."

"Workroom, actually," said the other. "He sent me to wake you. I'm Ronin, by the way."

"Poly."

"Josie's, um, niece."

Did *no one* believe the story? wondered Poly, a little tartly. The whole thing seemed to have been a colossal waste of time. She nodded and introduced Onepiece by way of distraction, unwilling to explain to Ronin the true state of affairs.

Onepiece said, "Yes," with great precision, though whether this was because he approved of the introduction or merely wished to say it, Poly wasn't sure.

Ronin said a more convincing "Charmed", making an elegant half bow that included Poly. When she asked what brought him to visit Luck, he held up a lightly spelled hat and added, "A faulty spell. I can't think where I went wrong, but I must have done *something*: instead of warding off rain, it attracts it. I only have to step out of the house on a cloudy day to make it rain."

Poly tried to hide her smile, but fortunately, Ronin was perfectly cheerful about his backwards spell.

"Oh well, at least you won't have to wait long," she told him. "Luck will fix it in a trice."

"That only makes matters worse," Ronin said gloomily, but he was still smiling. "I've seen you out and about with Josie's Margaret, haven't I, Miss Poly?"

"More than likely. We've been restocking my wardrobe with the latest fashions the village has to offer."

He gave her an amused look that suggested village fashions were far from high fashion, and said thoughtfully, "Pert girl, Margaret. Sharp and clever, and she's the darling of the village."

"She's been very nice to me," said Poly, feeling obscurely as though she needed to defend Margaret.

"I'm glad to hear it. I would have thought—" he stopped, gave a barely discernible half smile, and said, "She doesn't take competition very well."

Poly shrugged uncomfortably and repeated, "She's been very nice to me."

"Michael seems very fond of you."

"Does he?" Poly unwrapped Onepiece's skinny arms from her waist, hiding a small, pleased smile.

"Oh yes. He was busy fending off enquiries about you when I passed him last night: nearly every boy at Mistress Pritchard's wanted to know if you had a sweetheart, or what your schedule was for today. Michael and Margaret were like two dogs guarding a bone."

The charm of novelty, thought Poly, too surprised to do more than methodically wipe Onepiece's porridgey face clean. She'd seen it happen at the castle with visiting luminaries, whose meteoric rise in popularity had always grated on Persephone unbearably. She hadn't expected it to happen to her. It did make her wonder, however, in a small, uncomfortable part of her mind, whether Margaret would still be friendly in a day or two.

Poly picked up Onepiece and Ronin opened the kitchen door for them with as much easy grace as if he owned the house. In the other room, Luck looked up, sharp and glittering and interested. Poly wondered exactly what he'd been up to. He was alone, and although the front door set carefully ajar suggested that he had just seen off another supplicant, Poly suspected that, for reasons of his own, he'd been waiting for herself and Ronin.

Onepiece sneezed and Luck's eyes flickered to the puppy, then became green and glassy once again. "The dog can stay in the corner," he said. "Poly, fix Ronin's spell; it's not hard."

Poly almost asked, tartly, just what he would be doing while she did *his* job, but she found she could see what he was doing, clear and glistening, on the bench in front of him. Something that looked like magic but didn't seem to quite *be* magic. Whatever it was, Ronin didn't seem to be able to see it, so Poly took heed of the blanker-than-usual stare that Luck turned on her and pretended not to see it either.

Instead, she accepted Ronin's hat, turning it over in her hands to find the weak spot and listening with an indulgent ear to Onepiece's proud reiterations in her head that he could *-fix it, fix it, fix it, easy-peasy-*

"The dog stays in the corner," repeated Luck, without glancing at them.

Onepiece gave the suspicion of a growl in his gruff human voice. Much to Poly's surprise, however, he obeyed Luck without any other argument, settling down in a corner with various offcuts of magic and a lone, vociferous gremlin who seemed to be egging him on to build something noxious.

"An interesting child," said Ronin, a question hidden in the deep velvet of his voice.

Poly said, "Yes," noncommittally, straightening out the wrong patches in the hat spell and weaving them new. And then, feeling that she'd been rather prickly this morning, she added, "He's only just learning to be human again. He's my ah, brother."

"Mum," said Onepiece from his corner, crossly.

Poly felt Ronin's amused eyes on her and thought ruefully that between Luck and Onepiece, she wouldn't have a shred of reputation left by the time they travelled on to the Capital.

"He's a little confused," she said, meeting that amused look without a blink. "He lost his mother when he was very young. Your hat is finished."

Luck snatched it with a superfluous, "Let me see" before Ronin could take it, and Poly wondered if she had merely imagined something clear and fiery being done to the hat in the blink of an eye.

"Huh," said Luck, flipping the hat with one hand to inspect the other side of the brim. He tossed it back to Ronin. "Well done, Poly. Send in the next person."

"Well, you don't need to sound so *surprised*," said Poly, but she showed Ronin out anyway.

He gave her a smile and one last elegant bow, sweeping back gracefully with his newly fixed hat spell, and jauntily strolled down the main street. Further down, Michael was sweeping a shopfront porch with his apron tied on sideways; she caught his eyes and was treated to a swift, mad little dance in which Michael's broom nearly went through the front window.

Poly was still laughing when Luck poked his head around the door, his eyes gold and a little bit narrow, and said, "Stop flirting, Poly. Send in the next one."

. . .

THE LINE of villagers had dwindled to nothing by early afternoon. The earliest callers had been the serious ones, mostly complaining of field work that needed to be redone—power loss, some of them called it. Others said no, it was as if their spells were routinely being pulled sideways by something that they couldn't trace. Poly began to think that she hadn't been wrong about the faint skewed feel to the village's magic, and Luck's eyes became narrower and greener with each supplicant.

Most of the later callers were young, presumably marriageable females, much to Poly's amusement. They came, bewitching smiles in place, for reasons as varied and creative as cursed shoes to charming away a single, non-existent freckle. Poly gave full marks to the freckle girl—who, to her appreciative wonder, sat with an upturned face to Luck's close scrutiny and blinked heavy lashed eyes at him—but she would have been better pleased if the young girls had not also been accompanied by a fair assortment of males, who were becoming less tongue-tied and more persistent in their attempts to catch her attention.

Perhaps it was due to the lingering effects of the freckle girl's purple eyes that Poly was able to slip away shortly after, towing Onepiece and his resident gremlin. If so, she was very grateful.

When she passed Michael's storefront, hoping to catch a glimpse of him again, she was further pleased to find that she would have his escort instead: it was Michael's half day.

"So we've managed to abscond with you at last!" said his voice. There was a flurry of movement as Michael leapt the front railing, apron over shoulder, and landed with a flourish and a bow. He was trailing threads and tiny triangular offcuts of blue cotton. "Did I impress you, Miss Poly?"

"Oh yes, I'm terribly impressed. I don't think the man behind the counter thought much of it, though."

Michael grimaced comically, ducking out of sight of the store owner's glare. "He's merely jealous of my physical prowess."

"Oh, is that what it is?"

"It must be: who could be angry at this face? Hurry along,

Miss Poly, or he'll be after me to clean the dust from his front window."

So Poly hurried along, giggling at Michael's nonsense while Onepiece perched on her hip and made popping noises in her ear. Before long they had arrived at a small, clean scrubbed cottage that Poly recognised without Michael's unnecessarily flamboyant gestures, by the simple fact that Annie was in the front garden planting seeds.

Annie looked up at their approach and said with a smile, "I thought I heard trouble. Welcome, Poly: I hope Michael hasn't been wearing your ears to nubs?"

"Only one of them!" protested Michael as Poly laughingly denied it.

She *liked* Michael's chatter: it made a vast change from Luck's mostly silent, magically charged presence.

"Did you manage to sneak away, or did Luck give you a half holiday?"

"Luck's out repairing a few spells. He says there's something nattering at the steady magic around the village, and that it's giving him a headache. Besides," added Poly, unable to repress her amusement, "it was mostly young girls and their eyelashes today."

Annie climbed to her feet, dusting the rich, black soil from her palms, and asked curiously, "Don't you mind?"

"Good grief, no! Why should I? It's far too entertaining to be annoying, and if I wanted to learn how to flirt, I think it would be very instructive."

"Yes, but does *Luck* mind?" asked Michael, a mischievous gleam in his eye.

"Oh, Luck doesn't notice a thing! I suppose," added Poly with guiltily appreciative amusement, "that's what makes it so funny. The poor girls have no idea what they're up against."

"They do, you know," said Michael, opening the front door for Poly and his mother. Of course, being Michael, he did it with the lowest of court bows, wriggling his eyebrows at Poly.

"They're just beastly determined. I think they might have bets on it."

"You hush your nonsense," said Annie, while Poly was still trying to decide whether he was joking or not. "You'll have Poly thinking we're all escapees from the Frozen Battlefield."

"Well, some of them might as well be: they're as mad as a pair of wet gnau in a hole."

"Madgnau," said Onepiece, giggling. He wriggled vigorously to be let down and promptly grabbed Annie's hand, much to that lady's delight.

"Tea, I think. Michael, fetch the biscuits, will you?"

"I hear and obey, Mother Mine," said Michael cheerfully. "Nuts or raisins, Poly?"

"Nuts, please." Poly paused, considering a question to which she thought she might already know the answer. While Michael fetched biscuits, she asked diffidently, "Are they flowers? That you're planting out front, I mean?"

Annie didn't choose to misunderstand. "No, I'm planting as many strawberries as I can before the season passes. Slightly Sideways Strawberries are very picky about their planting time, and we're coming into the last week just now."

"I'll have a word with Luck," Poly said, sighing.

She expected Annie to make a polite demurral and was preparing to press her point when the other lady nodded once, relief clearly etched across her face. Poly was surprised, and then annoyed at her surprise.

"I'd take that very kindly in you," Annie said. "The wizard is a very great and kind man, but I'll be the first to admit that he's inclined to be forgetful."

"Oh, is that what it is? I thought it was plain boredom and a habit of forgetting everybody else but himself."

Annie smiled guiltily, but said, "Well, I suppose the centuries will do that to a person."

"Good grief, don't excuse him! You can feel free with me: I have no illusions about him, you see."

"So I see," observed Annie, but there was still a smile at the edges of her eyes, and Poly wondered why. "Oh well, let's not fuss about the wizard: today is tea and biscuits, and never mind our problems. We want to know all about you."

"Indeed we do," said Michael, leaning across the counter and the biscuit tin both. He looked as if he was prepared to hold the biscuits ransom unless he was satisfied that all his questions had been answered. "Don't listen to Mother Mine: she only wants to know such tawdry things as where you attended school, where you're really from, and what you're really doing here. *I* want much more pertinent information. For instance: I can't help but feel that such an entrancing young lady must have suitors under every rock, but *are* you spoken for? And that's a rather delectable spellpaper gleaming at me from one of your pockets—I would love to poke my nose in and see it. Thirdly and finally, how did you get the curse that's clinging to you like a shadow? Now, now, Mother Mine, don't hit me! You must admit they're more interesting than your questions!"

Since Annie really did look as though she was about to box the ears of her erstwhile offspring, and Michael had darted back behind the kitchen bench with the biscuit tin clasped to his chest in order to escape the wrath he had invoked, Poly said, proud to find herself not blushing, "No, perhaps, and it's a long story, in that order. And not under *every* rock, but one of them certainly crawled out from under one."

"Slimy?" asked Michael, pausing in his mad dash for long enough to offer Poly and Onepiece a biscuit.

"No: beautiful! And about as dangerous as a cockatrice."

"Now, cockatrices are much maligned creatures—"

"This particular one wasn't," observed Poly, dispassionately interrupting the flow of nonsense before it was fully begun. "In fact, if it was anywhere around, you could be sure that someone else around it was being maligned."

"Shame on you, Poly," said Michael, piously. "Just because a creature is poisonous at one end and sharp at the other, is no reason to cast aspersions upon its character."

"Oh, will you hush your nonsense! Michael, love, if you're going to hand out biscuits like fair favours, you should perhaps hang the kettle."

Michael gave one of his elaborate bows, suggesting another 'I hear and obey', and vanished briefly into the depths of the kitchen with numerous clatterings and clangings that were evidently designed to remind them of his presence.

"No village is without its own particular cockatrice," said Annie, dryly enough to make Poly think that she was referring to a particular person. "But you're not village, I think?"

"No. Is it obvious?"

"The court curtsey was a hint. Most mothers and finishing schools in the Capital still teach a version of it, but none quite so elaborate. You're from court, I suppose: but not Glausian or Broman, I'll be bound."

"No: Civet."

"Special," explained Onepiece, tugging at Annie's jerkin to indicate his need of another biscuit. "Old, *old* Poly."

Poly, a rueful smile twitching her mouth up at the corners, saw the brief, frozen moment when Annie understood.

"You poor child! You're the Sleeping Princess."

"Well, in a manner of speaking," said Poly cautiously.

"I knew it!" Michael said triumphantly, appearing in the doorway again with a dangerously tilting canister of tea in one careless hand. "An Elder Curse: The Mysterious Stranger: A Hidden Menace!"

"Stop talking in play bills, you horrible child! The Sleeping Princess, now: that had something to do with the Frozen Battlefield, did it not?"

"Luck thinks so."

"You don't?"

"Well, yes," said Poly doubtfully, unsure of how to explain that it was more of a personal connection than a magical one.

Her parents had been responsible for that, though it certainly hadn't had anything to do with her curse. Or, she wondered suddenly, remembering Mordion: had it? If Mordion was behind her own curse, it was more than passingly likely that he'd also been responsible for the fierce, terrifyingly joyful faces she'd seen captured in amber. What had Mum said? *They would have killed everyone. We had no choice.*

"I didn't mean to bring up unpleasant memories," said Annie's voice.

Poly blinked, becoming aware that Annie was leaning across the table, her face concerned, and drew her thoughts away from Mordion with a conscious effort.

"Not unpleasant," she said, smiling faintly. "But I don't seem to remember much."

"You looked like you were about to fall asleep," said Michael, startling Poly by being much closer than she'd realised.

He proffered a messy cup of tea that had sloshed into its saucer and placed a sugar bowl on the table with triumphant precision, indicating with a flourish that she could help herself.

"I probably was."

"Ah, the curse clinging! How exciting. Do you know that your hair is growing again?"

"Of course she knows her hair is growing! Very trying for you, my dear."

"Pretty," said Onepiece with a frown that only went away when Michael winked at him in agreement.

"Can a well-placed kiss break it?"

Poly tried not to blush, failed, and said, "I think so. I haven't had a chance to look at the spellpaper yet, but that's how Luck woke me up at first."

"Fortunate Luck," remarked Michael, with a sparkle in his blue eyes as he dodged his mother's hand. "Desist, Mother! After all, everyone loves a good love curse!"

"I don't," said Poly frankly. "It's a great nuisance, in fact. Luck's working on it, but every time we've think we've managed to corner it, it sneaks away."

"Just like Luck, in other words."

Poly gave a surprised gurgle of laughter. "Well, yes!"

"You're a pair of disreputable children!" chided Annie. "The wizard doesn't have to answer to any of us: anything we get from him is a windfall."

"Oh well, you'll let me know if you need any help, won't you, Poly? Spellpaper or kisses."

"I'll bear that in mind," said Poly. Her voice surprised her with its dryness, but Michael's innocent façade didn't even register a crack.

"Have a biscuit, Poly. Have a biscuit, Mother Mine. Now, out with the spellpaper!"

Poly took it out of her pocket with slight reluctance: she'd wanted to look it over by herself in private first. But Michael's blue eyes were very hard to resist, and even Annie's eyes, though not as compelling, glittered with interest. Annie, like Josie, was unrepentantly one of those who 'wouldn't mind if I *do*'.

When she smoothed the spellpaper out on the table, it crackled and became smooth and matte, the folds disappearing as if they'd never been. The snap of impersonal, clerical magic made Poly jump. She hadn't looked at a spellpaper in—well, more than three hundred years, and not so very often back then, either. Lady Cimone had made sure she knew all the treaties, of course: the Forest Treaty, which was the oldest of them all, and made of leafy parchment that somehow still glowed with the same pearlescence of the newer papers; the slightly scorched Treaty of A Hundred Days, which hadn't fared nearly as well due to a few treacherous Parrasians or Civetans (depending on which country you happened to be in); and the Three Monarchies Treaty, which Poly shrewdly suspected was no more than a pile of ash after the Enchanted Battlefield.

But studying the Treaties from behind glass and magic ward was very different from the crackling, powerful presence of an

Spindle

uncaged spellpaper, and Poly cleaned her glasses once, very slowly, before she began to read. Across the table, Onepiece's little human nose wrinkled and was firmly grasped in one small hand before it could sneeze into his tea.

Poly had only read four lines before she looked up, bewildered. "But this is nonsense!"

"Aloud, aloud, Poly," pleaded Michael, bouncing on his seat. "What's nonsense?"

"It's in rhyme!" She ran her eyes over the lines again, unreasonably irritated. "A trite little three verse curse, actually."

Annie's blue eyes had become very sharp. "Now what is a three-verse curse doing written in spellpaper?"

"That's exactly what I would like to know," said Poly, a little fiercely.

Across the table, Onepiece looked at her with watchful eyes and said guiltily: "Wasn't feeding gremlin."

"I'm not cross with you, darling," Poly assured him, watching the gremlin as it shoved the rest of a biscuit into its mouth. "It says,

Briar thorne and spindle's end
Spin a cage of sleep and time.
Now is lost, the past is teind.

DEATHLESS SLEEP *with endless night*
Lay you here until love's kiss
Ends the curse and breaks the light.

TWO POWERS GATHERED, *harnessed,*
Caught; within the will of state
On the monarch's shoulders rest.

. . .

"The rest of the spellpaper is just legal nonsense: hereintofore as such and such is referred to as such and such, the crown wishes it to be understood that...and so on."

Michael leaned perilously over the tea things to look at the paper. "Disappointing of you, Poly! I was hoping for something more helpful. Look, how did Luck manage to kiss you awake in the first place? According to the curse, anyone kissing you awake is supposed to already be in love with you: hence the sobriquet 'love curse'."

"Knowing Luck, he managed to wriggle around it somehow," said Poly. "He told me that he slipped around a tricky bit of wording, but he's still trying to break it properly."

"What I want to know is *why*," said Michael, absentmindedly tapping the spellpaper with a half-eaten biscuit. "Why you, and why *then*? And what's all this about the monarch's shoulders? What has it got to do with your parents?"

"And why are you only just now being woken up?" put in Annie. "I don't want to seem harsh on your parents, my dear, but it does seem a little remiss of them not to have found their own Luck. Or Luck himself: I'm sure he was around then."

Poly opened her mouth to protest the culpability of Persephone's parents, and closed it again under Michael's curious eyes. After all, she didn't owe the old king and queen anything.

"Do you know, I always have the feeling that you're about to say something and then think better of it," said Michael. "If it was a compliment you can feel free to express it: I promise to blush becomingly."

Poly gave an involuntary laugh, but she had begun to feel the danger of discussing her previous life, and she changed the subject as adroitly as she knew how, crumbling a biscuit into her saucer with suddenly restless fingers. Michael and Annie took it without a blink or a question, much to Poly's relief. The three-verse curse, which at first had seemed laughable, was now growing in importance at the back of her mind and making it difficult to converse sensibly. It suggested that Mordion had cursed her under orders from the Crown, and that the Crown had been under the impression that she possessed magic strong enough to be worth claiming under right of Monarchy.

Annie, noticing her distraction, kindly led everyone out to play with the baby chicks, and Poly left not long after that, tugging a reluctant Onepiece behind her. She felt, by and large, that she was escaping from an increasingly perilous situation.

The only question was, Poly thought ruefully, whether it was any less perilous with Luck?

11

Poly reminded Luck about Annie's dilemma at breakfast the next morning. Luck gave her a blank look and continued to mutter beneath his breath in a suspiciously magical manner while the breakfast glowed briefly and then quite simply disappeared before they could eat so much as a bite of it.

Luck said, "Huh," in a surprised tone, and likewise vanished into his study.

Margaret said, "Well, of all the—!" in indignant tones, and got up again to make more toast.

Poly reminded him again at lunch, when he gave her a prolonged look with his head tilted back and two of his chair legs off the floor and then said, "Where's my spellpaper, Poly?"

"It's not yours, it's mine. And *don't* change the subject."

"I'm not," said Luck unblinkingly, and when Poly went to look at her spellpaper later, it had disappeared as completely as breakfast had.

She was still annoyed at the loss of the spellpaper that evening, when she reminded Luck again at last bell that Annie's jinxed field needed seeing to.

"There's something different about you today, Poly,"

complained Luck. "Something picky and bothersome and annoying."

"I've probably been living with you too long," Poly told him, irritably. "It's probably catching."

Luck gave her another long, narrow look with a gold tint to the edges of his eyes that warned Poly she'd better not push things too far, and went back to studying what she was fairly certain was her spellpaper.

Trusting to Luck's tendency to forget everything and everyone once they were out of sight, Poly wandered the library for a few, quiet minutes before silently leaning over his shoulder to read it. It *was* her spellpaper. Luck must have done something fiddly and strongly magical to it, because it was glittering with a spiderweb of sharp golden tracery that looked as though it could possibly cut the air.

Poly found herself holding her breath as she studied it, fascinated at the power, the intricacy, the *Luck*ness of the spell. With his spell lifting the edges of the legality in the spellpaper, she could see the curse itself, words curled tightly in a coil of blackness that was slightly looser here and there. It looked intent and determined. But as determined as it was, Luck's magic was still more determined and insidious, and Poly could see where two battered words had been nudged so far out of their place that they were no longer part of it.

She wasn't aware that she'd reached out a finger to touch one of the words until she saw the iridescent *something* that rippled across her arm in a seamless coating from finger to shoulder, and felt the static fizz that stung her finger as it met the word.

"Yow!" said Poly frantically, snatching the finger back and instinctively putting it in her mouth.

Luck jumped, knocking over his chair, and said with a sharp snap of magic that made the iridescence disappear, "You can't do that! Poly! How did you do that?"

"What did you do to me!" demanded Poly, at the same time.

She watched with wide eyes as more of the iridescence disappeared from the rest of her body, but she didn't miss the covert flick of Luck's fingers that made the spellpaper vanish from his desk.

"Nobody listens to me anymore," he said plaintively. "Three types of magic, I said. You have one and two, and you can't have three, but you do. I need peace and quiet to work it out. And the village is still sideways."

Perfectly well aware that he was only trying to change the subject, Poly said crossly, "I wish you wouldn't do things to me without asking! And it's *my* spellpaper, after all!"

"I should start talking to the gremlins. At least *they* listen to me."

A muted *yik* followed by a shower of woodchips suggested otherwise, but Luck ignored them grandly. "Why are you sneaking around in my library? Where did you get an Invisibility spell? And how did you get it to do *that*?"

Poly, all at sea, sat down on the desk with her ankles crossed and tried to decide if it was worth making any of the protestations or asking any of the questions she wanted to ask.

Finally, she decided on a single question. "What are you talking about?"

"Unmagic. I *told* you, Poly. Three kinds of magic."

"Yes, I remember."

"Well, then; you should understand."

"Luck, I want my spellpaper back."

"Three kinds of magic that all work together but aren't ever found together. It's impossible. Except sometimes when it's not."

"Yes, I understand that," said Poly wearily. "But I want—"

"No, you don't," contradicted Luck. "You can't. Otherwise you wouldn't keep bleating about not having magic. Or doing spells that are impossible."

Bewildered all over again, Poly was betrayed into repeating the oft-repeated mantra: "But I *haven't* got magic!"

"Huh. I thought you'd stopped saying that. You didn't lose more of your memory when you woke up, did you, Poly?"

"Well, like you said before, I wouldn't know, would I?" said Poly, beginning to feel distinctly sulky. "What did you do to me?"

"It was an Invisibility spell with a Soundless clause, three kinds of dampers, and worked in unmagic." Luck sat back down in his chair, lounging at ease but with a sharper-than-usual gaze directed at her beneath his lashes. "A beautiful, impossible spell. And I didn't do it. But while you're *here*, Poly—"

"No!" said Poly hurriedly, careless of whether it was one of Luck's misdirections or an actual threat. "I'm going out. Please don't forget Annie's field! There's only a little planting time left now."

She left while Luck was still muttering something about flirting in the moonlight and negligent pet owners, which fortunately reminded her to look in on Onepiece before she left the house. Michael and Margaret had come by just after noon, while Michael was supposed to be eating his lunch, and had entertained Poly through the kitchen window while Luck did something fiddly with one of Norris' inventions. Before leaving they'd told her about a moonlight walk that was to stealthily occur tonight when the village was asleep, and between Michael's ridiculous pleading and Margaret's rather alarming prognostications of a great many stolen moonlight kisses, Poly hadn't found herself able to say no. It was too entrancing to be a part of the revels instead of an onlooker.

Onepiece was in his little boy form when Poly tucked the sheets securely around him, much to her satisfaction. He was uneasily asleep, but her instinctive pat on the head made him suck in a quick, sniffy little breath and open his eyes.

"Pretty magic!" he said, smiling up at her. "Not sneezy."

"Yes, darling. Go to sleep, now."

"Poly sleep, too?"

"Not right now. I'm going for a walk."

"*Onepiece* wants walks, too!" said Onepiece indignantly, pawing the sleep from his eyes.

"I know, darling. But you have to sleep now."

"Poly *sleep*. Not leave Onepiece alone!"

Fortunately for Poly's slender parenting skills, the puppy was still only half awake, and by the time she'd reiterated in a soft voice that he was staying in *bed*, and Onepiece had muttered sulkily into his sheets, he was all but fast asleep once more. Poly stroked his hair for some time after in spite of this, feeling a little bit sorry, and a little bit fond, and suddenly a little bit terrified, because all of Onepiece's sleeping thoughts said: *Mum*.

THE NIGHT WAS A PLEASANT ONE. Poly found herself dizzily talking to more young men than she could ever recall knowing before, and being ignored by nearly as many of the village girls, who tended to eye her in somewhat gloomy resentment and ask leading questions about Luck, his schedule, and even (from one bold, sparkling redhead) his preferences as to hair colour.

Poly gave the redhead a fascinated look and truthfully said that she didn't know, to which the redhead replied with another barrage of questions, each more personal than the last, until Poly was rescued by Ronin. His requests after her—nephew, is it, Miss Poly? Ah, *brother*, of *course*—made the redhead chuckle in a manner that she didn't quite like, but when Poly informed them both quite calmly that Onepiece was in bed and asleep she seemed to lose interest in the subject. Much to Poly's relief, the young lady was caught up in a sudden rush of young men who were determined to show off their magical prowess by levitating a select few ladies over the tiny stream they'd come upon, and was soon to be seen bobbing merrily over the foot-wide trickle with her ankles primly crossed.

"Lovely girl!" said Ronin with a cutting edge of sarcasm in his voice.

He swept Poly across the stream in one fluid motion, and she thanked him with some amusement. She could have stepped across it without breaking stride. How different it was from walking with Luck, who was more likely to plough into the middle of a stream without noticing it than he was to bestir himself to help her over it! Two village lads on the other side reached out eagerly to receive her on the other side, and Poly couldn't help laughing at their unashamed interest: they reminded her of Onepiece in possession of a new toy.

Ronin gave her up with a wry smile but said teasingly, "Miss Margaret won't be happy if you purloin *all* her beaux, Poly!"

Since she remembered these particular boys waiting impatiently for a dance from Margaret at the 'happening' not long since, Poly felt a twinge of unease that only intensified when she caught Margaret watching her thoughtfully as the evening progressed. After that, she stayed determinedly with Michael, who was outspokenly willing to have her with him—and, moreover, was quick to cook her sausages and provide her with chocolates.

Poly arrived back home in the wee hours of the morning, shutting the front door behind her and guiltily tiptoeing across the obstacle-strewn main room. Luck was still awake, his figure vaguely visible through the library wall. There were two gremlins on his desk, one *yik-yiking* in a vehement fashion as it pointed at a section of Poly's spellpaper and another, younger one attempting to make a meal of the topmost corner with its sharp teeth. To Poly's surprise, Luck did little more than poke the hungry gremlin away from the paper with one finger, producing a scrap of cheese for it to eat instead, and as she passed the library he said to the other gremlin, "Yes, I can see that. But there's nothing in there that deals with antimagic. It only mentions two powers."

She called out a sleepy 'good morning' in passing, grinning when she heard the startled "Morning?" from the library, and climbed into bed too early to catch Margaret sneaking in from the other side of the room.

. . .

Poly slept heavily and woke with difficulty to find her hair ominously long once again. Fortunately, Onepiece had prodded her in the ribs until she woke, and he trotted gleefully behind her with handfuls of hair as she wandered drowsily down the hall to find Luck. The halls were fuzzy, and though Poly was awake enough to be alarmed at it, she couldn't work up the will to do anything more than yawn and avoid the worst of the obstacles that littered Luck's floor. The fact that some of the obstacles seemed to be people, she was dimly aware of, and she was likewise aware that Onepiece's odd magic had gone very prickly.

He said, "No touch!" in a tight little voice to the fuzzy figures, defensively huddling her hair closer to his chest, and scowled at them all until he and Poly had passed through to the library.

The blurry swirl of green and gold that was Luck said, "Huh. Having trouble again? You may as well sit down in here: there's nothing I can do about it that your hair isn't already doing."

Poly did so, instinctively finding a comfortably stacked pile of books close to the reassuring presence that was Luck, and felt Onepiece climb into her lap.

"Poly should come to bed *earlier*," he said crossly, and Poly smiled faintly.

It was oddly comforting to watch Luck wandering the library with blue and white streamers of an unknown magic trailing after him. She let herself fall back into a half-doze, sleepily entranced to actually feel the curse pushing and her hair growing, cancelling each other out.

Luck came and checked on her periodically, muttering unintelligible things beneath his breath, but once she heard him say, "*That's* right, Poly. Let it push at you: I won't let it get too strong."

She became more and more awake by degrees; first to feel the growth of her hair slowing while the push of the curse became less irresistible, and then to feel the thin little arms that were wrapped around her waist. Onepiece's head, she discovered, was lying on her chest; he was fast asleep and snoring occasionally.

She hadn't fallen over, much to her own surprise, but when

she woke a little more thoroughly Poly found that this was because Luck had piled more books around her, effectively hemming her into her own little corner. She couldn't help feeling that this was uncharacteristically thoughtful of him, and when he wandered past again with a patchily spelled cloak dangling from one arm, Poly gave him the warm smile she usually reserved for Michael. This made Luck stop in his tracks and gaze warily at her, his head tilted back, and Poly wondered with a faint sense of shock if she smiled at him so little that it was an occasion for surprise when she did so.

"I haven't helped much today," she said, so that she wouldn't have to think about it. Everything with Luck was always just a little bit uncomfortable: he took liberties, he never listened, and he very rarely deigned to notice anything that didn't interest him. How could she help it if she'd scowled at him more than she smiled? But she still said, for that and for today, "Sorry."

"I didn't need you," said Luck absently, and even if that was insulting, at least it was reassuring.

He was still observing her, his eyes for once entirely and completely green with not a golden speck of magic to be seen, and Poly, finding herself uncomfortable and slightly flushed, asked, "Can you get rid of the hair again?"

"What? Oh yes, the hair. Well, I could do with a few more specimens: the last lot were no good at all. I might have to try something different this time."

He knelt in front of her, parting the gathered hair to find a bare spot on the floor for his knees. Poly, who had intended to rise and seat herself on Luck's chair in a civilised manner for the operation, found herself, as usual, with nowhere to retreat.

"Spell!" she said warningly to Luck, as the spelled cloak in his arms sent an arcing spit of blue-ish magic flying into her hair.

"Huh," said Luck, looking down at the cloak in faint surprise. "Where did that come from?"

"You were already carrying it. I don't think it likes me."

"It doesn't like anyone," Luck said dismissively, laying the battered thing carefully down behind the wall of books. "It's a Cloak of Hideous Aspect. Sooner or later all the grimaces and frightened looks sink into the lining with the spell and turn it sour. This one is very old. Lean forward, Poly: I need to be able to reach the hair at your nape."

Poly did so reluctantly, cupping Onepiece's suddenly restless head with her hands and feeling that the space was already entirely too crowded as it was.

"Much better," said Luck cheerfully, slipping one arm around her neck.

The other arm went around her shoulders, and Poly was able to renew her acquaintance with Luck's ink-stained collar while Luck muttered into her hair. Terrifyingly, Poly found that she could understand almost everything he was saying.

Finally, he said, "Give me your hand, Poly. Not the antimagic one."

"But—oh, wait a moment." Poly reshuffled Onepiece to rest against Luck's shoulder and wriggled her normal hand free, which Luck grabbed with more speed than gentleness and wrapped around a thick hank of hair.

"Think of it as magic," he told her, nudging his shoulder into hers to accommodate Onepiece's head. "Well, it is, but I mean the hair itself. Think of it as a skein of magic that you want to cut in half."

"Shall I cauterize it?" asked Poly dubiously.

Luck said, "No!" hastily, tugging her hand away. "Poly, you don't listen. I specifically want it *not* cauterized!"

Poly made a rude face at Luck's collar that had to be quickly smoothed away when Luck's collar was replaced with Luck's face, but the rather closer look he gave her suggested that he'd caught the tail end of it anyway.

Using her arm as a demonstration, he curled his fingers around her wrist and squeezed tight. "Cinch it, you see? Then twist and tug." He demonstrated that, too, prompting a muttered 'ow!' from Poly, and added, "If we're lucky, that'll do it."

Poly wanted to ask what would happen if they *weren't* lucky, but Luck was gazing at her expectantly, his nose mere inches from her own, and even being more or less hugged by Luck was better than being stared at by him. She reached back for the bunch of hair that Luck had scraped together again, caught hold of it, and *twisted*.

At once her head was lighter and her hand heavier, loose tendrils springing up to tickle her ears. When Poly shook her head in fascination, her freshly cut hair dusted Luck's cheeks.

He muttered but didn't move away, and Poly refused to feel apologetic. She was surrounded by Luck—Luck's arms, his magic, his sharp chemically smell—and if he was slightly inconvenienced by that, well, serve him right. He gathered the hair, which was longer again than she'd realised, and from the vague hum Poly sensed coming from it, he should be well pleased with the success of their experiment.

Poly didn't realise Luck had finished gathering hair until he said, "You'd better hold the dog, Poly," and it was borne in on her that they'd been sitting quietly for some minutes without moving, and that Luck needed her to hold Onepiece again in order to disengage himself.

She murmured her apologies, faintly surprised at herself for becoming comfortable enough with Luck's somewhat pushing presence to forget it, and curled her arms beneath Onepiece.

"Got it!" said Luck cheerfully, heaving up armfuls of hair.

Feeling somehow chilled now that Luck's warm presence had moved away, Poly climbed carefully to her feet with Onepiece's skinny legs dangling on either side of her hips.

She was wondering if she should wake him for breakfast—or was it lunch? Time had gone a little strange today—when someone in the kitchen screamed. It was a staccato scream: short, sharp and possibly angry, and in the astonished silence that followed, Onepiece muttered sleepily, "Wasn't me."

Luck said thoughtfully, "Huh. Margaret doesn't usually scream," and took off at a dash.

Poly, following more slowly with Onepiece, her antimagic arm swiftly ungloved, came across a scene as macabre as it was bright. Margaret, a chocolate held between two shaking fingers, was gazing wide eyed at the kitchen table, upon which a semicircle of gremlins were sprawled around a cheerfully coloured box. Their faces were smeared with melted chocolate, and they were quite dead.

"I almost ate one!" said Margaret frantically.

She managed to drop the chocolate at last, flinging it away in her haste to be rid of it, and it tumbled stickily past the gremlins. She wiped her hand furiously on her apron, scrubbing away the slightest trace of melted chocolate, and when Poly skirted the table to put a comforting arm around her waist, Margaret subsided into the hug with a shudder.

"Huh," said Luck, observing the top of the chocolate box. "They're for you, Poly."

"Thank you, I'm sure!"

"No, they're addressed to you. 'Miss Polly, from an ardent admirer'."

"How charming," Poly said, with a dry mouth. She passed Onepiece to Margaret, who seemed glad to have a warm body to cuddle, and tugged her glove back over her antimagic arm. "Can you do anything for the gremlins?"

"What? Oh no, they're dead as doornails. The others will probably come along later and collect them. I think they stuff them and hang them on their side of the walls."

Poly sighed, tugging her laces tight. "Well, you wanted someone to try and kill me. Now they have."

"Again," agreed Luck. "All very helpful."

"I'm so glad you think so," Poly told him, unable to repress a faint smile. Neither was she able to repress the shiver that followed a moment later. "Wait, what do you mean, again?"

"Third attempt, Poly. We had an explosive in a Journey spell the first time. The second attempt was more of a gentle brush, so I could only catch a trace of it: this time should be *much* easier."

"But when did someone try to kill me before?" protested Poly, interrupting Luck as he muttered something distinctly magical to himself.

She categorically refused to believe that the bomb in the Journey spell was anything more than mischief directed at Luck himself.

"When I put you to sleep in the kitchen two days ago," he said, between mutters. The chocolate box lid was luminescing faintly, swirls of Luck's golden magic putting coils of something else into sharp relief. "Someone tried to kill you then. I thought they might."

"Do you mean to say," demanded Margaret, in growing indignation, "that you put Poly to sleep and left her *in my kitchen* to be murdered?"

Poly, somewhat amused to note that Margaret was more concerned by the idea of a body in her kitchen than the thought of Poly's murder, was able to say calmly enough, "Well, it's done now. Ronin must have scared away the murderer before they had a chance to finish me off."

"Yes," said Luck thoughtfully, tilting the lid to gaze more closely at it. Poly wasn't sure whether his assent was to Margaret's indignant question or her own statement. "Poly, take your glove off."

"One day," said Poly, tugging once again at the laces of her glove, "one day you'll say please, and I'll probably faint with shock."

Over the chocolate box lid, Luck gave her a brilliant, dreamy smile that made Poly blink in surprise, and said, "Be a darling, Poly."

There was a stifled giggle from Margaret, and while Poly was still startled into immovability, Luck peeled the glove from her hand and tugged her forward.

"You shouldn't smile at people like that," Poly told him, becoming more or less coherent again. "Good grief, no wonder the redhead was peppering me with questions!"

This time, Luck's smile was more smug than breathtaking, but all he said was, "Poke about, Poly. See if there's anything there to dismantle."

Poly did so, her fingers running nimbly over the smooth surface of coloured cardboard in search of any traces of magic.

"Nothing," she said, at last. "Nothing magic, anyway."

"Huh," said Luck, unsurprised. "Didn't think so. Clever. He's filled the chocolates with poison: nothing magic to trace."

Poly pulled her glove back on, shrugging away disappointment and a slight quiver of fear. "We've no way to find him?"

"Oh no, I can find him," Luck assured her.

Since he followed this assurance by disappearing into the library with the chocolate box and one of the gremlins, Poly felt distinctly unconvinced. When she tried to follow him, she found to her indignation that he had somehow closed the library against her. She stomped back into the kitchen with something less than the fellow feeling she'd had toward Luck that morning.

"He's going to cut up that gremlin, you know," Margaret said, grimly scrubbing the kitchen table.

Poly whisked away the remaining dead gremlins, but there seemed to be nowhere appropriate to put them, so she lined them up in the garden outside, decently out of sight behind the butterflowers. She hoped that Onepiece wouldn't take it into his head to explore the garden as a puppy—in which form she had a feeling he would be more than capable of chewing on and then burying the gremlins.

The garden reminded her of Annie's front garden, hollowed out to serve as a tiny field for strawberries, and another source of ire against Luck raised its head.

"Does Luck ever actually remember to help anyone?" she asked Margaret irritably, working the kitchen pump vigorously to wash her hands.

She could still feel the tiny, stiffening limbs against her fingers, and the gremlins had left a sticky scum on her hands.

"Not unless you keep prodding him," said Margaret sympathetically. "Or if it's interesting. If it's interesting, just you *try* keeping him away."

"Yes. I've already discovered that."

"Did he really put a spell on you and leave you out as bait?"

"Well, it wasn't so much a spell as an experiment," Poly admitted, fighting off the desire to thoroughly berate Luck. "But yes. I suppose I'm just lucky that Ronin came along when he did."

Margaret snorted. "If you call *that* lucky. Don't let Ronin hang on your apron strings, Poly: you'll end up with the wrong kind of reputation."

"Oh," said Poly blankly. "Really? But he seems so nice!"

"Tell me he didn't murmur a word or two about Miss Margaret being 'a trifle overblown', or warn you that I'd scratch your eyes out? Just in passing, of course, and in the nicest way."

Poly grimaced. "Something like that."

"Well, I hope you didn't listen to him!" said Margaret, scooping up soap foam with a damp cloth. She shot a sideways look at Poly and burst out laughing. "You did! You thought I'd be upset that you're here and turning the head of every boy from one end of the village to the other!"

"You *were* a bit standoffish at first!" Poly protested, but Margaret's laughter was infectious, and she couldn't help her lips twitching.

"Yes, but that's because—oh, never mind! I decided you couldn't help it, so there was no use being upset, after all."

"Couldn't help what?" said Poly, bewildered, because Margaret had gone off into another peal of laughter.

"That's exactly it!" she said, and refused to explain any further. "Never you mind! As to the beaux, well, it's nice to have a bit of space every now and then! Only don't get attached to Michael, will you? He breaks hearts every which way."

"I'll take care," Poly said dryly. Now that she was thinking of it, she seemed to remember a remark or two that Ronin had made—one *to* her and another *about* her—that made her wonder why she hadn't been more careful with him in the first place. "My skills have gotten rather rusty."

"Skills? Oooh, *do* tell, Poly! Do you have delicious castle secrets to reveal?"

"There was a time when I could tell a scheming courtier at a glance," said Poly, irritated with herself. "How annoying! I shall have to learn it all over again!"

"Well, don't be too hard on yourself," said Margaret soothingly. "Dad had to pay Ronin a visit a few years ago, back when I thought he was rather nice. That was before the rumours started, of course. I still don't know if he thrashed Ronin or just threatened to do it, but it was all very archaic and lovely of him. Michael always said Ronin was a rotten apple," she added reflectively.

Poly nodded, remembering Mordion and the unsuspecting Mary Massey. "He reminds me of someone I used to know."

"They do say history repeats itself," nodded Margaret wisely.

And Poly, appalled, said, "Oh, I *hope* not!"

12

The next morning there were almost no villagers lined up. No serious ones, at any rate, Poly thought. There were the few assorted girls draped about the place in various sultry and elegant poses, but Luck seemed willing to let them wait. He was working on something quite different when Poly made her way into the library after convincing Onepiece to use the water chamber and *not* the backyard for his morning toilet run.

The smell hit her as soon as she stepped through the wall.

"Oh! *Oh!* Luck, what *is* that?"

"Our gremlin's stomach contents," said Luck cheerfully. "Chalk, cheese, poison, half a rusted tea kettle—actually, it's quite possible that the poison didn't kill it."

Poly, feeling her stomach about to revolt, asked hastily, "Luck, you *will* call on Annie today, won't you? They need to plant in the next few days."

"Annie," murmured Luck. "Oh yes, I'm due there at noon. It's a very boring problem, Poly."

"Not to them," Poly said grimly. "Do you need me for anything?"

Luck looked hopeful. "You can't get rid of a few of those girls, can you? No? Well, it was worth a try. Where are you going?"

"I'm taking Onepiece down to the mill stream for a paddle."

Luck nodded, his attention already straying back to the dead, spreadeagled gremlin that was displaying its stomach contents to the room. He did say, "Take Margaret with you. And a stout stick or a good spell," but by the time she was stepping through the library wall, he had already picked up a small glass tube with a soft bulb at one end and was applying it to the gremlin's open torso.

Poly repressed a shudder and found herself grateful to be in the open sunshine with Onepiece and Margaret, who sniffed and said, "He's there with his knives and tubers, isn't he? I can smell it."

"So can I," Poly said, hoping the smell wouldn't linger much longer. Her breakfast already sat with precarious unease in her stomach.

They collected a few stray children as they walked, much to Poly's satisfaction. Those children were barefoot, happy, and a little wild, and didn't seem to find Onepiece's lack of vocabulary an odd thing. They danced and skipped and threw inconsequential and entirely disconnected questions at the other little boy until his gruff voice could be heard almost as often as theirs, speaking in short, rough bursts to their birdlike tones. Poly, watching them, felt guiltily that she'd spent far too much time on her own social activities without trying to find Onepiece some of the same.

Sensing weakness, the children clamoured for ices at the sweet store—and got them. Really, it was Luck paying for them, but Poly, watching Onepiece's fascination with the frozen treat, couldn't find it in herself to feel guilty about that.

Margaret, watching shrewdly, said, "You'll never get rid of 'em now. No, you little beast, I won't have you dripping melted ice all over my skirt! Hold Poly's hand."

The child in question did so, provoking an indignant

response from Onepiece, who evidently hadn't been taught to share and had no intention of so learning.

"*My* Poly!" he said irritably, tugging at the other child's fingers. "Off, off, *off!*"

"I have two hands," said Poly peaceably, wiggling her free fingers at him, but this didn't please him either, and he spent the remainder of the walk to the stream in clinging fiercely to Poly's hand and glaring at anyone else who dared to approach her other hand.

He continued to hover suspiciously at the stream, but fortunately the mill wheel was new and exciting enough to capture his attention, and although he paddled close to her Onepiece seemed content to allow the other children to do so also. Poly, for her part, enjoyed the paddling as thoroughly as any of the children, and scandalised Margaret by kilting her skirts to the knee in order to join them in the deeper parts of the stream. The big mill wheel slapped at the water with heavy paddles, plopping huge, sulky drops of water into the stream to disappear with the current, and although the stream was sparklingly cold the sun was hot, and they splashed each other until they were too wet and too hungry to continue.

By the time they waded ponderously out of the water to eat their lunch, Onepiece was thoroughly wet from an accidental ducking, and Poly had ceased to tuck her skirts, since they were wet through anyway. The plunge to rescue Onepiece had seen her waist deep in the water before she knew it, with one skinny ankle seized unceremoniously in her gloved hand. In her further efforts to set him once more on his shaky feet, both sleeves had also seen a good deal more of the stream than she intended. Onepiece clutched and gasped and laughed, and all in all clung so effectively to her that in the end she was as completely wet as he was, though considerably more rueful at the fact.

Margaret laughed at her without sympathy, declaring that it was her own fault for paddling with the children, but Poly felt that she'd rather have been there to catch Onepiece than see him disappear beneath what now seemed to her a rather sinister paddle wheel. Ridiculous to think so, of course: the stream was barely deeper than Onepiece's waist at its deepest. Still, Poly found herself shivering, and when the dripping boy insisted on sitting on her lap to eat his picnic lunch, soaking her bodice once again, she didn't argue. He drummed his heels on her shins as he ate, sprinkling crumbs with abandon and making the occasional dart at a butterfly that wandered too close to be resisted.

Margaret, noticing Poly's occasional wince as Onepiece's bony rear wiggled and bounced, said with a grin, "You'll have to fatten him up, Poly."

"Yah," said Onepiece, nodding vigorously into his sandwich. "Shoc'lat!"

"No chocolate for little boys who can't sit still," Poly told him, attempting a stern tone.

Onepiece giggled and gave her a jammy kiss. "*Lots* of shoc'lat!" he said.

Luck passed them by some time later, crossing the bridge on his way to Annie's house. Poly smiled and waved gaily at him, relief putting a decided sparkle in her eyes, and to her surprise, Luck waved back. He also walked into the bridge balustrade, which made both Margaret and Onepiece giggle, but continued, Luck-like, without really noticing.

"Do you know, I didn't think he'd actually *do* it," said Margaret, with dawning respect. "How did you manage it, Poly?"

The idea that Luck could be managed by anyone made Poly giggle rather more than Margaret's disapproving face suggested was welcome.

"Well, there's no need to be smug!" she said, with a touch of indignation.

"Oh no, it's not that! What do you think *I* did about it? I only reminded him."

"I'm sure I've never seen him listen to anyone else before," sniffed Margaret, mollified. "He just looks through you, or around you, or—*or*, Poly—he changes the subject without notice. He's a horrible, horrible man. I can't think why I—oh, never mind that. Michael will be happy, at any rate."

Poly, considering ruefully that in *that* case, she should have accepted the merit for Luck's unusual dedication to duty, said, "Annie, too. She was seeding her front garden just in case Luck didn't come around."

Margaret's eyebrow quirked. "That bad, is it? I wonder why Michael didn't tell me."

"You're good friends," Poly said slowly, wondering if she had misread both Margaret's pert dismissals and Michael's lofty disregard.

She would have to watch them more closely next time they were together.

"Oh, we've been complaining about our Mums to each other for as long as I can remember. That, and scraping knees and throwing stones—not to mention the pranks we played. You wouldn't think it from the nonsense he spouts, but he's even better than Dad at taking a spell apart and putting it back together differently."

"Why would you put a spell back together differently?"

"Well, that's the game. I thought you'd seen Dad and Luck playing: it's a sort of clear shimmer in the air with figures to represent the two spells. You take it apart and use the parts to make as many different spells as you can. The more spells, the more points, and you subtract any leftover spell bits from your final tally."

"Picky-pecky," said Onepiece unexpectedly, his face sharp and interested. Poly looked at him questioningly, and he said again, "Picky-pecky!" making vigorous pincer movements with his fingers.

Margaret, with a narrow look, tossed him a tiny brooch spell. Onepiece fumblingly caught it, chuckling in his rough little voice, and said once more, this time gleefully, "Picky-pecky!"

The brooch spell remained in his lap, but his thin fingers made rapid dashes and pinches in the air above it. The spell went from soft pink to red, and then to brilliant orange. At his last pinch, Poly saw the colour jump in intensity, and even Margaret, who couldn't directly see the effects of Onepiece's effort, said, "Yow! What was that?"

"Tippin'!" said Onepiece, with a gratified look.

"It's *topping*," Margaret corrected him, but her eyebrows said she was impressed. "Poly, has he made this into three different spells?"

"Four," Poly told her, feeling absurdly proud. "There's nothing left behind, either. What was it before?"

"Just a tiny windbreak: something to stop my hair blowing about when I've just brushed it. What has he done to it?"

"I don't know exactly, but I think he's turned it into four tiny spells that work together to make another, bigger one." Poly gazed at the thing in fascination, following the flow of power until it stopped at the centre in one, pulsing, ready mass. "It looks like the first one somehow *catches* the wind, which the second one funnels somewhere, but I don't know where. The third has something to do with making things steady—equilibrium, I think. The fourth is—oh!"

"What, what?" demanded Margaret impatiently.

Poly giggled. "I think it might be a flying spell!"

"Whoosh!" agreed Onepiece. He breathed once on the brooch, and to his own delight, the spell harnessed enough power to lift him gently above Poly's head.

"Boys and their spells!" sighed Margaret. "That was the first thing Michael tried to do, too! Come to think of it, that was with one of my spells as well. He's going to love this."

"So will Luck," Poly murmured. She wondered if Luck knew that Onepiece could alter spells with little more than a few hand gestures and a few moments.

"Let's go show him off," Margaret suggested, her eyes dancing. "Oh, won't Michael be jealous!"

Since Poly wasn't averse to demonstrating Onepiece's prowess, they left the urchin children paddling noisily by the mill and took the scraps of their picnic with them to the edges of the village, where Annie's cottage stood forlorn. It was the only dwelling in the rambling street with bare dirt for a front garden.

"I don't see Luck," Poly said dubiously. "Perhaps they're at the field?"

"Annie's probably trying to fatten him up," said Margaret. She pushed cheerfully through the front door with Poly close behind, secure in her welcome.

Poly, who knew by a combination of sensory magic and sheer aggravation whenever Luck was in the vicinity, said, "No, he's not here."

"I can't stop to chat today, love," said Annie's voice, floating from the kitchen. "Oh, hallo, Poly: you too? I've just this minute stopped to wash up and have a quick bite to eat."

Poly and Margaret, together taking in Annie's discarded, dirt encrusted apron, said as one, "Hasn't Luck arrived *yet*?"

Annie brightened momentarily. "Oh, was he planning to call?"

"He passed us an hour or two ago," said Poly, and a creeping anger began to steal over her.

Some of the anger must have shown on her face, because Margaret said hastily, "You were probably right, Poly: he must have gone straight to the field."

"I don't think so," said Poly curtly. She had let her eyes glaze slightly to focus on the magical traces that ran through the village, and perhaps it was her annoyance at Luck that made his particular signature jump out at her. In any case, the location of the signature was unmistakable. "He's over by the forest. Someone's stables, I think."

Annie looked impressed and a little amused: Margaret seemed nervous.

Annie inquired, "Did you just sense Luck through the entire village?"

Margaret said, worriedly, "Poly—"

"He's hard to miss," said Poly, ignoring Margaret's unmistakeably anxious hand wringing.

"Bang-boom-crash!" Onepiece said gleefully.

"Exactly! Which means that you must stay here with Annie like a good boy. Do you mind, Annie?"

"Oh, it's my pleasure, my dear! Not but what I'd like to be there for the fireworks! No, my poppet, you can't go with Poly, you must stay to help me eat my honey apple cake."

Poly heard Onepiece say, "Cake!" happily as she left the house. Margaret wasn't so easily distracted and followed her into the road, but Poly was a determined walker and the other girl didn't catch up until they reached the end of the street.

"Poly! Poly, you're not about to do something silly, are you?" she panted.

"No," said Poly, with great precision. "I'm going to box Luck's ears!"

Margaret made a choking noise and snatched at Poly's arm. "Oh, no you don't! Poly, I'm doing this for your own good!"

Poly felt the spell before she saw it, a web of lethargy spreading along her arm. She peeled off the glove on her antimagic hand and swept the spell away without stopping, which made Margaret squeak in surprise and lose precious moments catching up.

When they reached the stable, Luck's head poked out of the stable door, his hair spiked with sweat and dust, trailing cobwebs. His eyes were already bright with magic, but when he saw her, they fairly blazed. "Poly! Finally!"

He dashed into the road, grabbing Poly's hand, and before she knew quite what was happening, Poly found herself being dragged into a stable that was more cobwebby and less smelly than she remembered stables being.

"You've gotten spiky again," said Luck unexpectedly, peering closely at her. "Why are you spiky again? No, never mind that: look at what I've found!"

"Annie's field, Luck!"

"What? Oh, yes, it was very useful: pointed me straight here."

Poly blinked in surprise, her anger momentarily arrested. "You mean you've fixed it?"

"Of course not. Why would I do that? I told you, it led me here. *Here* is where everything is happening. Can't you feel it? There's communication magic here that I've never seen before. It blazed up again a few minutes ago and everything got another little tug sideways."

A pulse of anger made Poly hot and cold at once. When she wrenched her hand out of Luck's, she thought that her fingers might be trembling slightly.

It was a new and unsettling feeling, and she was glad that her voice didn't tremble when she said, "What about Annie's field? You told her that you'd fix it. Luck, they need to plant!"

"But this is more interesting," said Luck, giving her the wide, glassy look that suggested she was babbling.

In another cold moment, Poly found something to do with her trembling hand that felt right.

Smack!

Luck's eyes were suddenly very awake and narrow above a brilliant red handprint on one cheek.

Poly had a moment to feel euphoric and oddly amused, her hand still tingling, before he said, very softly, "You shouldn't have done that, Poly."

There was no sensation of movement, but Poly found herself backed against the far wall with a decided thump, Luck's hands on her shoulders as if he was going to shake her. A cobweb tickled her left ear, but she wasn't entirely sure that the cobweb was responsible for the shiver that slid down her neck.

Oh well, she thought, looking into Luck's blazing eyes, it could have been worse. She wasn't in a spelled circle, for one thing. On the other hand, she wasn't sure that Luck wasn't going to retaliate in kind. His face was very close, his eyes very green and dangerous.

"Don't ever do that again, Poly!"

"If Annie doesn't plant now, they'll miss the season," Poly told him. She was surprised to find that she was still angry. Slapping Luck had been liberating, but not entirely satisfying. "If they miss the season, they won't have a crop; and if they don't have a crop they'll be running at a loss instead of a profit. That means there won't be any coal for the winter, and just barely enough food to go around."

If she was hoping to shame him, it didn't seem to work. Luck didn't answer. He was wearing one of the looks that she didn't understand yet, and if anything, she thought he might have moved closer. Poly thought she could feel her shoulders slowly bruising under his fingers and became irritated.

"Personal space, Luck!"

Luck blinked once, allowing the uncomfortable moment to stretch for a minute longer, then stepped away, digging his hands into his pockets. "Not everyone finds my kisses distasteful, you know," he said.

Poly felt the familiar sense of bewilderment that came with Luck's habit of metaphorically sweeping the rug out from under her feet. "Don't change the subject!"

"I wasn't," he said, sliding a brief, sideways look at her. "Now can we get back to work?"

Poly looked at him for a long, silent moment, trying to decide if it was worth being angry, and if she could get up the nerve to hit him again. The answer to both questions seemed to be no, so she turned on her heel and exited the stables, passing a wide eyed and open-mouthed Margaret at the door.

When Poly arrived at the contentious field, anger simmering, she could see the sideways pull of a great, big *something* dragging at the jinxed field. It was the same pull that she herself had noticed a few days ago, but now it was much stronger. Poly sucked in a deep breath, fidgeting with her glove as she surveyed the damage. There was certainly more than the sideways pull affecting the field.

She pinched away the sideways pull first, freeing the jinx from the draining influence that made it curl protectively in on itself. It relaxed slightly, a loosening of malevolence, and as she stepped over the stile, Poly felt it focus on herself. It was the questing, malicious feel of the jinx that made Poly tuck her glove into her pocket rather than put it back on. She turned in a circle, sweeping her antimagic hand through the air as a warning, and felt the jinx draw back carefully.

"Well, then," she said to it, feeling for a fleeting moment as if she were dealing with Mordion again. "What should I do with you?"

The jinx suggested, though Poly wasn't quite sure how, the idea of slitting her wrists and letting the blood seep into its soil.

"Aren't you lovely," Poly said, shocked. "No, I don't think so. I suppose that would help you in some nasty way."

Again, the jinx suggested in an indefinable way that, no, it would merely be amusing.

"I see." Poly crossed her arms over her chest. She found herself wishing, traitorously, that Luck was here. He would probably look at the jinx with golden eyes and say, "Huh. Interesting." Then he would flick his fingers in that annoyingly effortless way of his, and that would be that. In fact, if he had done that in the first place, thought Poly, feeling a resurgence of anger, she wouldn't be in this position.

Luck's voice said, "It's your fault anyway. Why shouldn't you fix it?"

"*My* fault?" said Poly, so astonished at the statement that finding Luck suddenly in the field with her didn't surprise her.

"Ever since I met you, things have been going wrong. There was the curse, to start with. How many people do you think it hurt when he used you?"

A familiar, sour taste seem to cling to the back of her mouth.

Poly recognised it as dread, and asked quietly, "Do you mean Mordion?"

"Ah. I thought you were self-absorbed," said Luck. "Apparently you're merely stupid. Why else do you think he picked you?

Do you really think you're important enough to capture his attention otherwise? He always wants something. In your case it was power—a *lot* of power. Enough to make an army."

"I didn't—it wasn't—" Poly blinked her eyes rapidly, but Luck's face still swam, cruel and almost unfamiliar, opposite her. "The Frozen Battlefield was my fault as well?"

"Of course. He must have taken on too much magic from you: he couldn't hold it all and they got away from him. Then there was the bomb, of course, and the chocolates that nearly got Margaret killed. Yes, you've stirred things up very nicely. And then there's the fact that someone's been using every power source in the village to send some sort of message out. The message tubes must be too public for them."

"They used the jinx as well?"

Luck heaved a quick sigh, impatience unconcealed. "I just *said* that. Good sources were drained of power, evil ones were drained of their checks and protections."

Poly, feeling a wave of hopelessness and guilt, said miserably, "I'd better try and fix it, then."

It was the fleeting look of angry surprise sweeping across Luck's face that gave it away. "All right," he said quickly, but it was too late.

"You're cleverer than I thought," Poly told the Luck-shaped jinx, drawing in a deep, shaky breath. "I should have known when you answered questions that I didn't ask out loud. And Luck doesn't know about Mordion, by the way."

Jinx-Luck shrugged and became slightly less formed. "It was a reasonable guess."

"You only know things that I know," nodded Poly. Her voice sounded surprisingly calm to her ears, even though there was a panicked, shivery feeling in her chest that threatened to overwhelm her. She stifled the renewed feeling of regret that Luck wasn't actually there and said, "I think it might be best if I unravel you."

There was a nasty laugh as jinx-Luck faded. To Poly, it sounded derisive: the jinx was daring her to do her worst.

"We'll see about that," she told it.

There was a sense of general fogginess about the field that made her think the jinx was up to something else. She ignored it and concentrated on the jinx itself, picking tentatively at the outlying patches of it that reminded her of a tangled ball of string. Some of the ends frayed when she picked at them, but since they re-joined the moment she turned her back, Poly soon gave up the exercise and turned to prying it from the ground instead.

Whatever strength or power she had (and Poly was determined not to call it magic), it seemed to work momentarily, her fingers twitching slightly with the suggestion of lifting while something bigger and stronger inside her grasped the jinx and heaved at it. The ground quivered minutely beneath her, and then Poly found herself surrounded by a vast jungle of woven vines that met high above her head and blocked out the triad. For a claustrophobic moment she thought she'd been transported back into the castle with the thorn hedge stretching high and sharp above her, but an unfamiliar gleam of dark, shiny purple to the vines caught her eye. Had the jinx really shrunk her, or was it playing with her mind again? Certainly that was the jinx high above her head, its creeper-like form evident at this scale.

Poly sighed. It was still playing with her: taking the power she'd used to lift it and blowing it out of all proportion until she did this to herself. It probably hadn't had to do anything more than amplify the power she was using.

Very like Mordion, Poly decided. There was still a pit of coldness in her stomach, but the dread had gone. Clever the jinx might be, and it might present a very good human front, but in the end, it was technically mindless. After the barrage of Mordion's relentless, cruel intelligence, that was something of a relief. The jinx could be beaten.

Poly wasn't sure if it was her own thought or the jinx that said into the back of her mind, *Then why haven't you done it yet?*

Poly didn't trouble to make herself bigger again. There didn't seem to be much point: if the jinx had tricked her into thinking she was small, the power would only be funnelled into something else of a more nefarious nature while she tired herself out. If she really *was* as tiny as it appeared, no doubt the jinx would manage to twist any spell she tried to reverse the damage, and Poly found that she didn't like the idea of being a giant among women.

Instead, she spent some time trying not to think too much about how to defeat the jinx. It had shown such an uncanny ability to garner knowledge from her mind that she wasn't sure it wouldn't manage to stop her if she *did* find a way to dismantle it.

The jinx caught that thought and agreed. Better not to unravel. Nasty things might happen. And what would Annie do with an unravelled jinx, anyway? The jinx was what made her strawberries slightly sideways: normal strawberries would be nothing like so profitable.

"Oh, shut up," said Poly wearily. She made herself comfortable on what should have been a small pebble but was now big enough to sit on, and let her fingers run aimlessly through the different threads that made up the jinx. "I'm not going to unravel you."

The jinx did something remarkably like purring, so Poly continued to stroke her fingers through it, an idea stirring in her mind. She held it back carefully, determined not to let the jinx know what she was thinking, and let her bare fingers work sweepingly in silence. And if her fingers felt light and cool and slick with something, well, what did that matter to the jinx? It knew magic, warm and brilliant, and it knew antimagic's sharp, cutting edge. Everything else was either fodder to play with or boring landscape.

And so Poly went on coating the jinx with a strong, clear *something* that she wouldn't dare think the name of, for her own peace of mind as much as for the success of her ploy. The jinx purred again, settled, and seemed to let her existence fade to its peripheral. Something else had begun to tug at its attention—something outside the field that distracted it at once from Poly, who felt with some relief that the reinforcements must have arrived at last.

However, if reinforcements *had* arrived, it soon appeared that the most they were capable of doing was distracting the jinx. Unwilling to waste even that slight advantage, Poly pressed on anyway, keeping her mind as busy as her fingers. It was nearly finished.

It? said the jinx, in its queer, non-vocal way. Then magic, big and bright, spluttered in the beginnings of a spell, enamel blue and dancing. Poly had a startled moment to realise that it was *her* magic, *her* spell, before the jinx pounced on it, swallowing the magic whole.

Something in the world around her went terribly, terribly wrong. Life corkscrewed painfully, twisting her with it, and Poly had the brief, unpleasant sensation of meeting herself through the back of her own head. She might have imploded—or perhaps *exploded*—for one painful second, but in that second Poly found herself more *complete* somehow. When the world untwisted and then twisted back the opposite way, it brought with it a sense of loss so overpowering that at first she didn't notice the distinct lack of jinx.

Poly gave a miserable little sniff and looked vaguely around at jinx-less soil. Only it wasn't quite jinx-less—in fact, the jinx was still running quite strongly through the soil. It was just that it was somehow...*backwards*.

Michael's voice hailed her from somewhere very nearby. "Poly, you beautiful woman!"

Poly stood up tiredly, just in time to find herself enveloped in a chalk scented hug. Even her tiredness didn't prevent the thrill at being swung gaily in Michael's arms, and by the time he lowered her laughingly to the ground, she was pink and pleasantly flustered. Fortunately, there was Onepiece to attend to, and the process of unwrapping his arms from around her knees gave Poly time to recover her complexion.

He was still muttering, "*Bad* Poly! Bad, *bad* Poly!" when she managed to heave him to her hip instead, and wrapped his arms around her neck in a stranglehold.

"I'm terribly sorry, dear," said Annie. "For someone so wobbly about the knees, the child puts on a terrifying turn of speed!"

"I'm only glad you managed to keep him out," said Poly gratefully. "I can't imagine what the jinx would have done with him."

"Dear me, no; it was the Wizard who did that," Annie scoffed. "I couldn't have stopped the little rascal if I tried: not after the spell he put on me!"

Poly found herself looking over Annie's shoulder with a distinct lack of enthusiasm. "Oh. It's you."

Luck gave her a particularly bland look that made Poly blush. She'd sensed Luck there all along, of course—childish to be caught showing her ire.

"Imagine, at my age! To be caught by a standard little Immoblio spell!" said Annie, shaking her head wonderingly. "It just shows you what a few years out of practise does to a mother."

"I hate to interrupt your cluckings, Mother mine, but I really must borrow Miss Poly."

"Oh, go along with you, then!" said Annie good-naturedly.

"Here, sit down on the stile, Poly," Michael said, sweeping her back toward the fence. "You look tired. That's right, mind your legs, pup!"

Onepiece made a rude noise at him but unwrapped his skinny legs from Poly's waist for long enough to let her sit down. She did so, and looked enquiringly at Michael, who was studying her in a mix of awe and fascination, a host of questions dancing in his eyes.

At last he sucked in a breath and said conversationally, "You know, I have so many questions that I'm not sure I won't choke.

There's *that*," he nodded at the inverted jinx, "and then there's *that*."

This time he nodded at her antimagic hand—which, Poly realised belatedly, was still ungloved and very noticeable.

"Perhaps we'll start with the jinx, then," she suggested, trying for the safer ground.

Michael gave her one of his sparkling smiles. "Very well, Miss Poly. How did you do it? No, on second thoughts, *what* did you do?"

"I *think* I turned it inside out. Things were a little bit confusing in there. Everything I tried to do, the jinx twisted and turned on itself, so I thought, why not let it fix itself?"

Michael looked like he was trying hard not to smile. "Why not, indeed? Poly, has anyone ever told you that you're beautifully, maddeningly understated? No? Luck must be blind."

"Well, it wasn't terribly difficult!" protested Poly, fighting off a blush more or less successfully. "It was mostly uncomfortable. Once I'd painted the jinx with—that is, once I'd attached a spell to its tail, it more or less ate itself and then spat itself out."

"Fascinating!" said Michael, his eyes sparkling. "Poly, you must never leave the village! Life would be far too boring without you."

"What else did you want to ask about?" Poly asked him hurriedly, one eye on Luck and Annie, who had begun to stroll towards them.

"This, of course," said Michael, lifting her antimagic hand with one of his own. He traced the spiral with one finger, and Poly's fingers curled defensively to stop the pleasant shiver that ran up her arm.

"What is it?"

"Time to go home, Poly," said Luck's voice. "Margaret's waiting. The pot's probably already boiling."

Poly's glove dropped silkily into her lap, and she looked at it stupidly for a moment before it occurred to her that it must have fallen from her pocket while Michael enthusiastically swept her in circles.

She tugged it on while Luck said cheerfully to Annie, "What? No, it was an easy fix: I knew Poly could do it by herself. No need for me to get involved at all."

Poly felt her fingers twitch with a renewed urge to slap Luck, and she looked up to find his eyes on her as if he was quite well aware of her thoughts. The next moment, he grabbed her hand and Shifted them away from the jinxed field, and into the main road.

Onepiece sneezed, then giggled.

Poly meant to say, "Why must you always be so rude!" What came out, however, was, "I think we should go on to the Capital very soon."

"Huh," said Luck, sliding a look at her. "Interesting. I wouldn't listen to anything *it* said, you know."

"Oh, well, the jinx was right about some things," said Poly wearily. The sense of loss was still tugging at her soul, continuous and almost unnoticeable. "Nasty things have been happening around me for as long as I can remember—even before you woke me. Now someone is trying to kill me. Perhaps next time it will be Margaret who gets to the chocolates first. And all those *people*, Luck! It was right: Mordion only chooses people who can help him. The Frozen Battlefield—"

"Not your fault," interrupted Luck, sharply. "What on earth did that have to do with you?"

"I don't know, but *it* did."

"Rubbish!" Luck said. "The jinx only knows what you know: it works on any pieces of information it can sneak out of your mind."

"I know," Poly said. "It also said I have magic."

"Well, you don't have magic, do you?" said Luck unanswerably. "What does it know?"

Poly opened her mouth to mention the robin blue spark of magic and the way it had twined with her unmagic to bring about the jinx's downfall. Then she shut it again. If it came to confessions, she may well tell Luck that she wasn't the princess at all, and she wasn't sure she was quite ready for that. Goodness knew it would be a relief if he decided that a mere lady-in-waiting wasn't worth the same time and attention that was accorded to a princess, but she found herself reluctant all the same.

Luck, mercifully oblivious to the pregnant silence, inquired unexpectedly, "Still have that spindle, Poly?"

A mild shock fizzed through Poly's mind, and she instinctively slipped her hand into one of her pockets. It came out clasping a spindle and Poly, gazing at it, thought that she might know what this particular oddity meant. The longing in her sharpened and focused.

She said quietly, "Yes, of course."

Barely aware that she had stopped walking, Poly breathed in the cooling afternoon air and looked without really seeing at Luck, who had also obligingly stopped. He was looking distinctly encouraging, which made Poly think that he had been egging her on to discover exactly what she had discovered. She ignored the annoyance the thought caused, because she did know, now.

It was even easy to ignore the faint smile he gave when she said decisively, "I'll need my books back, Luck. *All* of them."

13

When Poly woke the next morning, it was with the teasing thought that she had puzzled out something very important last night.

Mordion wanted me to forget it, she thought drowsily, stirring beneath the covers. Her movement toppled something off the foot of the bed in a series of thumps, and Poly sat up to find her books strewn on the floor beside the bed. Even *Angwynelle* was there. With them was a dusty note in Luck's handwriting. It said: *Don't forget the spindle. And wait for me.*

Spindle! thought Poly, with a fizz of confused awareness. *What spindle?* She would have thought it was merely Luck, talking in riddles again, but the framework of the idea she'd had last night was still there in the back of her mind, clever and sound and... missing something. The structure of it was there, but its object and conclusion were ungraspable, ephemeral. *That* must be the thing that Mordion had made her forget. Added to the certainty of what she had known last night was Poly's certainty that Luck, while odd, off-kilter, and annoying, had not yet been wrong about anything.

Poly began a systematic search of her clothes from yesterday, and at last found a small wooden spindle in the front pocket of

Spindle

her apron. She frowned at it in silence for a long time, turning it over in her fingers while her mind turned it over as well. If she was right, this spindle was very important—and it was likewise very important not to forget it again. Only how could she do that if, as she was beginning to suspect, she would forget it as soon as she was not looking directly at it? Poly was certain that she and Luck had already had a similar conversation several times now; if she didn't remember what the conversations had been *about*, exactly, she did remember that there had been such conversations.

Poly turned the spindle over once more and felt the corners of her mouth turn up. She searched for a sign of that deep blue flame she had seen yesterday and, finding it deep within herself, tiny and bright, pulled out a miniscule flare of it. After some moments of puzzled searching for the thing she had meant to attach it to, Poly found Luck's note again, and by default, the spindle.

"And that's enough of *that*!" she said to it.

The blue flare stuck nicely to the spindle, piercing the air of fuzziness that surrounded it, and to her delight, Poly found that it was now always in the corner of her eye, just as it must always have been somewhere about her person. Mordion had been very careful to make sure she didn't remember the spindle, and she very much wanted to know why. There were, in fact, a lot of things she wanted to know; and if the jinx had shown her anything, it was that there was a large part of her missing. Poly thought that she might just know how to get that missing piece back.

A cautious glance down at Onepiece showed that he was still asleep, and another at Margaret gave the same result, much to her satisfaction. The triad was only just peeking over the horizon with its first sun, so there was time to spare before either of them woke. Poly began on her investigations with a kindling hope.

Luck, as usual, had been entirely correct: it *had* been her fault every time his travel spells went awry. It had something to do with the spindle and her mother's books, and that exciting and unremembered part of her that had been missing for so long that she barely felt the loss of it any longer. She had been holding *Angwynelle* the first time a travel spell went awry. Poly remembered the bright, fuzzy unreality of the hermit with his indecently short cassock and remembered suddenly also the feather he had given her. Her fingers went instinctively to the place it usually occupied, just below her right ear, and ran lightly over the soft, thin edge. The unremembered bit of herself *was* trying to get somewhere—somewhere that meant something to the full Poly.

Experimentally, she tried to pull the feather out. It didn't budge, and Poly let her mind run forward to the next botched travel spell instead. *That* had brought them to the Frozen Battlefield, and to her parents. Only the spell hadn't been a travel one, she thought, frowning. It had been a spell for shelter that Luck put up to get them out of the rain. Besides, the Frozen Battlefield hadn't been frozen when she was cursed to sleep, so how would she have known where to send herself?

She was still gazing at the spindle with narrow eyes when someone tapped at the window. Poly jumped slightly, a nervous, half guilty thought suggesting that it was Luck, but when she pulled aside the curtain, it was Michael's appreciative smile that took in her chemise and bare arms.

Poly gave him a stern look, repressing the urge to snap the curtains shut again as a hopeless loss of dignity, and cracked the window open a smidgen.

Michael's blue eyes twinkled at her, defying the stern look. "Don't be cross, Poly. I ran away from work just to see you."

"I don't believe you," said Poly, managing to hold back both a smile and a blush.

"Well, perhaps Mr. Pinks was under the impression that he'd excused me from marking out patterns to help Mother Mine plough our allotment; but can I help it if I already did the ploughing last night?"

"Is Annie planting this morning?"

"Yes, and I'm under strict instructions to stay away, and to make sure you stay away, too. Mother Mine is under the impression that you've done more than enough for us and asks if you'll come to dinner tonight. Actually, I came to say thank you and see if I could reciprocate."

"Reciprocate?"

"Well, you've that nasty curse still holding on, and I'm tricky when it comes to magic. I'm even prepared to brave Luck's annoyance. I promise I won't send you to sleep again!"

Reluctance to reveal more than was prudent warred for a moment with anticipated pleasure at Michael's undivided attention. Anticipation won.

Poly asked, "Do you have any Shift spells? Small ones will do."

"Oh, a good handy couple. Where are we going?"

"That's what I'm trying to find out," said Poly. "I'll be right out."

Fortunately, Michael wasn't a slow learner. In fact, his brief head nods and the occasional 'yes, that makes sense', insensibly made Poly feel better about her reasoning. If Luck and Michael both thought she was on the right track, it stood to reason that she *must* be.

He was quick to understand the need for travel spells, too, though he seemed to think that the source of her effect on magic was within herself rather than her books or the spindle.

"They're not bespelled," he said patiently when they were settled on a comfortable little hillock just in sight of the forest. "They *can't* be doing anything."

"Yes, that's what Luck said," said Poly. "He still took *Angwynelle* away from me, though."

"And he gave it back? Will wonders never cease!"

"Yes. *And* he was looking smug about it. I hate it when people pat me on the head for a good girl."

"Did he—"

"Not actually. But that's what it felt like."

"Does he know what you're up to?"

"More or less," said Poly, ignoring the prick of paper in her pocket that bore the words *Wait for me*. She didn't particularly feel like pandering to Luck at the moment. "Wait until I've got the book open before you begin the Shift."

"What do you think will happen?"

"Last time, I met the hermit," said Poly. "Who knows? Maybe this time I'll meet Angwynelle herself."

Michael plucked a butterflower and swished it lazily at Poly. "Why the hermit?"

"I think that might have been the picture that flipped open when I nearly dropped *Angwynelle*."

"Oh good, we can add that to our calculations," said Michael, in a pleased voice. "The more information I have, the better our chances. Which picture would you like to use?"

Poly flipped through the pages gently, bypassing the hermit's mad, grinning face, and came to the second illustration.

"How about this one? Angwynelle's chambers, before the ball."

"Are there any guardsmen in it?"

"No. No assassins, either. We should be safe with Angwynelle."

"I certainly hope so," said Michael cheerfully, "because if we die, Luck's going to kill me."

The Shift went wrong straight away. Michael said he was trying for the allotment ('Give Mother Mine a shock, good fun!') but when his magic sparked, silvery and much weaker than Luck's, there wasn't even a moment's hesitation before everything went sideways.

"Oh, you're *pretty*," purred a voice behind them.

They turned to see Angwynelle climbing into the room through the large cathedral window behind them, her breeches rather the worse for wear and her feet bare. She was looking appreciatively at Michael through her lashes, which didn't surprise Poly. What *did* surprise her was the look Angwynelle shot her: complicit, understanding, and—yes, mischievous. She circled them slowly, returning a sparkling smile from Michael with one of her own, and came to a stop in front of Poly, twirling one red gold curl around her forefinger.

"Well, you took your time," she said.

One of Michael's brows went up. "Expecting us, were you?"

"Oh yes!" said Angwynelle easily. "The hermit told me you'd been to see him. I'm a bit hurt you didn't come to see me first, actually."

"The first time was an accident," Poly said, her lips curving despite herself. "Luck did a travelling spell, and it went wrong somehow."

"Well, it would, wouldn't it? What do you expect when you weave a book into the fabric of time and space?"

"*Weave*—I did? I only have the most rudimentary spark of magic: I can't even Shift without help!"

"I wasn't talking about your magic—though now that you mention it, there's more of that hanging about, too. No, I was talking about the Other Thing."

Poly's eyes flickered briefly to Michael. "Oh. That."

Angwynelle's amused gaze caught the look. She said casually to Michael, "Be a darling and find my cerulean skerry silk scarf, will you? It's in my boudoir."

When the door snicked softly shut behind Michael, Poly found herself the subject of a thoughtful look. "You don't want him to know?"

"No. He thinks I'm Princess Persephone."

"Good heavens! Really? How did that happen?"

"Mordion was playing games: I think it might have been his idea."

Angwynelle's mouth opened soundlessly. Then she said, slowly, "You still don't remember."

"Not very much, no," said Poly, a little curtly. "What do you know?"

"Only as much as you do. Did. Well, this is awkward."

Angwynelle pursed cherry red lips and narrowed her eyes at Poly. "You knew what I meant when I said *the other thing*."

"Unmagic, you mean? Yes. I found it yesterday."

The dismay on Angwynelle's face was plain to see. "Only yesterday? You were meant to remember much sooner. What about the hermit? Didn't you get his spell?"

Poly wordlessly twitched the feather from beneath her hair.

"Why haven't you used it?"

"It wouldn't come out."

"Oh," said Angwynelle again. "You know, I don't think you planned for this. You should know everything by now."

"I don't remember planning for *any* of it," Poly complained. "Look, what do you know about Mordion?"

"Oh, you had a *lot* to say about him. Let's see: when you wrote me he was trying to cut the spindle out of your mind, but you appear to have fixed that already. It was only a bit more than the standard Look Away/Forget Me spell to prevent it being any use."

"Luck said there was no spell on the spindle."

"You didn't put it *on* the spindle, exactly. You were trying not to let him see you do it, so you sort of spelled a part of your own mind. The spindle, plus a reasonable bit of magic, and *ha!* there you are! Hidden memories regained."

Poly's gaze sharpened on Angwynelle. "Oh! And to activate the process—"

"One pricked finger and a little bit of blood," nodded Angwynelle. "But when you wrote me, Mordion was being difficult, and you had to improvise awfully quickly. I don't know what else you did to that spindle, but I know there *was* something else."

"And the books?"

"You wanted somewhere to store all your magic so that Mordion couldn't use it. The curse on you was put to spellpaper to make it legally binding; you, as servant to the Crown, were at the disposal of the Crown, for the good of the Crown, etcetera, etcetera."

"How much did he get?" asked Poly, feeling suddenly very sick. She had been right—or at least, the jinx, in delving through her mind, had been right. "And how much was there?"

Angwynelle said frankly, "I don't know exactly how much there was, but it was an *awful* lot. You funnelled as much as you could into the books, and your hair took all the unmagic that wasn't helping the spell, but he got enough. That's the last information I have about Mordion: you were gone after that."

"Gone where?"

Angwynelle shrugged one shoulder elegantly. "You tell me."

"I can guess," Poly grimaced. "You said I wove this book through space and time. Why?"

"Not just this one: all of them." Angwynelle added, with simple pride, "I'm a trilogy, you know. There are hundreds of copies, too; all through the Three Monarchies. You didn't tell me why, though. I'm just to give you the magic and be generally helpful. I think you thought you'd remember."

"Well, I don't," grumbled Poly.

"I can show you the inside of the spell, if you like. It's all tendons and complicated time shuffle, though: *I* can't make head or tail of it."

"I might as well look," Poly said fatalistically. "I won't understand, but I might as well, since I'm here."

"That's the spirit," said Angwynelle encouragingly. "Anyway, it's your spell: that might help. Over here, behind the window seat."

They were still trying to shuffle the window seat out of its snug little alcove when Michael came back.

"Finished your little chat?" he enquired, wafting a blue scarf at them.

Angwynelle gave him an enchanting little grin and twitched the scarf from his fingers. "Quite finished. Help us move the seat?"

"With pleasure, dear ladies! What are we—oh. Well now. That's more than a bit frightening."

Poly looked into a dazzling array of curling, variegated threads that wove in and out of each other to form a terrifyingly powerful spell, and felt as though the spell might possibly be looking back at her. Michael was right: it was both vast and frightening. There was more of her missing than memories. This type of spell took *knowledge*. Where had that knowledge gone?

"What *is* that?" he asked, lounging across the window seat on his stomach. "It's—wait, is it *moving*?"

"Yes," said Poly, more briskly than she felt.

She ran one finger carefully along a strand that seemed bluer than its fellows, and knew with an oddly unbalanced feeling that wavered between familiarity and strangeness that this was certainly her magic. Her magic, and—

"The Other Thing," nodded Angwynelle. She was watching Poly steadily, but her eyes had lost their twinkle and were serious. "It's new and raw, and so is the magic."

"It can't be!" Michael said, sitting up. "That would mean the caster only just came into his power when he performed the spell. You can't make a spell like that on a month's notice. You couldn't on a *year's* notice."

"Not unless you knew an awful lot of theory to start with," said Angwynelle quietly.

The faint ache that spoke of missing pieces stung again, and Poly wondered bitterly just how much knowledge Mordion had taken from her.

Michael looked swiftly from Angwynelle to Poly, opened his mouth, and closed it again. Eventually he said, "Don't think I didn't notice your 'so is'! What else is it made of? I know that's not just magic."

"No, it's not," agreed Poly. She found herself thinking, ridiculously, Well, if Luck had been right, so had she. Before Mordion, and the curse, and Midsummer Night's Eve, she *hadn't* had magic. Not magic, nor unmagic. "It must have been something Mordion did," she said slowly. "Perhaps the curse woke something up."

Michael leaned over her shoulder, tickling her ear with his hair. "Is that part of the curse?"

"Oh, what a shame," sighed Angwynelle. "And you're so pretty, too. It's got nothing to do with the curse, simpkin: it all belongs to Poly."

"I might be a simpkin, but I'm certain I remember you telling me that you don't *have* magic, Poly."

"I didn't know about it then," said Poly, and thought, *How ridiculous! I didn't know it then, but I did **before** then.* She added, "Now I have a little bit again: it's not much, though."

"This should help," said Angwynelle, looping the blue scarf around Poly's neck. "Play with it later, Poly: what about the spell? Helpful or not?"

"I can see what little bits of it are for, but not how it all works together. Oh, I wish Luck was here!"

"Yes, about that," said Michael unexpectedly. "You didn't tell him where we were going, did you?"

Poly thought about it and then said carefully, "He knows where we are."

"But he was meant to come with you, wasn't he? Don't try to flummox me, Miss Poly!" he accused, eyes dancing in spite of the severe tone. "I know that look: I've seen it on Margaret scores of times. If we're playing hooky, I want to know when to run."

"I'll give you good warning," promised Poly. She sat back on her heels and sighed. Of Angwynelle, she inquired, "Will I be able to get back once we're out?"

"To this particular point in the book?" asked Angwynelle. "No. But there are dozens of illustrations: some more of me, even. Come back and see me when you can. You can access the spell from anywhere in the book if you know where to look."

"Good. Luck will want to see it."

Angwynelle's eyes narrowed. "Who *is* this Luck? Why didn't you bring him with you?"

"It's time to go home," said Poly hastily.

Angwynelle would only flirt with Luck anyway, and Poly

thought that such an exercise would be rather irritating to watch. It was bad enough to have to stand by stupidly while she flirted with Michael. What if, she thought rather wistfully, what if Lady Cimone had taught Poly how to flirt with her eyelashes and charm with her conversation, instead of stuffing her head full of history and language and how to read a courtier through the surface lies?

Then I'd be Angwynelle, and who would be me? said her thoughts.

"I'll find out, you know," sang Angwynelle. Her eyes, wickedly dancing, caught and held Poly's. "A pretty simpkin and...a Luck? Which one?"

"*Neither!*" squeaked Poly, mortified. Michael was grinning, which made it worse; but he also winked at her. "We have to go now!"

Angwynelle made a pout that only just escaped being a purse-lipped smile. "Oh, all right. You first, simpkin: through the window."

"A thousand pleasures to have met you, mistress!" said Michael, still charming from his straddled position on the windowsill.

"Yes, I know," said Angwynelle, and pushed him off. She grinned unrepentantly at Poly but said: "I won't push you. Promise. Wasn't his surprise delicious, though!"

"That wasn't nice," Poly said, but her voice burred on a laugh, and Angwynelle laughed along with her.

"You know you wanted to do it, too. You *had* to. Well, I mean, I *am* you, after all. Idealized and romanticized, but I'm you, all the same."

"Of course you are," Poly sighed. "I really think I must have been too clever for my own good. But I don't flirt, you know."

"I know," said Angwynelle, helping her over the sill in a sisterly fashion. Her face was already beginning fade, and the colour leached from her red gold hair as Poly slid tentatively across the sill into emptiness. "That's why I do!"

Reality hit with a gentle bump and nudged Poly into a flowery hillock.

"There you are!" said Michael.

His face was both pleasantly and frighteningly close, and he seemed content to tickle Poly's nose with a butterflower while she collected her scattered wits. His proximity made the exercise considerably more difficult. If Poly hadn't discovered the blue skerry silk scarf around her neck when her fingers automatically fluttered to check that she was still all in one piece, she might have lain there for some time still, gazing up into Michael's blue eyes. The cool, slippery slick of it around her neck made Poly sit up rather quickly, which seemed to startle Michael as much as being pushed off the windowsill had.

"Now that's interesting!" he said, surprise melting into curiosity in the blink of an eye. "How did you bring a physical something out of an ethereal something? That shouldn't be possible."

"Yes, Luck's always complaining about that. I don't think it's really a something, though: I think it just looks like a something."

Michael gazed at her limpidly. "Erudition fairly drips from your lips, Miss Poly! Dizzying, unfathomable...and, well, I honestly don't know what in the Two Monarchies you just said."

Poly gave vent to a little spurt of laughter. "I mean that it only *looks* like a scarf. It's a little bit of my magic: I seem to have stored bits and pieces of it through the trilogy to collect when I escaped from the curse."

"That really was your spell?"

Poly lifted one shoulder. "It must be. I recognised the magic."

"What about the spindle? You said it does two things: makes you remember, and pushes spells to take you somewhere you need to go."

"That's what I can't quite figure out," said Poly regretfully. "I seem to have spelled my mind to access memories that Mordion tried to take away, but the spell only works in the right conditions. Now that I know how, I should be able to get them back. It's the way the spindle hijacks Luck's spells that I can't figure out. The spindle itself isn't bespelled: there isn't even any magic in it."

"Nothing at all?"

"Not the tiniest—oh! Oh! I wonder if I was that clever?"

"Of course you were!" said Michael, pleasingly prompt. Poly couldn't help laughing, which made him grimace self-deprecatingly. "Habit, Miss Poly; sheer habit! What were you clever about?"

"I don't think I put a sneaky spell on the spindle. I think I took magic *out* of it."

"It must be clever: I don't understand it at all."

"It was one of the first things Lady Cimone taught me," explained Poly, feeling automatically for the tag of blue magic that flagged the spindle. "One of the lessons in theory that I seem to be able to remember. Magic abhors a vacuum. Almost everything and everyone has the tiniest bit of magic in them because an absolute absence of magic attracts magic. I think I pulled every last bit of magic out of it because I knew I'd need as much as I could collect after, or *if*, I managed to break free from the curse. It's pulled me from power source to power source and collected more magic every time."

"That's easy enough to prove," said Michael interestedly. "Obviously my magical education has been deficient. Out with it, Miss Poly! Only you will put your books away first, won't you? I don't think I could survive another encounter with Angwynelle: she may be beautiful, but she's the most terrifying thing south of the Forest."

"Do you have enough energy to work another Shift spell?"

"That hurts me, Miss Poly!" said Michael solemnly, and then grinned. "Honestly, no: but I have a small Shifter in my signet for emergencies."

"Is there a good strong magic source nearby?"

"There's the Forest, but we don't want to be stealing magic from there," said Michael feelingly, and Poly just as feelingly acquiesced. "The jinx is closer, and it's one of the stronger pulls in the village, but the village clock is the strongest of the two. Will the spindle look for the nearest source?"

"I don't think it *looks* for magic, exactly; it's just that magic is attracted to the emptiness of no magic, and sort of—well, reaches out. Then the magic pours in trying to fill the vacuum."

"Then the closest source should be the one that pulls us?"

"I assume so," said Poly dubiously. "But I don't know if there was anything closer than the Frozen Battlefield when it pulled us in, so I can't say for sure."

"Reasonable risk," Michael said cheerfully. "If we die in the attempt—"

"Luck will kill you," nodded Poly.

"Well, I was going to say that I wouldn't speak to you again, but that too. Are you ready?"

Poly briefly displayed the spindle between her fingers, and as briefly nodded. "Remind me to put the tag back on, won't you? Only I'll forget it if you don't."

She pulled the flicker of blue magic back into her hand, and just for a moment forgot why she and Michael were standing there, waiting.

Then Michael said, "Here we go, Miss Poly!" with a tiny blaze of sliver magic, and something vast and ageless and terrifyingly strong narrowed its gaze on them...and *pounced*.

The Shift happened either very quickly or very slowly, Poly wasn't quite sure which. All she was certain of was a sense of being lifted by the scruff of her neck like a recalcitrant puppy and deposited somewhere that was somehow alive and hard to breathe in. The shadows, velvety green, seemed to move without sound. Poly barely recognised the wild, living greenery as the quiet and really quite civilised forest she'd entered the night of the games.

"How did we end up in—"

"The Forest," said Michael hoarsely. "Poly, please tell your hair to stop sucking up forest magic. The Forest is very protective."

"I don't—oh, that's *strong!*" panted Poly. "I can't stop it, Michael! I can't—it's too strong and there's too much of it. Oh! Michael, please Shift us! It keeps pushing more in and *I can't fit any more!*"

Under the oppressive weight of too much, too strong magic, Poly only vaguely felt Michael prise something out of her hand. The light flicker of silver magic that Michael attached to the spindle helped her to remember that it was the spindle, but by then she was drowning in a surfeit of forest magic. She vaguely felt Michael slip his arms around her and was as vaguely grateful to be able to let her head drop onto his chest.

The Forest must have let them go. Poly wasn't sure if it was because the spindle was no longer so obviously magic-less, or if it was because Michael's Shifting spell blazed stronger than before in his urgency to get away; but after another, too full moment there was blissful weightlessness. Poly found herself able to appreciate the pleasure of being embraced by Michael for one delightful second.

Then Margaret's voice, quiet and a little bit scratchy, said, "Oh, Poly, not Michael too!"

Poly's dazed look around comprehended a dizzying catalogue: walls, house—*Luck's* house; Margaret, pale and big eyed; Josie, thoughtful and sharp eyed; Annie, cheerful but watchful; and Luck looking white about the mouth with Onepiece's skinny wrist grasped in one hand. She looked up and met Michael's blue eyes, which were startled and somehow undecided. His mouth opened as a flurry of skirts attended Margaret's dash from the house. Then Poly was let go abruptly, cold and shaken, and Michael dashed for the door.

"Margaret! Wait, it wasn't—Meg! Please!"

"Well done, Poly!" said Josie's fat voice, complacently. "I've been wondering exactly what it would take to shake a bit of sense into those two."

"I always like an autumn wedding," Annie said.

Poly blinked and smiled painfully, hoping that she didn't look as shocked and miserable as she felt. She found herself gazing stupidly at Luck, whose eyes had gone very green and narrow, and heard him say, "What do you mean by going into the Forest when I tell you not to?"

"Accident," whispered Poly, tears threatening to spill over. Josie saw the exhaustion, if not the tears, and became bustlingly supportive, calling on Luck not to be 'too hard on the poor mite'; and even Annie was bold enough to say, "Look at her! Pebbles and Primroses, she's all done in!"

"Out, biddies!" demanded Luck outrageously. "I won't have 'poor Poly' here and 'poor Poly' there! She sneaks out behind my back, steals magic from the forest, and won't share! Out!"

"Well, I never!" said Josie, but she said it on her way out the door, and Annie was even quicker to go, with a commiserating smile at Poly.

When the door shut behind them Luck dropped Onepiece's wrist and said, "Well, that got rid of them. Are you going to cry now?"

"Um," said Poly in a watery voice, not quite sure, herself.

She sat down by a pile of scalloped metal and Onepiece pattered over to cling to her knees, looking anxiously down at the tears that were trying to escape. His painfully worried look was at first touching and then amusing, and in playing games with his fingers to cheer him up, Poly found herself gradually regaining her composure.

Luck sat down next to them at some stage and said, "He was too young for you anyway, Poly."

Poly gave a slightly wet giggle. "Of course! I couldn't think of anyone under the age of four hundred!"

"That's right," said Luck. "And he'd never be able to keep up with you. Your hair is growing again, by the way."

"I know," said Poly, fighting back another wave of misery. "I really liked him, Luck. I thought—well, for a minute I thought he was—"

Luck was observing a violet stain on one cuff. "I thought so too. Thought his taste was beginning to improve."

"You yelled at me."

"Oh. Yes. Sorry about that. You needed a moment to—"

Poly stretched up to kiss him on the cheek. "Thank you. Onepiece, don't do that to my hair. I'm trying to tie it up."

Luck silently watched her tie her braid with the blue scarf and then asked, "Where did you find your magic?"

"Angwynelle had it. Did you know I wove—"

"—an entire trilogy of books into time and space? Yes. Well, I guessed. Nifty work, that."

"We were testing a theory with the spindle when the forest pulled us in."

"Told you not to go into the forest," said Luck mildly.

"Michael thought we'd end up at the clock tower."

"Huh. I knew he was an idiot. The spindle doesn't pull magic, magic pulls *it*. The stronger the pull, the likelier you'll end up with it."

"I know that *now*," said Poly. "I keep going wrong. I'm missing some memories I need to have."

"I'll get the dog to bite you again. So long as there's blood it should trigger your sensory programming."

"Not those ones. That's from the day before it happened." Poly paused, struggling with the concept, and at last said, "I don't think it's memories, exactly. I think it's knowledge. A big piece of knowing that I used to know, and don't know any more. Magic theory and court politics were the two things that Lady Cimone taught, but I only remember the politics and some basics of magic theory."

"Someone took them out of your head," nodded Luck. "They must have been very much afraid of you, Poly. There are three kinds of preventatives in the three-verse curse itself, two more in the spellpaper, and you're spelled to fall asleep again every time you think about the castle or your old life. They made certain you wouldn't wake up, and that if you *did*, you'd never be a threat to them."

"He always did like chess," Poly said. "It's all a game to him, but he'll always make sure he's at least six moves ahead of you."

"You're talking about Mordion again. I told you, it can't be him."

"It can't be, but it is. He was there, in the memories I don't remember."

"Then it must be a *different* one," said Luck stubbornly.

Onepiece, looking from Poly to Luck, said hopefully, "Bite?"

Luck said, "Yes," his eyes brightening.

Poly said, "No, darling. Maybe later. Luck, we really ought to leave the village: someone trying to kill me nearly killed Margaret."

"More importantly, someone knows you're the princess and has been sending messages to the Capital," said Luck, leading Poly to wonder who was the less important factor: herself, or Margaret.

She found herself faintly smiling. "Why does it matter what information gets back to the Capital? We'll be there soon, anyway."

"Yes, but there are over a hundred miles of bumpy road between us and the Capital, and highwaymen are a bore. They yell and wave pistols about, and sometimes a bullet is faster than magic and then your horse ends up dead. Besides, I prefer to know exactly how much the bunch of them know before I wander into the Council Hall. The communications magic I found wasn't linked to the message tubes: someone was talking face to face through magic, and I can't spy on that."

"You're not supposed to look at anyone else's messages, anyway," Poly said.

She knew this because she had been the uncomfortable spectator in a scene between Josie and Margaret, who was furious to learn that her mother had been briefly riffling through her messages when they arrived daily through the tubes. The tubes,

Poly had discovered quite quickly, were not really tubes but a stream of disseminated information. They disintegrated paper messages at the sender's end and reconstituted them in somewhat flimsier paper form at the other end. She had been fascinated by the idea, used as she was to colourful pages and liveried messengers, and had been startled to discover that there were laws, actual *laws*, made solely for the governance of the tubes.

Luck looked startled at the reminder, and said hastily: "Yes, well, never mind that, Poly. We'll leave tomorrow."

"Without travelling spells," agreed Poly. She'd had quite enough of travel spells for the time being.

"Oh, we don't need spells," said Luck blithely. "Didn't I tell you? I have a coach."

14

Poly dreamed the night pleasantly through and woke up in a room as unfamiliar as it was familiar. Instead of Margaret's bed there was a shelf of books, covers sharp and new; and instead of the window was something that shifted and glittered and tried to bulge forward.

Poly flopped back onto her pillow and groaned. Onepiece wasn't on the bed with her, but that didn't surprise her: the bed, after all, was only a metaphysical projection. Somehow or other, Poly had woken up in her own mind.

It hadn't changed much since the last time she visited, thought Poly, sliding from the bed and wandering cautiously about the room. Still, there was enough of a difference for her to notice it. That difference was mainly in the bookshelf, packed tight with a great many more books than she remembered, but the curse seemed to have altered a little, too. It was turbulent and somehow desperate, which should have worried her. Instead, it made her feel that in some inexplicable way, the curse wasn't so very far from being broken.

The books wouldn't open when she pulled them from the shelves to try one bright, stubborn tome after the other.

Poly said, "Bother," glumly.

It was obvious what the books were: they were the metaphysical representation of her knowledge in magical theory. She looked for any trace of magic or unmagic on the books, cautiously optimistic that she could break the spell if only she could see it, and fancied that she could see a tracery of crisscrossed, clear thread sewing up the edges of the book she held.

Unmagic, then. Poly had peeled off her glove and attempted to shake out her antimagic hand before she remembered that it wasn't her real arm, and that the antimagic wasn't really there. She felt her not-real face go pink just as it would have if it was real, and frowned, tapping the spine of one book with her forefinger. She could feel Luck's presence pushing hard at her from somewhere outside, making it difficult to concentrate, and Poly rather thought she'd prefer to remain asleep until she'd sorted a few things out.

Then Luck's voice said, very clearly, "Poly, if you don't wake up, I'm going to have to kiss you again."

"Go away," Poly said back, though she wasn't sure he could hear. She pulled at something ephemeral and whispy that she thought was the antimagic in her arm, and somehow it was actually obeying her.

"Well, I tried," said Luck's voice. This time it was closer: it sounded as though he was looking over her shoulder. "You're not going to like this, Poly."

This kiss was nothing like Luck's first kiss. It was just as insistent as the first had been, but this time it was also soft and pliable, and the feeling of being surrounded by it resolved into the comprehension that Luck's arms were wrapped around her. It woke her at once, with a shock and a clarity that Poly didn't remember feeling when she'd woken the first time, but when she sat up with life blazing through her limbs, Luck moved with her.

He didn't stop kissing her, in fact, until Margaret, who was kneeling beside the bed and looking prim, cleared her throat with a ladylike, *"ahem!"*

"Yow!" said Poly, when she'd got her breath back. "That *fizzed!*"

Luck, looking pleased with himself, disentangled himself from her hair and sat back at the foot of the bed.

Margaret gave a scandalized giggle. "Poly!"

"Well, it did," Poly said defiantly. "My head is much clearer now."

"I should think *so!*" Margaret said, but her voice had lost the scandalized note. "Oh Poly, I'm sorry about yesterday! Michael explained it all, and it was all a big misunderstanding, and we're as happy as a pair of hand fed skerry! Oh! And I got your frocks!"

Poly found herself bemusedly clutching a tightly packed bundle, much to the vociferous disapproval of Onepiece, who was also clutched in her arms, his skinny arms wrapped around her torso.

"Luck *squish!*" he said indignantly. "Now splat on head! Poor Onepiece!"

Poly put the package aside but laughed at Onepiece, which seemed to please him. He grinned his slack jawed grin up at her and loosened his skinny arms from her torso long enough to wrap them around her neck instead.

"That's not a dog, that's a limpet," said Luck. He was watching them narrowly. "Poly, you've done something else impossible, and I don't know what it is."

"If you don't know, I'm sure *I* don't. And Onepiece is not a dog, he's a boy."

"Boy!" agreed Onepiece, making a rude face at Luck.

Luck made one back, surprising a giggle from both Poly and Margaret, and stood up. "You've got a quarter hour, Poly," he said.

"A quarter hour for what?" said Poly to the closing door.

"That's how long it takes for him to assemble the coach and input the directions," explained Margaret. "I packed the frocks to travel, so mind you hang them as soon as you unpack them. The spell will stop when you untie the string."

Poly took a bewildered moment to realise that Leaving was

not just Today, but Now, and mechanically disengaged Onepiece's arms from around her neck. As she did, something that had been pressed between them dropped to the floor with a loud thump.

"You shouldn't read in bed," said Margaret, stooping to pick up a familiar book. "No wonder you can't wake up in the morning."

Poly took it from her dumbly: it was the shiny new unopenable book she'd been holding before Luck woke her up. It was still unopenable when she mechanically tried it, but Margaret's curious look and Onepiece's avid interest caused her to tuck it away beneath the parcel of clothes with a loop of Don't See Me magic, and then, when she was dressed, into her pocket.

THEY LEFT the village in style. True to his word, Luck had managed to produce some species of coach—fat, bulbous thing that it was—and although it was ridiculous, it also proved ridiculously comfortable. Besides, anything was better than another of Luck's Journey spells gone awry.

Once the coach appeared outside Margaret's window, the morning began to blend together in a blur of action. Poly wasn't sorry for it. Michael had come to wave goodbye along with Margaret, and when his blue eyes failed to meet hers for the third time in a row it occurred to Poly that for Michael at least, it had been a close thing. She tried to feel glad for the obviously happy Margaret, but she couldn't help wishing that she had a little more of the bounce and vivacity that had won Michael's heart.

Luck was busy muttering magical instructions to the thin air between the coach shafts, so Poly hugged Margaret, who hugged her fiercely back, and then smiled a friendly smile at Michael, who gave her one of his old grins and at last met her eyes.

"Look after the wizard," he said. She thought he might have been about to hug her, but Luck breezed around the corner, his muttering finished, and swept her along with him instead.

Spindle

"Up you go, Poly; we can't wait around all day. The highwaymen will be getting restless."

Poly allowed herself to be shooed along, hampered slightly by Onepiece—who, it turned out, did not care to ride in the carriage, and made realistic sick noises to illustrate his displeasure when Poly ordered him to climb in anyway. She pushed him up the three perilously steep steps into the carriage, but the calculating look she caught from beneath his lashes prompted her to wonder if Onepiece was at last beginning to test his boundaries. She wasn't sure if the thought terrified or pleased her.

A huge basket of provisions was given pride of place on the backward-facing seat, as was Poly's parcel of new clothes. Much to Poly's surprise, Luck seated himself beside both basket and parcel, one leg stretched across the gap between seats, his booted foot braced against the seat cushion and his arms flung comfortably over the basket and the back of the seat respectively.

Poly felt the coach lurch into motion and saw a row of smiling, waving townspeople. "Who's directing the coach?"

"You go pink when you're agitated, Poly."

"I'm not agitated," Poly said. "I'm terrified! Doesn't even a magically propelled coach need a driver?"

"I am driving it," said Luck, closing his eyes. "You'd know that if you knew what you were seeing."

"I see a swirl of magic that doesn't mean anything to me," Poly said. Her fingers automatically tapped the book in her pocket. If Luck was going to sit there with his eyes closed, there was no reason for her not to play with it. "Oh yes," she added, seizing Onepiece's waistband to prevent him from tumbling out the window. "And I want my spellpaper."

"Want to *ride*," said Onepiece crossly, clinging to the window despite Poly's admonitory tug.

Luck opened his eyes and said, "All right," with one of his sweet smiles, and after a brief search of his pockets, passed the gleaming paper to Poly, who had been expecting a fight and accepted it in astonished silence. She tucked it into her own pocket, half expecting it to disappear.

Luck was, in fact, in an entirely good mood. He stretched out on his side of the coach, closed his eyes again and, Poly presumed, drove the coach. It was hard for her to tell. She could see all the connecting threads of the spell—the ones that looped around the shafts of the coach, the ones that looped around Luck's wrists. She even thought she could see Luck doing something with the changing patterns. In spite of that, Poly couldn't make head or tail of it. The spell was utterly alien.

Still, she watched the swirls and concentric cogs of it until magic danced in her mind when she blinked. She tore her eyes away from it eventually, beaten, and her tightly shut book seemed to mock her with hidden knowledge from its pocket. Luck's eyes were still closed, so Poly tightened her hold on Onepiece's trousers as they bounced over a particularly rough patch of road, and slid the book from her pocket.

The loop of Don't See magic was still around it loosely, and she left it there, mistrustful of Luck's closed eyes. Even with it in place she could still pick at the seams of unmagic that bound the book closed, and though she didn't want to spare a hand to wrestle the glove off her antimagic hand, Poly felt the antimagic at the back of her mind where it had been earlier in the day, and drew on it.

It came to her willingly, and Poly, following Luck's lead, braced herself with one foot against the opposite seat and tilted the book against her knee. She didn't really need to use her fingers but she did anyway, delicately hooking an invisible thread sickle of antimagic through the strands of unmagic that were holding the book closed. To her pleasure, the antimagic cut through the threads with ease. Poly pinched them away from the book as she cut them, dropping each one carefully onto the floor of the coach until she realised that they were wafting into her hair anyway, where they made brief spangles of colour before fading to black.

Onepiece wriggled back down into his seat partway through the operation, his interest piqued, and watched her intently with wide brown eyes as she worked. Poly, finding it easier to unpick with two hands, gave him a piece of the unmagic to play with and was very soon plucking the last few threads from the boards of her book.

Onepiece stopped playing with his loose end of unmagic for long enough to bounce eagerly on the seat. "Open, open!"

Poly sneaked another look at Luck, who was still leaning against the wall of the coach, eyes closed. Well, what could it hurt? She slid one finger under the coverboard, and was faintly surprised when it lifted from the pages without effort. She exchanged a delighted smile with Onepiece and flicked the cover open completely.

"Pah," said Onepiece, his smile fading into a scowl. "Still tricksy."

The book was empty. Blank pages whirred beneath Poly's fingers as she flipped through it, each page as smooth and clear as the day the paper was made.

-*This can't be right!*- said Poly silently, stung by the unfairness of it all. -*Not when I've just got it open!*-

-*one missing*- said Onepiece, who seemed to be struggling to find the right words. He made silent shapes with his mouth before scowling and giving up. -*one half gone walking away. not far away now*-

Poly said crossly: -*Of course it is! And where is it, I would like to know!*-

"Not got it," said Onepiece immediately. "Maybe *per*haps string is in the way?"

"Perhaps," allowed Poly, charmed to hear a very nearly correct sentence from him. To her dismay, Onepiece took her approval as encouragement, and darted one hand toward the book. Before she could stop him, the Don't See loop was around Onepiece's skinny wrist, and the book had gone back to being very noticeable indeed.

Across the coach, Luck's eyes opened, gold and green in swirls. "Poly, I'm going to invade your personal space," he said.

Used as she was to Luck invading her personal space, Poly still wasn't prepared for him to lunge across the coach and kiss her thoroughly.

When she got her breath back, she said, "You're going to have to stop doing that, you know."

"No, I won't," said Luck. "Why should I? Poly, you are a beautiful, impossible woman. I knew you were hiding something."

"It's *mine*."

"Yes. Oh, yes, very much yours. You've bought back a corporeal something from meta-space again."

"I know," said Poly, eyeing him warily. He looked as though he might kiss her again. "It's my—"

"Knowledge. Yes. I know that. How do you know that?"

"I guessed. And she—"

"She? Huh. The other one was male. Why didn't you introduce me? More to the point, why did you go by yourself?"

"I didn't go by myself; I went with Michael."

"That's another thing, Poly. You can't go wandering off with strange men."

"I can, you know," said Poly, feeling argumentative. "I'm making quite a habit of it, actually. I wandered off with *you*."

"Yes, but I'm not a strange man."

"Yes, you are. You're the strangest man I've ever met," said Poly. "Why can't I wander off with anyone I want to?"

"Poly, you're deliberately being difficult!" complained Luck. "The curse is broken!"

Poly gazed at him in bewilderment. "I know it's broken! I feel wide awake for the first time in hundreds of years. What on earth has that got to do with anything?"

"It's broken," said Luck again. He looked distinctly offended. "Why don't you understand?"

"I give up!" said Poly, throwing up her hands. Onepiece

copied the action, chuckling in his gruff voice, and drummed his heels against the kickboard.

Poly endured Luck's scowl until it faded into thoughtfulness and gold began to rim his pupils. She was almost beginning to think that anything would be preferable to spending much longer in the same carriage as Luck, when something delicate pierced through the carriage spell and seemed to look at them.

Luck said, "Huh. That's interesting," and then the carriage was wrenched to a violent halt, tossing Poly and Onepiece into his arms.

Onepiece gave a doglike yelp and Poly gasped painfully, wincing in vicarious pain when her left elbow jabbed into Luck's stomach.

Luck exhaled forcefully somewhere around her ear, but still said quite cheerfully, "Oh, *here* they are! Poly, you can't sit on my knee right now: we're about to be boarded."

Poly tried to scramble herself into some semblance of order, and inadvertently elbowed him in the stomach again. "What? Why?"

"I'm beginning to think you're doing that on purpose," said Luck, hoisting her up by the waist. "Here, sit down before you hurt yourself. They're boarding because they want to kidnap you."

Poly automatically snatched up Onepiece. "I thought they wanted to kill me."

"The other ones do. These ones will want you alive. I told you about them before, Poly. Royalists, this lot: they're all mad, but at least they're stupid."

He kicked the door open and someone outside went reeling with a burst of invective. The air had grown thick with magic—magic of so many different kinds that Poly was hard put to distinguish between them all. And surrounding the carriage, in masks of various cut and hue, were roughly twenty men. Onepiece, who had been indignantly struggling to see outside, abruptly went still and dived under her arm in his puppy form.

"You can stay inside if you want," said Luck, climbing down. "It's a bit stuffy out here. *Don't* throw that at me."

An overeager kidnapper ignored the command and sent something buzzing and slightly blue through the charged air. Poly saw surprise in the eyes above the mask when the spell puffed harmlessly against Luck's ear and sent a reversed charge streaking back toward the caster. Three masked men in that general direction dived away from the offender just in time to avoid the messy capture spell that encased him in sticky black ropes of magic.

Luck said, "That's what you get for being rude. What do you want?"

"We want the Princess," said the nearest masked man.

"You can't have her. What else?"

The kidnapper who was still struggling to escape his own spell, yelled angrily, "You! Dead!"

"You can't have that either," snapped Poly, sticking her head out the coach window.

She was feeling very pink and annoyed, and it made her angry that Onepiece had been frightened back into his puppy form.

At the sight of her, a handful of the kidnappers dropped to their knees, and the leader bowed deeply. "I know not by which manner of lies this knave hath imposed upon thee, fair princess," he said. "But in our hands lies your succour. Plead not for the life of this varlet!"

The speech, cumbersome and archaic, took far too long to make sense in Poly's mind. It was something of a shock to realise that he was addressing her in Old Civetan.

"I'm very familiar with the current dialect, thank you very much!" she told him sharply. "Call your men off!"

He bowed again. "I regret that I can't, your highness. I'm sorry."

"He thinks I've bespelled you," said Luck. "Suspicious lot,

Royalists. Think anyone who doesn't agree with them must have been subverted by the Council."

"Well, they're upsetting Onepiece. Can you get rid of them?"

"Probably. Maybe. Someone has given them a few nasty toys to play with."

"All right, then," said Poly, and sat down again.

She tucked Onepiece under one arm and fumbled with her book until it was open on her lap. Outside, something vastly magic sucked at the air, popping her ears, and Onepiece whined.

"Oh, *won't* I teach you to frighten Onepiece!" said Poly wrathfully.

The book tried to slither away from her, obstinately unreadable, and she stripped the glove from her antimagic hand with her teeth, pinning the book ruthlessly between leg and palm. The book wriggled without much hope and eventually gave up, but not a word appeared on its snowy pages. Poly set her teeth and reached further in, pushing at the boundaries of Real and Not Real.

Magic was already flying outside the carriage, fast and thick, when she looked out briefly. After that one anxious look Poly concentrated on the book, sickened by the sight of Luck at the centre of a deadly, multicoloured whorl. The reality of the book had parted beneath her hand, and that was all that could matter, because it was slippery, illusive, and somehow *incomplete*.

Poly crooned, "You clever boy!" at Onepiece. The puppy had told her what the problem was, in his roundabout way: the book itself was only half of the spell. The other half, the half that would complete and break the spell, was missing.

The carriage rocked. Poly and Onepiece were hurled across the seat once again, and when Poly looked dazedly out the window, clasping Onepiece in one arm and her book in the other, Luck had disappeared. She was up and out of the carriage before she realised what she was doing, leaving Onepiece to scrabble on the cushions, and found herself plunging headfirst into a miasma of deadly magic that was only loosely being controlled by someone in the group.

Luck sat in the dirt, looking rather surprised and damp. "Better get back in the carriage," he said to her, his voice strained. "They can't get at you in there."

"What about you?"

"Some fool gave these madmen specialty target-oriented magic," he said. "The carriage has a failsafe clause that'll trip when—well, it'll send you back to the village."

"*What* failsafe?" demanded Poly.

She was trembling in a very unpleasant way, and she was quite sure she knew what kind of failsafe Luck had on the coach.

"Poly, get back in the coach!"

"Books," said Poly aloud, her eyes distant and shiny. "Books are for reading. But I can't read it. There are no words. Blank books are no use. Blank books are—oh!" She looked up at the leader and said icily, "Let Luck go."

"Can't!" panted the leader. He was quite obviously struggling to control the magic that spiralled from himself to Luck. Poly was coldly certain that before long he would be in the same situation as Luck.

She said, "Well, I warned you," and tugged the hermit's feather from her hair. This time the feather came out easily. Her mind, Poly was beginning to find, worked in a deceptively simple way. For example: the book was half a spell. The book was blank. Blank books were for writing in. Therefore, the other half of the spell must be a pen, and in Poly's time, pens were not the elegant, hollow tubes that Luck used. They were still proper quills. The hermit had told her what she needed to do when he gave her the feather.

She had thought he said, "Right, right, right!" but what he had actually said was, "Write, write, write!"

Poly didn't even try to write a word in the book; she simply stabbed at it with the feather. Something gave a great, messy *blurt!* like the splattering of ink, and Poly found that she could *understand.* She looked briefly down at her antimagic hand, revelling in the impossible wonder of it, then found the disintegration trigger in her book spell and wafted both book and feather into dust.

It felt as though she'd never forgotten. And when the joy of newly remembered knowledge began to seep away into contentment, there was the joy of truly understanding what it was that Mordion had woken in her.

Poly gave a low little chuckle and said to the masked men, "I think you will all be *very sorry*."

The spell they were using on Luck was a wind funnel, magic and oxygen twisting at such speed that it ruthlessly sucked the breath out of him. It was a shame to disintegrate it instead of studying it as Poly would have liked to do, but Luck was rather blue in the face. She corroded the piece that controlled the oscillation of the spell and then took out the safety clause and blasted all the collected wind at the masked men, bowling them into the trees.

When they began to gather themselves together again, groggy but determined, Poly flung one of the amber beads from her hair at them and said, "Oh, no you don't!"

The bead expanded and liquefied in the air, slapping against the men with a heavy, wet sound, and trickled around them until they were covered. In the heavy silence that followed, Onepiece said curiously rather than sorrowfully, -*wizard dead?*-

"Of course not!" said Poly, rather more fiercely than she meant to. She dropped to her knees by Luck's limp form and shook him. "Wake up, Luck!"

Luck's eyes opened at once. "No need to be rough," he said. "Knowledge all in order? Very good. We can go now." He lunged up and shooed Poly back to the coach, where Onepiece's trembling snout was poking out of the window.

"You should be resting!" she protested.

Luck said, "Hah!" and lifted her bodily into the coach. "If you'd been any longer breaking that spell, maybe."

"Speaking of spells," said Poly, confused and a little suspicious, "how did they manage to trap you with something that simple?"

"It was very strong," Luck said evasively. "Besides, you have your knowledge back now."

Poly, mechanically receiving Onepiece into her lap, stared at him. "You *let* them catch you!"

"Well, you don't like it when I experiment on you," protested Luck.

"You *let* them catch you!"

"Of course I did. You needed something to push you, and now you have your knowledge back. Don't complain."

"I thought you were dead!"

Luck eyed her warily. "I've warned you about hitting me, Poly."

Poly struggled for words briefly. It occurred to her that she wanted, more than she had ever wanted, to hit Luck. And then perhaps to hug him, and kiss him, and—

Oh, dear. Poly sat very, very still, panic tickling at her stomach.

I can't have fallen in love with him! she thought wildly. *I can't have! Oh, it's not fair!*

At last, she sagged against the plump seat cushions and said, "Just drive the coach!" glaring balefully at him over Onepiece's head.

For some reason, her glare only made Luck smile. To her irritation, when he closed his eyes to marshal the spell, the smile remained.

15

Poly had been asleep for some time when they entered the Capital. By then, it was closer to dawn than night, with a bold pink line from the first sun edging the monstrous walls that enclosed them, and the rattling of wooden wheels on cobblestone woke her at once. Onepiece had at last reverted to his boy form, his skinny legs curled up on the cushions and his head in Poly's lap.

"Go back to sleep, Poly," said Luck. His eyes were still closed, and both his feet were resting on the cushion opposite him, pinning Poly's skirts on one side. "We still have a long way to go."

Poly, sleepily stroking Onepiece's hair, went back to sleep with the hazy impression of having entered a vast, sprawling metropolis.

When she opened her eyes again, the impression was strengthened and expanded to include the idea of buildings formed from ice. Huge marble slabs of icy white seemed to make up nearly every building in the vicinity of the coach, carefully sculpted corners sweeping down to meet meticulously swept footpaths, and from thence to regular, well-kept circles of delicate foliage. The streets had been paved to look just like the marble around them, but Poly picked up the spell that turned ordinary brick to white marble and smiled a little derisively.

Luck pointed to the grandest of these: the only one with golden steps. "Council Hall," he said, his eyes green and very, very bright. "They like people to know. Home isn't far."

Caught up in a sudden, blind panic, Poly asked, "Are you leaving me here?"

"What? No, of course not. You don't want to face that lot until you've had a long rest and a full breakfast. We're going home. All of us."

Poly hunched away from the icy buildings and the frigid cold they exuded, shivering in mingled relief and coldness as the coach continued its journey. Before long the ice white buildings gave way to a more sensible yet still elegant brownstone, and not long after that, to plain brick and cobbles again. The cold didn't diminish, however, and the breeze picked up sharply when the coach took a turn to the east, sweeping down the walled streets and into the coach with piercing accuracy.

Onepiece shivered in his sleep, and Poly, belatedly casting about for blankets or furs, found that the coach was stopping.

"Wake the dog," said Luck, flinging open the door and springing from the coach without use of the stairs, eyes still bright. "We're here!"

Poly followed rather more cautiously with a half-asleep Onepiece draped in her arms, and found that they had pulled up directly between two brick houses. Both of those houses were tall, narrow, and rather pokey: neither of them were particularly inviting. There was a gate arch between them, though it held no gate, and it was through this archway, to Poly's bemusement, that Luck now walked. Through it she could see the narrow channel formed by the opposing walls of each domicile, rising high in chipped, dusty red brick.

"Here?"

"Don't dawdle, Poly. In you come."

The red brick alleyway felt fresh and cold, dappled here and there with leaf shaped shadows in the early morning light of the triad. Poly, looking up curiously as a whisper of breeze brought the scent of pepper tree to her nose, saw clear sky between the two red brick walls, and wondered. She wasn't really surprised when the alley ended abruptly at a wooden gate, beneath which grass seemed to peep.

Luck opened the gate without use of a key and marched on, redbrick path turning to grass between one step and the next, and redbrick walls disappearing in a riot of foliage. Poly walked into a pleasant glade, and the early, sharp yells and clatterings of the stone road outside immediately ceased. She squinted up at the triad, but it wasn't in a different position than it had been before they entered the gate. Very well. She knew what Luck *hadn't* done.

Luck was watching her expectantly, so she said, "Well it's not a piece of land from somewhere else, anyway."

"No. That would be too clumsy. Besides, a portal to Somewhere Else leaves you open to nasty things creeping in from the middle."

"It feels like Forest," Poly said, scrunching her toes in her shoes. She could almost feel the grass through her leather soles. "But not quite. It's sort of growing up the walls and spreading out."

"Yes," said Luck. He sounded quite pleased with himself. "I found a lonely little bit of land and seeded it here between the bricks. It's been growing ever since. I think it wanted to be Forest but couldn't quite manage."

"Did it build the house, too?"

"What? No, of course not. I did that."

"Oh."

"Well, what's the matter with it?"

"*You* built it?"

"Poly, you're being insulting again."

Poly said, "Oh," again, and gazed thoughtfully at the house.

It had appeared after they reached the top of a sudden swell in the grass; greenish, just marginally square, and somehow not very interested in *being* a house. It had the requisite two windows at the front, and a dutifully knockered front door, but Poly was shrewdly certain that at the sides and back, where it couldn't be seen, the house would be leaf and hill.

She was half convinced that the windows and door were painted on, and it was a mild shock when Luck opened the front door quite easily.

"They *all* open," Luck told her, with a narrow look that suggested he'd noticed her surprise. "And so do the windows."

Poly followed him across the threshold and looked around curiously. There was enough magic in the place to make Onepiece mutter in his sleep, and from the inside the walls were suspiciously leafy. The floorboards didn't even attempt to wood-like solidarity: they were green and gave slightly beneath her feet.

Grass, Poly decided, watching her own footprints vanish as the grassy floorboards sprang back. Typical of Luck's preferences for open living space, the room had no appreciable furniture.

"You used the land to make the house, too," she said.

"Of course I did. Otherwise I would have had to ferry bricks in here. I don't like bricks. They're stubborn and they don't like being shrunk and expanded."

"*Would* they have been shrunk and expanded?" asked Poly.

"Probably," said Luck carelessly, tossing his dirt stained long-coat onto a dusty hatstand. The hatstand staggered a little but held, the coat caught drunkenly by one sleeve. "The land isn't quite settled yet. Put the dog down somewhere, Poly. We have work to do if you want to survive the Council."

Poly looked around at the square room with its three doors and said, "Where are the bedrooms?"

"They're here somewhere," said Luck vaguely. "Open a door. Explore."

The first door Poly tried led to the bath house. It was huge and leafy and cool, and the bath itself was more akin to a pool than it was to a bath, its sides built with mortared rock. Poly even thought she saw a stream glittering away somewhere underneath the green floorboards, feeding happily into the bath and out again.

The second door led to a hall that was more promising, with two doors to each side and one at the very end. These, in succession, led to the water closet (which was none the less terrifyingly modern for Poly's introduction to those in the village); a curiously springy room that gave under her touch in all directions, walls and floor alike; two rooms stuffed full with books and other dangerously magical artefacts; and, at last, the kitchen. Since it was unlikely that the third door in Luck's main room led to anything but the back garden, Poly settled for what she had and decided to help herself to breakfast.

She was looking for a suitable place to lay the slumbering Onepiece when she noticed a small fire growing swiftly bigger in the depths of a square, tidy stove. That was curious, since Poly was certain there had not been a fire there when she entered the kitchen. She laid Onepiece on the lid of the woodbox where he was close enough to the stove to keep warm but far enough away not to burn himself on it if he tossed in his sleep and set about exploring the cupboards.

The cupboards were as helpful as the stove had been. The first provided her with a small but surprisingly matching set of cups, bowls and plates, and a variety of wooden cutlery. The second showcased three adorably tiny saucepans and two bigger pots, and the third held stoppered pots of oats, millet, barley, sugar and thick molasses.

"Porridge, then," said Poly to herself.

A spelled coldbox held a bottle of milk, though how it got there, Poly wasn't sure: Luck didn't seem the kind of person to remember about keeping milk. Still, it was fresh when she dubiously sniffed it, so Poly used it.

She would have taken a bowl of porridge to Luck except that when she opened the door she'd entered by, it opened into a room instead of a hall. It seemed to be the cloakroom, hung about with various coats and hats, all of them in a state of disarray. Amidst the coats and hats were myriad parcels of all sizes and shapes, some of them leaking magic into the surrounding wall and any hats that were too close for comfort. Finding the space above her head rather empty, Poly looked up to see that the roof was far above her head, and that the pegs on the walls extended all the way to the ceiling, nearly every one of them filled. She stepped carefully back into the kitchen, unwilling to be separated from Onepiece as well as Luck, and ate her porridge alone.

Onepiece stirred a little when she washed her bowl out but was still sleeping heavily enough not to wake when she picked him up and opened the kitchen door again. This time, instead of cloakroom or hallway, Poly found a small bedroom with a narrow white toned bed and an empty fireplace.

"Mine," said Onepiece in his sleep.

Poly laughed softly and laid him on the bed. Like the milk in the coldbox, the sheets were improbably fresh when she gave them a short, sharp sniff, and she had no qualms about tucking the boy in. On her way to the door the fireplace burst into tiny warm flames. Poly eyed it thoughtfully and twitched a thread in the house as she left so that Onepiece would be able to find her when he woke. Then she set out to find Luck again.

He was still in the main room when she found it again, sprawled among a pile of dusty crates with his hands cupped behind his head.

When Poly entered, he sat up and said, "You took a very long time, Poly. Where's the dog?"

"Asleep in bed."

"Good. We have a lot of work to do."

Poly sat cross-legged on a crate opposite him and said, "You said that. What work?"

"You can't sit like that, for a start. You're meant to be a princess."

"I won't sit like this in the Council Hall," said Poly, somewhat indignantly. It wasn't her fault that Luck didn't care for chairs and tables. Something in Luck's tone made her blink a little, and having done so, to think better of her intended reply. "How long have you known?"

"Known what?"

"That I'm not the princess."

"Oh, that. I was reasonably sure when you kicked me. Princesses usually rely on their guards to do their kicking. Besides, princesses aren't known for their powers as enchantresses."

"Oh." She asked, "Are we staying here? Onepiece and I, I mean?"

It was Luck's turn to be mildly indignant. "Don't you like it here?"

Impossible to explain that she'd rather get away while it was still possible to do something about falling in love with him. "Yes, of *course* I—"

"Well, you can't stay in the Council Hall," pursued Luck, unheeding. "The Old Parrasians would probably try to blow it up, and we've just rebuilt it from last time. Besides, the Royalists would only say you'd been corrupted by that time Black Velvet would have gotten to you, so you probably *would* be."

"I don't know what you're talking about," said Poly rather faintly. It seemed suddenly as though it might be simpler just to say, *Look, I've fallen in love with you and I'd rather not stay here and make it worse, thanks very much.*

"*That's* why we have a lot of work to do," said Luck in some satisfaction. "The Wizard Council are the ones who sent me after you."

"They're the ones who want me to solidify their position against the Elder Parrasians."

"*Old* Parrasians. And it's the Royalists that the Wizard Council are thumbing their collective noses at."

"Oh yes, the Royalists are the ones who want to put me on the throne," said Poly. "It won't work, though."

"Why? Because you're not the princess? Try telling them that. Just see if they'll believe you."

"And the Old Parrasians are the ones who want to bring back the Parrasian capital," Poly continued. "But who are Black Velvet?"

"Sneaky people with too much money and too many influential friends. They're more annoying than evil. They like dabbling in international affairs and general spyness."

"Well, what do they want with the Sleeping Princess?"

"Who knows? Just don't encourage them. And *don't* accept any invitations of shelter, hospitality, succour, or refreshment. Any or all of 'em will try to get you under one of their roofs, and once that happens, you'll never get out. Much safer to stay here with me."

"When will I be presented to the Wizard Council?"

"As soon as I figure out how to get us both back out of the Council once we're in. They'll get wind of you soon enough, but nothing will be formal until we present you. As long as you don't wander out of the grounds or open the gate to anyone until then, you should be safe."

"I won't wander," Poly said fervently.

"Yes, you will," Luck said gloomily. "You're always wandering and getting into trouble. I'd lock you in if I thought it'd work."

Poly tried to feel offended but could only manage to feel a rather pleased warmth. "Well, I won't wander this time. Onepiece and I will—oh." She faltered to a stop, and said, "Oh," again, this time more ruefully.

"I was wondering when you'd think of that," said Luck.

"I could tell them all he's a puppy you picked up in a dirty little town, who thinks I'm his mother," said Poly defiantly. "It is true, after all."

"They don't care about truth. They care about their truth. If it suits the Wizard Council or any of the others to put it about that the dog is your son, your brother or your slave, it'll be in the news sheet by last bell tonight."

"He's not a—"

"He'll have to stay at home," said Luck, ignoring her. "The house will look after him. I won't have him turning into a dog or sneezing every time someone gets a bit too excitable with their magic."

"He can't stay at home alone," Poly protested. "What if he gets stuck in one of the rooms? Or falls into the stream?"

"Stream? What stream?"

"I saw it out the kitchen window," said Poly, exasperated. "*And in the bathroom. You can't*—"

Luck said, "Huh. So that's where it went. I've been looking for that stream for the better part of a year. I think a bit of Don't See I was working on leached into the water."

"The point is—"

"You'll have to be kitted out, of course. No good going to the Council looking like a village girl. And you should try to put a few more spells into your hair: they'll be intimidated by that."

"Luck—"

"Something gold and magnificent, I think," said Luck thoughtfully. "Make 'em sit up and pay attention."

There was a familiar whisper of magic around Poly. She shivered pleasantly and found herself in an exceedingly heavy gown of gold threaded cloth with slashed sleeves, a properly whaleboned bodice, and a deliciously soft chemise. Persephone herself would not have scorned to wear it.

"Luck, I *can* do this by myself now."

"Yes, but this is more fun," said Luck. "Put your chin up, Poly. The dress is no good if you don't look like you're considering executing everyone. If they see any weakness, they'll go for the throat."

"It seems to me that they've already gone for the throat," said Poly.

"Poisoned chocolates are more of a hello-and-pleased-to-meet-you. Here in the Capital things will get more interesting."

Poly felt a tingle of cold unease. "I can hardly wait."

. . .

Luck left early the next morning, suited and top-hatted. Before he left, he gave Poly and Onepiece a narrowed green look and said, "Don't let anybody in—even me. I have a key. Well, a spell."

"If you have a key, I won't need to let you in," said Poly.

"Yes, exactly," said Luck, and disappeared into the streets.

It wasn't until late morning that Poly discovered what he meant. Determined not to miss him, she romped around the garden with Onepiece, paddled in the stream, and persuaded a chair or two to grow in the grassy living room. It was while she was growing the second bushy chair that someone activated the hailer on the gate outside. It buzzed obnoxiously to announce the fact, a surprisingly practical piece of magic for Luck to have about the house, and Onepiece sneezed. Poly left him playing with one of the chairs and took herself down to the gate to see who had come calling.

It was Luck. Or rather, she thought, looking narrowly at a cobweb of magic; it was someone pretending to be Luck. And not very well, at that.

In her coldest voice, she said: "Yes?"

Not-Luck blinked back at her through the peephole. "Let me in, princess," he said.

"I am not," said Poly very distinctly, "an imbecile. Go away."

Not-Luck was still gaping when she snicked the tiny door shut in his face. She treated the second Luck to the same outraged dignity, but by the time the third imposter tried to convince her to open the gate, Poly had decided that enough was enough. She tweaked a small corner of the imposter's spell and sent him away as a wrinkled old woman, hobbling angrily with a stick in each hand. Onepiece, perched on her right hip, gurgled with delight and clapped his hands, which inspired in Poly such creativity that she sent away from the gate in quick succession a small, freckled child, a mournful bloodhound, and a fat white sheep.

Not all the visitors were spelled to look like Luck. One, a

Spindle

pompous old man with magnificent side-whiskers and a Comply spell on his well-modulated voice, told her in tones dripping with condescension to 'be a good girl and open the gate'. It was with great satisfaction that Poly sent him away barking like a seal. The other was a young man following close behind the older, and since he hurried away very quickly after seeing the reception of his predecessor, Poly chose to let him alone. He seemed to have more sense than the others.

After that it seemed wise to ignore the hailer, since Onepiece was rapidly showing signs of learning how to throw off spells. Accordingly, Poly ignored the frequent buzzes and concentrated instead on keeping Onepiece in sight and in one piece around Luck's rather perilous house.

Poly ignored the hailer, in fact, until she could ignore it no more. Most callers seemed to press the hailer either once or twice: if twice, leaning on it rather a long time the second time. This time, however, the buzzer sounded exactly once, after which a silence of some seconds elapsed, then an autocratic female voice said in disembodied tones, "Let me in immediately! I refuse to wait on the doorstep!"

Poly sighed and approached the gate once again. This time it was an angular lady who appeared to be in her late forties. Her face was narrow but handsome, and if it wasn't for the spell at present clinging to her hat and swirling around her person, Poly thought she would have quite liked her face. But the spell was there, and though it was unfamiliar, Poly could see quite clearly that it had concealment and transformation clauses attached to it.

"You're a goose," she said to the woman, and where the woman had been standing was now an equally angular goose.

Outraged, it said, "*Honk?*"

Someone burst into a peal of laughter. Poly blinked in surprise and saw a thin, red haired girl a step or two behind the goose.

"Oh, *poor* Aunt Oddu!" said the girl, with tears of laughter in her eyes. "I don't think she's ever been so surprised in her life! She won't stay like that for long, you know."

"She'll have to," said Poly grimly. "I altered her spell. Who are you supposed to be?"

"I'm Isabella," the girl said gaily. "That's Aunt Oddu. She's rather strong, you know, and that wasn't her natural form."

"I know. That's why I changed it. Who sent you?"

"The enchanter did. I mean she's not exactly *people*, princess. Whoops, there she goes!"

Rather to Poly's shock, the goose seemed to be growing. No, not growing: *changing*. Scales in bright green rippled from white feathers, spreading and dancing with variegated light, while the goose's bill grew huge nostrils and faded from bright orange to a delicate flush of pink.

Poly took a deep breath and tried not to sound flustered. "She's a dragon."

"Yes. Rather beautiful, isn't she?"

"How is she *fitting* in here?" The alley was filled with dragon, but the dragon didn't seem to have spilled out into the roadway. It wasn't even a concealment or illusion spell: it was all real, flesh-and-blood dragon.

"It's got something to do with Luck's alley," said Isabella. "He explained it to me once when I didn't ask about it. It's ridiculously hard to understand, but what it all comes down to is that the space is slightly stretchy here because it's almost-Forest, and Forest loves its mythics."

"Oh yes," said Poly. "I should have remembered that."

Isabella looked slightly envious. "How interesting! That made sense to you!"

"After ten years of magic theory with Lady Cimone and two weeks of travel with Luck, it should!" said Poly. "Is she going to stay like that?"

"Oh, I shouldn't think so," said Isabella blithely. "You took her by surprise, that's all. Speaking of surprises, why *are* you Transforming hapless callers at Luck's gate?"

Spindle

"Luck told me not to let anyone in, even himself."

"I see," said Isabella. To her credit, it sounded as though she *did* see. "They've all rather dashed for the gate, haven't they? Do you know who delegated whom?"

Poly shook her head. "Four Lucks showed up, one after the other. I can only assume that they've all had a go."

"It does sound like some of the Royalists," said Isabella. "And the Old Parrasians would certainly try something that stupid, but it seems a little clumsy for Mordion. I wonder who the fourth was?"

"Perhaps it was Black Velvet," Poly said, prompting a narrow-eyed look from Isabella.

"Now where did you hear that name?" Behind Isabella, the dragon rumbled and emitted a few, scorching sparks. "Oh, all right, Aunt Oddu! I wasn't being rude. I was just being, well, nosy."

Poly gave a surprised giggle, but Oddu merely snuffed a few more sparks and began to shrink again. When she was once more human, spell intact about her hat, she said quellingly, "Isabella, how many times have I told you that young women ought to be seen and not heard?"

"If you include this time, once," said Isabella, not quelled. "In fact, I believe you rather encourage me to talk. I manage to find out all the gossip that you don't know."

"*Or* that you've become distressingly pert?"

"Oh, that you've said many times, Aunt Oddu."

"Young woman," said Oddu to Poly, "I am far from commending your attack upon my person. However, I must say that you show remarkable form for so young a person. I do not refer to you as Princess, you understand."

"Of course not," said Poly in polite fascination. "I suppose you're an Old Parrasian."

"Certainly not! I am neither Old Parrasian nor Royalist."

"Aunt Oddu thinks it's nonsense to try and reclaim a country once it's lost," said Isabella. "And she doesn't approve of putting redundant royalty from a past age on the throne. Isn't that right, Aunt?"

"Word perfect," said Oddu, with an angular, amused look. It made her look much nicer. "Are you under instruction, my dear?"

"That depends on what you consider to be instruction," said Poly. "Luck has been throwing bits and pieces of magic at me for the last two weeks, and some rather unpleasant Royalists attacked our carriage before we got here."

"I see. As usual, Luck has been regrettably deficient in his duties. I will have words with him. Come along, Isabella."

She sailed away commandingly, followed by Isabella, who shot a grin back at Poly over her shoulder in parting. Poly was left feeling as though she had not successfully withstood an attempt upon her defences, but that Oddu had come, decided that she would prefer to remain outside, and left again at her own leisure.

16

Luck didn't come back until the next morning. When he did return, he woke Poly from outside the gate with the gale force of his anger. Onepiece whimpered and shrank to a puppy in his sleep, and Poly dashed for the alley, muttering threats and imprecations. The gate blasted open before she could get to it, sending a storm of magic and splinters flying into the glade, and Poly threw up a shield more by instinct than decision.

"Stop that at once!"

"No," said Luck. "I'm angry and I want to break things."

"Not in here! Onepiece is sleeping!"

Luck looked obstinate. "It's *my* allotment. I should be able to break things when I want to without worrying about the dog."

"He's *not*—oh, never mind! What's gone wrong?"

"Nothing's gone wrong. Everything is just as usual. The Council is a blood-sucking collection of leeches, the Old Parrasians are slavering wolves, and the Royalists are terrifyingly insane."

"You forgot Black Velvet," said Poly.

Luck's agitated magic was quickly settling where it reached out to meet with hers, gold mingling with blue.

"Yes, well, they're just as sneaky as usual. You'll have to come out with me tomorrow."

"Today."

"What? Oh, yes. Today. The dog stays at home."

"Luck, you sent a woman around yesterday."

"Did I? Huh. I did. Oddu. Knew you'd like her."

"It's more of a question of whether *she* likes *me*," said Poly. "After I dismantled her human-shape spell, anyway."

Luck looked surprised, banishing the last signs of anger. "Why did you do that?"

"You told me not to let anyone in. *Anyone*. There were four Lucks before her."

"Huh. Clumsy, that."

"Yes, I thought so," agreed Poly. "I expected something a bit cleverer, actually. Only then Oddu and Isabella came to visit and I could see the spell on Oddu's hat, so—"

"Well done, Poly! Tricky spell, that."

"Yes, but *not* something to be doing to invited visitors," said Poly pointedly. "Why didn't you tell me you were sending her around? I wouldn't have turned her into a goose if you had."

"Oh, the old tartar likes someone who can best her every now and then. You'd better get dressed, Poly; it's going to be a long day and you can't wear your nightdress to the council buildings."

Poly worked a piece of Dressing magic, encasing herself in the golden dress that Luck had made for her. In addition to the heavy skirts, Poly added a queenly ruff, a few jewellike spells to enhance the bodice, and then, sighing, turned her attention to underthings. The delightfully soft chemise, she kept. After that, it was merely a matter of adding the correct number of stiff petticoats and forming a series of hoops into the once-fashionable *cage*. The result was stately, imposing, and decidedly stifling.

Poly sighed. "Ooof. I forgot how uncomfortable court dress is."

"You look a bit stiff, Poly. You'll have to do something about your hair, too."

"Bother!" grumbled Poly, striving to catch her coiling hair. It was at present stirring around her waist, tendrils exploring the laces and gems of the gown she'd just magicked, but it proved to be remarkably acquiescent for a wonder, and let her form a not-too-ridiculously-ancient bouffant that must have looked heavy but was delightfully light.

"I never liked that fashion," said Luck, offhandedly insulting. "Anyway, you look nicer with your hair down."

"Maybe so, but I don't look like an ancient Civetan royal with my hair down," said Poly. "Are we going *now*?"

"Yes. Well, as soon as the little firebrand gets here."

"The little firebrand is already here," said Isabella's voice, sweetly.

She was leaning in the gateway, crossing her thin ankles to display rather delightful green shoes with shiny silver buckles. The rest of her was clothed in green and silver, too, bodiced tight but not in stiff whalebone, and her sleeves were both simple and elegant. Poly looked over her ensemble and felt a pang of bitter envy.

"You're very Ye Olde Civet today, princess," Isabella said. "Elegant! Not my sort of thing—*or* yours, if you'll excuse me. But excessively imposing. How long will you have to keep it up?"

"Just today," said Luck. "That's what you're for."

"I thought I was here to entertain a dog-boy."

Poly smiled involuntarily at Luck. "Really?"

"You'd only spend the whole day muttering and glaring at me if I didn't find someone," said Luck, but he looked pleased with himself. "The dog is in his room, sleeping. Come along, Poly."

"Oh, no you don't!" said Isabella. She held out her wrist expectantly. "Spell please. If I get lost in that cavernous monstrosity you call a house just *one* more time, I'll haunt you from far flung rooms for the rest of your life."

Poly watched curiously as Luck drew a small Navigate spell on Isabella's wrist and noticed something rather surprising. "You don't have magic!"

"Well, not much," said Isabella ruefully. "Such a trial! I've enough to pick locks and be generally annoying, and just enough so that I don't attract every magical entity in the land by creating a vacuum, but I'll never be able to really work my own spells."

"Oh dear," said Poly. Isabella was so commanding for such a young girl: it hadn't occurred to her that the girl wouldn't be able to keep up with Onepiece magically. "Onepiece likes to play with magic and if he changes into a puppy again—"

"Oh no, that's quite all right," said Isabella serenely. "Children, I can manage. It's magic I'm no good at. You'll see."

"Yes, I suppose I will," said Poly. "All *right,* Luck, I'm coming."

Luck was dragging her inexorably away by the elbow, and she had the feeling that if she resisted for much longer, he'd Shift them both bodily into the street. Now that she had enough magic and knowledge of her own to conceivably prevent him from so doing, Poly found that it didn't annoy her as it once would have.

The hooped edges of Poly's skirts swung gaily as Luck pulled her through the alley, threatening to sweep strands of ivy from the red bricks as they passed. Thanks to the inflexibility of the whaleboned corsets, Poly found herself out of breath uncomfortably soon, and greeted the sight of Luck's horseless carriage with a relieved gasp.

"Why are we in such a hurry?" she said, once they were seated more or less sedately in the carriage. The stiff dress was still tidy, but Poly felt flustered and hot, and decidedly out of breath.

Luck said, "Pay attention, Poly. Don't agree to anything. Don't smile. *Don't* nod. They'll try to get you to agree to things, especially in the Council Hall itself—"

"Why?" interrupted Poly, since it didn't seem that Luck was about to stop for either breath or explanation.

"One of the Arbiters imbued the Hall with a Binding spell. Makes it difficult to go back on what you agreed to do while you were in there."

Poly felt a touch of panic. "I thought it was just the Council,

Old Parrasians, Royalists and Black Velvet! What's an Arbiter? And why would they let one put spells on the Hall?"

"They probably couldn't stop him. Very powerful enchanter, Rorkin."

"And who's Rorkin?" asked Poly in despair.

"I told you: he's an enchanter. Powerful. Sneaky."

"So Arbiters are enchanters?"

"Can't be an Arbiter unless you're an enchanter. No agreeing to things in the Hall, Poly. No agreeing to things anywhere. In fact, don't speak at all."

"I can't stand there mumchance, Luck. Who or what are Arbiters?"

"Yes, you can. And don't let anyone touch you, either. Also, keep your glove on."

Poly felt her hair stirring in irritation and took a deep breath. "Luck, why would I take my glove off? What are Arbiters?"

"You're always doing dangerous things. Don't take off your glove. Don't accept any gifts. Keep close to me and don't wander off."

"Arbiters, Luck!"

"We're here," said Luck, and darted from the carriage. "Come along, Poly."

Poly wrestled her stiff skirts through the door of the carriage, and emerged, breathless and slightly askew, on the golden steps of the Council Hall.

"Hair, Poly," said Luck.

He charged up the stairs, leaving Poly to attend to her hair and follow in a significantly statelier manner. The Council Hall exuded a potent blend of magics that called to her, and it was rather difficult to keep her hair in the bouffant when every strand of it hummed to reach for the magic. At last, Poly contented herself with form but not stillness, and allowed her hair to move within its bouffant. It wasn't until the thin little door attendant looked at her with wide eyes and she caught sight of herself in the sheen of the glossy marble halls that Poly realised how very disconcerting the effect was.

"Well done, Poly," said Luck, sounding pleased. "That'll get 'em talking between themselves."

Poly favoured him with a repressive look, and Luck smiled his sweetest smile at her. "Yes. Do that look at 'em, too. Here we go."

The door attendant led them into a small antechamber some way down the hall. "The Head Wizard will be with you shortly," he said, and with a last, less than covert glance at Poly and her hair, he hurried back down the hall.

The antechamber wasn't empty, to Poly's dismay.

Luck said, "Hullo Melchior. Hullo Pettis. Session not out yet?" and crossed the floor to shake hands with two men in severe black-and-white.

"Not even close," said the older of the two. "They've been at it since you left. It's all *The Council needs to turn the Royal Personage over to the Guild of Old Parrasians* on one side, and *The Royal Personage has returned to claim her throne* on the other."

Luck said something dismissive in return, but Poly saw his golden magic stir and sharpen.

"Well now," said a soft, amused voice beside her. "Something seems to have annoyed Luck. I wonder what that can be?"

The younger of the two men had strolled away from Luck and was now standing beside her. Poly turned her head in what she hoped was a stately manner and took in the faintly challenging hazel eyes that glinted at her above a thin, sarcastic mouth.

"I can see why Luck likes you so much," said that sarcastic mouth. It wasn't said sarcastically, however: unless Poly was very much mistaken, those hazel eyes took her in with distinct appreciation. "I'm Melchior," he said. "That's Pettis: he and Luck will talk for hours if left alone. Foolish of him, I think, when he could be whispering in *your* ear. You do speak, don't you?"

"You're very forward, sirrah," said Poly. She was pleased to hear that her voice sounded thoughtful and quite cool. "Why are you addressing me?"

"Four reasons," said Melchior. "One, I have a great interest in the Sleeping Princess. You're something of a hobby of mine. Two, your hair is delightfully unusual. Those *are* spells, I take it? May I touch your hair?"

"Of course not!" said Poly, ruining her aloof tone of voice with an unfortunate squeak.

Melchior's eyes lit with wicked amusement. "Three, you're quite obviously an enchantress of some power; and four, well, I haven't seen anything quite like *this* before."

He was holding her gloved hand in his own, and before Poly quite knew what was happening he had kissed her fingers lightly.

"Stop that!" hissed Poly, her eyes flying to Luck. He hadn't noticed, still deep in his conversation with Pettis, and Poly wasn't sure whether to be annoyed or relieved.

"Why? Because Luck isn't intelligent enough to do it?" This time there was certainly a sardonic edge to Melchior's voice. "You must have so many questions, princess: I'm certain that Luck hasn't answered them all. Allow me to be of service."

"He warned me about you," Poly said bluntly. She was rewarded by a lightning-fast grin from Melchior and was a little annoyed to find that she *felt* rewarded.

"Did he so! Clever Luck. Me in particular?"

"Not in particular, no. He did warn me against accepting any gifts, agreeing to any arrangements or allowing people to touch me, however."

One of Melchior's hands spread wide, indicating innocence, but the other didn't release Poly's gloved hand. Poly saw a brief glint of magic obscure his hazel eyes like the flash of light across glass and knew that he was studying her antimagic hand. The magic was obsidian black, but it didn't frighten her.

"No hidden costs, princess. Ask, and I'll tell you anything you want to know."

"That would be easier to believe if you weren't using magic to study my hand," said Poly.

"You can see magic," said Melchior delightedly.

Poly had the uncomfortable feeling that she'd told him entirely too much without meaning to do so.

"Tell me about the Arbiters," she said, taking a leaf from Luck's book.

"The Arbiters?" One of Melchior's brows went up, and his eyes flicked from her hand to her face. "Yes, you were asleep for that, weren't you? They were all enchanters: Rorkin, Glenna, Peter—I'm sorry, did you say something?"

Poly shook her head soundlessly, and he continued, "They brokered the peace between Civet and Parras and formed New Civet from the debris that was left."

"I see. Luck said something about Rorkin putting spells on the Council Hall?"

"They all did," said Melchior, and added with an especially sarcastic twist of the lips, "They seemed to think the Wizard Council might be subject to corruption. Odd, eh?"

Poly, trying not to hold her breath, asked, "What happened to them?"

"Old Rorkin was assassinated, or so they say. *I* think the sneaky old goat's still toddling around somewhere. His staff hasn't ever been found."

"And um, Peter and Glenna?"

"No one knows," said Melchior, looking down at her curiously. "Know them, did you?"

"What makes you say that?" asked Poly, just a shade too quickly.

A slight curl of the lips. "They were young, but not so young that they wouldn't have been to court at least once. By all accounts Rorkin was the oldest of them. Funnily enough, he was the only one I ever met: Glenna and Peter vanished long before I was born. There was some talk of segueing through time, but most people don't believe that."

"Yes. Well, it's impossible, isn't it?"

"Mm. So they say."

"Might I have my hand back now?"

"Since you ask so nicely," said Melchior.

His eyes flicked past her to the door, and Poly realised with a fizz of what could have been either fear or excitement, that the big double doors were opening.

Three men in blue emerged first, and though there were others behind them, Poly didn't see them. All she could see was Mordion—*her* Mordion—not aged a day and smiling as charmingly as ever as he trod across the carpet toward her. She heard Melchior suck in a breath between his teeth and realised that she had pinched his fingers painfully between hers. She would have let go immediately, but he curled his hand around hers instead of pulling loose, and Poly hid their linked hands behind the panniers of her gown, allowing herself the dubious comfort of clinging to him.

"Your Highness," said Mordion.

He bowed deeply, his eyes laughing up at Poly in a way that was horribly familiar. Over his shoulder, she was pleased to see that her marble reflection was cold, calm, and utterly devoid of the panic that raced through her veins.

She said, "And you are, sirrah?"

"Head of the Wizard Council, Highness. I am at your service. My name is Mordion."

"Is it really?" said Poly, with cool unconcern.

There was an indulgent tone to Mordion's voice that told her he didn't really expect her to remember him, and that made her furiously angry. Across the room, Luck's eyes found hers, very green and narrow, and Poly looked away.

Melchior inquired, "How goes the session, sir?"

Poly noted the *sir* with a sick feeling in her stomach and glanced sideways to find Melchior watching her with a warning in his hazel eyes. Behind the panniers of her skirt, his hand squeezed hers once and released it.

"Slowly," said Mordion, shrugging. "Now that you are here, Highness, perhaps we can come to some kind of agreement—"

"There you are, Poly!" said Luck's voice, suddenly and firmly. "It's time to go in. Mordion. Melchior."

He nodded to both wizards and swept Poly into the Hall, where it seemed that a thousand eyes were suddenly upon her. The sedate roar of conversation dropped immediately, leaving Poly to follow Luck with a hideously loud rustling of starched petticoats. The carpet beneath her feet was red with gold trimmings and ran in nine spokes from a circular centre to the edges of the room. Each spoke was a series of stairs that climbed between tiers of seats until it met double doors: the one that they were currently descending cut through tiers numbered one through thirty.

By the time they were seated in one of the tiers, Poly was feeling decidedly raw. The stares had not abated during their walk, and Mordion had taken his place in the centre of the room, sleek and smooth and handsome. Across the Hall, Melchior winked at her, which made Luck look sharply at Poly, and Poly feel rather naughtily better.

After that it was easier to listen to Mordion's purring voice as he recognised speakers across the hall. As far as Poly could tell, it was all a very polite, very correct fight about who would claim *the Royal Personage*, which seemed to be herself. After a little while, it even became amusing. Poly would have enjoyed herself if it wasn't for the fact that, every so often, she would look up to find Mordion's eyes on her. She was quite sure that he didn't know she had remembered everything. She was just as sure that she didn't want him to find out.

I wonder, thought Poly, chilled and a little elated, *I wonder if he was the one who tried to kill us as well? Is that why he sent Luck to get me?*

The noise in the room sank to a mere babble in the background as she thought about it, and it wasn't until Luck whispered in her ear, "Nominate me as your champion, Poly," that Poly regained some sense of the room about her.

She said a startled, "Pardon?"

The room fell silent. Poly flicked her eyes up and found that Mordion's eyes were on her, mockingly.

He said, "Will you have a champion, your Highness? Or will you speak for yourself?"

"Luck will be my champion," said Poly carelessly, and had the small, frightened satisfaction of seeing a startled look in Mordion's dark eyes. He knew her. He'd expected her to manage, independent and alone, as she'd always done. She said more clearly, "Luck speaks for me."

The babble in the room rose to an immediate roar.

"Right!" said Luck, surging to his feet. "That's that, then. Come along, Poly." He flung open the short wooden door at the end of their row, thoughtlessly trampling toes and squashing hats on his way, and Poly swept out grandly in his wake.

They were halfway up the aisle again when something distinctly magical went *pop!* very, very loudly. Poly felt a huge, warm inrush of air that buffeted her hair and pushed her a step forward, then Luck turned, his eyes golden and wide as a pounding of sound began.

Poly heard the screams and shouts that broke out above the pounding, but only managed to turn herself halfway around in her ridiculously stiff gown before Luck wrenched her close and pulled her bodily into the air.

A cacophony of sound and vibration thundered beneath their feet as they dangled in the air: Poly dazedly saw the backs of a herd of lowland cattle that stampeded below herself and Luck. She also saw the few, unlucky wizards who had not managed to vacate their seats in time, huddled and bloody beneath the hooves as they trampled, and lifted the rest of the men and women in the hall without thinking about it. Mordion's dark blue eyes flew to her face in arrested question, but Poly was too distracted to feel as sick as she should have felt. She released her hair from its bouffant and let it waft easily around herself and Luck, taking in magic.

"I'm fine. You can let go now," she said to Luck.

"Don't be silly, Poly," said Luck, in a reasonable tone of voice. He adjusted one of his arms, but only to pull her closer. "Mordion is looking. Put your arms around my neck and step onto my feet."

"What happened?" Poly asked, wrapping her arms around his neck.

With the bulk of her skirts, it was difficult to get to Luck's feet, but she managed to get the tips of her toes precariously balanced on his.

"Someone Released one of the paintings in the hall. Can you keep holding everyone up while I Bind everything back into the painting?"

"Of course," said Poly.

"Very good. *Back you go.*"

The lowland cattle that were milling about below their feet seemed to flicker and become less real. Poly, looking over Luck's shoulder, saw an imperfect picture through the strands of her hair: golden magic in tiny, hairlike filaments was sticking to the cattle and irresistibly pulling them back toward a canvas across the hall. In their wake, tumbled benches and splintered timber became apparent, as did the few crushed bodies. Poly waited until Luck Bound the painting once more, then gently set down everyone else in the room.

There was a moment's silence, then voices burst into wild, hysterical gabble. Poly heard someone's voice calling for a Healer, another howling for everybody to get out, and as Luck's feet touched carpet again, she heard the sudden, venomous whisper that slithered through the whole assembly, *The Old Parrasians have done it again. It's murder this time.*

"Poly," said Luck's voice in her ear. His arms were still wrapped around her, warm and close, and her feet were still on his, arms around his neck. "Poly, we should go now."

But he didn't let go, and he didn't move.

Poly said, "Be quiet, Luck," and listened as hard as she could. Around the room a susurration of voices lapped against each other, and then against her moving hair.

It's the Old Parrasians. They've taken it too far this time. Who would try to murder the Sleeping Princess?

More interestingly ran a current that said, *Well, Mordion's back. The accidents started very quickly, didn't they?*

And then Poly heard, "May I be of assistance, Princess?"

"No, we're quite all right," she said, stepping back briskly from Luck.

He blinked and seemed to sway.

It was Melchior beside them, looking very sarcastic. "A little excitement for your first session in parliament, Princess."

"Are those men dead?"

"No, I think not. The healer is with them. We'll be breaking for the day after this debacle: mind you don't get caught with the reporters at the front door."

"We're not going out the front," said Luck, tugging Poly away. "Come along, Poly."

"Yes, go along, Poly," said Melchior, quick and sharp and impudent. "Be a good girl. I'll see you tomorrow."

Poly meant to give him the icy look she'd been practising, but a smile slipped out instead. And instead of *No*, she found herself saying, "All right."

"Poly, you're not to encourage the Wizard Council," said Luck, dragging her down the vast marble hallways of the Council building until Poly had no idea where they were.

"I wasn't encouraging the Wizard Council, I was encouraging Melchior," Poly said. She wondered, for a brief, mad moment, if it was possible that Luck was jealous, and it seemed good to her to stir the coals a little. "He's very useful for answering questions."

"Answering questions is not what Melchior does best," said Luck. His eyes were all green, without a trace of gold, and very narrow. "Besides, we'll be going out again tomorrow, so he can't come to see you."

"Well, I like him."

"You're not to like him," said Luck irritably, gratifying Poly greatly. "In fact, you're not to—"

"Luck, sweeting," said a husky female voice, interrupting Luck before a highly interested Poly could find out what else she was not to do.

Luck ceased in his headlong rush and pivoted to greet an occupied doorway. "Melissa. What are you doing here?"

Poly, who had stiffened at the drawling, intimate greeting, found that Luck had let go of her hand. It left her feeling cold and abandoned, and in no humour to appreciate the beauty of the woman who had accosted Luck.

She *was* beautiful, no doubt. Her delightfully proportionate curves were set off by a gown of deep green that cinched tight at the waist and plunged almost scandalously deep at the neck. The skirts of the gown pretended to a fullness at the back, but the cut of it, Poly noticed, was set to brush against her legs as she walked and emphasize the curve of her hips. Her hair was gracefully caught up in a series of stately waves in burnished gold, and the heavy-lidded caramel eyes that spoke promises above plump, cherry red lips only made her appear riper and more mature.

"I came to see you, sweeting," said those cherry red lips. "What, no kiss for your oldest friend?"

Poly was annoyed but unsurprised to see Luck take a step toward Melissa and kiss her. She was almost certain that Luck meant to kiss the woman on her cheek; if so, Melissa turned her face so smoothly and naturally that the kiss fell on her lips instead.

This was who Luck had meant, then, thought Poly, curling the fingers of her antimagic hand into the lace of her glove, when he had complained that not everyone found his kisses distasteful. She felt small and scrubby and school-girlish.

When Melissa had finished kissing Luck—and did they *have* to take quite so long about it? thought Poly irritably—she turned her heavy-lidded eyes upon Poly and gave her a curtsey that was deep and, Poly suspected, entirely mocking. Poly found that she resented mockery from Melissa in a way that she hadn't when it came from Melchior.

"This must be the Sleeping Princess," said Melissa, in her husky voice. "That is a magnificently classic ensemble, Princess."

"Sadly outdated, I believe," Poly said carelessly, but she felt the sting. "I shall dress myself new tomorrow."

The caramel eyes lost interest and turned from Poly to Luck. "Why this hurry, Luck?"

"There was an accident in the session," said Luck. "Someone Released a painting and tried to trample the Wizard side of the Hall."

"Indeed? I hope the princess doesn't think us all as barbaric as the Old Parrasians."

Poly would have answered with another polite court nothing, but it was evident to her that Melissa was talking to Luck, and Luck only.

"No one is as barbaric as the Old Parrasians," said Luck. "They were taught that a long time ago and it seems to have stuck. Come along if you're coming, Melissa. We have to go now."

"At your turn of speed? Certainly not! Dine with me tomorrow instead and tell me all about everything."

Luck's eyes flicked momentarily to Poly before he said, "All right. Poly's staying home tomorrow anyway. Out or in?"

"Oh, in, of course," purred Melissa. "Since I saw you last I've acquired several little knick-knacks you might find interesting."

"Tomorrow," agreed Luck, his eyes bright. "Come along, Poly."

It was a rather silent drive back to Luck's alley. Luck, his eyes bright and green, was unnoticingly deep in thought, and Poly was in no mind to talk. She was cold and sick, and couldn't quite bring herself to the point of convincing Luck that his Mordion was her murderous Mordion. He hadn't shown any signs of believing her yet, and Poly didn't have the energy to try again. She was also full of other unpleasant thoughts.

As they passed through the gate, there was the distant sound of a door slamming, and Onepiece came lurching across the grass to throw himself at Poly.

"Polypolypoly!" he burbled, in dizzy glee, and though Isabella said, "Well! There's gratitude for you! You'd think I beat and starved him!" her smile was affectionate.

Poly, her arms full of skinny little boy and a feeling of lightness dispelling some of the ache in her heart, said, "Yes, I love you too, Onepiece. Luck, am I staying home or going out tomorrow?"

"Staying home," said Luck, his eyes glazed and distant. "I have a dinner engagement. I shall not be home until late."

"Very well. Do you have any fashion plates, Isabella?"

Isabella's eyes danced. "Oh yes. Just a few. Should you like to see them?"

"Yes please," said Poly.

17

It was borne in on Poly, some time after Luck left the next day and Isabella arrived, that Isabella's airy assertion of owning 'just a few' fashion plates had fallen very far short of the truth.

In fact, she seemed to have several hundred.

"But if you want the very latest," she confided in Poly, "You need only look at these ones."

Poly looked at the fat little pile of drawings and smiled faintly. "That narrows it down."

"You mean to say it doesn't at all!" said Isabella frankly. "Never you mind, princess: you'll be grateful for them by the time we've done."

"I'm grateful now," said Poly. "I'd be more grateful if you'd call me Poly, though. Luck does, and there's no princesses and kings in New Civet now, anyway."

"Not unless the Royalists get their way," agreed Isabella. "All right, Poly: would you prefer a fringe or a lace front?"

"Lace, I think," said Poly. She studied one of the plates: an exaggerated sketch of a simple enough dress that had a draping, graceful top of lace, a narrow waist, and a full skirt with just the suggestion of a bustle. Then she created one for herself, feeling the familiar whisper of magic across her skin as her clothes changed.

"Oh, what I wouldn't give to be able to do that!" sighed Isabella. "I was going to suggest one of the modistes that Aunt Oddu patronizes, but I don't think I'll bother. Luck didn't tell me that you're an enchantress."

"Luck doesn't tell anyone very much," said Poly, rather grimly.

Isabella shot her a knowing look. "Where is Luck today?"

"Having dinner with an old friend."

"Yes, I knew that. Melissa has been looking for him for days. I meant what *else* is he doing?"

"Else?"

"He's been in a bate for the last two days, ever since he got home: you must have noticed!"

"Well, yes; but he's been out all the time."

"Yes, it isn't like him at all. Luck doesn't like—"

"Going out," finished Poly. "Or people. He has been spending rather a lot of time at the Council Hall, though. He took me there yesterday for the most ridiculously short amount of time."

"What did you do while you were there?"

"Listened to Mordion talk, mostly. Oh, and I was asked if I would name a champion. Luck told me to nominate him, so I did."

"How very clever of him!" said Isabella approvingly. "In that case, whatever he's doing will have to do with you."

"I thought he was going to hand me over as soon as we got here," admitted Poly.

"So did I," said Isabella. She was studying a drawing with great attention. "So did everyone. Curious."

"What does it mean, nominating someone as champion?"

"It means that neither the Royalists nor the Council can claim you. And if I know Luck, the Old Parrasians won't get a look-in either. It means you've set up as your own person, and that any agreements you enter into will be bargained through Luck. No one can claim anything from you."

"Except Luck."

"Except Luck. It's a partnership. I'm surprised that Luck thought of it, actually: it's an old statute that no one has used in decades. The Arbiters put it in place."

"Of course they did," said Poly, with a small, bittersweet smile. She wondered if it had been Mum or Dad who thought of it. For absentee parents, they certainly looked after her very well. "Isabella, who is Melissa?"

Isabella again gave her full attention to the drawings. "A highly intelligent, excessively powerful, and incredibly sticky leech. Enchantress, of course: she's been around for at least a hundred years. She and Luck were rather close at one stage, I believe."

"Allegiance?"

"Herself, really. But professed to the Council—and, I believe, most *especially* to Mordion."

Poly shivered involuntarily and found Isabella's eyes on her.

"Yes, exactly. He's very beautiful, but I've never met anyone who scared me more."

"Nor I," said Poly.

A thread pulled tight from somewhere in the house, and she wasn't surprised when Onepiece stumbled through one of the walls, yawning and muttering. The wall swished back behind him with a leafy rustling and became solid once again.

"Oh, it's just not fair!" sighed Isabella. "You beastly child, you!"

Onepiece, naturally enough, took this as a compliment, and gave his rusty little laugh. "Belle come play!"

"Certainly not! I am here to help your mama."

"Mum," grunted Onepiece, and climbed into Poly's lap.

Since he didn't seem inclined to any other mischief than to make faces at the fashion plate she was holding, Poly let him stay.

"You said Melissa and Luck *were* close," she said to Isabella. "What happened?"

"Nothing that I know of. They were close, and then they weren't. Hullo, is that the hailer? Loud, isn't it?"

Poly felt a touch of warmth in her cheeks. "Oh! I forgot! Melchior said he would visit today."

"Goodness me!" said Isabella admiringly. "You do have good taste! No, I'll keep Onepiece here: you go ahead. Despite what Aunt Oddu may say, I *am* occasionally tactful, and I *can* occasionally mind my own business."

Onepiece said, "No!" grumpily when Poly deposited him in Isabella's lap. Poly heard Isabella say, "Ingratitude!" as she left the house, and was both pleased and a little regretful to hear Onepiece chuckle up at Isabella again. It was silly to feel regret, of course: Onepiece must be encouraged to be fond of other people, after all.

Poly found Melchior almost nose-to-nose with her when she opened the hatch, his mouth curled in a half smile and his hazel eyes laughing at her.

"Did you miss me?" he asked through the hatch.

She said, "Certainly not!" and opened the door. Luck and his orders to keep everyone else out be hanged. It was undoubtedly Melchior, and Luck was out with Melissa, after all. "Do come in."

"No, no," said Melchior. "You're coming out with me."

"Oh, but Luck—"

"Yes, you're a very good ComealongPoly and StayathomePoly, but Luck doesn't own you, after all. Don't you wonder what he's up to? I do. That's what I'm doing today: I thought you might like to join me."

Poly gazed at him for a long, silent moment, while Melchior gazed back mockingly. She could see his obsidian magic tucked away neatly inside him and, partly to shake his mocking smile and partly to see what would happen, Poly let her hair waft forward and wrap lightly around his wrist.

The smile vanished from Melchior's lips. "Now that's very interesting," he said.

He'd gone quite white.

"I shall come with you," Poly said.

Melchior's magic was strong, but it wasn't enchanter strong. He was a wizard, nothing more.

"I wish I could think it was for my charm," said Melchior. "But I have the distinct feeling that you've just found out that I'm no threat to you. Oho, did Luck leave you with a nursemaid? Well met, firebrand!"

"Yes, hullo," said Isabella. "Here to make mischief, are you?"

Melchior winked at Poly and murmured, "Of a kind. Shall we go, princess?"

"Do try to be back before Luck gets home," said Isabella. "He'll only sulk at me, and he's very tedious when he does that."

"Luck is always tedious," said Melchior, seizing Poly's hand and pulling it through his arm. "However, if we can annoy him at all I won't feel the day wasted."

And when they were strolling down the street arm in arm, he said, "I really must congratulate you, princess. Your ensemble is up to date and entirely delightful."

"I was spurred on to modernise myself," said Poly, entirely truthfully.

"Yes, I heard that you'd met Melissa," said Melchior.

He paused: looked up the street, then down it.

Poly, much amused, said, "No one is around to hear. Besides, fashion is hardly a state secret, is it?"

"Not at all," said Melchior, with one last look up and down the street.

Then, seizing her by the waist, he whirled her right through the solid wall they'd been strolling beside. Poly blinked rapidly in the sudden half-light and found herself in a cold, narrow corridor with Melchior's arms snugly around her.

His voice murmured in her ear, "Much better!"

"So it's not just Luck rearranging the city allies," said Poly. Melchior had neatly pinned her arms across her chest, and it was a little difficult to move. "Are you going to let me go?"

He gathered her closer. "I was just trying to make up my mind."

With more interest, Poly inquired, "Are you going to kiss me?"

"Not yet," said Melchior and, regretfully (it seemed to Poly) he released her.

"Why are we in a hidden alley?"

Melchior pulled her hand through his arm and nudged her into a stroll. "I felt the need for privacy."

"Oh. Why?"

"I'm going to tell you a story."

"Oh," said Poly again. "Why?"

"Will it help if I tell you that I'm quite certain you're not actually the Sleeping Princess?"

"Not really," sighed Poly. "It seems to be the worst kept secret in the whole of the three—that is, the whole of the two monarchies. Is your story an adventure?"

"No: a romance. It begins fifteen years ago, when I was a boy of eight or nine."

"Started young, didn't you?" observed Poly. "Not very surprising."

Melchior's hazel eyes glittered. "Do you recall me saying that I wasn't going to kiss you yet?"

"Clearly."

"If you keep that up, I'll find it hard to help myself. Picture me, a child of eight or nine; charming as ever, and on the cusp of being sent away to one of the best boarding schools in New Civet. Every young schoolboy knows the story of the Sleeping Princess, of course: we all dreamed that one day *we* would be the ones to wake her."

"Then how did Luck end up with the job? You can't expect me to believe that he dreamed about rescuing me too."

"I've never been sure that Luck does dream," said Melchior, his lip curling. "As a matter of fact, I had the distinct impression that he doesn't sleep at all. I assumed that he draws energy from free magic like a rather eccentric vampire. However, to continue my romance: by the time I left for school, I wasn't nearly as ignorant as the other boys when it came to the Sleeping Princess."

"Do you mean the real princess, or me?"

"Well, that's the crux of the matter. By then I knew that you weren't the princess at all."

"That was clever of you," said Poly politely. "Considering no one else but Mordion knew."

"Ah, yes, but I had an informant—in fact, I had two."

Poly stopped and wheeled to face him. "My parents told you?"

"Does Luck know that your parents were both Arbiters?" enquired Melchior.

"You told me that you'd never met them," Poly said crossly. "You knew perfectly well when you told me about the Arbiters yesterday that they were my parents!"

"And very adorable I found you! Didn't I tell you that I'd answer your questions, no payment required? Admit it, you had no idea."

"None at all. They've been turning up in such odd places! And what did you mean by telling me you'd never met them?"

"Strictly speaking, I never did," said Melchior. "There's an old oak tree on my estate; an ancient, sprawling thing with a nest of branches. I wanted to climb it the moment I saw it, but my legs weren't long enough until I was eight. When I made it to the nest of branches, this was waiting for me in a bespelled piece of oilskin."

This was a folded piece of paper between his long fingers. It looked old and faded and a little bit fragile. His name was written on the front of it in familiar, blunt handwriting.

Poly looked at it, frowning. "My father and mother wrote to you. Why?"

"First, to tell me everything that had ever happened to me, including a few things that no one except myself knew. Secondly, to enlist me in the rescue of their daughter. They went into it quite thoroughly; told me where you were, how to get there, and what it would take to rescue you."

"Well, why didn't you rescue me, then?" demanded Poly.

"Believe me, it's a grudge I'll hold against Luck until my dying day," said Melchior. "Your parents' letter—amongst others I found later at school—instructed me to wait until I was contacted by a group known as Black Velvet: they also went into the details of when and where you would appear in the Capital. I didn't understand why until I met you yesterday in the Council Hall. They must have known that someone else might get there before me."

"And were you contacted by Black Velvet?"

"Yes: on my sixteenth birthday."

Poly gazed up at him curiously. "You kept this a secret for eight years? Even when your school friends were talking about the Sleeping Princess?"

"Never told a soul," said Melchior, with a half-smiling shrug. "You were *mine*, you see. Something special and delightful and secret. I fell in love with you years before we ever met."

"It must have been a nasty surprise when Luck was sent instead of you."

"Not nearly as nasty as the surprise I got when I realized you'd fallen in love with him instead of me," Melchior said meditatively. "Hm. If Luck hasn't told you how adorably you blush, he's been wasting his time. No, it's no use protesting, I knew it as soon as I saw you together. It *was* meant to be me, you know: Black Velvet was pretty sure Mordion was up to his old tricks, and by then I'd managed to worm my way into the Wizard Council."

"You're not really part of the Council," said Poly, in some relief.

"Good grief, no! They're a throat-cutting bunch of vermin. No, I'm there on a purely informational basis."

Poly said accurately, "You mean you're spying on them."

"Well, yes. We needed to know when Mordion was going to move. We had a pretty good idea of the spells he used to bind you, and why: Peter mentioned the Frozen Battlefield in my letter as well. I was almost certain that things were coming to a head, and I was just where I was meant to be. Mordion was making overtures to offering me the job and I'd gathered everything that I might need. Then Luck showed up again."

"Mordion approached him instead of you."

"Only to be expected, I suppose," said Melchior. Poly thought his voice was a touch bitter. "Why send a wizard when you can send an enchanter? On the other hand, it meant that I was here to see things happen when the truth leaked out to a few influential people."

"Someone tried to kill us before we got to Luck's village."

"Yes, it got out faster than Mordion expected. He had me make friends with a few people around the Capital—"

"More spying?" Poly couldn't help laughing up at him, and his eyes laughed back at her.

"Exactly. It turns out that I have a talent for it. I knew that the Old Parrasians were in contact with someone from the village, so I set myself to finding the link. I thought that if I couldn't be there to look after you, I could at least try and keep you safe from here."

"We found a big piece of communication magic in the village," said Poly. "Well, Luck did, anyway. It looked like it'd gone wrong somehow."

Melchior grinned. "That's because I sabotaged it from this end. They call it a comm-link. It's not much good unless you've got a spare room to set it up in, but when they work out how to link it all up without the need for so much space, it'll be the next big thing."

"Yes, Luck got very excited about it. Melchior, where are we going, exactly?"

The alley was certainly not merely for privacy. Distracted as she was by the conversation, Poly had nevertheless felt the way it *squeezed* improbably between buildings and turned impossible angles. At one point she had been almost certain that they were walking along the alley walls instead of the floor, and now that they were back on the cobbled ground again, it felt distinctly as though the alley was coming to an end.

Poly's hand slipped instinctively away from Melchior's arm, and she realised that she'd half unlaced the glove that covered her antimagic arm only when his fingers covered her own.

"I wouldn't do that in here if I were you," he said softly. "Not unless you want to crush us both midway between two houses."

Poly's hair spread out questingly and told her what she should have realised much sooner. "It's your magic. There wasn't a secret alley: you *made* it. You made a path."

"If you're going to rescue an enchantress from an enchanted castle, you learn to think about secret doors and magic pathways," shrugged Melchior. "I had a long time to think about how I'd manage it. It's about the only thing I can do really well, as a matter of fact."

Poly gave a sudden chuckle. "Rather fitting, isn't it?"

Melchior grinned. "Being such an untrustworthy and generally sneaky person, you mean? Mind the step, Poly."

There was a slight jolt between one step and the next, and then Poly found herself in a small, neat sitting room with street-facing windows.

"We've arrived," said Melchior unnecessarily. "Yes, that is Luck out on Curzon Street. Didn't I tell you he was up to something?"

"Luck is always up to something," murmured Poly. She let Melchior slip the unlaced glove from her hand and waited until he was studying her antimagic arm before she said, "Regarding Black Velvet—I'm sure there isn't a secret organisation dedicated simply to the task of rescuing one bespelled enchantress."

Melchior flicked a glance at her. "Charming and exquisitely mystifying as you are: no. Black Velvet has a range of projects. As a matter of fact, I have a range of objectives myself."

"Which are?"

"Do you know, I thought you'd be more interested in what Luck is up to."

"I *am* interested," said Poly. "But if you *will* offer me bait!"

Melchior's lips curved in a faint smile. Poly had the idea that he was pleased at her interest. "When I was first recruited, I thought my only focus would be you. It turns out that Black Velvet has fingers in many, many pies. I will say merely that they wouldn't be sorry to see the Wizard Council dismantled, Rorkin's staff found, and a royal on the throne."

"Goodness! Very modest in your aims, aren't you? What is Rorkin's staff?"

"Exactly what it sounds like," said Melchior. "A staff belonging to Rorkin. Legend says it's the only thing that can choose the next king or queen. It vanished at the same time that Rorkin was said to have been assassinated."

"You haven't had much luck, have you?"

"Not particularly, no," said Melchior amusedly. "Why do you suppose Luck is visiting a contractual specialist, Poly?"

"Is that what the shop is? I thought it was a lawyer's shopfront."

"Doctor Shore specialises in contracts magical and normal, with a distinct tendency toward finding loopholes in untenable requirements. Does that sound familiar?"

"My enchantment was bound with a governmental spellpaper that makes me property of the state," said Poly slowly. "I haven't looked at the spellpaper in days: Luck probably pinched it when we got here. And Isabella did say that whatever Luck was doing, it was bound to have something to do with me."

"Clever little firebrand," said Melchior approvingly. "She's entirely correct. In that case, we can assume that Luck is trying to find a way to make your contractual spellpaper null and void."

"Why would he do that?"

"I can think of a few reasons. If it was me, I'd be trying to weasel out of the clause that claims you as property of the state. Luck was clever enough to get you to acknowledge him as your champion, which means you're temporarily bound to him and that the state has to negotiate through him, but I wouldn't put it past Mordion to try and have him killed."

"Nor would I," Poly said, and she shivered.

"Have you told Luck about Mordion?"

"I tried to tell—well, not really, I suppose. He went out today before I could talk to him."

"Tell him as soon as you can. If I read the spellpaper aright, the kind of power he could get from doing this particular spell again will be more than enough to rule New Civet for centuries to come. *If* he does it right this time."

Poly felt the familiar tug of dread at her stomach. "Luck is leaving now," she said, trying to quell it.

"No need to follow him, I think," nodded Melchior. "He's off to see Melissa: that's her street he just turned into. Where would you like to go from here?"

"Does it matter?" asked Poly, a little listlessly. "The things I need aren't out here, anyway."

"I suppose not," said Melchior, and his smile was rueful.

"I NEED the rest of my memories," said Poly. She had been playing rather absentmindedly with Onepiece ever since Melchior brought her back home, much to the puppy's satisfaction.

"I can bite," said Onepiece. He thought about it and added, "You. Can bite you. Blood is good."

"No, darling, you don't need to bite me. A nice sharp pin will do the trick." She sighed and looked wistfully at the gate to the alley. It was almost dark, and Luck still wasn't back. "Time to go in, darling."

"Don't want bed," grumbled Onepiece.

Poly was about to tell him that he would have it whether he wanted it or not, but caught a faint murmur of movement outside the gate. She sprang to her feet with a lighter heart, reaching out to sense Luck's magic and—someone else.

"Go to the house, Onepiece," she said, and ran to the gate.

Through the hatch she could see the lit street and a carriage. Luck had already climbed out, but instead of driving on, the coach deposited another passenger. Melissa was dressed in russet today, and as provocative as ever. She said something in Luck's ear as Poly watched, and he smiled.

"Come to me tomorrow, sweeting," she said, this time loud enough for Poly to hear.

A whisper of magic accompanied the words, soft and sly and warm.

Luck said vaguely: "Yes. That will be...nice."

"Until then," Melissa purred.

She kissed him, spreading more of the insidiously sticky magic, and to Poly's dismay, Luck didn't push away either the kiss or the magic. She shut the hatch and went to bed.

18

"Luck, I want to go out today," said Poly.

Luck said, "Huh," and looked bemused. Poly wasn't certain that he'd heard her. She'd been trying all morning without success to detach Melissa's clingy magic. It felt as though Luck, at some level, was holding on to it.

"I want to go out," repeated Poly.

This time Luck looked up with entirely clear eyes. Then he said, "No," with such completely unexpected authority that by the time Poly gathered her startled wits, he had left the house.

She was still fuming when Melchior rapped on the gate.

"You'd better come in," she said crossly.

"Thank you, I'm sure!" said Melchior, greatly amused. "Have you told Luck yet?"

"No," said Poly tightly. "Luck isn't going to be any use."

Melchior sauntered through the gate. "Luck's never any use. I'm surprised that you're only just discovering it. After all, you have been travelling with him for quite some time now. What happened?"

"Melissa."

"I see. Do you need a shoulder to cry on? Perhaps a comforting arm around your waist?"

Spindle

"Not yet," said Poly. "She had to use magic on him."

Melchior gave a soft hiss of laughter. "Very promising for you! Her appeal certainly hasn't vanished, so I can only assume that Luck has become impervious to her charms. You must have made quite an impression."

"Don't," Poly said quietly. "I'd rather not hope, if it's all the same to you."

"Oh, live dangerously, Poly! So Melissa has been reduced to ensorcelling Luck's affections. Perhaps I should stir things up."

"Help me, instead," said Poly. "There are still memories I need to find, and Luck—"

"—is busy elsewhere. Very well. What do you need me to do?"

"Nothing very difficult. I'll be...elsewhere...for a little while. Make sure I don't fall off my chair. Keep Onepiece from worrying. Does blood bother you?"

"Only if it's mine," said Melchior, and followed her into the house.

Poly settled herself comfortably in one of the leafy chairs opposite Melchior, who held an anxious-eyed Onepiece.

"Ready?"

"Yes," Poly said. Her hands felt cold and clumsy, and she drove the needle further into her finger than she'd meant to. She reached to pull the second amber bead from her hair, but it slid through her blood-slick fingers and tumbled to the floor, sprinkling droplets of blood as it fell.

When it hit the floor, Poly found herself in a different chair. This chair, instead of being leafy and a little bit flexible, was cold and hard. Her younger mind was racing, her breath in and out far too fast. It took Poly far too long to realise that her younger self was tied to the chair, palms up.

Somewhere behind her, Mordion's voice said, "Useful things, spellpapers. They have the benefit of turning legally binding contracts into magically binding ones."

"That's very interesting," said the younger Poly's voice. "But what's the point of binding me into a legal contract, let alone a magical one? I haven't got anything of value."

"Now, that's where you're mistaken. You're very valuable to me. Try not to move, won't you? I'd hate to cut off a finger by mistake."

Poly felt the shuddering intake of air as her younger self saw the knife in Mordion's hand. Both incarnations of herself understood the meaning of that. Younger Poly held very still but couldn't help the gasp when Mordion slit a shallow cut in the palm of her hand and pressed a pearly white spellpaper flat against it.

"Thank you, darling," he said.

"I don't have magic," younger Poly told him. There was a burning in her eyes, but she refused to give in to the tears. "You're wasting your time."

"Young enchantresses are always the best. Magic bottled so tightly inside that most of them think they haven't got any. That's unfortunate for you, darling, but it's very helpful to me. I don't need it to be active, you see. I can draw it out of you like marrow from a bone whether it's active or not. And this little paper makes it all legal. You're an asset to the crown, Poly."

Poly felt her younger self open her mouth to reiterate wearily that she didn't have magic, but the thought fizzled away. Something was stirring deep inside of her.

"You can feel it, can't you? The tugging? I'm afraid it will be quite painful for you, darling."

It felt as though her soul were being torn from her body. Poly tried to pull away from the pain, but she was hooked fast in the memory, and she suffered along with her younger self. And there, amidst the pain, was a cold, hard thought that she had to do whatever was necessary to stop Mordion. Poly let herself sink deeper into the memory and became one with her younger self.

"Are you going to kill me?" she asked, through jagged, painful breaths.

"Dear me, no! You'd be no use to me dead. You'll live for a

remarkably long time, I'm afraid. You won't be aware of it, but it'll be a productive life nevertheless. You can go to sleep with the satisfaction of knowing that you're the means of creating the most powerful ruler Civet has ever seen."

"I see," said Poly. She was shaking now, in waves of tiny, wracking shivers. Mordion was going to use her, use her magic, as a power source. It stirred to life within her, but not quickly enough to be any use, for as it woke, Mordion stole it away.

Yet beneath it, uncomfortably pushing, was an unfamiliar something that stirred to life with much greater vigour. Poly's thoughts split distractingly. Her younger self felt the surge of unmagic but didn't know what it was, and fatalistically waited for that to be noticed and stolen away, too. Poly's current self knew the unmagic for what it was, and her heart sang. So *that* was how she'd managed to do the thing!

She felt her eyes fasten on Mordion. The thoughts that flowed past said, *He must have sensed it. Why didn't he react?* and as Mordion busied himself with an egg sized amber stone, the thought wandered through her mind with a sense of lightness, *He hasn't felt it!*

Poly was pleased to find that her first thought was the question of how this new, unexpected power could be utilised. Both aspects of her could see the way it curled through her magic: a strong, clear, lacy kind of thing that at once supported and surpassed the blue magic around it. Her younger self reached out tentatively to it, her fingers barely twitching in sympathetic effort, and as it slipped into her thoughts, she knew what to do.

Older Poly watched the flow of thoughts, her own conclusions leaping to keep up. There was desperation there, because younger Poly knew that, do what she might, she couldn't escape. A lethargy had already overspread her limbs, and while her mind was still awake, fog crept in from the edges.

So her younger incarnation didn't try to escape. Instead, she matched and overtook Mordion's draw upon her magic, feeding it into something big and terrifying and *new*.

In the moment between waking and sleeping, the divided aspects of Poly both saw time and causality spread out before them like a map. They tore their magic apart piece by piece, put it together in a different form laced with unmagic, and scattered it into that vast spread of possibility. When they woke, it would be theirs once more, no matter where they went.

Into the bitterness of defeat, they searched for the last necessary piece, and remembered the bodily discomfort of something hard and sharp pressing against their left leg.

Our spindle, said their thought. They slid the spindle from their pocket with a sliver of unmagic, and it slipped into their blood-slicked palm. *Blood to bind the memories,* they thought, and they pieced the memories at the back of their mind, linked to the pain and the blood.

"Now, now, that's no way to behave," said Mordion, quick as a snake. They hadn't thought he'd been watching, but his fingers wrenched the spindle from their hand. He cocked an eyebrow at them but dropped the spindle again. "I'm not sure exactly what you think you're attempting, my dear. However, just to be safe—"

They saw him reach for them in the last moments before sleep claimed them, hands coated with their own magic and the universe in his eyes.

"Forget," he said, and as he said it, they stripped the spindle completely of magic, every last drop, until they could feel it calling out its emptiness to the world.

Then they rested, hopeful and despairing; bitter and satisfied.

"Forget," said Mordion again, the command impossible to refuse.

They tasted the sourness of defeat, and when Poly woke, she was one again.

"Sweetheart, don't cry," said someone's voice remorsefully.

A smaller voice was shouting "Mum! *Mum!* No! Let Onepiece *go!*"

"We're all right," whispered Poly, with great weariness. "I mean, I'm all right. Come here, Onepiece."

Melchior released the Onepiece's skinny wrists, and the boy dived into Poly's lap, wrapping his arms around her with feral intensity.

"Mum is safe now," he said, clumsily patting her hair.

Melchior sat back, visibly exhaling in relief. "Unpleasant memories?"

"Very," said Poly quietly. She lifted a hand to wipe away the tears, but Melchior caught it before she could do so.

"That's not a good idea, sweetheart," he said. He fumbled in his breast pocket and produced a handkerchief, with which he dabbed her tears away and wiped the blood from her hand. "Did you get what you needed?"

"I think so."

"Mordion?"

"Yes. We—that is, I—hid away as much of my magic as I could, but he got a lot. I don't think he was expecting it to be as strong as it was, and he only expected magic. That must be why everything went so badly wrong when I went to sleep."

"Were your memories clear?"

"Very extremely," said Poly.

"Good. That means we can use them as evidence. I know someone who can help with that."

"A friend of yours?"

"Yes, not that he knows it. I can't come with you when you see him: each of us is under strict orders not to attempt to find the others. It's safer if we don't know who the others are."

"Then why do you know?"

Melchior's thin lips curled. "I'm special."

Poly gave a sniff of laughter. "What does your friend do?"

"He collects impressions and memories. He's quite the artiste, actually. He's one of the few practitioners whose work is legally acceptable as evidence in criminal or legal matters."

"He'll *collect* my memories? Will I still have them?"

Melchior looked faintly amused. "Of course. Brackett only copies the memories. Can you take Luck with—"

"No."

"In that case, I'll take you as close as I can," said Melchior. "The streets are a bit lively at the moment, or you'd probably be safe enough alone."

"Yes, I seem to bring out the worst in the general populace," said Poly, thinking of the ambered faces at the Frozen Battlefield, terrifying in their joyfulness.

"Oh, they've been rioting for the last hundred or so years," Melchior said easily. "Gives them something to do. They mill about in the streets holding up signs that say *'Give back Parras'* and *'Parras for the Parrasians'* and all that sort of thing. Occasionally one of them does something like what happened in council yesterday, but none of them ever seem to want to run for council."

Poly shivered, prompting Onepiece to burble nonsense into her neck from where his head was resting. "At least no one has tried to kidnap me again, I suppose."

"I did hear that you'd been waylaid by a pack of Royalists. What happened?"

"Luck used it as an opportunity to ah, develop my skills," Poly said dryly. "I very nearly hit him again."

Melchior's eyebrows flew up. "Again? You've hit him before? *This,* I want to hear!"

"Well, you're not going to hear about it!" said Poly firmly. "And speaking of Luck, what exactly is he up to today? He wouldn't tell me anything. As a matter of fact, he only said one word to me this morning."

"Hm," said Melchior. "I know what he's up to, but I don't particularly want to tell you."

There was a leadening sense of gloom in her stomach, but Poly couldn't help smiling. "Why is that?"

"You might hit me," he explained, surprising a giggle from her.

"Then I assume he was on his way to visit Melissa again."

"I believe so. Don't worry, sweetheart; we'll give him a bit of a hurry-up when he gets back tonight."

"We won't do anything of the kind. You'll be gone before Luck gets back, thank you very much."

"Do you really think so?" Melchior said affably. "Well, we won't argue. I get far too much enjoyment out of being the amiable party for once. Feeling better?"

"It's stopped bleeding," said Poly, observing her hand.

"Good. Let's do something fun."

AT ONEPIECE'S INSISTENCE, they went paddling. Poly, who could feel the stream wending its way through Luck's yard, not quite where it should be and oddly unsettled, had told him that if he could find it, she would let him paddle.

Onepiece gave a deep chuckle and darted away across the grass, lurching between hillocks and unexpected patches of briars.

"I hope he knows where he's going," said Melchior, offering his arm to Poly. "I don't! I never could find that blasted stream of Luck's. I swear it's somewhere different every time I visit."

"Yes, he said a bit of Don't See must have dribbled into the water. I don't think he's right."

"That must be rather good for Luck," Melchior said reflectively. "I can't remember the last time someone told him he was wrong."

"Well, it's quite easy to see the stream," Poly pointed out. "I can see it from the window every time I look out, and most times I can see it when I walk in the gate. The trouble is getting to it. I don't think it exactly stays still—in fact, I don't think it's really *here* properly. It feels more like Forest."

"As much as I love to think myself magically competent, Forest has never been one of my strong points. You'd better lead the way."

"That must have been very painful for you," said Poly, with dancing eyes.

"It was, thank you! I prefer not to admit weakness. Hm, your boy seems to have found the stream."

It would have been more correct to say that Onepiece had pounced on the stream and, having pounced, held it down while it wriggled wildly in an attempt to escape. That attempt proving unsuccessful, the stream had evidently decided to play dead, and was now glimmering more or less solidly not twenty feet away.

"Paddles for Onepiece!" shouted the boy and leapt into the shallows without regard to his trousers.

Melchior, less careless of his clothing, stopped to roll up his trousers and remove his shoes. Then he pretended not to watch while Poly tucked up her skirts and joined Onepiece in the shallows.

"Considerate of Luck to arrange for such beautiful weather in his little patch of the world," he said. His thin lips were more than usually sarcastic.

Poly, equally so, said, "Yes, wasn't it? I think the land does it, actually: Luck doesn't really notice weather."

"No!" marvelled Melchior. "I would never have guessed! Sweetheart, must you splash my second-best waistcoat?"

"Yes," said Poly, feeling wonderfully lighter for the laughter. "Yes, I really must!"

It was late afternoon before it occurred to Poly that she ought to be sending Melchior on his way. She would have remembered sooner if Melchior hadn't been so delightfully and determinedly entertaining. By the time she *did* remember, it was all but impossible to usher him out. He merely sauntered and smiled and looked mockingly at Poly when she hit him in the arm with one clenched fist.

"A person could think they weren't welcome," he said.

"A person would be right," said Poly crossly. "You're being deliberately unhelpful!"

"Don't be like that, sweetheart. Look at the progress you've made: you've managed to chivvy me past the house already."

A laugh escaped before Poly could quite help it. "You're up to something, and I don't trust you," she said. "Go home before Luck gets here!"

"Behold me, going! I'll come for you again tomorrow, shall I?"

"Yes, please," said Poly, relief warring with amusement. Onepiece had already capered off toward the house, and if she was *very* lucky, Melchior would be outside before Luck got back.

"Oh, and one more thing," said Melchior. His eyes were dancing with mischief and Poly automatically narrowed her eyes at him. "Now, Poly, it's for your own good. Please don't struggle, I don't think my ego could take the sting."

Poly wasn't quite surprised to find herself being kissed. Melchior's kiss was really very nice—warm and deep with no stand-offishness to it—so she let herself enjoy it without wondering too much what he was up to.

He let it linger pleasantly and then whispered in her ear, "You're welcome."

She followed the direction of his gaze and saw Luck sweeping toward them through the grass, his eyes very green and narrow, and his magic standing out around him in sharp golden shards. Poly valiantly choked down a giggle, feeling at once elated and nervous, and saw Melchior wink.

He said, "You might need this, sweetheart," and tugged loose the knot that kept her glove laced.

He bowed and made himself scarce before Poly could accuse him of cowardice, which might possibly have been a good thing, since at Luck's closer approach she swiftly put a tree between him and herself, and it would have seemed perilously close to hypocrisy.

Luck dealt with the tree by exploding it into splinters, and when Poly automatically grew another, he disintegrated that as well, striding through the dust without stopping. Poly's eyes, wide and startled, took in the way his magic leapt in intensity, and hastily threw up a protective wall that was strong and see-through, and not entirely steady.

"Poly, come out of there!"

"No," said Poly. "You'd only start throwing magic at me."

"I'm not going to throw magic at you," snarled Luck. To his credit, he was holding his magic in very tight check: Poly could see it straining to break against her wall. "I'm going to give you a good spanking!"

"Oh. Well, I think I'll stay in here, then." Poly looked at him speculatively and added with more than a hint of mendacity, "I don't see why you're so upset."

Luck's eyes locked on hers, glowing with molten gold, and Poly found that she couldn't look away. He said tightly, "I told you not to let anyone in! These people are raving, cannibalistic, prairie-creepers. I *told* you, Poly. The Royalists want to chain you to the throne, the Old Parrasians want to kill you, and the Council wants to—"

"Yes?" prompted Poly, well aware that Luck had tumbled over the reminder that Melissa was very much a part of the Council.

"Well, at least they're honest about it. Nobody has ever known which side Melchior's on."

"He's on my side," said Poly.

It was the one thing she was really sure of when it came to Melchior.

Luck said something rude not entirely under his breath, and added, "You've no business consorting with him. I won't have people sniggering behind their hands at us."

"Nobody is sniggering at us!"

"Melchior is sniggering," said Luck obstinately.

Fairmindedly, Poly said, "Well, yes, probably; but Melchior sniggers at everyone, I think."

"And what do you mean by letting him kiss you?" demanded Luck, reminded of her perfidy. "You didn't hit *him*."

"Well. No," said Poly, and added hastily, "Luck, I need to talk to you about Mordion."

"I don't want to talk about Mordion. I want to know why you hit me every time I kiss you and don't hit Melchior."

"Luck, it's the same Mordion I used to know. He's the one that—"

"Rubbish. I told you that before, Poly."

"Don't tell me 'rubbish'!" said Poly heatedly. "I *remembered* it!"

"Then you must have got the magic wrong," said Luck.

"I didn't get the magic wrong. Mordion was—"

"Mordion's not an enchanter. He's not even a particularly good wizard. Your magic must have gotten too old and decayed."

Poly very precisely pushed her glasses up on her nose. She had a feeling that she would hit Luck if she didn't do something else with her hands.

"My magic is perfectly fine, and I remembered perfectly clearly," she told him.

"Poly, you're not to go trysting with wizards when you've nominated me as your Champion."

"Don't change the subject!"

"And you're not to keep going out for the day as soon as I leave."

"Why not?" demanded Poly. "And if it comes to that, why can't I talk to whomever I please? *You're* off with Melissa all day!"

There was a brief moment of pause. Then Luck said, "Yes. Well. That's different."

"No, it's not," said Poly bitterly. Melissa's magic was still twined in and around Luck's—and, if anything, only seemed to have multiplied in amount and tenacity since the morning.

"*Completely* different," said Luck. "Poly—"

"What?" Poly prompted, when it became evident that Luck wasn't going to continue the thought.

"You're being very difficult today. You don't listen to anything I say, and you've gotten prickly again."

"I'm not prickly!"

"And you haven't been paying attention! If you'd been paying attention, you wouldn't be making things difficult."

"*Me?*" gasped Poly. "*Me* making things difficult!"

"Yes," said Luck, with dignity. "I'm tired, and I'm going to bed. I will be out all day tomorrow, and I expect you to stay at home."

He swept away toward the house, leaving Poly dumbstruck for just a moment too long. "You can expect what you want!" she shouted after him. "I shall be out all day as well!"

By the time she got back to the house Luck was nowhere to be seen. Poly, sitting down crossly in one of the chairs she'd coaxed to grow in the living room, thought that it was just as well. She laced her glove again, conscious of a feeling of grating disappointment as the unmagic spiral disappeared beneath a layer of lace.

"Angry wizard," said Onepiece's voice, making her jump. He was crouched in one of the corners, dismantling a small, rusty spell. "Angry mum."

"We're not—oh, well, I suppose we are angry. Don't worry, darling; we're not angry with you."

"Not bedtime," said Onepiece, correctly anticipating the result of being brought to her notice again. "I am splashy-wet and will catcherdeath."

"You won't catch your death because I shall dry you," said Poly firmly. "*Must* you take that messy thing with you?"

"Yus," he said, gathering all the pieces of the spell with surprising care. "Wizard doesn't like little pieces everywhere."

"Very well, but no playing with it when you're supposed to be sleeping."

"Pft," said Onepiece in dissatisfaction, but he followed her to his bedroom obediently enough. He stood still to let Poly dry him off, turning his pieces of spell over in his hands, and when she was finished, he put each piece precisely on the washstand, making a semicircle.

"Can do it myself," he said, when she went to unbutton his shirt.

"We'll see," said Poly, but she resisted the urge to help him when he attempted to put his head through the arms of his nightshirt. She chivvied him into bed, cocooning him tightly in the blanket to make him giggle, then left a tiny moonshine glow of magic to keep him company and went in search of the kitchen.

She was still simmering with annoyance, so when her attempts to settle in front of the gently glowing stove with a cup of tea failed, Poly brought out the fashion plates that Isabella had brought her, and crossly made frock after frock for the pleasure of disintegrating them with a wave of her hand. The process was obliquely satisfying, and by the time she began to think that she could sleep, Poly had amassed five or six of the ensembles that she had not been able to bring herself to destroy.

Now let Melissa try to look down her lovely nose at Poly! The militant thought brought with it a renewed sense of sourness, but Poly pushed it aside. After all, it wasn't as though she had made a push to interest Luck when she'd had the chance. If she had, Luck might not now be ensorcelled to Melissa.

Poly thought about that, then thought about Luck's utter obliviousness to any of the young ladies in the village.

"Oh, what utter nonsense," she said to herself. "He probably wouldn't even have noticed."

19

Luck was already gone when Poly and Onepiece finished breakfast the next day. Poly wasn't surprised by that, but she was surprised that Isabella hadn't yet made an appearance, and a sneaking suspicion made her stroll to the gate with Onepiece prancing beside her. Having done so, she found Isabella leaning elegantly against one of the alley walls and sighing at her polished fingernails.

When she saw the gate open, Isabella said resignedly, "What's Luck done this time?"

"Silenced the hailer, by the looks," said Poly, giving the door's magic a brief overlook.

She ushered Isabella in, finding in the process that when open, the doorway strenuously resisted any attempt she made to approach closer than a foot towards it.

"Dear me!" said Isabella. "Luck *has* been busy, hasn't he?"

Poly, struggling to close the gate again, gave her an expressive look.

"How wonderful!" Isabella said, laughing delightedly. "Luck is becoming more interesting than ever! Shall you be confined to the premises, then?"

"I don't think so," said Poly grimly, succeeding at last.

"Good for you! Will you be going out straight away?"

"No: I need your advice first."

"Even more wonderful! I delight in giving out advice!"

"Amongst other things," said Poly, with a rather dry laugh.

Isabella was younger even than Margaret, but her quickness of mind made it difficult to remember that she was two years younger than Margaret, and some three or four years younger than Poly herself—if one were to count only the years Poly had spent awake.

Isabella's grey eyes danced. "Oh yes! Amongst many other things! But I do believe you and Luck are my favouritest thing at the moment. Shall you be wanting advice on matters of dress?"

"Yes: I made a few things last night."

"Just made a few things last night!" sighed Isabella enviously. "Oh, what I wouldn't give for your talent! Very well: show me to the goodies."

Much to Poly's secret satisfaction, Isabella immediately pointed to Poly's favourite emerald green ensemble. "This one, without a doubt. Lengthen the cuffs a trifle and make the bustle more of a suggestion than an actual bustle, and you'll be the most fashionable lady traversing the streets of the Capital. Excepting myself, of course."

"Of course," agreed Poly, making the suggested changes with a few tweaks. "Anything else?"

"Well, that depends."

"On?"

"Well, were I making this particular ensemble for *myself*—and do feel free to take that as a hint, by the bye—I'd put in an extra fall of material just here, beneath the bustle."

"That'll make it heavier, won't it?" said Poly curiously, making a few more tweaks.

Her experience with Isabella's sense of style had led her to believe that Isabella preferred a certain simplicity and elegance of cut.

"Oh, certainly; but the benefits far outweigh the drawback of an extra pound or so of weight. The cut will still look slim and tight, but should you need to run—"

"Now, where would you get the idea that I might need to run?" asked Poly, her eyes bright with amusement.

Isabella met them, her own dancing. "An extensive knowledge of Luck. Besides, the extra fall of material is decidedly elegant, don't you think?"

"I do," agreed Poly, observing the difference. She made a little blue flicking of magic that slithered around her and curled out into green velvet.

"The world is an unfair place," Isabella sighed, watching with envious interest. "Shall you be walking out with Melchior today?"

"I shall."

"*So* unfair! Oh, not those shoes, Poly! You can't wear slippers out for daywear!"

"What if I need to run?" countered Poly.

"Learn to run in heeled boots, naturally! Black, of course, tooled with an elegant version of spats—*not* real ones, thank you very much. If you're *very* sophisticated you may have a red or gold heel, but I suggest leaving those for evening wear."

"I'll probably break an ankle," said Poly; and then, observing Isabella's shoes, "Yours aren't black and white."

"No, but I am *excessively* sophisticated."

"And very modest," agreed Poly.

Isabella gave her an enchanting grin. "So Aunt Oddu says. Is that someone yelling at the gate, do you suppose?"

"Melchior!" said Poly in dismay. "I'd better go. Onepiece is working on a spell: don't let him experiment with it in the house, will you?"

"Certainly not," said Isabella cheerfully. "Do have a lovely day! I'm sure you will: after all, you'll have some delightful scenery to look at."

Poly met Isabella's saucy look with a narrow-eyed one, and hurried off to do battle with Luck's gate once again.

. . .

"I really approve," said Melchior. "In fact, I congratulate Luck."

"You *could* have helped," said Poly. Her cheeks were still hot and flushed. The enchantment Luck had put on the gate hadn't been easy to bypass. In the end she had been forced to shove through it by sheer brute force, leading to some disarray of her new ensemble and a very high flush. Luck's enchantment had fared much worse.

"And miss that particularly luscious little blush? I think not. Is the firebrand responsible for your new outfittings?"

"By and large," said Poly, growing a little pinker. "Melchior, is it really necessary to put your arm around my waist?"

"Rhetorically, or essentially?" asked Melchior, his thin lips curling. "I've a feeling that my time with you is fleeting. I therefore feel it incumbent upon me to take up every opportunity of putting my arms around you."

"I'm not going anywhere, you know," said Poly. "Not with Mordion and Luck, and everything."

"Yes," said Melchior, still with that twisted smile. "*Everything.* However, things must eventually change, whether or no I will, and until then I shall enjoy the moment."

"I thought I was in love once before Luck," Poly said. "It was silly, now that I come to think of it. Only he was so beautiful, and so much fun, and I got a bit carried away."

"Are you sharing life lessons, sweetheart? Life goes on, and so on?"

"No," Poly said slowly. "Only by rights, I should have fallen in love with you: you're obviously cut out to be the hero of the piece. I'm sure it would have been more comfortable than being in love with Luck."

"Ah, the double-edged sword," said Melchior. He was grinning. "One wonders if one is supposed to be inordinately flattered, or mildly insulted. One likes to think that one would be an exciting lover."

"You're exciting in all the right ways," Poly said comfortingly. "Luck is exasperating and annoying—oh, and wonderful and *home*. I've never felt at home before. Melchior, you've made me maudlin!"

"Then do feel free to consider this arm a comforting rather than a romantic gesture."

"Very kind of you."

"Altruistic, in fact," nodded Melchior. "No, Poly, I think we won't go down that street."

Poly looked around him. "Are those people holding sticks?"

"Signs. Someone must have arranged a protest. Shall we go by the back way?"

"Another of your secret passages?"

"I've only one talent," said Melchior, his mouth more than usually sarcastic. "I flaunt it where and when I find myself able. Stay close."

This hidden corridor was stone instead of brick and didn't curve as circuitously as the first had. Poly paid attention this time, running her fingers idly through the sable strands of magic that forged an impossible path through stone and wood and mortar, and thought she understood how it was done.

Melchior gave her a swift look beneath his lashes, but only said, "Here is where you and I part ways, Poly. It would be unfortunate if anyone inconvenient were to see us together in Brackett's vicinity—especially when it leaks out that he's Preserved your memories as evidence. I have something of a reputation to uphold."

"All right," said Poly, feeling absurdly abandoned.

It was ridiculous to feel anxious about something as relatively normal as paying a house call. Luck had dragged her into far more perilous situations.

Only if Luck was with her, Poly thought, she wouldn't feel anxious. Because Luck, for all his throwing magic and suspicious lack of attention, had always been paying attention at just the right moment.

"I'll be right here waiting for you," said Melchior encouragingly. "And Brackett doesn't bite, after all. He's a bad tempered, penny-pinching old miser, but he knows his job. Number eight."

The memory business must have served Brackett well—his house was the finest in the street, and the street itself was finer than any Poly had yet seen, excepting only the Capital Square. It was certainly nothing like the ordinary little street that Luck's house was attached to. There was no door knocker, nor was there a bellpull, but when Poly dubiously pressed the little button beside the door, she heard a faint buzzing from the other side of the door. She sent out bright blue tendrils of magic to explore this new phenomenon, and discovered to her surprise that unlike Luck's hailer, this buzzer was not magical. It sparked with a sharp metal life all of its own.

While she was still surveying the metal-wired buzzer the door opened, a soft, inward tug of air that disconcerted Poly.

"The Sleeping Princess to see Doctor Brackett," she said, startled into a brief staccato of words.

The butler's face went slightly blank with shock and then firmed into lines of immense rigidity. "Will you come in, Your Highness? I will place you in the sitting room, if I may be so bold. Doctor Brackett will be with you *immediately*."

He wheeled in as grand a manner as any steward, and Poly followed his poker-straight back down the grand hall and into a large receiving room. The windows were tall and thin and clear, streaming sunlight into the room from the road: the effect was at once warm and slightly chilling.

Poly sat down in one of the elegant chairs, careful of her half-bustle, and was composed enough to cross her ankles and incline her head graciously when the butler said, "May I say, your Highness, what an honour it is to welcome you. I shall fetch the Master."

BRACKETT'S EXAMINATION room above was as contradictorily warm and chill as the lower rooms had been. Poly, sitting more gingerly than ever on the leather chair she was offered, watched Brackett pour tea. He was a small, white-haired man in very precisely mended clothing, as if after the extravagance of the best house in the street, he had felt the need to economise. His face was sharp and acquisitive, with clever eyes and a sly smile that Poly wasn't sure she liked. He looked capable.

"I've been expecting you," he said at last, offering one of the teacups to her.

"So I understand," Poly said, refusing to be impressed.

Brackett gave a sharp grin. "Friends in high places, Your Highness! Friends in high places, eh? You have some memories for me?"

"I believe so. Our friends would like them—well, *copied*, or whatever it is you do to them."

"Evidence, is it?" Brackett's eyes were sharp. "Sorry, highness: I forgot the sugar cubes! Allow me!"

Poly opened her mouth to protest that she didn't take sugar in her tea, but a cube had already tumbled into her cup from Brackett's silver sugar tongs.

"Help yourself to biscuits, your Highness," he said. "I have a few things to prepare."

Interested, Poly sipped her tea and watched him. There were magical things about the room, mostly small, uninteresting charms, but Brackett wasn't tinkering with any of them. When it came right down to it, he didn't seem to be doing much except moving things around on his desk, and that was curious.

Poly blinked at his quick, clever fingers, her teacup tumbling to the carpeted floor, and thought, *That's funny. The room's gone dark.*

She felt a soft, distant tickle of fear in her stomach. The curse was broken: why was she falling asleep? *What had Brackett put in the tea?*

She moved one heavy hand, fingers tangled in the laces of her other, gloved hand, and somewhere across the room, a small magical something sparked a huge magical Something Else.

"Sit. Still," said Brackett's voice. There was something stiff and wrong about it. "I. Will attend. To you. Shortly."

He was moving his fingers again—this time curiously, jerkily—and Poly thought she understood. The magical Something Else that surrounded Brackett like a haze, seeping into skin and nail, was Someone Else gradually taking over his body.

Poly fumbled at the laces of her glove again, cold and heavy and clumsy, and felt the warmth of antimagic spiralling up her arm. It pricked at the lethargy in her limbs, sending a shock of wakefulness through her, and Poly gulped in a breath that felt fresh and blissfully alive.

"Don't bother struggling, darling," said Brackett. It was still his voice, but Poly knew the cadence of the words—the slightly mocking tone to the endearment. "It's not a spell; it's tincture of lilly-pilly. There's no fighting that, I'm afraid."

"Mordion," said Poly, curling the fingers of her antimagic hand. She was quite certain that she would need it before long. The lilly-pilly, now—that was easy enough. "There's magic in everything. You should know that, but I'm glad you don't."

From somewhere in the depths of her stomach she found the specks of ambient magic in the lilly-pilly and pulled them upwards. Then she vomited them onto the floor until she was headachy but awake.

"Well," said Mordion, through Brackett's face. "I have to say, darling, I didn't expect such an er, *earthy* solution from you."

He lunged for her, and Poly tumbled out of the chair, her legs trembling but supportive. Brackett's body was old and slow, and he was far behind her when she dashed for the door.

"Locked, I'm afraid," he said, panting.

Poly tried the knob anyway, jabbing with her magic at the lock, and found that her magic didn't work. It was there, and present, and powerful—and then sucked up as soon as it touched the door.

That was familiar.

"Heavily soaked in antimagic," said Mordion, confirming her

suspicion. He held a small tube filled with something dark and fluid, the tip of which looked unpleasantly sharp. "So is Brackett's body. I had a suspicion that you might have got back your magic, and I couldn't positively count on the tincture working. You're a resilient young woman, Poly."

"I've had a lot of practise fighting off unconsciousness," said Poly, rather bitterly.

Behind her bustle she rested the palm of her antimagic hand on the door. It tingled where it rested against the wood, like recognising like, but didn't suggest any way of unlocking the door.

"This will be much more pleasant for you if you sit down again," said Mordion, leaning casually on a chair top with Brackett's hand. "If you make me chase you around the room, I will be less inclined to be gentle with you."

"I remember sitting down for you once," said Poly. "It wasn't very pleasant. I'll take my chances."

Mordion pushed a thumb against the end of the fluid-filled tube, and a tiny spurt of dark liquid leapt in the air, scenting the room with lilly-pilly.

"I've measured the dose myself this time," he said. "It works rather devastatingly quickly when injected. No time for any of that nastiness."

His voice was thoughtful and calm, and despite herself Poly wasn't ready for him to toss the chair aside and leap at her. She dodged away with desperate slowness, and Brackett's fingers bruised her arm where he grasped at it, throwing her off balance and into the cluttered occasional table.

Mordion caught her as she tried to scramble up, Brackett's stubby fingers clawing at her shoulder and his weight heavy across her legs. She kicked desperately, her breath loud in her ears and the floorboards rough and unforgiving beneath her. There was hot breath at her neck, fabric tangling her legs, and then Poly's heeled boots found soft, sensitive flesh and she kicked once more, viciously.

Glass flew and shattered as Brackett's body jerked away and into something else, and Poly scrambled to her feet, dress tearing and palms bleeding. Mordion swore behind her in a groaning gasp, horribly close.

There was a warmth in Poly's antimagic hand that wasn't from the bloody scapes across her palm, and she threw a wild look around the room. Antimagic door. Antimagic Brackett. No windows. Solid block walls of quarried stone. There was no way out. But Melchior opened passageways in the space between mortar and brick, and he had shown her how.

Poly ran for the wall ahead of her and didn't stop. Then she was running down a shadowed passage at impossible angles, her gloveless antimagic arm clenched tight to her chest where her heart beat hard and fast. Mordion stumbled into the passage after her, the sound of Brackett's footsteps spiralling behind her, heavy and irregular.

He caught up so quickly that Poly only had time to give one short, startled scream as he spun her roughly around. Her glasses jerked off her nose and clattered to the ground somewhere out of sight. Poly, reverting to instinct, plied her black-heeled shoes with such vigour that Mordion abruptly released her once more.

She fell, backwards this time, her antimagic arm flying up and out in a vain attempt to catch herself. Brackett's body fell with her, and Poly felt her fingers scratch flesh and then magic. The passage collapsed in on itself, but Poly was already falling free. She landed heavily in a familiar brick alley and sent something skittering sideways with her skirts.

Mordion said something that sounded like, "Urk!" in Brackett's voice and slumped to the ground, a blurry muddle to Poly's unaided eyes. Poly felt frantically for her glasses and found them against the alley wall. She put them on with shaking hands and straight away wished she hadn't.

Brackett was sprawled out on the ground—the half to three-quarters of him that had been outside the passage when it collapsed, that is—but the rest of him had vanished with the passage. Poly caught a fleeting glimpse of slick red, and white bone, and took her glasses off again.

She climbed stiffly to her feet, feeling the warmth of tears on her cheeks, and carefully made her way to the familiar alleyway that she had homed in on as if it really was home.

All she needed to do was go back through the alley and get through the gate. Something stirred her hair as she stumbled over the alley entrance, but when Poly twitched herself around in fear, she found that it was only Brackett's magic following her. It sank into the strands of her hair and made a single white streak from the crown of her head to the end of her hair.

"What a waste!" said a familiar voice.

Poly dried her tears with cold hands and put her glasses back on her nose. She felt sick and stiff and not quite real.

"I could have found a good deal of use for that," said Mordion, strolling into the alley behind her. "I don't think you appreciate how much of an annoyance you are."

"I'm always glad to be of assistance," said Poly, through her teeth. She was shaking from head to foot, and it was difficult to stop her voice from shaking as well.

"I don't think I've seen anything quite like *that* before," he said thoughtfully, nodding at her bare antimagic arm with its silver spiral.

Poly laughed before she knew what she was doing. "That's ironic. You're the one who gave it to me."

Mordion's eyes sharpened on her face. "That's the dog leash? Now, how did you manage to do that, I wonder?"

"You can tell me if you ever find out."

"You do me an injustice, darling. I merely *heard* about it: I wasn't the author of the scheme. I did allow it to go forward without interfering, I'll admit. I hoped it would give Luck a few moments of unpleasantness."

"You don't know Luck very well, then," said Poly. "He got me to unleash the dog."

"And thus we come to the crux of the matter," said Mordion

affably. "I *don't* know Luck very well. But Melissa does, and I flatter myself that I know you quite well now."

"Do you?" asked Poly, opening the gate and slipping through before he could get any closer. "Then you should know that I'm about to shut the gate in your face."

Mordion said to the closing gate, "Have you seen Luck today?"

Poly's fingers froze around the latch. "He's been busy."

"Oh, he has. He and Melissa have been very, very busy."

"What's your point?" asked Poly coldly.

"Luck is otherwise engaged tonight. You won't see him again. And unless you present yourself at the Council Hall tomorrow by ten, I'll use him instead."

"You're nothing like strong enough to control Luck," Poly said, with a coldness growing in her.

She remembered Melissa's sticky magic curled parasitically around Luck's and found herself unsure.

"I'm not," agreed Mordion. "Melissa, however, has him well in hand. I wouldn't be able to get all of his magic, of course: he has none of your delightful pliability. But I'll take him if I can't take you."

"I see," said Poly. Mordion was smiling at her in a friendly sort of way that stopped far short of his eyes. "I'll be there."

She closed the gate on him and sat down in the grass, deathly tired. With her eyes closed and her head resting against the gate, she heard Mordion walk out of the alley, his footsteps clicking against brick. She didn't open her eyes again until she heard quick, uneven footfalls through the grass and Onepiece tumbled into her arms.

"Mum!" he said, and made a sticky *mwah!* against her cheek.

"Terribly sorry," said Isabella, her eyes sharp. She was only a few feet away. "Toffee, I'm afraid. I'm sure there's a more comfortable chair in the house, you know, despite Luck. And I have a suspicion that a very strong cup of tea is in order."

"No," said Poly wearily, rousing herself sufficiently to climb to her feet with Onepiece clasped in her arms. "That is, not yet. Melchior is waiting for me in one of his created passages."

"Shall I tell him that you were called away? I think you shouldn't be out and about right now."

"Please."

"Very well," said Isabella. She opened the gate and said, "Dear me. What would you like me to do with the body on the street?"

"Oh." Poly blinked foggily. "Can you get rid of it?"

"Certainly. Aunt Oddu has some very useful connexions. I take it we are *not* reporting the matter?"

"Not yet."

"Very well," said Isabella again. "Go to the house, Poly. You're worrying Onepiece."

Poly, belatedly realising that Onepiece was patting her head and murmuring, "Good Poly. Good mum. Good, good, good. Good mum," smiled at him to take the anxious look from his eyes and said to Isabella, "Yes. Thank you."

When Isabella returned, Onepiece was napping across Poly's shoulder. Unwilling to wake him, and still more unwilling to lose the comfort of his dead weight, Poly took him with her to let Isabella back in.

The girl looked her up and down and said frankly, "You still look awful. Tea, I think. Then you can tell me all about it."

They made tea in the kitchen, sitting on the kitchen table with their feet dangling, while Isabella asked sharp questions and Poly held Onepiece close, comforting herself with his warmth.

"Luck isn't coming home this afternoon?"

"No. I'll fetch him tomorrow."

"Melissa?"

"No. Well, yes, directly. Indirectly, Mordion."

Isabella's eyes narrowed. "Blackmail?"

"Yes. Will you spend the day with Onepiece again tomorrow?"

"Of course. What shall you do?"

"I'm not exactly sure yet," said Poly. "Last time I was taken by surprise. I think Mordion might regret giving me time to think things over."

"How did you come to be involved with such a disreputable character? I can't help feeling that Mordion isn't at *all* the sort of man to interest you."

"He and I met a long time ago," Poly said. "He seems to be a collector of powerful things. He decided that I was a powerful thing to be collected long before I knew I was an enchantress. The first I knew of it was when he cursed me and bound most of my magic to himself."

"So *that's* how he's lived so long!" said Isabella, in satisfaction. "There have been rumours, and I did wonder—only there always *are* rumours and they're not always true. But Poly, if he *did* curse you, why send Luck to wake you up?"

"He didn't get it quite right the first time. Some of that was because I managed to work a rather big bit of magic, and some of it was because he didn't realise how much power he was trying to take on. Something went very badly wrong and almost the whole of Civet—"

"Went mad overnight," finished Isabella, her eyes sparkling. "Goodness! You've made quite the impression over the centuries, haven't you?"

Poly laughed bitterly. "I really have."

"Yes, that was rather thoughtless of me, wasn't it? What can I do to help?"

"Keep Onepiece safe for me. I hope—that is, I might not make it back. If I don't, I need to know that he's cared for. And I need you to look after something else for me."

"Anything," nodded Isabella, her young face for once entirely solemn.

Poly felt around the threads of the house and plucked her books from beside her bed. They appeared between herself and Isabella a heartbeat later, making Isabella jump.

"Keep these safe for me, too. If things don't go as well as I hope, I'll need them."

"What are they?"

"Guidebooks. Receptacles. Something to help me remember."

"Very well," said Isabella. "They'll be safe with me. Poly, what's the worst that could happen?"

"Me asleep again," Poly said, shivering. In his sleep, Onepiece clung closer. "Luck enchanted not to rescue me. Mordion in power again."

"Best case?"

"Mordion, dead," said Poly, her voice as sharp as glass.

20

Isabella stayed through the afternoon and all that night, a sharp bolstering presence and conscientious maker of tea, to Poly's distant amusement. It seemed that there wasn't a problem Isabella didn't consider could be solved by the constant application of tea. Since she couldn't sleep, Poly accepted the tea and used the time to think. It was a regrettably frustrating exercise: if she *knew*, thought Poly, really *knew* that Luck was entirely useless in this situation, then she could plot a course of action with reasonable ease.

The question was, *was* Luck entirely useless? And then there was the question of Melchior—who, as lovely as he was, and as useful as he could be if everything *did* go wrong, was nothing like strong enough to help if it came right down to a contest of magic.

As the morning broke and grew later, Poly laid Onepiece out in her bed. Her arms ached with the loss of warmth and fullness, but the time for thought and rest and comfort was gone. Now it was time to fight.

Isabella helped her to dress, an unnecessary and almost ceremonial attention that Poly found bolstered her courage immensely. She wouldn't allow Isabella to braid her hair into a coronet, however, despite Isabella's protestations that hair worn down the back was neither elegant nor fashionable.

"I may need it," she said.

And Isabella, eyeing askance the ominous way that Poly's hair undulated of its own accord, said, "Hm. Perhaps you're right."

True to Isabella's promises, Brackett's body was gone when Poly set out. The blood was gone, too, leaving no sign that anything untoward had ever happened.

Despite that, Poly chose to walk to the Council Hall, eschewing hidden passages and horseless carriage alike. It was nice to feel the triad on the crown of her head, and if a small, dark part of her suggested that it could be many years before she again felt the warmth of the suns, well, that only enhanced the delight of it.

When she was standing on the golden steps of the Council Hall, Poly allowed herself a small sigh. It was done. There was no backing out now. But she did wish that she could have seen Luck one last time without the threat of Mordion and Melissa between them. She thought of Onepiece sleeping in her bed, unaware that he might not see her again, and felt such a physical pain at her heart that she nearly sat down with a gasp on the stairs.

Isabella would take care of him, Poly knew. Isabella had promised, and Onepiece was already very fond of her. If only he wouldn't revert back to being a puppy when he found out that Poly wasn't coming back. Or, more hopefully, if only Poly could make this work, and things went well. Then—oh, *then*—but it wasn't helpful to think about it. She wouldn't think about it. Wouldn't hope for it. Not yet.

Poly stood still for a moment longer, sick but determined.

Then Mordion's voice said behind her, "Not getting cold feet, I hope, darling? Luck will be arriving shortly. I wouldn't like to have to change my plans at such short notice, but I will if I have to."

Relief fizzed in Poly's stomach. So Luck *would* be there. "I'm ready to come in," she said.

The hall passed in a white, marble blur until Poly's fixed gaze informed her that she was in the Council Chambers, where she had declared Luck her Champion. The room was confusingly full of people, clumps of wizards talking nervously until the door opened, and the room muffled as all faces turned to Poly and Mordion.

Melchior's face jumped out at her first. He was frozen mid-word, his face stunned, then sick, and finally blank. Poly gave him the tiniest shake of the head and saw with relief his eyelashes drop in acquiescence. He couldn't help her now, but there was still hope that Black Velvet could salvage something of this later. Perhaps even wake her again. Poly found herself fiercely grateful for his presence: she hadn't expected quite so many people. Her eyes flicked from face to face until it occurred to her that the whole wizard council, man and woman, was present.

"Everyone is eager to see what you can bring to the council," said Mordion, without troubling to lower his voice. "Last time we tried this little experiment I made the mistake of trying to take on too much by myself. I didn't expect you to be quite so potent, you see. I very nearly burned myself out. That won't happen this time."

"I see," said Poly, and she *did* see. Every wizard here was willing to tear her into pieces so that they could each have a piece of her power. "You'd better get on with it, then."

"Don't be impatient, darling. We're waiting on Luck. After all, he's still your champion: we need a release from him first. Ah, here he is."

Poly turned her head, feeling a nasty lurch in her stomach as Luck walked through the door with Melissa on his arm, his eyes vague and preoccupied. Melissa, dressed beautifully in cerulean blue, looked plump with satisfaction and power, her blue painted fingernails making patterns on Luck's arm.

The wizards parted for them instinctively, making a channel through which they swept, gaudy, bright, and powerful, until they were at the centre of the hall with Mordion and Poly.

"Have you got your part under control?" Mordion asked Melissa.

"Of course!" she said, laughing.

The stickiness of her magic was in and around Luck's golden magic, a fuzzy crimson haze that surrounded and suffused him. And yet, somewhere underneath it all, Poly thought she heard the *tick, tick, tick* of something counting down. She caught her breath and stared up at Luck, who returned the look with one of his blandest, gold-eyed looks.

"He's mine, now," said Melissa, misunderstanding Poly's fixed gaze.

She gave a tiny, proud smile that Poly saw and hated.

Poly flicked her eyes briefly to Melissa's face and said, "Oh? I must have misunderstood. I thought you had to use magic to interest Luck this time."

Melissa went pink with anger and took one darting step forward, but Mordion laughed, low and delighted. "Darling, your claws have grown sharper. You're one of the few women of my acquaintance who becomes more interesting on further acquaintance. Such a pity I can't keep you."

"I'd rather sleep for another three hundred years," said Poly, "if it's all the same to you."

"Oh, that's not up for debate, darling. I've never been one to sacrifice self-interest to pleasure. You are a very necessary part in my plans. Is he ready, Melissa?"

Melissa caressed a finger down one of Luck's cheeks and said to him, "Now, sweeting, what is it you have to say?"

Luck's mouth opened just as someone said, "Mum!"

Poly's heart stopped. Onepiece, thin and uncertain and angry, was pushing his way through wizards with sharp elbows and sharper magic. Poly's heart started again with a shockingly painful thump, and her eyes went to Luck, who stood silent and unresponsive. Beneath the thunder of Poly's heart, an unwinding magic went *tick, tick, tick*.

Luck said in a voice that brooked no refusal, "Dog! *Heel!*"

Onepiece scuttled to his side and allowed himself to be picked up, wrapping skinny arms around Luck's neck and watching Poly with wide eyes. How had he gotten away from Isabella? More importantly, how was she to keep him safe?

Tick, tick, tick.

"How delicious!" said Melissa. "He'll make a lovely accoutrement for evening parties! Do go on, Luck. What is it you have to say to everyone?"

"I resign my claim," said Luck readily. "I pass the right of championship to the Wizard Council."

Poly would have felt sick at the ease with which he said it if she couldn't still feel the spell unwinding beneath the veneer of Melissa's magic.

"Wonderful!" Mordion said briskly. "Spellpaper?"

Melissa flourished a pearly paper at him with languid fingers. "Of course. Though why you didn't just draw up a new one, I'll never know."

"Sentimental value," said Mordion. "Besides, the curse is a good, strong one. The enchantress who drew it up for me met with an unfortunate accident at the hands of two children: we won't see her like again."

Probably Mum and Dad, thought Poly, with a distant, sick amusement. Onepiece was making tiny, magical spurts with his fingers, and she desperately hoped that the haze of Melissa's magic surrounding Luck would render it unseen.

Someone else in the room was forming magic, too. Poly, her eyes darting around the room again, saw a burgeoning cloud of obsidian behind Melchior and felt her heart sink. Complications were springing up more quickly than she could think how to deal with them.

"Do sit down," said Mordion. He was looking at her curiously, which would have worried Poly greatly if it didn't mean that he hadn't noticed either Onepiece or Melchior. "I'm afraid that we must dance this little dance once again. You must find this rather a bore."

"Oh no, I understand," said Poly. She looked past Mordion and into Melchior's hazel eyes, and said very clearly, "It means you get a second chance. It didn't happen the way you thought it would the first time. This time you can make sure it does."

"Exactly so," said Mordion. "Palm please, darling—no, I *don't* think the antimagic one is a good idea, do you? Glove on, please."

Poly, silently pulling her glove back on, saw Melchior give the barest nod in her direction, and felt a flood of warm relief. If everything went wrong and Luck couldn't or wouldn't wake her a second time, there was still hope.

The knife pricked, sharp and shallow, pooling blood in Poly's palm. And Mordion, as he had done three hundred years ago, turned her palm over again and pressed it to the spellpaper, slicking blood across its bone white surface. Her heart was beating fast and hard, but all that Poly could hear was *tick, tick, tick,* layered beneath the babble of surrounding magic.

And as she listened, the spell gave a final *tick* and was silent.

Into the silence, Luck, his eyes very golden and awake, said, "Right. You're all under arrest."

Wizards all over the hall froze.

Mordion laughed, an incredulous sound that broke the silence, and a few uneasy titters of laughter rose around the room. "Is that so? Forgive my disbelief, but even if you had the manpower—not to mention the authority!—to arrest *all* of us, it seems remarkably foolish to wait until I've sealed the curse again. Melissa's enchantment notwithstanding, I think even you will have a hard time fighting off Poly's magic."

"Oh, she's at least as strong as I am," said Luck affably. "That's why I thought it was better not to let you have it. Sorry."

"Don't be dire, sweeting," said Melissa, her honeyed tones full of sticky magic and soft promises.

"Huh," said Luck interestedly. "I don't remember you being so boring before. That's a pity. Stop doing that with your voice. It's irritating."

Melissa gasped in outrage, but Mordion, smiling with eyes as hard as granite, said, "I have the spellpaper. The curse is completely bound. I *have* it all."

Poly looked into Luck's bright eyes and gave herself a hasty internal check. There was no loss in her—no pain, no draining pull, no irresistible lethargy.

"You don't, you know," she told Mordion. She felt light and free and powerful. Something had been done when her blood sealed the spellpaper, but it certainly had not been a curse that activated.

"I have the spellpaper," said Mordion again, but his eyes were cold and watchful.

"Yes. About that," said Luck. "I fiddled with the spellpaper a bit. And the curse is null and void anyway."

Mordion, his gaze fixed on Luck's face, said, "You broke the curse? Impossible! She was still falling asleep in the village."

"Everything about Poly is beautiful and impossible," said Luck. "You of all people should have seen that. It's one of the reasons you chose her, after all."

"How?"

"Oh, I just kept kissing her," Luck said dreamily. "It worked out surprisingly well."

"I see," said Mordion. His eyes were without even a touch of his usual cold amusement. "Then I will just have to draw up another paper. I'm sure Melissa and I can come up with something suitable. After all, you *did* just turn Poly over to the Wizard Council's Championship."

"Yes. About that," said Luck again, and Poly swallowed a mad little giggle. "I did give her over. But you did, too. That was one of the things I did to the spellpaper. You made a pact of blood, turning Poly over to her own Championship with perpetuity. And if you don't know what that means, you can go and visit the little grey man in Curzon Street. He told me all about it. Gave me a lot of good advice, actually. Oh, and Black Velvet will be here shortly: they were very interested to find out what you were up to."

"I see," said Mordion again. This time his voice was curious, even thoughtful. "This complicates matters. Let me clarify for you all."

The Wizard Council, who to a man had begun to look very uncomfortable indeed, looked variously at their feet, Mordion, and the middle distance.

"There are only two outcomes for you all today," Mordion told them. "One, you give yourselves up to Black Velvet and accept lifelong imprisonment or worse for treason."

There was an immediate, low buzz of conversation, and magic flared into being around the room.

"Naughty wizards!" said Onepiece. He had made a cat's cradle with loops of frighteningly strong magic that stuck to the ceilings and walls and threatened to fall at any moment.

None of the wizards around them seemed to have noticed it, much to Poly's relief.

"I don't think we ought to let him keep talking," she said to Luck.

"It'll be fine," Luck said cheerfully. "You look very pretty today, Poly. What did you do to my gate spell?"

"Two:" said Mordion, his voice low and hypnotic, and somehow managing to cut through all the surrounding noise, "we all join our magic and take not only the enchantress but the enchanter. Twice the profit with no more risk."

"Huh," said Luck, as Melissa's aura of magic expanded in readiness. "Didn't think of that."

Separate strands of magic rose all over the room, combining in a vast, piebald reservoir of power. Melchior, surrounded by wizards as he was, did something deadly and black with his own magic that would have him killed by the closest wizard as soon as it left his fingers. Poly swept him effortlessly into a corner of the room, boxing him in with impenetrable, invisible unmagic, and left him calling her name in frustration as he vainly tried to escape. She was so busy doing that, in fact, that she didn't throw up a protection around the three of them quickly enough.

Poly saw something fierce and poisonous and scarlet in her

peripheral, then Luck did something quick and twisting with a snarl. Melissa screamed once, sharp and fearful, and as Poly blazed a wall of protective unmagic into being around them, she saw a crimson cloud stain the air. Mordion pounced on it, quick as thought, and drank it in greedily.

"Mine this time, I think," he said to Poly. His voice was oddly muffled through the barrier of unmagic, and the piebald mixture of magic seemed to push more heavily against it. Poly threw an extra layer of protection over Melchior, finessing it with a coating of invisibility, and found that he had stopped struggling. Instead, his obsidian magic steadily grew, flowing freely around him—an offering for her use.

When she was finished, Poly asked in a voice that wasn't quite steady, "Luck, did you kill Melissa?"

"She threw something nasty at you," said Luck. "While you weren't paying attention. Why weren't you paying attention?"

"I had to make sure Melchior was safe," Poly said briefly, swiping with her antimagic hand at several surprisingly strong spells that had managed to get through the unmagic.

One of them disintegrated an inch from Luck's nose, much to his surprise and Onepiece's disapproval.

"Ooof! That's a bit strong for Mordion's talents," he said.

"It's some of mine," Poly said, unwinding the magic from its spell form. It slithered up her fingers and into her hair, comfortably hers again. "Look out!"

Luck ducked a poisonously yellow spell. "They're getting through faster. What's wrong with your unmagic?"

"Nothing's wrong with it," panted Poly, snatching curses from the air. "It's just that they're getting stronger, and there are *lots* of them. Shouldn't Black Velvet be here by now?"

"You've got to stop mollycoddling Melchior," said Luck. He covered Onepiece's eyes with his hand just as one of the spells exploded in a blinding flash of light. "He's Wizard Council, too, you know."

"He's Black Velvet!" snapped Poly, trying to blink the glare from her eyes. Her hair expanded in response, tangling enchantments and curses in its coils before they could land, but she couldn't see Luck and Onepiece, let alone single magics. "When will they get here?"

"That might have been an exaggeration."

Something hissed between them, sharp and deadly.

"An exaggeration?"

"Well, a bluff. I couldn't go to Black Velvet with Melissa's magic all over me—she would have known. I had to leave them more of a clue than a message."

Poly closed her eyes and studied the dancing lights that still burned there. "They're not coming?"

"Maybe. They're clever; they'll figure it out. Eventually."

There was a flutter as a small, thin spell slipped through the tendrils of Poly's hair. Luck gasped, then groaned, and Poly reached blindly for him.

"Luck? Luck, are you all right? Is Onepiece all right?"

"Strong!" said Luck hoarsely. "Shouldn't have missed that one. The dog is fine."

"I can hold this," said Poly, blinking madly. There were still bright, black ringed spots in her vision, but she could vaguely see Onepiece and Luck again. "Get Onepiece somewhere safe, *quickly.*"

To her surprise, Luck didn't argue. He merely disappeared, surprising shouts from half the wizards present, and returned a moment later without Onepiece. He did something big and netlike to the Chambers around them, and when Poly looked at him curiously, said, "Don't want them getting ideas about Shifting out and back in again. Some of them have spells from me that could give us a bit of trouble. Besides, I want 'em all here when Black Velvet arrives."

"I see," panted Poly. The push of magic had grown significantly stronger. "*If* Black Velvet arrives, do you mean?"

"Did you know the dog's done something to the room?"

"Yes. It's on the ceiling; it'll fall in a few minutes."

"Whoops! Careful, Poly! Too late, another one's got through. Do you know what he did?"

Poly tried in vain to remove the latest curse from her sleeve. "No. Ooh, Luck, this one's sticking!"

"I've got it. Stand still; you keep moving just as I've got it."

Poly felt her knees threatening to give way beneath her and caught a look of fierce exultation on Mordion's face through the unmagic barrier.

"Oh! Get it off! Luck, *get it off!* He's using it to draw on my magic!"

Not just her magic, she realised a moment later, when her unmagic shield flickered and then disappeared. She felt the tail-end of it as it was sucked into Mordion's orbit, immeasurably expanding his reservoir of power.

There was a moment of absolute quiet. Then Poly flung herself at Luck, wrapping her arms around him, and saw her hair rise, growing and shifting around them as a furore of magic began.

Her hair grew. Spells and curses, large and small, fed into it while tiny clever little curses knifed right through the strands. The sense of power building popped her ears and made her dizzy, and before long it wasn't Poly protecting Luck, but Luck supporting Poly as she blindly took in spell after spell.

Through her teeth, she said, "Luck—"

"I'm here."

"It's too strong."

"I know," said Luck. His magic was twisted and tarry from the onslaught. "Hold on just a little longer."

Poly felt the quick in and out of breath above her ear as Luck set an enchantment spinning around them. The barrage of tiny, stinging curses ceased, and Luck began to unlace her glove.

"Oh!" said Poly, drunk on magic. "Don't need to do that. Can get to it without that."

"I know," said Luck again. "But I can't."

The glove slipped to the floor, eddying on currents of loose magic, and Luck threaded his fingers through hers, sparking a warm glow of antimagic from her fingertips to her shoulder. The moment he touched Poly's hand his enchantment died.

Mordion said, "I have you!" his voice thick with satisfaction.

"No," said Luck. "I *have* you."

He seized Mordion by the throat and used Poly's antimagic to bring down every piece of wizard magic in the room. Mordion choked, grasping for the remainder of Melissa's magic, and Luck brought that down, too. It wasn't enough: spurts of magic were already beginning to restart around the room as wizards discovered that only their spells and not their magic had been dismantled. Above, Onepiece's intricate enchantment quivered in response.

"Luck," Poly said warningly.

More magic flared into life, building and dangerous.

Poly gripped Luck's hand, tugging him toward her. "*Luck*."

"Together, you fools!" snarled Mordion, around the chokehold of Luck's fingers.

"Luck!"

"Whoops!" said Luck, ducking back into the cover of Poly's hair as magic pelted at them again. "There it goes!"

Onepiece's spell fell on them, sticky, insidious, and strong. A babble of confusion grew in the room, rising over the deadly hum of magic, as wizard after wizard shrank and lengthened and —grew *fur*.

Mordion, a scarlet and blue blur of magic, fought tooth and nail but shifted and changed with the rest of them despite his best efforts.

"Huh," said Luck, looking around. "They're all cats. Who did that?"

-*cats!*- said Onepiece's gleeful voice in Poly's head, from some distance away. -*yowly spitty cats. run, cats, run! onepiece will catch you and bite you!*-

"Onepiece," said Poly, her voice wobbly with laughter or exhaustion. "He did it. He wants to chase them."

Spindle

"Well, he can't. They have to stay here until Black Velvet comes for them."

"All right," Poly said, wearily. "I can make sure of that. It would be nice to lose some of this weight, anyway."

She pinched away the hair at the nape of her neck, heavy and lustrous with magic, and tossed it outward. It stuck to Onepiece's magic, snaring cats all over the room, and when she drew it back toward herself, cats snarled and scrabbled through the forms, scratching wood as they came.

"That's no good," said Luck. "Now you have a parliament of wizard cats on leashes."

"They're not leashes," Poly told him. "They're threads."

Luck followed her eyes to the tapestry across the room, a firelit scene of home and hearth with a dog curled by the fire at his master's feet. "Huh," he said. "That'll work."

Poly bound the cats into the tapestry—thread by thread, cat by hissing cat—until all fifty-eight cats were still and thready by the woollen hearth fire.

"That should hold them for a while," she said. There was a coiled resistance to her binding somewhere deep in the tapestry—Mordion fighting back, Poly supposed. It wasn't strong enough to worry her, however, and she tied off her enchantment without taking the time to subdue it. "Can they see in there?"

"See us, you mean?" said Luck. "I don't think so. I'm not sure they could even if they were human."

"What do you mean, even if they were human?" Poly asked uneasily. "They *are* human. They're just cat shaped."

Luck shrugged. He was examining the unmagic box in which she had encased Melchior, and she had the feeling that he wasn't quite paying attention.

"Mordion might be. The rest are proper cats: I doubt they'll even remember being human. We'll have to get that dog of yours some training before he does something unfortunate."

"But what about their magic?"

"Oh, they'll love it," said Luck. "They'll probably use it to enchant mice and magic balls of string. What is this spell, Poly?"

"It's not a spell, it's unmagic," said Poly, belatedly considering Melchior's imprisonment again. "I'd better let him out."

She dismantled the box of unmagic that had kept Melchior safe through the storm of magic, and found that he was wearing the sarcastic, self-mocking look that she didn't like.

"Oh, is it safe for me to come out now? Or would you prefer me to cower a little longer?"

"Don't make me apologise for keeping you safe," Poly said severely. "And thank you for the magic."

A smile swept across Melchior's face, softening his hazel eyes. "I'd never make you apologise for anything, sweetheart. Thank you. I believe my ego will limp on."

"I see you survived," said Luck irritably. He was leaning on the first row of seats, gently swaying, and his magic had blackened further. "Stop cuddling Poly."

"Oh, I'm pretty resilient," said Melchior, smiling faintly and withdrawing his arms. "Poly, should your Binding be doing *that*, do you think?"

Poly's eyes went involuntarily to the tapestry. It was bulging, stitches straining at the frame, and within the worked picture, cats were moving. They seemed to be chasing a ball of robin blue string—no, wool. And in the background, one smoky grey cat watched, twitched its tail, and waited. "It's Mordion. He's done something."

"Told you they'd use it to make balls of string," said Luck in satisfaction.

"I don't think *they* did," said Poly, watching the ball of wool with narrow eyes. "I think *he* did. Which means that the ball of wool is—"

"Unravelling."

"*Magic!*"

"And unravelling," reiterated Luck.

"My Binding! Luck, help me catch it!"

But there was no catching it all. Poly tried, grasping at the threads as they flew apart, but then the Binding was unravelled, and the threads were gone. The magic Mordion had been using was her own: the last dregs of what he had once stolen from her. He had used it to spark up what remained of the other wizards' magic, tricking them into unravelling the Binding for him.

Cats streamed past, yowling and hissing and scratching, and flowed out the door.

Melchior's eyes met hers, and Poly saw resolve there. He kissed her, quick and hard, his hands cupping her face. "I'll miss you," he said. "I can't—I wish—but you have Luck, and I have to finish this."

Then he was leaping over rows of seats for the door, and on the last leap Poly saw only a lithe black cat, springing lightly to the floor and darting through the door.

"Hey!" said Luck, swaying in the sudden silence. "Stop kissing Melchior!"

"Luck, we've got to stop them!"

"I don't want to stop them," said Luck, but Poly was already running for the door.

She could see cats at the end of the hall as she ran, flowing toward the front entrance; Melchior was with them, leaping high and fast to catch up with the leaders. She hoped to corner them when they reached the grand front door, but when it came in sight it was open, cats pouring over the threshold and into the street. Poly dashed after them, catching one side of the doorframe to keep her balance before the stairs, and stopped short on the top step, her heart pounding.

On the golden steps of the Council Building were twenty precise men in twenty precise grey suits. They were prim and proper, and carried behind them a storm of magic that obscured the street. Through their legs the cats streamed, yowling and spitting.

Luck stumbled into the daylight, blinking, and hung on the doorframe behind Poly. He said, "You took your time!"

"Where are the detainees?" asked the first precise man.

"That was them. The dog turned them into cats."

The precise man blinked precisely once. "Cats. Hmm. We might need to keep an eye on that."

"I wouldn't bother," said Poly wearily. It was too late to catch them, and too late to stop Melchior. "Melchior is with them. I'm sure he'll be in contact when he's able."

The precise man seemed to consider this. Then he said: "Very well. We'll tie all this up."

"That's their way of saying 'thanks and run along now'," said Luck, as two rows of precise men marched quietly through the doorway and into the Hall.

"Do we want to run along now?"

"Might as well. It'll only be paperwork and statements for the news sheets. Maybe some cleaning. We splashed a bit of magic about in there."

"Where did you put Onepiece?"

"What? Oh, second floor," said Luck, just as Onepiece himself trotted into sight along the hall, hotly pursued by two of Black Velvet's number.

Onepiece said crossly, "Muuuum! More naughty wizards!" and held out his arms to be lifted up.

Poly lifted him and glared at the two Black Velvet wizards. "Why are you chasing my son?"

"I'm sorry, your highness, but you can't take him," said one of the wizards.

Poly said coldly, "I beg your pardon?"

"Mr Pennicott says to detain him until we can determine what he is and if he's a threat," said the wizard.

"I wouldn't do that if I were you," said Luck.

The wizard, persevering, added, "There's also the matter of the Transformation magic he worked: we need to know what it was. Those cats were *cats*. They weren't Transformed. Not really."

"You're not keeping Onepiece here."

"But Mr Pennicott says—"

Spindle

"If you so much as lay a finger on my son, I will Bind you into the stairs of the Hall until every person in the Capital has walked over your face."

"Now, Poly, don't pick a fight with these wizards as well," said Luck, in a reasonable tone of voice.

"They said they're going to keep Onepiece!"

"Well, they can't," said Luck. "We're going home."

And much to Poly's appreciation, he Shifted the three of them directly back home.

There was a shriek as the parlour appeared around them. Isabella, her eyes wide with shock, gave vent to her relief in a long, quivering breath. "I'm exceedingly glad you're both safe!" she said.

Poly thought that there might be a slight glimmer of moisture to the girl's eyes. She hugged Poly and even Luck, who suffered it with the dim listlessness of one who has endured so much that one more indignity scarcely matters.

Isabella, eyeing him shrewdly, said, "Oh, very well! I'll leave you both alone!" Her eyes fell on Onepiece, and she went from understanding to wrathful indignation in a moment. "*What* did I say about running away, you repellent little boy!"

"Smack me inna head and throw me inna stream," said Onepiece obediently, wriggling to be let down.

"Exactly!" said Isabella. She boxed Onepiece's ear gently while Poly watched, highly diverted, and demanded, "Come with me."

"Inna stream!" said Onepiece happily.

"Yes, inna stream," Isabella said severely, shoving him out the front door. She turned back to Poly with a smile that was still somewhat crooked with relief, and added, "We'll be down at the stream. We'll be gone for quite some time, I imagine."

She gave them a pert nod and was gone.

Luck, blinking at the curls of his own blackened magic and then at Poly, asked vaguely, "Where's she gone?"

"Sit down, Luck. She's taken Onepiece to the stream."

"All right." Luck sat down, hunching his abused magic around him. "Why?"

"To throw him in, apparently," said Poly.

"Oh. Good. What are you doing?"

"Straightening this mess out, of course. Sit still."

"All right." Luck sat in silence for some minutes before he said moodily, "You were kissing Melchior again, Poly."

"*You* were kissing Melissa!"

"Yes, but that was just work," said Luck. "I needed to know what she and Mordion were up to, and Melissa is a lot more careless when she thinks she's in control. I had to let her enchant me. And then all you wanted to talk about when you got back every day was Mordion."

"So *that's* why you kept cutting me off every time I tried to tell you about him! Luck, why didn't you tell me what you were going to do?"

Luck flopped onto his back and stared at the ceiling. "Melissa was too quick for me. Took me by surprise. And then once the enchantment was there, I couldn't tell you anything without her learning about it, too. Good thing I'd already sorted out the spellpaper by then."

Poly smoothed out threads in silence, stripping black from gold.

Luck said, "My head hurts."

That wasn't surprising, Poly thought, caressing each strand of magic back into place. Luck's magic was in a worse state than she'd ever seen it. Some of her own magic, repurposed by Mordion, was responsible for a lot of the damage: she could see the familiar yet alien shards of it amidst Luck's magic.

"Poor darling," she murmured.

Luck sat up, blinking, and said, "What did you call me?"

Poly froze, fingers caught in a web of magic that seemed to grip suddenly around her fingers, warm and tight.

"Poly. Poly, don't you dare ignore me. Do you know how long I've waited for you to call me darling instead of the dog?"

"He's not a dog," she said automatically, hot and cold by turns because she'd slipped and *Oh, how embarrassing!* but Luck had said—*what* had he said?

"Well, I know that," said Luck, in an entirely reasonable tone of voice. "But what else was I supposed to say when you were lavishing all those *darlings* on him instead of me?"

"How could I know that hurt you?" demanded Poly. "You were kissing Melissa and ignoring me all day!"

"I broke the curse long before that!" complained Luck. "You were supposed to understand that. I had to butcher the curse just to wake you up the first time but when I kissed you in the village the curse really broke."

"Oh. *Oh!*" Poly gazed at him. "*Love's Kiss!* It was in the curse!"

"That's right," said Luck, smiling sunnily.

"I see," said Poly. She felt breathless and light, and as free as she had felt the moment she knew she was released from Mordion's claim on her.

"I hope you don't mind my not asking your parents for your hand in marriage, by the way," said Luck. His magic curled tighter around her fingers and coiled up her wrists. "I'm fairly certain they know, anyway."

Poly gave a little spurt of laughter. "I'm sure they do."

"I did want to ask you something, though," said Luck. His hands, gilded with magic, seized her by the waist and pulled her closer. "If I kiss you, will you promise not to hit me again?"

Made in the USA
Middletown, DE
04 January 2023

21370060R00205